# BOUND
# BY
# EARTH

## CENTALLIAN GUARDIANS
## VOLUME II

# BOUND BY EARTH

CENTALLIAN GUARDIANS
VOLUME II

## ROSE SARTIN

LAGAN
PRESS

an imprint of
**OGHMA** CREATIVE MEDIA

# OGHMA

C R E A T I V E   M E D I A

Lagan Press
An imprint of Oghma Creative Media, Inc.
2401 Beth Lane, Bentonville, Arkansas 72712

Library of Congress Cataloging-in-Publication Data

Names: Sartin, Rose, author
Title: Bound by Earth/Linda Sartin | Centallian Guardians #2
Description: First Edition | Bentonville: Lagan, 2019
Identifiers: LCCN: 2019942403 | ISBN: 978-1-63373-515-6 (hardcover) |
ISBN: 978-1-63373-516-3 (trade paperback) | ISBN: 978-1-63373-517-0 (eBook)
Subjects: | BISAC: FICTION/Romance/Science Fiction
FICTION/Romance/Action & Adventure | FICTION/Science Fiction/Space Opera
LC record available at: https://lccn.loc.gov/2019942403

Lagan Press trade paperback edition October, 2019

Cover & Interior Design by Casey W. Cowan
Editing by Mari Mason

*Dedicated to my mother and father, Helen Marie (Lundy) Brown and William Chester Brown who believed I could live my dream.*

As always, I wish to thank my daughters, Melissa and Angela, for the time and energy they've put into making this book possible, and to my son Eric and daughter-in-law, Honnah, for their scientific and tech expertise. Thank you to my critique group, Barbara, Susan, Prix, Sherry, Rachel, Melinda, and Wendy. And thank you to the Grand Canyon Fire Fepartment EMS responders, Ron and Kelso (whose name was remarkably close to my book's protagonist, Keeso) for coming to the rescue of a lady in distress. A special thanks to the wonderful Hopi people I met on my journey through the Hopi reservation in Arizona, including Lisa Lomavay from the Hopi Health Care Center, Anna Silas, from the Hopi Museum, Darlene Quavehema, and Sandra Hamana from the Hopi Cultural Center. And, of course, thank you to Oghma Creative Media, my publisher, Casey Cowan, who designed my gorgeous book cover, Chief Operations Officer Venessa Cerasale, Editorial Director Cyndy Prasse Miller, and editor Mari Mason. What would I do without you all?

# PROLOGUE

Keeso leaned his shoulder against the porch post of his log home and sipped dark coffee as he watched the sun set behind the mountain range. Six Earth months had passed since the *Novaria*'s emergency departure for his home world of New Centallus. Rhyel, his commander and friend, had been wounded while protecting his bond-mate, Amber. As second-in-command, Cintar had assured him the commander was in healing stasis and out of danger. Keeso hadn't been worried. But *Novaria* failed to arrive as scheduled for its late spring supply run. The colony's desperately-needed supplies were crated and stored in the ground-to-ship shuttle hidden behind a holographic image. Crates of New Centallian gold also lined the small cargo ship's interior walls.

He'd watched the sky for his people's return, though it was as likely one or two of his friends would simply materialize in his kitchen.

*Something had gone wrong.*

The question was what. Had the unknown assailants who'd destroyed his home planet, and annihilated all but a handful of his species, found them and finished their job? Was he the only Centallian left alive?

No.

To believe such an atrocity bordered on blasphemy. More likely, something had happened to the *Novaria*. Hopefully, something the technicians could repair.

Clouds, etched in silver, hovered above the ramparts. Bright streamers splayed like a fan above the peak before dimming in the receding light. He took a final swallow of coffee and tossed the dregs on the ground before going inside. Rinsing the cup, he stacked it on the draining-rack, and sank into the easy-chair across the room. His attention centered on the blinking green dot on the transceiver that sat above the sink.

He checked it several times a day. When his friends approached Earth, he'd know it. Until then, he'd remain the semi-reclusive gold miner most people in Connor, Colorado knew.

# BOUND BY EARTH

CENTALLIAN GUARDIANS
VOLUME II

# 1

✧

The gunshot cracked like a whip. A terrified scream cut short when a second shot splintered the air.

Emma scrambled to her feet, and raced through the door of her upstairs bedroom, skidding to a stop at the landing banister.

Downstairs, John's study door stood open, the light filtering into the wide hall. Everything seemed normal. Where had the gunfire come from?

Four-year-old Levi wandered out of his bedroom, sleep-rumpled and confused.

"Mommy?" His cry echoed overloud in the large area.

Emma scooped the little boy into her arms and hurried to his room. "It's okay, baby. We're playing a game of hide and seek. It's your turn to hide." She set him on his feet in front of the closet. "Crawl way back in here and don't make a sound."

He hesitated. "But Aunty, you'll know where I'm hiding."

"I won't tell. Get behind those boxes and don't come out unless mommy, daddy, or I call you. Do you understand?"

"Why?"

She knelt in front of him. "Those are the rules. We have to play by the rules, don't we?"

Levi nodded, and she gave him a fierce hug. "Good. Remember, don't come out for anyone else, just us. Don't talk to anyone either—promise me."

"I promise." He turned and blended into the dark shadows. She closed the latticed door, praying he wasn't afraid of the near-dark. He didn't make a sound.

Easing the bedroom door closed, she sprinted to her room and grabbed her cell phone before returning to the landing. Should she dial 911? What if the noise she'd heard came from outside—screaming kids playing with fireworks? It was close to the fourth.

Still no sound from the study. John brought work home from the lab most nights, made a habit of late-night projects. Denise had probably gone to bed.

The panic subsided a degree. Cautious, she crept down the stairs. A shadow passed in front of the lamplight. She froze. Someone slammed a cabinet door, or maybe a drawer. *Another of John's habits.* She smiled, relieved.

"John?" No answer. She walked around the doorway into the room.

Denise lay sprawled on the floor inside the entry, her arms splayed out in front of her, as though she'd tripped and tried to catch herself. Blood poured from a gaping hole in the back of her head.

"Denise!"

Sliding to her knees at her sister's side, she swallowed down the acid in her throat. So much blood. She had to stop the bleeding.

"Please, God, not Denise," she prayed, even as her mind registered the truth. Her sister was beyond prayer. She struggled to her feet, searching for something, anything, to staunch the blood.

That's when she saw John. Her brother-in-law slumped forward over the desk, a growing pool of blood seeping from beneath his body, soaking the papers haphazardly strewn across the workspace. John was usually so neat. She shook her head at the errant thought and turned back to Denise.

"She's dead. Don't waste your time with her."

Emma started at the disembodied voice. A man moved from behind the door, his gun pointed at her head, its polished steel-gray barrel gleaming in the lamplight. She held her breath and waited for her own death. Why didn't he pull the trigger? He'd killed Denise and John. Why didn't he shoot her too?

*Run.*

Her body refused to obey.

*He's going to kill me, and I can't move. Why can't I move?*

She dragged her eyes from the weapon. The man holding the gun looked like anyone on the street—medium height, thinning brown hair. Unremarkable, though she'd never forget him.

"You couldn't stay upstairs with the boy, could you? I got what I came after. Two more minutes and I'd have been gone." He drew a deep breath and released it on a sigh. "But you didn't stay with the kid. You trapped me in here. I kept waiting for you to go back up to the boy. Where'd you hide him? In the closet?"

She whimpered.

He laughed. "Yeah, he's in the closet. It's the first place I'da looked."

The man glanced from John's prone body to her sister's still form. "I've never killed anyone before. John should have taken the money I offered him. People sell industrial secrets every day. He could have been a rich man. His stubbornness cost him his life—her life, too." He shrugged as he looked down at her sister. "I couldn't leave a witness, could I?"

His eyes locked with hers. "And now there's you—another loose end I have to tie up." He stepped over Denise's body. "Turn around."

Emma backed away. "No."

"Turn around. I promise you won't even know what happened. I'm a good shot."

She was suddenly furious. He'd killed Denise, the sweet, gentle sister she loved so dearly. He'd killed John too, making Levi an orphan.

"If you murder me, you'll have to look in my eyes when you pull the trigger."

Sirens—lots of them—wailed in the distance, growing in volume. Tires squealed on the pavement in front of the house. The man must have tripped John's silent alarm.

The killer stiffened, his attention drawn to the window as he reached out to grab her arm.

"Aunty? Where are you?"

"Levi, run!" Launching herself at the gunman, she grabbed the hand holding the weapon with both of hers. "Hide!"

She struggled to keep the gun barrel turned away from her. He closed his fist and slammed it against the side of her head. The force of the blow staggered her and pain exploded behind her eyes. She held fast to her assailant and prayed she'd stay conscious.

Someone pounded on the front door. The killer growled something, but the ringing in her ears distorted all sound. He jerked and twisted the wrist she grasped, clawing at her fingers. He wanted to get away—she wasn't going to let him. Emma pressed closer, blocking his free hand to keep him from hitting her.

The gun went off, the shock-wave shaking both their bodies. Emma stared into the man's eyes and waited. Neither of them moved. The pounding at the front door intensified, then heavier thumps vibrated the room. Someone was breaking down the door. It sounded far away.

The killer pulled free from her numbed fingers. His white shirt and pants glistened crimson. He watched her, the strangest expression on his face, before he turned and lumbered through the study door toward the back of the house.

He'd left her alive. Why had he left her alive? She knew what he looked like—could identify him. Her hands began to shake, and she held them in front of her face. His blood stained her fingers.

The front door buckled under a crashing blow, and uniformed men poured into the hall, handguns drawn. They came to a halt at the study door. Their eyes swiftly took in the room—her sister, John—but they came back to her and stayed.

"He ran to the back of the house. There's a door...." She barely recognized her shaky voice. "He's wounded."

The lead officer gave a quick nod and most of the men took off in the direction she'd indicated.

"Miss, you'd better sit down." His voice was overly calm, as if he expected her to bolt.

"I'm okay. It's his blood."

"No, Miss, it's not." He grabbed her arm, easing her into a chair, then yelled over his shoulder, "Get the paramedics! Now!"

Emma looked down—at the bloodstain spreading across the lower, left side of her skirt, at the bullet-sized hole in the fabric. Her body tightened, her breathing reduced to short gasps of air. Searing pain shot through her middle, radiating outward.

*Her* blood had stained the killer's shirt.

Her blood... He'd known she'd been shot.

*He didn't leave me alive. He left me for dead.*

Two paramedics rushed into the room, navigating a gurney through the doorway, maneuvering it around her sister's body, lowering it so they could move her from the chair to the backboard.

"Try to stay calm," a voice said from behind her—the officer who'd helped her into the chair. "They'll take good care of you."

"Be careful, boys. We don't know where that bullet is. We don't want it moving on us." The female voice seemed far away.

Denise? No, Denise was dead—wasn't she?

The pain was gone now, and a beautiful, tingling numbness enshrouded her. But her mind wouldn't settle. She had to remember something. Something—*important.*

What was it?

"Levi!" He must be hiding somewhere, terrified—or did the killer have him?

Emma struggled to lift her leaded body out of the chair. A pair of hands held her in place.

"You have to listen to me—"

They lifted her to the gurney. She screamed.

"I'm sorry, sweetie." It was the woman's voice again. Not Denise. "You'll be more comfortable in a moment. We'll get you into the ambulance and—"

"No." Emma reached out and grabbed the woman's sleeve. "Wait. Please."

She bent close. "What is it?"

"Levi." The light faded. She fought to stay conscious. Levi needed her. Someone had to save him.... Her eyes drifted closed.

The young paramedic leaned closer, her voice urgent. "Stay with us, honey. Keep those pretty blue eyes open for me, okay?"

She tried to ignore the pain that had reawakened, scorching her body. She wanted to reach out to the woman, but her arm wouldn't move, had been strapped down. A plastic tube was attached to her forearm and ran to a bag of clear fluid hoisted on a rod above her head. When had that happened?

The gurney was moving. They were taking her outside. She couldn't leave without Levi. They stopped at the back doors of the ambulance. "We'll have you at the hospital soon." The woman's voice again.

"Please."

The girl paused. "What?"

"Levi."

She put her ear close to Emma's lips. "Who?"

She sank deeper into the swirling, black vortex. Surging against the void, she tried one last time.

"Levi... find him."

# 2

✧

"Aunty!" Levi tore away from the social worker holding his hand and lunged toward his aunt. Fortunately, the woman caught the little boy around his midsection before he crashed into Emma.

"Levi, remember what we talked about? Your aunt just got out of the hospital this evening. She doesn't have her strength back yet. You can't jump on her."

The uncertainty in her nephew's eyes went straight to Emma's heart. "It's okay, honey. I'm getting better every day. You can still give me a hug."

Cautious now, Levi moved into her arms. The social worker slipped out of the room as Emma pulled Levi into her lap. The twinge of pain the action caused didn't matter. She needed to hold him as much as he needed to be close to her.

"Aunty?" His voice wavered.

"What is it, sweetie?"

"I want mommy and daddy."

She pulled his little body close and rested her cheek against the top of his head. Shutting her eyes tight against the pain, she fought the tears his plea wrenched from her heart.

*How do I tell him?*

"I know, honey."

Emma shifted her nephew so he rested against her uninjured side and brushed the hair out of his eyes. How did you tell a four-year-old his parents were never coming back? How long could she keep him from learning they were taken from him by a ruthless killer?

"It's hard to understand, but even though you can't see them, they're still with you, watching out for you." She pressed her hand over his heart. "They will always be here. And whenever you feel scared or alone, all you need to do is think about something happy that you did with your mom and dad, and you'll feel better."

"Is that what you do?"

"Yes, sweetie, that's exactly what I do." She touched her lips to his forehead. "It's okay to feel sad sometimes. Everybody gets sad."

He lifted his head and gazed into her eyes. "And when I'm sad, Aunty, or when I'm scared, can I talk to you, too? Will you be with me for always?"

The fear in his voice and in his eyes tore at her heart. She wasn't ready for this conversation. She needed more time to prepare him.

The detective had convinced her that while the killer was at large, Levi had to stay away from her. Leaving her nephew was the only way she could protect him.

Everything had been arranged. He was going to live with his father's cousins, people Levi had never met before—people she'd never met either. And she was going into witness protection. It might be years before they would see each other again.

She wouldn't lie to Levi. She refused to assure her nephew she'd be there for him and then send him away. The lie would eventually be more traumatic.

"Levi, I—"

"'Cause, Aunty, I'm scared of that man." Her stomach twisted. Had the trauma already caused a problem? She prayed not.

"What man, honey—someone here?"

"No, Aunty—the man at my house. Remember, we played hide-n-seek. You told me to stay in the closet, but I didn't. I snuk'd out."

Emma shivered, knowing what was coming. "And?"

"You was mad at the man, and... and I was gonna come downstairs and help you, but I heard a really loud noise and I got scared and stopped."

"Where did you stop, honey?"

"I was on the stair steps and—and you know what? Someone was hitting the door real loud. And that's when the man came out of Daddy's office room." Levi buried his face against her chest and mumbled. "He scared me."

She snuggled him closer. "I'm here baby, you don't have to be afraid. He isn't anywhere around."

"You sure?"

"I'm sure. Did the man see you?"

He bumped her chin when he nodded. "Uh-huh. We looked at each other. He said a bad word and I thought he was going to chase me, so I run'd back upstairs and got under my bed so he couldn't find me. I stayed real quiet until the policeman came and got me."

She hugged him tight, closed her eyes, and thanked God her nephew was safe and hadn't been caught in the middle of the violence, that his last memory of his parents wouldn't be the horror she'd witnessed.

What now? Sending Levi to the cousins was no longer an option. He needed protection as much as she did. They'd be safe here tonight. Tomorrow, she'd arrange for Levi to travel with her.

Sometime during the night, Levi crawled into her bed. He snuggled his warm little body against hers and immediately fell back to sleep. She pulled the covers over him and tried to do the same, but the twinge in her side made it difficult. She was finally dozing when urgent voices in the living room roused her. A second later, someone knocked on the door.

"Ms. Kent?" The social worker's voice was filled with panic. "Ms. Kent, Levi isn't in his room."

She got out of bed and hurried to open the door a crack. "It's okay. He's here with me. He's asleep."

"Thank God. We thought—never mind. We need to leave right away. Get dressed. I'll bring Levi's clothes and shoes.

"What's wrong?"

"Detective Hartman called. The safe house has been compromised. An informant told him something was going down tonight. I'm not sure what that means exactly, but the detective wants us out of here now."

"Yes, okay." Emma bolted to the bathroom where she'd laid out her clothes for morning—a pullover shirt and loose slacks she'd chosen to accommodate the still-tender scar from her gunshot wound. She grabbed socks and her running shoes and headed back into the bedroom.

The social worker was slipping Levi's shoes on his feet. He was sleepy and confused, but cooperative. Emma sat on the bed beside them and put her own shoes on. As soon as she finished, Levi reached for her. She took him on her lap, and Jean, the social worker, closed and picked up their bags. "I'll put these in the trunk and come back to help you with Levi." Jean didn't wait for a reply but moved through the door and down the hall to the living room.

"What's the matter, Aunty?"

"I'm sorry we disturbed you, honey. We need to get an early start and it's time for us to get in the car. You can go back to sleep once we're on our way. Okay?"

"Okay."

He reached for her hand as the first shot rang out.

# 3

Emma rolled off the bed, pulling Levi down with her. Another shot, and Jean cried out. Had she been hit? More shots, this time from inside the house. Emma hoped the officers in the living room had returned the fire. How many policemen were here? She remembered two, maybe three. She'd been so anxious to see Levi she hadn't paid much attention. Would they be able to keep whoever was out there from getting to them? So many gunshots. The killer must've brought help.

Levi whimpered, and she hugged him close to her body. He was trembling—or was it her? Probably both.

"Stay here, and keep down," she told him. "I've got to turn off the light, so no one can see us." The little boy nodded. Emma crawled to the closed door, reached up and flipped the switch beside it. She stood up, locked the door, and ran across the room to the dresser for her purse. They were getting out of there, and she'd need her ID and credit cards if she had any hope of getting very far.

Everything went quiet. Not a sound—except the jackhammer-pounding of her heart.

"Aunty?"

Emma flinched. Levi's whispered plea was like a shout in the dark. She grabbed her purse and raced to him, sliding to her knees. "Shh, baby. Don't make a sound. We're leaving. Hold my purse while I check the window." He clutched the bag to his chest as if his life depended on keeping it safe. It might, she thought, as she climbed over the bed and peeked out the window. No moon tonight, or maybe the clouds hid it from view. Good. If she couldn't see anything, neither could someone with a gun.

Still no sound—outside or in. No one had tried to come through the door. Was anyone alive in the next room? Had the shooter been killed? Was that why it was so silent? They weren't waiting around to find out. She turned the lock on the window and lifted the sash. The glass glided up without protest. There was no screen.

"Levi, come on." She kept her voice low.

He skittered over the bed, landing with a thump on the other side. Grabbing him up, she leaned through the window, bending low enough to get him close to the ground, then let go. He landed on his feet. She followed him out, closing the window behind her. Crouched low, she grabbed her nephew's hand and ran with him away from the house, stopping only when they reached the temporary safety of a tall, thick hedge that separated the safe house from its neighbor. The streetlight at the front of the property would give them away if they ran in that direction. Even if the killer had someone covering the back door, following the hedge through the backyard was their safest option. She took her purse from Levi and they moved adjacent to the hedge, deeper into the darkness

Glass broke, and a renewed burst of gunfire mixed with excited shouts. She glanced over her shoulder. A light flickered in the window of what she thought was the living room.

*Fire.*

Emma picked up the pace, half-dragging Levi behind her. They had to find a way around the prickly obstruction. If the fire got out of control, the burning house would light up the neighborhood.

The hedge gave way to a privacy fence at the end of the long backyard. Still no access to the other side. At least no fence separated the safe house property from the yard behind. She stopped beside a large tree to catch her breath. Her weakened condition made the short sprint from the house feel like a marathon.

Where were the killers?

The gunfire quieted, but people were still yelling. Using the tree for cover, she glanced back. Nothing moved, but smoked puffed from under the eaves, highlighted by the fire's glow. Someone had to have reported the shots and the fire by now. Why wasn't anyone responding?

As if she'd conjured them, sirens whined in the distance, the sound jarring her memory. Levi shivered, and pressed against her side. He remembered too. She bent to give him a quick hug, ignoring the twinge the action caused, and took his hand again.

The property ahead of them was smaller, the distance to the house shorter. They made it to the end of the back porch when a light came on. Emma gasped, and pulled Levi against the house out of the light.

A door opened and closed. Someone shuffled across the porch. From the sound of the footsteps, it was a man. For a moment Emma considered calling out, asking for help—but only for a moment. He would call the police. Someone in law enforcement had betrayed them. Until she knew who was working with the killer, she couldn't afford to trust anyone in authority.

"Laura!" He shuffled back to the door. It squeaked when he opened it. "Laura, call 911. The house behind us is on fire." He moved to the end of the porch. Emma pictured him staring intently at the growing blaze. Lighter feet clicked against the porch floor. "They've already been notified. Look, you can see the emergency lights flashing on the other side of the house. Are those flames coming through the roof?"

"I can't tell. Let's get a little closer."

The couple stepped down from the porch into Emma's view. She pulled Levi into her side and pressed as flat against the house as possible. If either person turned around, they'd be seen. She edged toward the front of the house, keeping her nephew close. The privacy fence across the drive ended before it reached the sidewalk that paralleled the street. Could they make it that far without being seen?

She'd feel better if she knew where the killer was. For all she knew, he might be waiting on the other side of the fence. She shivered. It was still her best option. Clutching Levi's hand, she was about to cross the drive when she saw the headlights of a slow-moving vehicle. A spotlight's beam danced from one side of the street to the other, lighting the shadows, pausing here and there before moving on. Was it a squad car—someone searching for the shooters? The beam arced across the front yard of the house, catching the privacy fence and following it. The car pulled even with the drive and stopped. The green sedan looked too old to be an unmarked car. Emma saw two men watching the light as it moved along the fence, drifting deeper into the yard. If one of the men looked away from the light, even for a second, he'd see them. Levi shifted from one foot to the other. She tightened her hand around his. He must have understood her silent message. He held still. If the beam shifted to the side of the house they huddled against, they'd be exposed with nowhere to run.

The light moved from the fence into the darkest part of the backyard, catching the couple in its beam. It paused long enough for the men to see who was there—long enough for the man in the yard to become irritated and start for the car. The woman grabbed his arm, preventing a possible confrontation. The light blinked off. The car moved on.

When the man turned back to the fire, Emma pulled Levi with her to the front of the house, watching for the green car. No taillights, no dancing beam. She drew a deep breath. They were safe for the moment. But the car might circle back.

She knelt in front of Levi. "Are you okay?" He nodded. "I know this is scary, honey, but I won't let anyone hurt you. We'll find someplace safe."

She took his hand and walked him to the next intersection. With luck, she could hail a cab.

But then what?

# 4

The bus ascended the off-ramp right, from I-70 to what appeared to be a state highway. Turning left, it crossed over the interstate at a crawl, following the smaller highway around a long curve.

Leaning against the window, Emma strained to see any sign of a town, or the lights from a cluster of service stations and convenience stores that usually dotted interstates. No lights or town appeared in the distance, only a dark highway running through the rural countryside. She checked her watch, surprised to see it was almost nine p.m.—eight Colorado time. They were over halfway to California.

Several passengers mumbled to each other. Obviously, something was wrong with the vehicle, but where on Earth was the driver taking them? They had to be two or three miles off I-70 by now.

The murmurs grew louder, and she saw lights in the distance. A few minutes later, the driver pulled the bus into a convenience store parking lot. He pulled himself out of his seat and turned to face his passengers.

"We're having a problem with the transmission, folks. I've already called for help and another bus is on its way. Dispatch says it'll take a couple of hours to arrive. They suggested we wait here. It's a little out-of-the-way but transferring from one bus to the other will be safer."

He glanced out the window to his right, then to his left. "I can see some booths in the convenience store, so I imagine they have food. The restaurant across the street is open too. You've got plenty of time to eat and stretch your legs, or you can sleep on the bus 'til they get here." He opened the door and stepped off the bus, heading for the restaurant.

The noise of people leaving their seats woke Levi. He sat up rubbing his eyes and looked around. His gaze darted to her.

"It's okay, honey. We're stopping to change buses. Are you hungry?"

"Uh-huh. Can I have a candy bar and chips?"

She laughed. "Nice try, kiddo. How about sharing a sandwich with me, instead? You can have an apple for dessert if they have them, and maybe a granola bar."

"With chocolate chips?"

"We'll see what they have." The bus had cleared, with only three people sleeping in their seats. "Put your backpack on, honey." Grabbing her purse and duffel, she nudged him into the aisle.

The convenience store bustled with bus passengers. There was a line in front of both restrooms, another in front of the counter too. But the man behind the register took the unexpected business in stride, and the line at the counter moved quickly. Two hard-plastic booths lined the store's front windows. One was empty. She aimed Levi in that direction.

"Scoot in there and I'll get you something to munch on." She set her duffel beside him and walked to the cooler for a bottle of orange juice, then carried it to the counter, glancing at her nephew every few seconds. Even the fifteen or so feet between them made her uncomfortable. He must have felt the same. He sat on his knees, leaning over the table to watch her every move.

By the time she made it to the counter, most of the bus crowd had left the store. She ordered a turkey sandwich and a roast beef. It would probably be a while before the bus stopped again. She took a banana from the small basket on the counter, placing it with her other purchases.

"I'm getting a cup of coffee, too—a small one." She handed the clerk a twenty. "What town are we in?"

The clerk smiled as he counted her change back. "Connor. Actually, the town's about six blocks south of here."

Something tugged at her blouse. She looked down into the fearful eyes of her nephew. Kneeling, she took his shoulders with both hands. "What's the matter, honey?"

The boy grabbed her neck and held tight. "There's a man."

Lifting him into her arms, she glanced toward the two booths. A broad-shouldered man had taken a seat in the booth in front of theirs. He'd set his western-style hat in the seat beside him and his long, ebony-brown hair was tied at the back of his neck. He ignored the crush of customers as he drank his coffee and read his paper.

She patted the little boy's back to comfort him. He'd grown fearful of strangers, especially men. She couldn't blame him. Too many horrific things had happened in his short life.

"It's all right, Levi. He isn't the man who hurt your mommy and daddy."

"He didn't hurt you, either?"

"No, honey. He didn't hurt me. You don't have to be afraid."

"Okay. Can I have the banana first?"

She gave him a squeeze. "Sure, you can."

She caught the concern on the clerk's face before he turned his attention to the next customer. She needed to be more careful. The fewer people who noticed them, the better.

Levi wriggled to get down. As soon as his feet touched the floor, he grabbed his banana and ran to the booth, sitting with his back to the stranger—a sign he no longer considered the man a threat. She wasn't sure that was a good thing. How did she teach him to be cautious without frightening him? She carried their food to the table, glancing at the man in the other booth as she sat down. She wasn't the type to go weak in the knees at the sight of a good-looking man, but, heaven help her, with his slumberous eyes, broad shoulders and long, auburn-black hair tied at his nape, he might just be the exception to her rule.

Looking away, she busied herself with unwrapping one of the sandwiches. Levi's sigh caught her attention.

Her nephew was frowning at his banana.

"Need some help?"

He held the offending fruit up. "It don't wanna be open."

She reached for the banana. "Would you like to know a trick I learned from a monkey?"

Levi's eyes rounded, and he nodded. "A real monkey?"

"A real monkey at the zoo. Can you guess how he peels his bananas?"

He shook his head.

She turned the fruit upside down. "A monkey peels his banana from the bottom. It's easier." She peeled a strip a quarter of the way down the banana then handed it to Levi. "Why don't you try it while I get my coffee?"

He watched her walk to the coffee urn before turning his attention to the banana. He'd refused to let her out of his sight since she'd returned from the hospital. Her once innocent, carefree nephew lived with constant separation anxiety. She understood why. She shared the emotion. The thought of losing Levi terrified her.

Her cup was half full when the bell on the door rang. A man in jeans and a t-shirt walked in with a boy who looked maybe three or four years older than her nephew. The boy dashed past Levi on his way to the drink cooler. She finished filling her cup and pulled a lid from the dispenser before heading back.

She'd almost made it to her booth when the man at the front counter called out, "Jake, hurry up. I'm leaving."

The cooler door slammed. It was the only warning she had. A second later, the boy slammed into her side, twisting her off balance. She didn't have time to stop her fall and landed hard. Her back slammed against a rock-hard chest and she ricocheted into a pair of warm arms.

"Are you okay?"

She nodded and looked up at him. He had the richest dark brown eyes she'd ever seen on a man. She couldn't seem to look away.

They crinkled at the corners. "I'm impressed."

"What?"

He leaned over and took the coffee cup from her hand. "You didn't spill a drop. I expected a hot caffeine shower."

"It's decaf." *That was dumb.* She started to sit up.

His arms tightened. "Tom's son hit you pretty hard. You all right?"

"I'm fine."

His hold loosened, and he chuckled.

She looked over her shoulder at him. "What's so funny?"

"Tell me, are monkeys smart enough to take creases out of a Stetson?"

It took a minute to figure out what he was really saying. She groaned. "I'm sitting on your hat."

"Yeah, you are." She tried to jump up.

His hand on her shoulder stopped her.

"I'm sorry about your hat. I'll pay for it."

"No." He tilted his head toward the front of the booth. "They will."

The boy and his father were practically on top of them. She would have collided with the child again if the man, whose hat she was perched on, hadn't prevented it.

"Ma'am." The big man standing in front of her touched his own hat and nodded to her. "My son has something he wants to say to you."

The youngster's hat was in his hands. "I'm sorry for bump'n into you."

His father gave him a gentle push toward the door. "Go wait in the truck." He returned his attention to her. "My son didn't hurt you, did he?"

"No, I'm fine."

"Good." He looked above her head. "Send me the bill, Keeso."

"I will, Tom. Don't be too hard on Jake."

"I'll make him work off the cost of your new Stetson. That should teach him not to go tearing around places he shouldn't." He touched his hat and nodded to her again before following his son outside.

The hand on her shoulder lifted, and the cowboy leaned close to her ear. "Your son looks worried."

Levi stared over the back of the booth seat, looking more than worried. His eyes brimmed with tears and his lower lip trembled. She forgot everything else and rushed to comfort him. If he'd just turned around, he'd seen her between two giants, one with his hand on her.

As soon as she slipped into the seat beside him, he crawled into her lap burying his face in her neck. She rocked, and patted him, soothing him with assurances—they were not bad men, only big.

The cowboy—Keeso—set her coffee on the table in front of her. "It's probably cold now. Frank won't mind if you get a fresh cup." He squatted in front of Levi. "You don't have to be afraid," he soothed in a low voice. "No one's going to hurt your mom."

Levi lifted his head from her neck. "He already did."

Keeso's gaze met hers in question. She closed her eyes and shook her head, letting him know she didn't want to talk about it. She heard him stand and walk to the counter. A moment later, the bell on the door indicated he'd left.

The bus crowd had filed out earlier. No lines formed in front of the restrooms. She patted Levi's back. "Let's go into the bathroom to wash our hands before we open our sandwich. Okay?" He nodded, hopped off her lap and took her hand.

When they returned, the clerk was placing a steaming cup of coffee on the table. He smiled. "Keeso told me your cup got cold. He said you take decaf."

"I do. Thank you." He returned to the counter while she unwrapped the roast beef sandwich, placing half on a napkin for Levi.

They ate in companionable silence. Her nephew's eyes were getting heavy. Hopefully he'd stay awake until the replacement bus arrived. She finished her half of the sandwich and stowed the extra sandwich in a zippered compartment of her duffel. She leaned back, sipped her coffee and occasionally encouraged Levi to finish his meal.

What was she going to do once she reached California? She'd asked herself that question a dozen times since they'd boarded the bus in St. Louis—and still didn't have an answer. Chancing a trip to her bank when it opened yesterday, she'd tried to close out her accounts. The clerk had raised an eyebrow when she asked for cash. She retreated into the bank president's office before returning to explain they didn't have that much cash on hand. The most she could get on such short notice was five thousand. They could issue a cashiers' check for the remaining amount.

She and Levi had walked to a department store a few blocks away to purchase a couple of changes of clothes each, a few essentials and a duffel to use as luggage. They hailed a cab to the bus station, bought tickets for the next bus out of town, and thirty-six or so hours later, here they were—somewhere in the middle of Colorado on their way to California.

"Ma'am." The clerk walked around the counter. "The other bus pulled in the lot a few minutes ago. They're about done loading up." He carried a white square of paper to the door and taped it to the glass. "Can I help you with the boy? No one's in the store right now."

"Thanks, but I've got it." She tossed their trash in a nearby can and came around to wake Levi, who had curled up on the seat. "Come on honey, it's time to get on the bus." He roused enough to let her help him with his backpack. She lifted him into her arms and grabbed her purse and duffel.

The clerk held the door open. Smiling, she mouthed the word 'thanks' as she passed. She noticed the sign on the door read, 'Help Wanted' and her smile broadened. He'd certainly needed help tonight.

They were out the door and halfway across the parking lot when she stopped. The bus driver motioned for her to hurry. She shook her head and made a U-turn. Maybe this town had an answer after all.

# 5

✧

Emma turned at the convenience store entry to watch the bus pull out of the parking lot, heading east toward interstate seventy. The door opened and the clerk leaned out.

"Did you forget something?" He glanced through the window at the booth where she and Levi had been sitting. "Wouldn't the driver wait for you?"

"I've decided to stay."

"Ma'am?"

She pointed to the sign. "You need help, and I need a job."

He stepped back and held the door open for her. "Why don't you sit down again, and we'll talk?" He followed her to the booth and sat across from her. She eased Levi onto the seat using her duffel to cushion his head. Levi, she'd learned, could sleep anywhere this time of night.

"You do know the bus doesn't stop here regularly, don't you, ma'am?"

"Please, call me Emma." She'd considered using a different name, but he would need her ID if he gave her a job.

"Emma's a pretty name. My wife's sister has a daughter named Emma. She's about your age I'd guess." He smiled. "My name's Frank. Frank Martin."

His smile was contagious. She extended her hand. "It's nice to meet you, Frank." After shaking her hand, he slipped out of the booth and went to the coffee pot. A moment later he returned with coffee for each of them. He'd remembered she took decaf.

"So, you need a job, do you?" He moved back into the seat across from her.

"Yes."

He pulled a package of creamer from his shirt pocket, tore open the corner, and sifted the powder into the steaming liquid. She waited as he used a red plastic stick to turn the black brew into a creamy mocha color.

After taking a sip, he leaned back in the booth and studied her. She was afraid he was already making up his mind about hiring her. He probably didn't intend to make her nervous, but he was doing a fine job of it.

"You're in trouble, aren't you?"

She wasn't sure what she'd expected him to say, but that wasn't it. Was she so transparent? She grabbed her purse and started to reach for Levi.

"Wait." He pushed his coffee aside and leaned forward, folding his hands on the table top. He glanced at Levi. "I overheard you and the boy talking. It's obvious you're both afraid. Is there something I can do?"

She caught her lower lip between her teeth, debating how much, if anything, she should divulge. His expression mirrored genuine concern. Something about him reminded her of her dad. She stared out the window at the empty parking lot. He had always been easy to talk to. Even strangers seemed to know they could depend on his discretion.

Frank was like that. She instinctively knew she could trust him.

In the end, it came down to doing what was right. Hiring her could put him in jeopardy. She'd already seen what the killer was capable of. He wouldn't hesitate to hurt anyone who stood between him and what he wanted. And what he wanted was her and Levi dead. She needed to tell the man the truth before he made the decision to hire her.

"I'm running from the authorities. I haven't done anything wrong."

"I didn't think you had. I'm a fairly good judge of character. You don't work with the public as long as I have and not get an education in humanity. If I'd thought you'd done anything wrong, we wouldn't be having this conversation."

"Mr. Martin—"

"Frank."

"Okay, Frank. Levi isn't my son, he's my nephew. My sister and her husband named me legal guardian in their wills. Before they were…." She clenched her cup, the white foam crinkling as she lifted it to her lips and gulped the still warm liquid like an alcoholic gulps his first whiskey of the day. Talking about her sister and John still hurt.

She finally set the cup down. "Levi and I… we saw someone we shouldn't have—someone dangerous. He saw us too."

"How dangerous?" Frank's low voice filled with dread.

Her gaze met his. "He'll kill us if he finds us."

The storekeeper glanced at Levi. "Please tell me that boy's folks weren't murdered by whoever you're running from."

She shook her head. "I can't."

"Did your nephew see it happen?"

"Levi and I were upstairs when we heard the shots. I made him hide and went downstairs to John's study. I found Denise and John dead—they'd both been shot. Their killer shot me too and left me for dead when the police broke down the front door.

"After I recovered, I joined Levi in a safehouse. The authorities were going to relocate us, but the killer found us anyway. In the confusion, I took Levi and ran. I didn't know who to trust. Someone must have told him where we were." She took the last swallow of coffee.

Frank leaned back in the booth. "So now you're looking for a job."

"I am, but it isn't going to be easy. I don't know why I thought I could work here. I can't use my identification. My Social Security number can be traced. I suspect the St. Louis police department has been compromised, or maybe the FBI. They share information. Regardless of who it is, if the good guys find us, the bad guys will too."

He nodded in understanding. "What did you do before your sister and her husband were killed?"

"I'm a teacher. I taught first and second grade."

"I imagine you're a fine teacher. You're good with the boy."

"Thank you." She reached for her purse again. "I don't know what I was thinking when I asked you for a job. I can't have my personal information put in the system. If you offered me work, you could be putting yourself in danger. I don't think I can handle it if anything happens to you or anyone else because of us. I'm sorry I bothered you."

"Hold on now. I'd like to help you, but I think we need to figure a few things out first." He nodded toward Levi. "You have any idea where you're going to stay tonight?"

She felt blindsided. What was the matter with her—dragging Levi off the bus, asking for a job she couldn't have, and stranding them for the night?

"I don't suppose Connor has a taxi service, does it? And a motel or bed-and-breakfast, maybe?"

"There's a small bed-and-breakfast on Main Street, but I imagine it's filled. It usually is this time of year. People start coming out to see the aspens turn gold about now. No taxi, though."

"How far is the bed-and-breakfast?"

Frank tilted his head at her. "Too far for you and that boy to walk there, especially this time of night. How long have you been out of the hospital?"

"About a week."

He looked like he thought she was crazy and shook his head. Then he sighed. "I know you're desperate, but you need to be reasonable, too. I may have an answer for you, but I need to call my wife, Molly, first. We never make any decisions without consulting each other. Stay right here." He got up and walked around the counter, picked up his store phone and punched in some numbers. He stared out the front window, and conversed quietly with the person on the other end of the line, nodding occasionally.

After no more than five minutes, he returned to the booth and sat down.

"I usually hire a high school kid during the summer when tourists show up. Can't always depend on them, though. That's why I put up the sign."

He smiled. "You can have the job if you want it. We'll figure a way around the identification problem. I can't afford to pay more than minimum wage."

He inclined his head toward the hall that led to the bathrooms. "But there's an apartment in the back you can use if you'd like, and the electric and water are connected to the store, so they wouldn't cost anything."

Her vision blurred. This kind man was an answer to her prayers. "Yes, I want it, but you need to understand. If I stay in one place more than a month or two, he might find me. I won't be here long."

"Don't worry about that. I can always put the sign back up if I need to."

There was still a worry. "You're not... concerned about your safety? Or your wife's?"

"I doubt there's much chance of anyone finding you way out here. Even if someone figured out what bus you were on, they'd be looking for you at your tickets' destination. No, I'm not afraid."

He unfolded his tall, thin frame and stood. "Why don't you gather that boy up and I'll show you where you'll be living."

"Thank you." She lifted her nephew onto one shoulder, hooked the strap of her purse over the other and scooted out of the booth.

Frank picked up the duffel and led the way, moving past the counter into the hall and through a swinging door. The hall on the other side was well lit. An open door on the left led to a large room full of supplies and case goods. He stopped a few feet down the hall at a door on the right, pulled a set of keys from his pocket and unlocked it.

"It's nothing fancy." He switched on the light. "But it's clean. Molly is a bit obsessive about keeping it that way. She cleans it once a week—even changes the sheets. Says you never know when a member of our family will show up."

They walked into a combination living room and kitchen. The south end of the room housed a stove, refrigerator and counter area with cabinets above and below the sink. A small window, framed with white lace curtains, had a small potted plant on the sill. An oval table covered with a red and white checked cloth completed the area. Her eyes were drawn to the door next to the counter.

Frank set the duffel on the sofa to their right. "That door leads to the backyard and drive. He fished in his pocket and retrieved two keys. "The silver one's for the deadbolt to the outside door. The gold one fits the hall door. I'll find you a ring for these. Molly has some at the house." He nodded toward the TV across the room, hanging on the wall between two doors. "We get a few channels out here. I never bothered with trying to get cable or satellite."

"I'm sure it will be fine. We won't need more than the basics. Is there a library in Connor? Levi likes to have me read to him at night, and he's getting tired of the ones in his backpack."

"There is, and a community center too. We also have a nice park with a playground. Lots of kids for your nephew to play with."

He glanced at the sleeping child and pointed to the door on the right. "I imagine you want him to have the smaller room. The one on the left is larger. They both have plenty of closet space."

She decided to put Levi in the larger room with her tonight. She didn't want him waking alone in a strange place. After removing his backpack and shoes, she pulled the blanket over him, and returned to the living area.

Frank hovered at the hall door. "Take a couple of days to get settled in. Molly will want to meet you, and she can take you to the store to get a few things when you're ready.

"I appreciate everything you're doing for us. I hadn't expected a place to live as well as a job."

He shrugged. "No sense in this place being empty when you can use it. We open at six in the morning and close at eleven p.m. I'll open and close. You can work from eight to noon, take a break, and return at two. You'll have some time to spend with your nephew in the afternoon that way. Then you'll work until six.

"I don't leave any money in the register overnight and leave it open so anyone looking through the window can see it's empty. You shouldn't have to worry about break-ins." He stepped into the hall. "I'll be right back."

She listened to his footsteps recede. Five minutes later, he returned with a plastic bag. "I thought you might need a few things until you can get to the store. I'll leave you to settle in. Sleep as late as you want tomorrow. I imagine you and the boy both need your rest. Either Molly or I will be in the store, so if you decide you need anything, let us know."

He paused with his hand on the doorknob. "This is a good community. Lots of fine people live here, and we all help each other. Connor's a small town in the middle of nowhere. It doesn't have much to draw attention to itself, but we get our share of tourists. Except for a few regulars, we seldom see anyone more than once or twice. Seems to me Connor would be an easy place to get lost, if a person needed to. You might consider staying more than a month or two. I hope you do." He went into the hall and turned. "Have a good night."

She walked to the door. "Thank you again."

He nodded and headed for the store.

She closed and locked the door behind him, then hurried to lock the deadbolt on the outside door and pull the curtains closed. Leaning against it, she closed her eyes to offer a prayer of thanksgiving for the kind man. His parting words were more than she could hope for. She couldn't imagine being able to settle anywhere. But for now, she and Levi had a roof over their heads and time to figure out what to do next. Temporary though it was, Connor, Colorado, had become their safe haven.

# 6

✧

Keeso's home wasn't really a cabin, though he thought of it as such. The original cabin used by the man he'd bought the property from had been one room and falling in. The old timer was lucky it hadn't collapsed in on him.

Granted, the home he'd built had a solid log exterior, but the interior was as modern as they came, except for the huge wood cook stove in the main room that served as kitchen, dining, and living room. The large master bedroom boasted a full bath and Jacuzzi. The smaller bedrooms shared a second bathroom at the end of the hall. Those rooms were used to accommodate his fellow Centallians, who aided him on occasion—friends he hadn't seen in over six Earth months. Something had happened to them.

An odd sound interrupted his dour musings. At first, he assumed it was the wind, moaning through the Ponderosa Pines beside the cabin. But when the eerie sound continued, he walked to the door and opened the screen. The familiar yipping call of a lone coyote nearly covered the high-pitched whimper coming from the corner of the porch. Reaching for the flashlight he kept on the stand by the door, he stepped outside, and swung it in the direction of the sound. A pair of eyes reflected in the light, and the whimper changed to a soft, half-hearted growl.

"Easy, friend. Let's get a better look at you." He eased toward the timid animal. The beam exposed a young dog. It backed away. Keeso decided a little bribery was in order.

He returned to the kitchen and opened the refrigerator. Not much to offer in there. He grabbed the dish of leftover oatmeal from this morning's breakfast, the carton of eggs and a gallon of milk. Taking a metal bowl and spoon from the dish drainer, he dumped in the oatmeal and half the milk, cracked three eggs over the top, and stirred everything together. He carried the mess to the porch, set it by the door, and went back inside.

It didn't take long for the pup to discover his offering. The young dog slurped and skittered the bowl across the wooden slats. Keeso grinned as he turned out the lights and headed for the bedroom. If the dog was still there in the morning, he'd check in town. Hopefully, someone knew where he belonged.

Emboldened by the offering, the pup scratched at the door a couple of times, plopped down in front of it, and started howling. Before long, a chorus of coyotes joined him. Keeso figured a couple of wolves added their voices to the choir.

He told himself the dog had to settle down and go to sleep before long, but that long-eared, gangly half-hound didn't give up. Not for a couple of hours, anyway.

The little mongrel greeted him at the door the next morning. Keeso made a special trip into Connor to find out if anyone was missing a dog. Nearly everyone he talked to mentioned the fact that remote places like his were prime targets for people wanting to get rid of an animal. The idea disgusted him. Anyone capable of leaving an animal to fend for itself lacked character and honor.

He ended up buying a twenty-dollar dog bed and a fifty-pound bag of dog food. Spending money on a bed didn't mean he intended to keep the pup. The first person to offer the dog a good home would get the bed to boot.

The pup was waiting on his front porch, tail thumping. The relief he felt surprised him. A dog his size wouldn't last more than a day alone in the mountains—too many large predators roamed the area looking for an easy meal.

The dog followed at his heels while he checked the ore crates and supplies at the mine. When he caught himself talking to the pup, he decided he needed to get to town more often. He had to admit the little guy's company made the day less tedious.

At sunset, while he stood on the porch drinking his coffee, his new best friend sniffed the dog bed and tested it out. Circling twice, he plopped down, resting his head on the bed's high edge. When the air took on a decided chill, he turned to go inside. The pup tried to beat him to the door.

"No, you don't. You've got a perfectly good bed out here." The pup tilted his head in question. Keeso started to explain, then remembered he was talking to a dog. Shaking his head, he walked into the house.

The heat from the cook stove drew him like a magnet. Would he ever get used to this world's penchant for lower temperatures? He'd never get used to high country winters and didn't look forward to the next few months. Pouring the last of the coffee into his cup, he crossed the room to the big chair he'd purchased at something called a yard sale. He was easing into the cushions when the howling started. The pup sounded lonely tonight. Sighing, Keeso got up, opened the door, and laughed. The dog had pulled his bed in front of the door and sat waiting. As soon as the screen opened he tried to drag the bed inside.

The message was clear. As the old prospector would have said, he'd staked his claim. Keeso gave in gracefully. Carrying the bed into the house, he set it between his chair and the wall—out from under foot.

Keeso smiled to himself as he sat down. How often had he heard one of the locals say that? Even his thoughts were beginning to carry the local flavor. When he'd first taken over the mine, the residents continuously commented on his manner of speech, assuming he 'haled' from a different state, or maybe from another country. Hiilani had noticed immediately and asked where he had grown up. She'd told him his English was too perfect. After two years of listening to the people in Connor, his English had deteriorated—according to Centallian standards. He'd picked up the locals' dialect and some highly colloquial words and phrases.

*Hiilani.* She'd been the first woman from Earth to become a Centallian bride—his. How often in the last year had his thoughts strayed to his former bond-mate? The genetic incompatibility that sometimes occurred between their species had resulted in the loss of their son and forced them to dissolve their bonding. She had chosen to remain with his people on New Centallus, using her nursing skills to aid the Earth-born brides of his Centallian brethren.

He had opted to stay on Earth to run the mine. Their Hopi friends had suggested salting a played-out gold mine in Colorado with ore from mineral-rich New Centallus. Their bogus operation made it possible to convert Centallian ore into Earth currency that could buy desperately needed supplies for their colony.

He drained the cup and set it on the stand beside the chair. Thoughts of Hiilani no longer haunted him. While he still delayed choosing a compatible bond-mate, the thought of his lovely Hawaiian flower bonding with another Guardian didn't hurt as much.

Cintar, his friend and second-in-command of the starship, *Novaria,* had approached him on his last trip. He'd asked for his permission to court Hiilani, and for his blessing as well. He'd willingly given his blessing. His permission had only been a formality.

That was the last day he'd seen or heard from them. Something had happened to the ship, or the colony. He willed it to be the ship. After everything his people had lost, everything they had suffered, the colony had promised a new beginning.

But in the long, sleepless pre-dawn hours, his faith waivered. Were they still alive? The colony numbered less than two hundred, including the brides. So few Centallians. He knew every name, could picture every face. To his knowledge, they were the only survivors of his race. Earth had a phrase that described their circumstances—the Centallians had become an endangered species.

Were they still out there, fighting for survival? Or had the demons who'd destroyed Centallus attacked the colony, defeating them with greater numbers, and more powerful weapons? Did New Centallus still exist?

Faces cluttered his mind—his sweet Hiilani, Rhyel and Cintar, the Elders. Did they live only in his memories now? Was he the last Centallian, the only person in existence who remembered a beautiful planet named Centallus?

His mind refused to accept that possibility. They were still out there, building a new world. He'd know if they were gone.

If the problem was the *Novaria,* it might take the technicians months to repair it. A small voice in his mind reminded him that it *had* been months— long enough for any repair.

The *Novaria* might never return.

And *his* future? Healing stasis would provide for his medical needs. Barring an accident, the chances of anyone discovering his alien physiology was negligible. The leftover Centallian gold would sustain him, preventing the necessity of contact with more than a handful of associates and the acquaintances he'd made in Connor.

In more personal matters, choosing an Earth mate was out of the question. The possibility of genetic incompatibility would haunt any relationship he formed. Hiilani's anguished eyes filled his memory. He never wanted to see that look in a woman's eyes again. He had to spend his life alone.

A cold nose nudged him from his thoughts, and he reached down to scratch the pup's ear. Suddenly, he was glad the dog had found him. "Well, Pup, it's just you and me."

# 7

✧

A dark green sedan pulled up in front of the gas pumps. Emma held her breath and watched a man in a brown suitcoat get out of the car and begin filling the tank. An older woman got out of the passenger seat and walked toward the glass doors.

She could breathe again.

After working nearly three weeks for Frank, she still couldn't control the apprehension that gripped her every time a car she didn't recognize pulled into the parking lot—she hadn't been working long enough to recognize many vehicles.

The bell rang, and the woman mouthed the word 'bathroom' as soon as she entered the store. Emma nodded, and pointed her in the right direction.

A few minutes later, the couple paid for gas and two bottled waters. "Your town is quite lovely, dear." The woman's smile was contagious, and Emma responded with a genuine smile of her own.

As they walked out, she skirted the counter and headed through the swinging door to check on Levi. The bell chimed the couple's departure. Her nephew had tossed a pillow on the floor and sprawled across it to watch his favorite afternoon cartoons. He jumped to his feet when she entered the room, fear dominating his expression when he swung around. Seeing her, he propelled himself into her arms and she held him until the tension in his little body eased. Was his anxiety based on his parents' murders and their flight from St. Louis, or was it a reaction to her own fears? Probably a little of both.

She had to make sure he would have a normal, carefree childhood. The question was how to do that.

In her darkest moments, she'd even considered leaving the country. But again, the question was how. It took documentation to acquire a passport, documentation she didn't have at hand. Obtaining the necessary papers would lead the authorities—and the killer—to their door. Would she ever find a safe haven, a place where Levi wouldn't be haunted by the specter of death?

"Can I have a snack?" Levi had recovered from the moment and was ready to move on to important things like snacks.

"Sure. How about a yogurt?"

"Blueberry?"

"Blueberry it is." He followed her into the kitchen area and grabbed a teaspoon from the silverware drawer while she retrieved an individual-sized yogurt from the refrigerator. A few minutes later, he was back in front of the TV, spooning purple yogurt into his mouth.

She double-checked the lock on the back door. It was obsessive, she knew, but she never left the apartment without checking it.

She glanced out the small window toward Connor. She'd been to the little burg once to buy groceries, clothes, a few toys, and activity items to keep Levi occupied. The woman had called it her town. She couldn't claim the town, but the thought of belonging somewhere again appealed to her.

The small business district lay about five blocks south of the state highway and Frank's store. Few highway travelers saw the actual town. Most were on their way to one of the abandoned gold mines listed on a brochure they'd picked up from a rack somewhere. A few came for the area's spectacular scenery.

She was grateful for this out-of-the-way hiding place—and for Frank and Molly. Their kindness made it possible for her to give Levi a reasonably normal life. This job was a godsend.

But she couldn't get past her fear. In the beginning, the anxiety hadn't been as bad. Frank stuck around the first few days, helping her learn the routine.

He knew the locals and introduced her to what he called 'the regulars'. Lately though, she'd begun to anticipate trouble every time a car she didn't recognize pulled into the parking lot, or up to the pumps. Every day that passed felt like a day closer to being discovered. She told herself it didn't make sense. Reasonably, the more time that passed, the less likely someone would come looking for her. But reason didn't prevent her heart from racing a dozen times a day.

On her way back to the front, she stopped at the supply room for a box of what Frank called crankcase oil. She found the case of oil and lifted it. The slight twinge on her still-tender side warned her to be careful.

Keeso heard footsteps in the back hall of the store, and turned, expecting to see Frank walk out. Instead, a young woman, struggling under the weight of a heavy cardboard box, came out, heading for the counter. He rushed up the aisle behind her.

"Let me get that for you."

She screamed, pivoted, and lost her hold on the box. He caught it, preventing it from careening into an endcap display of A&W Root Beer, and looked up, laughing. The terror in her eyes caught him off guard, and her pale face made him think she might faint. He set the box on the floor and reached out to support her.

She backed away. "Don't touch me."

Keeso raised both hands to placate her. "I won't, but you need to sit down before you fall down. I didn't mean to scare you." She shook her head and kept backing up.

A short blur barreled out of the back room and attacked Keeso's knees, nearly buckling them. "Leave my Aunty alone."

"Levi, no." The young woman grabbed his assailant's arm and peeled the boy off his leg. "It's okay, honey." She knelt in front of the boy. "He didn't hurt me."

"But Aunty, I heard you holler."

"I was surprised, that's all. It's really okay."

She turned the most incredible blue eyes on him—eyes he remembered. He also remembered the feel of her warm, soft body pressed against his. The memory had caused him several sleepless nights. They were still clouded with fear. She clung to the child as though she expected him to be wrenched from her grasp at any moment.

"I'm not going to hurt your son, ma'am." She didn't move. "I won't hurt you either. Is Frank here?" It was a dumb question born of desperation. If Frank had been in the store, he'd have investigated the commotion.

Wariness replaced the fear in her eyes. "Frank will be back in a minute. Can I help you with anything?"

"I remember you from the night that bus broke down. You sat on my Stetson." She flushed, apparently remembering him too. "Do you work here?"

"Yes." She glanced out the window. "I don't see your vehicle."

"I pulled to the side of the building. My dog was hot, so I stopped to get him a drink." He grinned. "I should have known he'd refuse the free drink at the hydrant. He doesn't like the taste of Connor's water." Keeso bent and picked up the dented bottle of water and package of mixed nuts he'd dropped when he caught the box.

She stood with her hands on the boy's shoulders. He couldn't decide if she were protecting the boy from him, or him from the boy.

"The bell didn't ring." Her voice was tense.

"The what?"

"The doorbell. It didn't ring when you came in."

He didn't know what she was accusing him of. "Sure, it did. I heard it ring when I pulled the door open for the man and woman who left a few minutes ago." He nodded toward the door in question.

"A puppy!" The boy tore away from the woman and raced toward the glass door. She was right behind him, grabbing his arm before he reached the door and the dog.

"Levi, what have I told you about taking off like that?" She knelt so her eyes were level with the boy's. "Sweetie, we've talked about how important it is for you to think before you act. The dog doesn't know you."

The pup scratched at the door. "Get down," Keeso ordered. The young dog immediately sat back on his haunches, his tail thumping the sidewalk. "He won't hurt the boy."

"Can I pet him? Please? Can I?"

The young woman looked from the boy to the dog and back to the boy, obviously uncertain. Keeso decided to tip the odds in the kid's favor. "They both look like they could use a friend." He regretted his interference the second her amazing eyes clouded with guilt. "Of course, you know better than I do about what's good for your son."

It took a few seconds for her to decide before she finally relented. "Levi, you can pet—" She turned back to him. "What's your dog's name?"

"I just call him Pup."

She faced the boy again. "You can pet Pup but stay on the sidewalk where I can see you."

The boy hit the door running. "Thanks, Aunty."

She watched as the two got acquainted, her hand on the door as if she waited for something to go wrong. Finally, she turned toward him.

"He's not my son. He's my nephew."

Keeso smiled. "So, your nephew's staying with you for a while? He probably misses his folks. Is that why he was so upset earlier?"

"Levi isn't… His parents died two months ago. His mother was my sister. I have custody of him now."

He felt like he needed to go outside and clean off his boots. He just kept stepping in it. The loss probably explained the pain in her eyes, but her fear bothered him. He had the sudden urge to protect her.

"I'm sorry to hear about your loss, ma'am. I know what it's like to lose family. If I can do anything for you and the boy, all you have to do is ask."

She gave him a noncommittal nod, glanced at her nephew, and moved to the counter. "It isn't ma'am. It's miss."

That information pleased him, though it shouldn't have.

"Is the water all for now?"

"And the nuts." He set his purchases on the glass top and pulled a ten from his wallet. She rang up the items and counted back his change. Before he had time to return the wallet to his pocket, she'd moved from behind the counter to the door. Keeso followed but paused. When he didn't go out, she tilted her head in question. "Did you need anything else?"

He needed to know who or what she was afraid of. He removed his hat. "I never introduced myself. I'm Keeso Smith."

She hesitated a moment before extending her hand. "I'm Emma." She glanced toward the boy. "My nephew is Levi." Keeso shook her hand, noting she hadn't given him their last names. He peered through the glass. The boy and the pup sat side-by-side, the boy's arm draped over the dog's neck.

"I meant what I said earlier. If you or the boy need anything, let me know."

She avoided his eyes as she opened the door. "Levi, Mr. Smith is ready to go now. Tell the puppy good-bye and come inside." She stepped back so he could leave. Her nephew gave the dog a hug and ran past him into the store. He turned to watch her walk to the counter, her attention on the boy who was talking nonstop.

He grinned as he and the pup ambled toward the Jeep. She hadn't exactly tossed him out, but she'd come close.

# 8

✦

"Good morning, Frank."

The store owner looked up from his paper. "Mornin' Keeso. You're early today. She isn't working this morning."

"Who?"

Frank glanced at him over the newspaper. "You can't fool me, son. You've shown up here at least four times this week, and it's not to see me."

Keeso walked to the coffee machine to pour himself a cup. "How do you know how often I'm here?"

Frank nodded toward a security camera perched in a corner. "I play the recordings a couple times a week to see who needs a little closer watching when they come in. I've noticed you and the pup stop'n by more often since Emma started working here." He folded his paper and picked up his coffee cup. "I haven't seen you this interested in a woman since you dated that cute little nurse at the clinic. What was her name?"

"Hiilani."

"Whatever happened to her? I thought sure you two would get hitched."

"She went home for a visit and decided to stay." Keeso wasn't lying to his friend. Hiilani had gone home, but it was to his home, not hers.

"Guess the Colorado winters were too cold for her."

"Could be. I came in early to ask you about Emma and the boy."

"I can't tell you much. She's only worked here two months."

"It doesn't take two months to know she's afraid of something. She tenses every time a car pulls into the lot. She relaxes if a couple or family get out, but if it's a single man, she stays alert until she gets a good look at him. If he's wearing a suit, she stays tense until he pulls onto the highway. Something has her running scared."

"You're worried about her?"

"Aren't you?"

Frank waved away the money Keeso handed him for the coffee. "I am, but there isn't anything I can do about it, except keep an eye out."

"You know why she's frightened?"

Frank nodded. "I promised to keep it to myself. I'm afraid you'll have to hear it from her."

"Are they in danger?"

"That I can tell you. If they're found, they won't survive."

Rage caught him by surprise. Why would anyone want to harm an innocent woman and child? "We have to protect them."

Frank lifted an eyebrow. "We?"

"I'm not going to stand by and let them get hurt."

Frank nodded. "The question is, how do we keep them safe?"

Keeso tilted his head toward the corner of the room. "Do you have remote access to that camera of yours?"

"It has Wi-Fi. I check the recordings with my computer at home, but I've never used the live feed."

"You can do both. We'd keep a better eye on them that way. I'll find an excuse to drop by more often." He took a swallow of coffee and considered his options. "Her nephew likes the pup. That's excuse enough for me."

"Pup!" Levi raced out of the back hall to the front door, Emma right behind him.

"Levi, stop." She caught the boy before he opened the door. "What have I told you about tearing through the store?"

He didn't take his eyes off the dog. "I'm sorry, Aunty. Can I go out and see him? *Please?"*

"Only after you've apologized to Frank and Mr. Smith for interrupting their conversation."

The boy managed to drag his gaze from the dog long enough to mumble, "Sorry," and swing around to her. "Now can I go out?"

Sighing, she nodded in resignation. "You can pet him for a few minutes, then we have to go—" she glanced over at Frank, "—that is if we can borrow your truck to go to the park."

Frank was fishing in his pocket for the keys when Keeso spoke up. "I can take you to the park. Levi and the pup can wear each other out instead of us."

Emma started shaking her head.

The keys in Frank's hand disappeared into his pocket again. "That sounds like a great idea." He grabbed a plastic bag and opened the cooler at the counter. "I'll send some sandwiches and drinks along for lunch. Emma, why don't you pick out a bag of chips?"

Keeso tossed a twenty on the counter. "I'll need a bag of ice and a six-pack of water." He turned to Emma. "What does Levi like to drink?"

"Apple juice, but—"

Keeso repressed a smile at the confusion on her face. They hadn't given her a chance to say no. "Apple juice it is." He walked to the drink cooler. "What do you want to drink?"

"Mr. Smith, I don't—"

"Keeso."

"What?"

"Call me Keeso. You're getting apple juice too." He carried his choices to the front. "Keep the change."

Emma watched Keeso walk out the door, then turned to Frank. "What just happened?"

The man grinned. "You got an invitation for a picnic. It's a nice day for one."

Invitation? It felt more like she'd been railroaded, and her boss was a co-conspirator. "What's really going on?"

Frank sobered. "Keeso knows you and the boy are in trouble." He held his hands up when she opened her mouth. "I didn't give him any details, just confirmed his suspicion that you were in trouble. He knows someone is after you, that's all. From our conversation this morning, I think he's determined to keep you safe."

She followed Frank's glance to the front door. Levi was jumping up and down with excitement. Frank chuckled. "Looks like he intends to do it with or without your agreement."

She didn't like losing control, especially where Levi was concerned. Frank must have read her expression correctly.

"Keeso's a good man. All he wants to do is help protect you and your nephew. Take my advice and let him. This is too serious to take on by yourself. Allow him to shoulder the burden for an hour or two. His shoulders are broad enough."

Levi ran into the store. "Aunty, Keeso says he's going to the park too and we can ride with him. Can I go help put the ice in the cooler?"

She caved. Levi hadn't been this excited about anything since before his parents had been killed. She didn't have it in her to disappoint him. Besides, Frank vouched for the tall cowboy. The man certainly looked capable of taking care of them. She sighed. "Stay with Mr. Smith until I get there."

"He wants you to call him Keeso."

"Okay… Keeso. Don't leave his side. Understand?"

"Yes, ma'am." He ran outside, waited for Keeso to get a bag of ice from the freezer in front of the store, and walked with him to the Jeep.

Levi strutted beside the big man, chattering a mile a minute. Keeso nodded a couple of times at something her nephew said.

He should be sharing moments like this with his father, not some stranger—even if the man had good intentions. Regret tightened her throat and she fought back tears. It wasn't fair.

"You'd better get out there. That boy's ready to bust with excitement." Frank's grin widened as he stared out the window. "The pup's as excited as he is. Look at him race in circles around them."

"I'll get my purse."

"It's on your shoulder."

# 9

✧

The small park was lovely and completely theirs. Keeso's gaze did a full three-sixty as he circled the jeep to give her a hand out. Emma unclipped Levi's harness and helped him down while Keeso unhooked the pup.

"Can Pup and me go play on the slide?"

"Pup and I," she corrected as she looked where he was pointing. Several pieces of state-of-the-art playground equipment were contained in a large circle cushioned by wood shavings. Trees shaded the area, but the underbrush had been cleared away, leaving a wide, open space.

"All right." She started to follow her nephew, intending to sit on one of the benches edging the playground, but Keeso grabbed her hand.

"He's fine." He pulled a quilt out of a metal box in the back of the Jeep and handed it to her. Lifting the cooler to his shoulder, he led the way to a shady spot in the grass. "We'll spread the blanket here where we can see the playground and the creek. The pup's bound to lead him to the water eventually." He set the cooler on the ground. "I'll go check the creek."

"Check for what?"

"Critters."

She didn't ask what kind of critters, didn't want to know. "Maybe he shouldn't get close to the creek." She'd rather he didn't get near the water, anyway.

"He'll be fine. I'll scatter whatever's there and they'll stay away while the dog's around. He won't let them bother your boy."

Holding the quilt against her chest, she shook her head. "Levi's not my boy. I told you, he's my nephew."

"He may not have started out yours, but he's yours now, isn't he?"

The man turned and headed for the creek before she could reply, which was just as well. He'd guessed the truth, or perhaps Frank had told him.

She watched her nephew run from the slide to the swings, the young dog at his heels. Levi was hers now, making her responsible for his safety.

In a way, she was responsible for Frank's safety too—and for the big man kicking rocks and brush by the creek. They were getting too involved for their own good.

It was time to leave Connor.

"Can't find a spot to spread the blanket?" She jumped, startled. She hadn't heard him come back. He took the quilt. "This is flat enough." Tossing a couple of rocks toward the creek, he shook the cover out and spread it on the grass.

Her attention was drawn to the quilt. "That's too pretty to put on the ground. It looks hand-sewn."

He shrugged his shoulders. "I bought a couple of them from a shop in Connor. At the time, I was more interested in how warm they were. I guess they could be handmade."

"Do you always have a quilt handy in case of a picnic?"

He laughed—a booming, carefree sound. "I make a habit of carrying a warm blanket in my Jeep for emergencies. Winters can be unforgiving at this altitude. Make yourself comfortable while I get the food."

She settled onto the quilt, making sure Levi was in her line of vision. Her nephew giggled, and she smiled in reaction. There hadn't been much to laugh about recently.

Her gaze shifted to Keeso. She'd dubbed him a cowboy but realized he didn't fit the profile. Most of the ranchers in Connor had weathered, sun-browned skin. Usually lean and wiry, the few who'd spent a good part of their lives on a horse generally had a slight bow to their legs.

Not that she hadn't met a few tall, ruggedly handsome ranchers during her stay in Connor, but except for the Stetson he was fond of wearing, Keeso Smith didn't fit the image. He was too tall and broad shouldered. The long dark hair he tied at the nape of his neck didn't fit either. Nor did the footwear. The high-topped suede moccasin boots didn't exactly shout cowboy.

Now that she thought about it, he looked more Native American—except for his straight nose. His coloring certainly added to the impression—well, almost. His skin had a red-bronze cast and she wondered what heritage mix attributed to the unusual skin tone.

He retrieved the sack of food and carried it to where she sat. She returned her full attention to Levi before Keeso caught her watching him.

"Frank packed enough for two meals." He dropped to the quilt, his big frame taking up most of the space. "Are you hungry?"

She shook her head. "I'll wait for Levi. He's having too much fun to stop and eat. But you go ahead."

"I can wait." He set the bag aside and opened the cooler. "Thirsty?"

She nodded. "A water sounds good."

He reached into the cooler and pulled out two bottles, handing one to her.

"Thanks." She shook off the water droplets clinging to the outside of the bottle, removed the cap, and took a swallow. "You're not a rancher, are you?"

He stretched out on the blanket and faced her, leaning on an elbow. "No. I own a small mining operation."

"What kind of mine?"

"Gold."

"You own a goldmine?" She didn't know why it surprised her. People had been mining gold in this part of the country for over a century.

He smiled at her reaction. "A *small* goldmine. It's pretty much a one-man operation." He shrugged. "It's not making me rich, but I do all right."

Her nephew's laughter drew their attention to the boy and dog. The two were playing tug-of-war with a stick. Keeso levered himself up from the quilt and sprinted to the Jeep. He opened the metal box, rummaged around in the bottom, and came up with a blue frisbee. He pursed his lips and emitted a short, shrill whistle. The pup let go of the stick and whirled around toward his master. Levi landed on his backside.

Keeso tossed the frisbee in a long, high arc. The dog raced under it, lunging high to catch it out of the air.

"Wow!" Levi still sat in the dirt, his attention on the pup. "He's a really good catcher."

The pup lumbered over and dropped the frisbee in his lap, obviously wanting him to join in the fun. Keeso walked to the boy and knelt in front of him to say something. Levi nodded vigorously, grabbed the toy, and jumped up. He threw the blue saucer overhand, like a baseball. It landed in the dirt and rolled about five feet. The dog fetched it anyway and dropped it in front of them. Keeso picked the disc up, said a few words to Levi, then sent it flying. When the pup bounded back, it was Levi's turn. The disc wobbled but flew a little farther. The dog retrieved the frisbee again. Keeso gave it to Levi but placed his hand on the boy's and guided the throw.

And so it went, one toss after another with the man demonstrating the art of the frisbee, and the boy hanging on every word and action. Finally, Keeso patted Levi's shoulder, walked to the blanket, and sat down. He took a long swallow of his water and heaved a contented sigh.

"He's a good kid."

She smiled. "I know. He didn't deserve what happened to him—no child ever could."

"You're doing a good job with him."

"Sometimes I have my doubts. It isn't easy. He has a lot of fears."

"I imagine you have a few yourself."

She looked away. "A few."

Levi skidded to a halt at the blanket's edge. "I'm hungry."

She held a hand up when he started to get on the blanket. "Shoes off first. You don't want to get Mr. Smith's quilt dirty."

"He wants us to call him Keeso. Remember?"

Were all four-year-old's experts at changing the subject? "I remember. You still have to take off your shoes."

"You guys don't have your shoes off."

She sent up a silent prayer for patience. "We don't have our feet on the quilt."

He gave in with as much grace as a four-year-old can muster. "I don't like to take off my shoes cause then I havta put'em back on." He removed his shoes and settled himself between the two adults. Keeso opened a bottle of apple juice and handed it to him. She unwrapped a ham and cheese sandwich, offering him half.

Keeso retrieved an egg salad on rye. "Frank knows I'm partial to these." He removed the cellophane wrapper and took a large bite.

She nibbled on the other half of Levi's sandwich and watched the pup trot down to the creek for his own drink. "Is the water cold?"

"Most creeks around here are fed by snow melt. They're not quite as cold this time of year, but cold enough."

Levi perked up at the mention of the creek. "Can I go swimming?"

She shook her head. "Not today, honey. We didn't bring a change of clothes for you."

"I could take my clothes off. You could take yours off, too, and come swim with me."

Keeso choked on his sandwich and took a swallow of water. Her cheeks heated, and she refused to make eye-contact with the man.

Levi was blissfully unaware. "Maybe Keeso—"

"Nobody's going swimming today, Levi. The weather isn't warm enough. Finish your lunch."

"Can I at least put my feet in the water?"

Keeso cleared his throat. "The stream's shallow in the park. It gets deeper downstream where other tributaries feed into it, but here it's safe if you keep an eye on him."

"Can I, Aunty? I ate all my food, 'cept for the crust. I saved it for Pup."

"Okay, but only your feet."

"I promise."

Keeso leaned over and picked up a stick. "Here. The pup likes to fetch sticks out of the stream." The boy grabbed the stick and took off for the water.

She put the sandwich wrapper in the bag and picked up Levi's shoes and socks before getting to her feet. Having him out of her sight, for even a few minutes, made her anxious. The creek worried her too, and she hurried to the small rise overlooking the stream.

Keeso came up beside her, and they stood in companionable silence as the boy and dog romped at the water's edge. Levi kept his word. Only his feet touched the stream. The dog, on the other hand, splashed into the stream after the stick multiple times. Her nephew shrieked with laughter when Pup ran up and shook the moisture from his coat.

She laughed too. "Levi's having fun."

"They both are. We'll have to get them together again soon."

She frowned. "That isn't a good idea."

"Why not?" He tilted his head toward the stream. "Look at them. They're best friends already."

"That's the problem." She folded her arms and sighed. "If they get too close, they'll be miserable when we leave." She started down the hill.

He stepped in front of her. "Leave? You aren't happy here? You don't like working for Frank and Molly?"

"I love Frank and Molly. They're wonderful people. That's one of the reasons I have to leave." She didn't say anymore.

"Explain it to me."

"Frank said he told you about my… circumstances."

"He only told me you were in trouble. He said someone wanted to kill you and Levi."

"It's all you need to know. The only way we can survive is to run—to keep a step ahead of them."

"Them? There's more than one killer after you?"

"No. Only one killer."

"Why did you say them?"

She started to brush past him, but he put his hands on her shoulders. "I can't help you if I don't know who's after you."

She shrugged his hands away and stepped back. "The bad guys and the good guys are trying to find us. The case has been turned over to the FBI. I'm sure they're looking for us, too."

She stepped back. "I don't want your help. Other people tried to help us, people who were trained to take care of situations like ours. I'm positive some of them are dead now." She hugged her arms across her chest and took a deep breath. "I think someone in the police department, or maybe in social services, told the killer where to find us.

"I haven't told Frank yet, but we're leaving next week."

"Why would you do a crazy thing like that?"

"It isn't crazy. It's the only way I can protect Levi, and everyone here. The sooner we leave, the sooner we'll all be safe."

He removed his Stetson and whacked it against the side of his leg a couple of times. "Have you thought this out? Where will you go?"

"I don't know yet."

"Be reasonable, Emma. You can't keep dragging that boy all over the country." He slammed the hat back on his head. "You can't hide indefinitely either. They *will* find you. And when they do...."

A single tear rolled down her cheek. She turned away from him, swiping at the proof of how vulnerable his words made her feel. "What choice do I have?"

He groaned, and pulled her around, pressing her head against his chest. She pulled back enough to gaze into his eyes—deep brown and concerned—and was nearly lost. Unlike her, he wasn't trying to hide his emotions.

"Please understand, I have to run. I don't know what else to do." His face blurred, and she blinked back the tears.

"Aw, Emma, don't cry. Let me protect you."

His warm body felt strong enough to keep her safe. For a moment, she pretended everything could be all right, relaxed and let him draw her close enough to hear the steady beat of his heart. She'd been so frightened for so long. It would be wonderful to let someone else carry the burden, if only for a little while. But it was a fantasy, a foolish dream she couldn't afford to indulge.

Pushing out of his embrace, she wiped her eyes with the back of her hand. "No one can protect us and stay safe." She started toward the creek.

He grabbed her hand. "Get the blanket and food to the Jeep. I'll bring the boy."

Shaking out the quilt, she carried it and the bag of food to the vehicle. Keeso wasn't far behind. He'd hoisted Levi onto his shoulder and deposited the giggling child in the back seat to adjust the harness.

Emma and Keeso were silent on the ride to the convenience store. The boy and the dog had worn each other out. By the time the Jeep pulled into the apartment driveway, they were both asleep. But Levi woke as soon as Keeso unbuckled his seatbelt.

"I'm hungry." He scrambled out of the Jeep and ran to the apartment door. "Can I have a snack?"

She unlocked the apartment's deadbolt. "You can have a piece of fruit for now. I'm fixing supper early tonight. I don't want you to spoil your appetite."

Levi ran into the apartment ahead of her. She paused to look at Keeso. He stood beside the Jeep with the driver's door open. They stared at each other for a long moment before he tipped his hat, got in the vehicle, and backed out of her drive. She watched him turn onto the highway, waiting until he was out of sight before going inside and locking the door.

From an embrace to a nod. That was how it had to be.

# 10

✧

Three days later, Keeso walked into the convenience store with the dog at his side. The door to her apartment was open and the pup loped in that direction. His owner went directly to the coffee machine.

"Why are you here?" It wasn't the friendliest of greetings, but then Emma wasn't in the mood to be friendly. She thought she'd made herself clear the last time they'd parted. She didn't like the way her heartbeat picked up the minute he stepped into the store. She'd almost convinced herself she didn't miss his daily appearance.

Keeso glanced up from filling his cup. "I'm sorry, what did you say?"

"I asked why you were here."

"The pup wanted to visit Levi."

She was surprised he could say that with a straight face. "The dog told you he missed—" She took a deep breath. "Keeso, I thought we agreed it wasn't good for them to become too attached."

"We didn't agree. You just assumed—" He carried his coffee to a booth and sat down.

A car careened into the parking lot, throwing gravel before it skidded to a halt in front of the store. The glint of sunlight on the sedan's windows prevented her from identifying its occupants. She grasped the counter, tensing until the first gangly teenage boy climbed out of the vehicle. Weak-kneed, she drew a deep shuddering breath and slowly released it.

'What's wrong?" Keeso was half way to his feet.

She shook her head. "I'm okay. I was startled, that's all."

He didn't look as if he believed her but sank back into his seat as the bell on the door rang.

"Hey, pretty lady." Five teenage boys in ragged jeans and long-sleeved flannel shirts jogged through the door and spread out. The vocal one—a large, burly kid—stayed at the counter and attempted to flirt with her. He wasn't good at it. Staring at her chest a little longer than appropriate, he asked for her phone number. She folded her arms and shook her head.

The other four descended on the counter at one time and plopped down an arm-load of snacks and a twelve-pack of Budweiser.

"You guys wait for me in the car." Romeo nodded toward her in a not-so-subtle message to the others. He obviously thought he needed a little more time to wear down her resistance. As his buddies left, one acne-burdened youngster glanced at her, wiggled his eyebrows and gave his friend a thumbs-up.

Her not-so-secret admirer tossed a credit card on the counter. "Give me a carton of your cheapest cigarettes."

She picked up the card. "I'll need to see your ID."

"You don't think I'm old enough to buy cigarettes?"

She shrugged. "Looks can be deceiving. Show me your ID."

Grumbling, he fished another plastic card from his pocket, flashing it in her direction.

Irritated, she gave him a try-it-again look and extended her hand, palm up.

He tossed the driver's license on the counter in a childish show of vexation.

Lifting it, she glanced at the picture, then set the beer on the floor behind the counter. "Do you want the snacks?"

He shook his head and nodded toward the cards in her hand. "I need those back."

She held them out of his reach. "Who do these belong to?"

"They're mine."

"You want me to believe you're forty-seven, and balding? Who do they really belong to?"

He looked toward the parking lot and the boys watching through the window. "My dad. You'd better give 'em back."

She didn't like the boy's attitude. Apparently, Keeso didn't either. He'd left the booth and moved behind the teenager.

Opening the register, she placed the cards under the cash drawer. "Tell your dad he can get them from Frank in the morning."

"Hey." He grabbed her wrist. "I said give 'em to me."

"Let go. Now."

"Do what the lady says. Release her."

The hard voice directly behind him startled the bully. He let her go to swing around, his beefy fist raised to strike.

Keeso moved with a viper's speed, closing his hand around the boy's fist, twisting it at an odd angle, holding him in place. He was half a head taller than the teenager, his body considerably more muscular. He didn't appear to be exerting much effort, but his young opponent strained to free himself, using his other hand as leverage.

Jaw clenched, the boy dropped to his knees groaning. Keeso still didn't let go. He glanced at her. "Did he hurt you?"

Stunned by his response, she shook her head. "I'm okay." A quick glance outside assured her the kids' friends weren't on their way in to help him. They were already hopping into the car. This one would be lucky if he had a ride home.

"You're sure you're not hurt?" She nodded, but Keeso wasn't satisfied. "Do you want to call the sheriff?"

She glanced at the young man. His entire body shook, but she didn't know if it was from pain or fear. "No. Let him up."

"Not before he apologizes to you."

"I'm sorry." The boy squeaked. "I promise it won't happen again."

Appeased, Keeso released him. He scrambled to his feet, cradling his abused arm against his chest, and took off without looking back. A minute later, his car threw gravel as it careened out of the parking lot.

She turned to Keeso. "Thanks, but I could've handled him."

"I don't doubt it, but I was tired of his insolence."

"They can be pretty cocky at that age." She shrugged. "Most of them grow out of it, though."

He moved closer to the counter and took her hand, gently turning it to examine the angry red finger marks on her wrist. Growling, he turned toward the door.

She kept hold of his hand. "I'll probably have some colorful bruises, but no real harm was done. Let it go." She picked up the beer and came around the counter.

"Let me put those back for you."

She shook her head when he reached for the twelve-pack. "I've got it. Why don't you sit back down? The least I can do is buy you a cup of coffee."

After returning the beer to the cooler, she stopped at the coffee machine, filled a cup for each of them and grabbed a packet of creamer before sitting across from him.

Levi's giggle floated in from the back room, bringing her thoughts back to the previous subject. He was going to be devastated when they left, but they had to leave soon. Regret made it difficult to breathe.

She opened the package of creamer, stirred the contents into her steaming coffee, and set the cup aside to cool. He had already taken several swallows of his. The hot liquid didn't seem to faze him. "Keeso, you have to stop coming here."

"Can't. I gas up the Jeep here." He held up the coffee cup. "And I like Frank's coffee."

"You know what I mean. Don't you have a mining operation to take care of?"

"The mine's doing okay. Have you told Frank you want to leave?"

She took a sip of her coffee and set the cup down with a sigh. "No, not yet."

"Don't."

"I can't leave without giving him notice. And I won't go without telling him and Molly good-bye."

"Stay with me."

"What?"

"You and Levi can move into my cabin. It's big enough—two extra bedrooms and two full bathrooms."

"You want us to move in with you? Why?"

"It's the only way I can protect you."

She picked up the red straw and stirred the coffee in her cup. "I never asked for your protection."

"And I didn't ask to worry about you and that boy, but I do." He took a deep breath and another swallow of coffee before meeting and holding her gaze. "The only time I can relax is when I'm here, with you and Levi." He shook his head and set his empty cup aside. "I got out of bed at two o'clock this morning, drove ten miles and parked the Jeep on the side of the road where I could watch the parking lot and your back door, just to make sure you were safe." He shook his head. "I'm beginning to feel like a stalker."

The store's bell rang, and Frank walked in. He nodded at the two of them and went straight to the coffee pot.

Emma scooted over to give him a place to sit. "You're early."

"Forgot to mention we've got a grocery truck due in sometime this afternoon. You can watch the store while the boxes are unloaded, then call it a night. I'll probably be here until closing, going over the inventory manifests. I can sit behind the counter to do the books. No sense in both of us being out here. Take some extra time with Levi."

Keeso grabbed his hat and moved out of the booth. "Time for me to go home." His eyes locked with hers. "Consider my offer—for the boy's sake, if for no other reason." He turned toward the door, calling the dog as he walked.

The pup darted out of the back hall, his feet skittering on the tile floor. Keeso caught him before he crashed into a display. Levi was right behind the dog. Keeso caught him before he collided with them both.

"Do you hafta go?"

He knelt in front of the boy. "We do." He glanced her way. "But I'll bring him back tomorrow. You can spend all day together." He stood and looked toward the booth. "I'll see you in the morning." He touched his hat to her and walked out, the pup at his heels.

Frank watched him leave, then glanced at her. "He seemed a mite agitated. Did I interrupt something important?"

"Not really, just a minor disagreement. Nothing important."

She spent the afternoon cleaning the apartment and playing educational games with Levi. The truck arrived a little before three, and she watched the store while Frank and the driver unloaded boxes of canned goods. A few tourists stopped in, but none of the regulars who usually took time for small talk, which was probably a good thing. Her mind was fully occupied with Keeso and his outrageous offer.

The idea of taking refuge in a mountain cabin appealed to her sense of self preservation. She smiled. That the cabin came with all the amenities was particularly appealing. Her smile faded. Levi would love having the pup with him round-the-clock, but she'd probably go stir crazy alone in the mountains.

Then again, she wouldn't be alone. Keeso would be there. She liked his company, liked him… more than she should. More than she had a right to.

Still, his offer was tempting. They would have a protector. She shook her head. But at what cost? There was no doubt the imposing man could keep them safe—from everything but a bullet. Even he couldn't stop a bullet. He would end up making himself the target.

She wasn't going to give him the chance.

If circumstances were different, she'd stay in Connor, maybe encourage a big-brother relationship between Keeso and Levi. He had been so good with her nephew at the picnic, so patient and gentle. Levi needed a role-model to emulate.

She remembered Keeso's strong arms surrounding her, comforting her. For those few moments, she'd felt safe, secure, maybe even….

"You look a million miles away."

She jumped at Frank's unexpected comment and laughed. "Sorry. I was lost in thought."

"Good ones, I hope."

"I was thinking about how much fun Levi had at the park the other day."

Frank smiled. "That boy couldn't stop talking about Keeso. I think he's got a good case of hero-worship."

"It worries me."

"Why? Keeso's a good man."

"I know, but, Frank… it's time for us to leave. We should've left before now. "

"You won't be any safer anywhere else."

"You can't know that. It feels like I'm sitting beside a time-bomb. The longer I stay, the closer I come to catastrophe."

"Keeso told me he had a plan. Did he talk to you about it?"

She nodded. "He wants us to move in with him."

"Sounds like a good plan to me. It's unlikely anyone would find you there, and if they did, Keeso wouldn't let them hurt you or Levi."

"What makes you think he could protect us against someone with a gun? You know whoever comes after us will have a gun."

"I get the feeling he can take care of himself and anyone he cares about."

She'd had the same feeling. His physical build and strength conveyed confidence and capability. But a big man made a good target. She pictured John, sprawled across his desk, blood draining from his lifeless body. The image morphed into Keeso, laying prone in a crimson pool. She shuddered. They had to leave.

Frank interrupted her thoughts. "You understand what I'm telling you, right? Keeso cares about you and that boy."

"I know." That was the problem. People who cared even a little about her and her nephew were likely to be hurt—or killed. And as cold-blooded as the thought was, a dead man couldn't keep Levi safe.

She left Frank to his books, turning toward the apartment. Time to fix supper and spend some quality time with her nephew before his bedtime.

Later that evening, she removed a load of laundry from the dryer. She should have time to fold the clothes and put them away before going to bed.

Levi had been restless tonight but had finally dozed off halfway through the second storybook. Hopefully, he'd sleep through the night, untroubled by the nightmares that haunted him.

The store's doorbell rang—probably Frank doing something outside. It was late for the locals and there weren't many tourists now. The days were getting shorter, the weather less predictable. Mountain peaks were already snow-covered and tonight's weather forecast called for the first heavy snowfall of the season.

Returning to the apartment, she walked to the back door and looked outside. Snow had been falling for the past hour. It wasn't deep yet, but the ground was covered. Had she waited too long to make the break from Connor and find another temporary destination?

# 11

✧

When the store's bell rang, Frank looked up to see a man in a dark business suit. He moved straight to the counter. Since he hadn't looked around the store before coming to the counter, Frank guessed he probably needed directions. "Can I help you?"

The man extended his hand to flash a badge. "I'm looking for a woman with a child. We have reason to believe she may have been on a bus that stopped here a couple of months ago."

Frank leaned closer to get a better look at the badge. He straightened. "Buses don't stop here, Agent Johnston. Are you talking about the bus that broke down around the end of July?"

The agent pulled a photo from his lapel pocket and handed it to Frank. "Did you see this woman and boy?"

Keeping his face void of expression, he stared down at the grainy image of Emma and Levi. "I might have. There were a lot of people on the bus and everyone came in at once.

"You don't remember seeing this particular woman and boy?"

"There were a bunch of children running around, but they weren't causing any trouble, so I didn't pay much attention to them. I had a line of people at the counter."

The agent returned the photo to his pocket. "I'll be in touch." He left the store and climbed into the black sedan out front.

Frank watched him pull from the convenience store lot to the parking area across the street. As soon as the man entered the restaurant he picked up his phone and dialed Keeso. His friend answered on the first ring.

"You need to get over here. We've got trouble." The call disconnected, and he knew Keeso was on his way.

He called Molly next. She didn't answer until the third ring. She barely had time to say hello. "Molly, listen to me. Someone's asking about Emma and the boy. We've got to get rid of any evidence they've ever been here. Erase the store videos. Make sure there's no archive backup in the computer. Do it now. I'll tell you about everything when I get home tonight."

He hung up and looked across the street. Stan, the restaurant's owner, was from back east and minded his own business. He was civil enough when they met at the mailbox or in town, but he wasn't talkative. Hopefully, he wouldn't know much about Emma and Levi.

The sedan was still there. At this distance and in the dark, he couldn't tell if anyone was in the car. In case he was being watched, he picked up an empty box behind the counter and ambled to the back hall. Once the door closed behind him, he tossed the box into the supply room, hurried to Emma's door, and knocked.

"It's Frank. I need to talk to you."

The urgency in Frank's voice made her stomach lurch. She dropped the shirt she'd just folded and ran to open the door. The look on Frank's face confirmed her fear. "What's happened?"

He stepped in, closed the door, and looked around. "Where's the boy?"

"He's in bed sleeping. Tell me what's wrong."

"An FBI agent was here asking about you."

She clutched Frank's arm for support. "You're sure it was me?"

"He had a picture of you and Levi. I pretended not to recognize you and sent him across the street."

Her breathing escalated into short, quick gasps, yet she couldn't pull enough air into her lungs. "We've got to leave, now."

He made her sit in the recliner. "Don't panic. We'll get you to safety. Take a minute to calm down while I check to see if he's still over there. Don't leave the apartment. He might see you."

She nodded.

No more than a minute passed before he returned. "His car's not over there now—not anywhere I can see. Get your things together. Let the boy sleep. Don't come out front. Anyone watching the store could see you. I'll call Molly. She'll come get you and take you to Denver. You can decide where to go from there."

She stood and hugged him. "Thank you for everything."

His arms tightened around her. "I'm going to miss you both." He reached for the doorknob. "I need to stay out front, in case someone's watching the store. Molly will pull around back. You can leave from the apartment." Opening the door, he stepped into the hall, but stopped for a moment. "Stay in touch."

He pulled the door closed, but she didn't move. She was going to miss Frank and Molly—and Keeso. She'd never see them again. A deep sense of loss engulfed her. She shook her head and hurried to her bedroom. She'd have time later to regret what might have been.

Pulling the duffel from the closet, she opened it on the bed, and tossed her things in, then jammed her feet into her boots and carried it into the living room. She piled the clean shirts and pants she'd been folding for Levi on top, struggling to close the over-stuffed bag. Levi's backpack stuck out between the couch cushions. Grabbing it, she jammed his books and toys inside.

She stuck bottles of juice and snacks into her purse and opened the freezer. Retrieving an empty, pint-sized ice cream container, she popped the lid and removed the sandwich bag containing her money.

The money belt was in the side compartment of the duffel. Unfastening her blouse, she secured the belt around her waist, put the bills in a zippered pocket, and rebuttoned the garment.

The duffel weighed enough to fell a horse, prompting her to consider leaving a few clothes behind. After a moment's thought, she decided to wait. If it became too heavy to drag around a bus depot or airport, she could dispose of some later.

Setting the bag and backpack beside the outside door, she peeked through the curtains to see if Molly had pulled up, but her white Honda wasn't there yet. Huge flakes of snow were beginning to fall. The forecast called for the first big snowfall of the season with an accumulation of around twelve inches. She hated making Molly drive in bad weather, but they couldn't stay.

Someone pounded on the hall door. She froze in place and held her breath. The second round of knocking rattled the door—and her composure. She grabbed the broom. It was the closest weapon in hand.

"Emma, let me in."

Keeso.

She ran to the door on wobbly legs, opened it, and launched herself at him.

His arms tightened around her. "Are you okay?"

She was now. The tension coiling in her stomach eased. She pushed out of his arms. "I will be as soon as we leave." Pup brushed past her on his way to Levi's room. He sniffed at the closed door and whined.

Keeso ignored the dog and looked at the broom. "You're cleaning?"

She tossed the broom away and shook her head. "I thought you were… never mind. Why are you here?"

"Frank told me what happened. He said Molly was on her way. I had him call and send her home. You and Levi are coming with me."

"Where?" Pup was still whining and scratching at the back door now.

"To my house. I know you didn't intend to accept my offer but right now it's the only place you can hide. The roads are getting treacherous. You and Molly might not make it to Denver, and I don't want you stranded on the highway, or worse. Stay with me. It will give you time to plan. When you've decided where you want to go, I'll take you there."

Pup whimpered again and barked. Keeso pushed her behind him. "Stay here." He switched off the light on the wall by the hall door and moved to where the pup stood. He opened the curtain enough to glance out. After a minute, he returned to her side. "There's no one out there. No footprints." He moved to the hall door. "Dress Levi in something warm. I'll bring the Jeep around. He glanced toward the dog. "Come on, Pup." He ignored his master and continued scratching at the wooden frame.

Emma opened the door to her nephew's room and turned on the light. The pup was right behind her.

Levi's bed was empty.

# 12

✦

Levi's pajamas were on the floor and the clothes she'd left for morning were gone. "Levi?" Emma glanced around, expecting him to jump out at her. It was a favorite game of his.

He wasn't there.

"Levi!" She tore out of the room and headed for the hall door, then reversed and ran toward the back entry. "He's gone—Levi's gone!"

She was fighting the deadbolt when Keeso grabbed her arms. "Calm down. He has to be here. You haven't left the apartment, have you?"

"No, not since I put him in bed."

"Then he's—" The pup had picked up on her panic. He was frantically scratching at the back door, now. Keeso let her go and sprinted to the door. He checked the deadbolt. "Did you unlock this door?"

"No, it wouldn't turn."

"That's because it had already been turned—it isn't locked."

"He can't be out there." She was so desperate, she ran to the door even as she denied the possibility.

"Pup seems to think he is." Keeso caught her before she opened the door. "Put on your coat and keep the dog here. I'll pull the Jeep around."

Her coat and Levi's were with the duffel. Did Levi take his jacket? She ran into his room and glanced around. No jacket. Hopefully he was wearing it. At least he'd have something besides his shirt to keep him warm.

The sound of tires on gravel alerted her, and she ran to the door to look out the window. Keeso's Jeep sat in the drive with the motor running. When she opened the door, the dog charged outside. Keeso caught him by the collar to keep him from running off.

"Get in the Jeep." She grabbed the duffel and backpack. Once outside, she ran around the vehicle to the passenger's seat. He clipped the pup's collar to the seat behind his, stowed the bags behind her, and got in.

"We'll let Pup go when we get out on the road and see if he can find Levi." He backed the Jeep out of the drive, straightening the wheels before it skidded into the ditch, and shifted into park. "Frank knows what's going on. He'll call us if the boy shows up at the store."

The dog was fighting his restraint by the time Keeso reached behind the seat, opened the door, and unclipped his leash. He shot out of the vehicle and took off running. Keeso aimed the Jeep in the same direction. A moment later they were racing over the snow-covered road to keep up with the dog.

Snow limited visibility, but they heard the hound-mix baying in the distance. Despite the blowing snow, they rolled down the windows to listen.

He stopped the Jeep in the middle of the road and shut off the motor. "I can't hear him. Can you?"

She shook her head incapable of uttering a sound. Levi was so small. How would they ever find him in this massive land of blowing snow? How long could he survive the blizzard?

He reached under the seat and retrieved a large flashlight. "Stay in the car." He circled the vehicle, the light beam dancing across the snow in front of him. She knew he was looking for footprints—human or canine. He whistled, a loud piercing sound she remembered from the picnic. He whistled again.

A long, mournful howl drifted through the snow-shrouded night.

"I hear him!" She leaned out the window straining to catch sight of the dog. Had he picked up Levi's scent, or was he just responding to Keeso's summons?

Keeso was already sliding into the driver's seat. "I hear him too. He's behind us." He made a fast U-turn. The Jeep fishtailed as he hit the accelerator. "I think there's a side-road about two hundred yards from here. It's hard to tell in this blizzard. They must have gone that way." He slowed the vehicle, straining to see through the windshield. The wipers whipped back and forth across the glass, barely keeping the surface free of snow.

He almost missed the turn and jerked the wheel, the Jeep doing a three-sixty before he got it under control.

They drove maybe an eighth of a mile when the pup's baying grew louder. Keeso stopped the vehicle again, grabbed the flashlight and got out, this time aiming the beam toward a distant line of trees. Green eyes reflected the light, and a sudden frenzy of barking greeted him.

He opened Emma's door and grabbed her hand. "Come on." Neither of them had thought to put on gloves, yet his hand warmed hers as he clasped it.

She ran to keep up with his long stride, but that was okay. They needed to get to Levi as soon as possible, and Pup was their only hope. She refused to believe the dog couldn't find his new best friend.

Gasping for breath as they ran, she nearly fell to her knees when Keeso stopped abruptly to shine the light around. Pup raced out of the darkness, jumped on Keeso and barked furiously, then bounded into the line of trees. The dog was soaking wet. Was Levi in the water? He couldn't do more than a dog paddle.

Please, God, don't let him drown.

Keeso took her arm and pulled her with him into the dense underbrush, the flashlight's beam aimed at the animal's tracks in the snow.

"How could he get this far?" She tripped on a hidden rock and almost fell.

He pulled her up against his body and put his arm around her waist without stopping. "It isn't as far as it seems in this snow. I recognize where we are. Frank's store is less than a mile from here." They broke through the trees at the edge of a fast-flowing creek.

"Levi!" Panic seized her body. If he was in the water....

"Aunty." The shivery cry came out of the dark and gripped her heart.

Keeso swept the light in the direction of the voice and caught the boy and the dog in its beam. Levi was neck-deep in the water, hanging on to a sapling branch that hung down into the water on the creek's opposite bank.

Her knees nearly buckled. Relief and terror swept over her at the same time. "Hang on, baby! We'll get you."

Keeso had his boots off. He shoved the light into her hands. "Keep the beam on him." He tossed his jacket over her shoulders and waded into the freezing mountain stream.

The bottom of the creek seemed to drop out from under him, and he disappeared below the surface, but his head and shoulders bobbed up seconds later. He swam across to Levi.

The boy wrapped his arms around the big man's neck and held on. Keeso back-paddled across to the bank where Emma waited at the water's edge. He handed her nephew up to her and levered himself out of the creek. His jacket had fallen on the ground. He picked it up and tucked it around the shivering boy, then took him from her arms.

"Grab my boots. Let's get him back to the Jeep."

The vehicle was a welcoming sight a few minutes later. He set Levi on the passenger's front floorboard.

"Get his wet clothes off and stick him under your coat. Your body will warm him faster than any blanket can. I'll get the quilt to put around you both." He moved to the back of the vehicle.

Levi's teeth were chattering by the time she dragged his soaked shirt and pants off and stuffed him under the coat with her, buttoning it to his chin. The child wriggled closer to her heat and sighed.

"Are you mad, Aunty?"

"I'm not mad, sweetie, but you shouldn't have left the apartment alone. It got you in trouble."

"In trouble from you?"

"No honey. You were in danger. That's the kind of trouble I meant. You're too young to go off by yourself. Never go anywhere unless I'm with you."

"What about Uncle Keeso? Can he take me places?" Apparently, saving his life had elevated his rescuer to family member status.

"We'll talk about it later, after we get—"

"To my house." Keeso spread the quilt over them and secured the seatbelt.

The pup shook off the snow blanketing his back and jumped onto the floorboard, nudging under the cover to snuggle against her legs.

Keeso slammed her door and sprinted to the driver's side. When he slid behind the wheel, she noticed he'd taken time to put on his boots. He'd put on his coat, too, but it was probably as wet as the rest of his clothes.

"You're shaking. You'd better turn on the heater."

"Heater doesn't work. I have an appointment next week to get it fixed."

"We're closer to the store than your place. Maybe we should go there. Frank has a dryer in the supply room. It wouldn't take long to get your clothes dry."

He shook his head. "Can't take the chance of being caught by the FBI. It's only ten, maybe fifteen minutes to the cabin."

"You're sure? You look…."

"I am not the one you should worry about. Keep Levi warm until we get home. I'll be fine once I've had a hot shower." She couldn't argue with his logic.

His estimation of the time it would take to reach his home was off by about an hour. The road became treacherous, particularly after they left the main highway and started climbing higher into the foothills.

Keeso was hunched over the steering wheel, peering through the snow-streaked windshield occasionally using his coat-sleeve to wipe the fog off the inside glass. Strapped in with Levi, she was helpless to offer any aid except prayer.

After what seemed like forever, Keeso pulled the Jeep in front of an imposing chain-link gate. He reached into the glove compartment for a remote, punched in the code, and the gate inched open, dragging an accumulation of the snow with it. They drove through, and the gate moved a little faster as it closed behind them.

The Jeep followed a winding lane for another two thousand feet before he pulled the Jeep in front of a single-story, rambling log home with a wide porch across the entire front. This was what the man called a cabin?

He got out and stumbled up the steps of the cabin. His fingers must have been stiff from the cold. He dropped the keys twice before finally opening the door and reaching in to turn on the porch and house lights. Returning to the Jeep, he unclipped her seatbelt and helped them into the house.

The warmth was wonderful.

Lifting the quilt from her shoulders with trembling hands, he tossed it on the couch. "The bathroom is at the end of the hall, on the left. The two doors on the right are spare bedrooms. I have a bathroom off my bedroom I can use. Take all the time you need in the other one. I'll get your bags." He was shivering so hard she could barely understand what he said.

"Are you okay? Maybe you should get warm before going back out. I won't need the clothes right away."

"I'm fine. Take care of the boy. I'll put your things in the bedroom across from the bathroom." He opened the door before she could argue, closing it behind him.

Stubborn man. She carried her nephew down the hall to the bathroom, the pup at her heels.

A few minutes later, she heard one of the doors across the hall open and close. Her relief at knowing Keeso was okay surprised her. She couldn't understand why she'd even worried about him. Someone that big and strong would never allow a little cold to get the best of him.

# 13

The cold was going to kill him. He'd have laughed at the irony if he'd had the strength. His higher body temperature apparently made him more vulnerable—not less, as he'd hoped—to freezing temperatures. Either he was in danger of going into hypothermia, or his extended exposure to the cold had triggered healing stasis.

It was hard to tell since stasis lowered a Centallian's body temperature during the healing process. It also slowed the heart rate. He should have been able to control the process. Stasis was supposed to be self-induced, but this reaction spiraled out of his control.

Shaking off his coat, he stripped out of his wet clothes and left them on the floor. He'd never make it to the shower. He hoped he'd make it to the bed.

"Why did you leave the apartment?" Emma wrapped Levi in a large, soft towel and carried him from the bathroom to the bedroom where Keeso had placed their bags.

"Frank said we couldn't stay there anymore. I was going to get Keeso, so he could make Frank let us stay. How come Frank doesn't like us no more?"

"Oh, honey, Frank still likes us. He doesn't want us to leave, but we have to go so the bad man won't find us."

"Are we going to live with Uncle Keeso and Pup now?" The eagerness in his voice told her he was fine with the idea.

"Keeso isn't your uncle, honey, and no, we can't live with them. But we will stay a few days, until we decide where to go next." He looked crushed, and she wanted to cry for him. He desperately needed a father figure to fill the void left by the man who had been brutally snatched from his life.

She pulled him onto her lap and held him close. "We'll be okay, sweetie. I promise."

"Can Pup sleep with me tonight?" The young dog had already curled up at the foot of the bed.

She'd used one of Keeso's towels to dry the dog off while Levi played in the tub. Like her nephew, he seemed no worse for wear from his late-night swim.

"He can stay with you tonight, but Keeso will have to give his permission for tomorrow night."

"Okay." Levi scrambled out of her lap and crawled between the sheets.

She pulled the covers to his chin. "I'm going to have my bath, then find Keeso's laundry room and wash our wet things. I won't leave the house."

"Promise?"

"I promise. You don't have to worry, honey. I won't leave you."

"Okay." Satisfied, he turned on his side and murmured, "I love you, Aunty."

She kissed his cheek. "I love you, too. Goodnight."

She opted for a quick shower. The chill had left her body about halfway through Levi's bath, but a deep weariness took its place. She'd opted to change into slacks and a pull-over sweater. Walking around Keeso's home in a nightgown and robe seemed a little too casual.

Bundling the wet clothes in one of the damp towels, she carried them out of the bathroom, pausing at Levi's bedroom door to look in on him. The young dog had crawled up beside her nephew and Levi's arm hugged Pup's neck. Separating those two would be painful for everyone.

The laundry room was off of the mud room near the back door. She decided to wash the wet towels tomorrow with the quilt, but Levi's clothes smelled fishy. No doubt the creek he'd fallen into was full of them. Keeso's clothes probably smelled the same. There was more than enough room in the washer's tub. She'd ask if he wanted his things added to the load.

She knocked on his door. It must not have been completely latched because it swung open enough for her to see he was already in bed. He was lying on his side, the blanket around the lower half of his body, his chest bare. One foot and calf hung off the bed, out from under the covers. It looked as if he'd fallen asleep while climbing into bed. That would explain why he hadn't pulled the blanket over his shoulders. He'd been shivering when she'd seen him last. He should have been buried in blankets.

She was about to close the door when she spotted his soaked clothes on the floor. That couldn't be good for the gleaming hardwood finish. He probably wouldn't mind if she went in long enough to retrieve the wet garments.

The shirt and jacket were together, and she held them out to keep from getting her own clothes wet. The jeans were closer to the bed. And the briefs—he was naked. She whisked the last two garments from the floor, closed his door behind her, and sprinted to the laundry room.

As she loaded the washer, she thought about the man in the bedroom. Knocking on the door hadn't disturbed him. Neither had her presence in his room—not that she'd made any noise. Still, she couldn't picture him sleeping through it.

Concerned, she returned to his door and knocked. No answer. She knocked again. When he didn't respond, she opened the door a crack and called his name. Still nothing. She pushed the door open. He hadn't moved since she'd seen him last. Walking into the room she called his name again. He didn't move a muscle. Was he breathing? It was difficult to tell.

"Keeso? Can you hear me?"

No response.

Something was wrong. Heart racing, she touched his neck, feeling for a pulse. She couldn't find one.

His body was cold. Was he breathing? She shook his arm and ordered him to wake up. When he didn't respond, she reached over his side and put her hand flat on his chest. There, did she feel it move? She was shaking so hard it was difficult to tell. She took a couple of deep breaths and willed herself to calm down and concentrate. There it was again... and again. He was breathing slow—very slow—but even.

Hypothermia. It was the only answer she could come up with. He'd been fine before he jumped in the water. She pulled the single blanket up over his shoulders and tucked it around his exposed leg. It wouldn't be enough.

Blankets.

She searched the room, pulling out drawers, looking on the shelves over the closet. She ran to the empty bedroom, dragged the thick quilt and covers off the bed, and hurried back to spread them over Keeso, enshrouding him.

What else could she do? An electric blanket or even a heating pad would help, but she'd seen neither of those in her search for blankets. If he were conscious, she might be able to get him to drink something hot, or maybe he could make it into the bathroom and get into a hot tub.

But he wasn't conscious.

She went to check on Levi. His deep, even breathing indicated he was sound asleep. The pup was snoring. He had snuggled as close to the boy as he could manage, so they were both toasty warm.

Keeso still hadn't moved. She crossed to the bed and placed a hand on his head. He hadn't warmed at all as far as she could tell. Slipping her hand beneath the covers, she rested it on his chest. His breathing remained the same—slow but steady. He'd be okay if he'd just warm up a little. The pup should be in bed with him instead of Levi. She remembered Keeso telling her to take Levi's wet clothes off and share her body's heat with him, that it was the quickest way to warm him. Unfortunately, the puppy was too small to warm a man Keeso's size.

But she wasn't.

She was going to have to share her body heat with the man... and she had to remove her clothes to do it. Clothes were intended to keep body heat *in*.

Giving herself no time to reconsider, she pulled her sweater over her head and set it across a chair. Her pants joined the sweater and she paused to consider how much heat a bra and panties held in. Not much, she decided, and opted to keep them on, though the thin wisps of cloth offered little in the way of modesty.

Lifting the covers back, she slipped in beside Keeso, scooted closer, and drew her body against his, throwing an arm around his waist. It was like embracing a snowman—a very muscular snowman. She pressed closer, against his broad, powerful chest, her hand stroking the corded muscle of his back. How could anyone this imposing be as gentle as he'd been with Levi.

She'd often heard the term *gentle giant*. If anyone ever fit that description, this man did. Her head rested against his chest. She couldn't hear a heartbeat, but slightly lower and more centered, she felt the slow, strong pulsing against her breasts.

"Please God, let this good man live." She whispered the prayer out loud, in the silent darkness of his room.

# 14

A warm, nearly-naked female body embraced him. His muddled mind accepted the stasis-induced dream. His body welcomed it. Her head rested on his shoulder. One arm circled his neck, her fingers tangled in his hair. A silken leg draped across his hip, a wisp of cloth the only barrier against what his aroused body craved.

Burying his face in her hair, he inhaled the sweet scent of flowers and woman. He rolled her back against the sheets, nestling between her thighs. Nuzzling her neck, he sighed her name.

"Emma…."

She came awake slowly, drugged by the erotic dream. Her phantom lover's big warm body covered hers—his male scent exotic, compelling, exciting. His lips nibbled on her neck and she angled her head, inviting more. He touched her breast, his hand sliding downward, his fingers catching the elastic of her panties, tugging them lower.

"Emma…." His mouth covered hers.

Her eyes snapped open. Keeso was kissing her, the kiss deep and sensual, his tongue teasing, tasting her. And she was kissing him back, her arms tight around his neck, her fingers gripping his hair, pulling him closer. Their bodies touched from chest to hips, her thighs spread wide to accommodate his muscular frame. His arousal rested intimately against her, his fingers relentlessly tugging her panties past her hips. He was about to....

She shoved at his chest and dragged her lips free of his. "Stop!"

Eyes still closed, he was slow to respond, seeking only to regain possession of her mouth.

She turned her head to avoid his kiss. "Keeso, stop."

He stilled and leaned back. She turned her head to find herself staring into eyes the color of molten gold. Neither moved. He looked as stunned as she felt.

"Your eyes...."

He rolled away from her. The covers had ended up on the floor and he reached down, grabbed the sheet and tossed it over them both. She'd kept her gaze on the ceiling, but she still got a peripheral view of his incredible body. The man was all muscle—perfectly formed. She closed her eyes and took a deep, calming breath.

"Are you alright?"

She flinched at the unexpected sound of his voice.

"I'm not sure."

He rolled to his side, facing her. "What do you mean you're not sure?"

"I mean I'm not sure. Do you need a translator?" He coughed and she glanced at him. His eyes were normal. Had she imagined the gold she'd seen? It might have been part of the dream.

"You're upset."

"I'm more than upset. I... we almost...."

"I am aware of what we were in the process of doing. My body aches with the memory."

Her body might have remembered a few things itself if she weren't so horrified by her behavior. He was practically a stranger, yet she'd nearly let him make love to her. Granted, it had been a dream, or at least she'd thought it had been. In her mind, dream and reality were still blurred.

"Why are you in my bed?" His gruff voice brought her back to the present.

"I thought you were dying."

He leaned up on an elbow and tilted his head. "Do you make a habit of climbing into bed with dying men?"

His question was ridiculous. She answered it anyway. "I don't make a habit of climbing into bed with any man. You... you were the exception. You were hypothermic. I piled enough blankets on to crush the average man. And you were still cold. Then I remembered you saying body heat is the best method of warming someone."

"You certainly warmed me." She didn't miss the double meaning, or the teasing note. "Tell me. Isn't the body doing the warming supposed to be naked as well?" Obviously, he was trying to lighten the mood.

"Apparently, it isn't a requisite. You seem fully recovered."

She took a deep breath and tried to change the subject. "I didn't have a chance to thank you for saving Levi's life last night. I'll never be able to repay you."

"You have already thanked me."

Heat rushed to her cheeks and she looked away. "I didn't... I mean we didn't... do anything."

He leaned closer and tilted her face toward him. "I do not speak of what almost happened between us. During the night, you did everything you could to keep me alive." He bent and briefly touched his lips to hers. "For that, I thank you." He leaned back against the pillow.

The kiss was over before she had time to protest. Would she have protested? The kiss was innocent enough, considering they were in bed together—she almost naked and he wearing nothing at all. Neither of them had made a move to remedy the situation.

"I'm not the type of woman to allow men I hardly know to—you know."

He turned toward her. "I never thought you were. Nor am I inclined to take advantage of a sleeping woman. I was in the midst of an extremely vivid dream."

"You said my name."

"Not surprising. I was dreaming about you."

"I was dreaming about you too. I don't know why."

"It's easy to understand. We shared a tense few hours looking for Levi. That, and our intimate sleeping position, would naturally lend itself to dreams of each other." He brushed the hair away from her face and gazed at her. "You look tired. I imagine you didn't get much sleep last night."

She ducked away from his hand. "I spent most of the night shivering. How can someone be as cold as you were and survive. I swear you're not human."

"The boy is well?" His abrupt change of subject and sudden formality caught her off guard. He acted as if they were sitting in a Victorian parlor sipping tea instead of sharing a bed, him naked and she nearly so.

She could do the same. "He's fine. He was worn out last night, though. The dog too. They were both sound asleep when I checked on them during the night."

"Did he tell you why he ran away?"

"He was looking for you."

"For me? Why?"

"Kids get the craziest notions sometimes. He thought Frank was forcing us to leave. He wanted you to make Frank let us stay." She smiled. "He has a good case of hero worship." She looked into his beautiful eyes and sobered. "After last night, I'm inclined to agree with him. You are a hero."

He leaned back on his pillow, stacking his hands behind his head and stared at the ceiling, clearly uncomfortable with her praise. "Anyone would have gone after him. It wasn't so dangerous."

"You nearly died."

"That's a matter of opinion." He glanced in her direction. "We have to talk about the FBI agent."

"There's nothing to talk about. I told you last night. We have to leave."

"Stay here. Frank's the only one who knows where you are and he won't say anything to anyone."

"Frank." She sat up, clutching the sheet to her chest. "I forgot about him. He needs to know we're safe."

"He knows. I called his cell last night before I brought in your bags. I was shaking so hard I had trouble talking, but I'm sure he understood. I told him you'd be staying with me."

"Keeso, we can't stay."

The man moved so fast she only had time to gasp and fall back against the pillow. He leaned over her, his hands planted on both sides of her head. The sheet had fallen to his waist, barely covering him. She slapped her hands against the bare skin of his chest to hold him back.

He allowed the restraint, but it didn't stop his words. "You can't face that monster alone. Let me protect you and Levi."

He'd started out angry, his voice harsh, but his last words were a whispered plea. He genuinely cared about what happened to them. Her vision blurred, one tear trickling into the hair at her temple.

"Ah, Em...." He dropped to her side and pulled her into his arms. "It'll be okay, I promise."

She sobbed against his neck. "I'm so frightened."

"I know, baby. I know." His fingers slid into her hair and he kissed the top of her head. "But you don't have to face him alone."

She leaned back, gazed into his dark, gold-flecked eyes, and tried to control her emotions. She needed to clear her mind, think rationally. Giving in, letting this man into her life, was tempting. He was tempting. She'd never been as aware of a man as she was at this moment. Keeso was like a magnet. If she let him get close, she'd never be able to escape the attraction.

As if he'd read her mind, he raised up on an elbow and leaned closer, his eyes growing gold again.... What was there about the lighting in the room that gave that impression? Slowly—agonizingly so—he lowered his head. His mouth closed over hers, his tongue immediately teasing her lips apart, thrusting inside to taste her. He moaned his pleasure when she rubbed her tongue against his. He tasted good.

"Aunty?"

They froze, each turning to look at the boy and his dog standing in the open doorway.

Her nephew took in their intimate position, tilted his head in question, then smiled. "Can I call him Uncle Keeso now?"

# 15

✧

Frank watched the snow plow cut a long swath down the highway. Plows had been out all morning, clearing as many roads as the crews deemed safe. He'd spent the night at the store, sleeping in the apartment after he'd closed. He and Molly had decided he shouldn't try to make it home.

There wouldn't be much business today. Most folks in the area planned ahead, knowing how unpredictable snowstorms could be. They were prepared to dig in and wait the storm out if necessary.

He already missed Emma and Levi. Thank God Keeso and that pup had found the boy. He hoped they were okay. Keeso hadn't sounded normal when he'd called last night to tell him they'd made it to his place. His voice had been slurred, probably from the cold and exhaustion.

He knew Emma and the boy would be safe with Keeso. He'd do everything in his power to protect them—if she'd let him. She had the insane idea they needed to leave to keep safe.

He sighed and turned away from the window. Well, she wasn't going anywhere for a while. The pass leading to Keeso's mine would be one of the last to be cleared. They wouldn't be leaving for two or three days. It might take up to a week.

At least the heavy snow would prevent anyone from getting to them, unless they used snowshoes. Even then, the attempt would be daunting for anyone unfamiliar with the terrain.

Maybe by that time Keeso could talk some sense into Emma. Frank sighed, the sound heavy in the empty store. If she took off alone with that little boy, he'd lose a lot of sleep worrying about them.

He went into the storeroom and grabbed a box of bagged chips to restock the shelf. The bell on the door rang as he returned to the front. Tom Jackson and his son, Jake, were stomping snow off their boots onto the mats he'd put down.

"Didn't think I'd see anyone out today." He set the box on the floor beside the chip display. "What can I do for you?"

"Jake's been waiting for the first good snow to try out the new skis he got for his birthday. Thought I'd take him to the foothills and start him on a low slope. Need to gas up the truck and the snowmobile. We'll need some sandwiches, too."

"Haven't made any yet today. Thought I'd make 'em to order if anyone was crazy enough to leave their house." He grinned. "No offense."

Tom laughed. "None taken. Fix us a couple of roast beefs?"

"Sure. Go ahead and get your gas while I make the sandwiches. Number three's on."

Frank had just wrapped the sandwiches in cellophane and put them in a plastic bag when Tom and Jake stomped their feet on the sidewalk outside the door and came in. A black sedan slid into the snow-covered lot. He recognized the man who got out and walked in behind the father and son. What was the FBI agent doing back so soon?

Tom stopped at the counter to hand Frank a credit card. "Put a large coffee and hot chocolate on there, too." He moved to the drink island and pulled two cups from the dispenser.

The agent moved in front of the counter, waited until Frank had run the card, then said, "I thought I'd drop back by before I left for Denver. I thought you might have remembered seeing the woman and boy after our talk yesterday."

Frank shook his head. "Like I said, a lot of people got off that bus that night, and not all of them came in here."

Tom looked up from handing Jake his drink. "I remember those two. They were sitting over by the windows. Keeso would remember her. She fell in his lap when my boy ran into her. Sat on his hat."

The agent turned to face Tom. "You saw a woman with a boy that night?"

Tom nodded. "In fact, I saw Keeso with them no more than a week ago, when I drove by the park."

Frank was quick to shake his head. "That was Molly's niece, Emma and her boy. They came out from Ohio for a visit. Arrived the same day. Molly brought them by a few minutes before the bus limped in."

The agent gave him a suspicious glance. "Emma isn't a common name. It's interesting that your niece and the woman I'm looking for share it."

"It isn't all that uncommon, either." He shook his head. "Look her up. Her name is Emma Kinslow. They live in Dayton."

The agent pulled the photo he'd shown Frank out of his pocket and handed it to Tom. "They look anything like this?"

Tom took a quick glance at the picture and shrugged before handing it back. "Look, if Frank says I saw his niece, then I saw his niece." He turned to Frank. "She's not here?"

Frank shook his head. "Molly took her to the airport yesterday morning."

"Too bad. She'd be able to clear things up for the man." He paid for his sandwiches and drinks and left with Jake.

The agent followed them out and spoke with Tom a moment before returning to the store.

He glanced at the camera mounted in the corner. "Do you have security video footage?"

Frank shook his head. "It erases itself every seven days."

"Would your niece be on it right now?"

"I doubt it. Like I said, she left yesterday. The camera was set to delete at midnight last night."

"That's real convenient."

"Not really. If it hadn't deleted the file you could have seen my niece and her boy. You'd know she wasn't who you're looking for."

"That remains to be seen." The agent started to leave but turned to look at Frank. "We'll talk again soon." He left the store and got in his car.

As soon as the car was out of sight, Frank dialed Keeso. When he didn't answer, he called his niece and warned her not to answer any phone calls from a number she didn't recognize.

# 16

✧

"I was about to make a pot of coffee. Would you like a cup?"

"Coffee sounds nice. I noticed you went out earlier. Did I hear the Jeep's motor?" She glanced out the window. "Where is it?"

"I moved it into the mine."

"Your mine's big enough to drive a Jeep into it?"

"The front entrance is. It makes a good garage." He carried the tall granite coffee pot to the sink to fill. "Have you had breakfast?"

"Sort of. I ate a slice of toast before you came in. Levi munched on one of the granola bars from his backpack. It was all I could get him to eat. He's anxious to go out and play in the snow." She laughed. "You should've seen the look on his face when I told him he had to wait until it warmed up a little. He's in the bedroom coloring. I doubt that's going to keep him occupied for long."

"It won't get much warmer today." He set the pot on the ancient wood stove. The big black monstrosity radiated heat. An overhead fan circulated warmth throughout the central room.

"I thought I'd give it another half-hour. Where in the world did you find a stove like that?"

He grinned.

"It came with the property." Retrieving a can of Folgers from the shelf above the stove, he opened it and poured a healthy portion of ground coffee straight into the pot. She wondered if he kept teabags anywhere.

"The old prospector I bought the property from lived in a small cabin closer to the mine. The stove took up most of the space. When I built this house, I decided to put the stove in the central room. I like how it feels on cold winter nights." He carried two coffee mugs to the table.

"How do you heat the rest of your house? I don't see any registers or vents. That stove can't heat every room."

"It doesn't." Another grin. "The roof has solar panels. They take care of my electric needs and keep the house warm in the winter. The heat radiates from the floors and walls."

"You must have a top-of-the-line solar set-up. Do you have any problems when it's cloudy for several days in a row?"

"The battery array is the latest technology. I haven't had a problem so far." He returned to the stove, lifted the lid on the pot, and moved to the refrigerator. When he pulled a carton of eggs out of the refrigerator, she assumed he'd decided to make his own breakfast. Instead, he removed one egg before returning the carton to the refrigerator and moving back to the stove. She watched in fascination as he lifted the lid from the pot, cracked the shell, and dropped the raw egg into the boiling coffee.

She couldn't believe what he'd just done. "Who taught you to make coffee?"

He looked over his shoulder at her. "The same man I got the stove from."

"Why the raw egg?"

"It settles the grounds."

"You know there are automatic coffee makers that filter the grounds, don't you?"

He nodded. "I've got one in the cabinet. Don't like the way the coffee tastes." Wrapping the potholder around the handle, he carried the pot to the table, and filled both cups. The steaming liquid in her cup resembled ink.

He sat across from her and was already putting the rim of his cup to his lips. She started to pick up her own cup and pulled her fingers back. The cup was too hot to hold. The coffee was probably hot enough to scorch her tongue.

When she didn't pick it up, he looked at her and raised an eyebrow. She shrugged. "I'll have to let it cool." He nodded and took another swallow from his own cup.

"Aunty, is it warm enough to go outside now?"

Levi's timing was perfect. She could make her escape and leave the coffee without insulting her host. She lifted her shoulders in a nonverbal apology and smiled. "I'd better check on him." Keeso's cell phone rang as she made her escape.

Keeso stood at the front window of his cabin, gazing out at the pristine white landscape, broken only by the Jeep tracks in the snow. If they did have to leave fast, the vehicle was near the ship, where it needed to be. But he'd be forced to reveal his secret.

Pup's excited bark echoed from Levi's bedroom. The boy's laugh followed when a ball bounced into the hall, the hound right behind. Grabbing the ball, the dog made what the locals called a beeline back to his new best friend. Emma's laughter joined Levi's a few seconds later.

Emma.

She was never far from his mind. Even now, when there was so much that needed to be decided, his thoughts turned to this morning, and what had almost happened. He turned away from the window. Emma's warm, soft body had invaded his dreams, beckoning a response his body was eager to provide. Her arms embraced him, her legs…. If she hadn't come to her senses…. Even after his head cleared, and he was fully awake, he'd wanted her.

He wanted her now.

He needed to keep his distance, but it was impossible to do when they lived in the same house. And it was too dangerous for them to leave without him. They couldn't elude their pursuers forever—not without help.

The boy came tearing down the hall toward him, dressed to go outside, his hooded coat zipped high. Pup, as usual, was at his side. Emma followed them into the central room. She'd put on her boots and carried her coat over her arm.

"Aunty says I can play outside in the snow. She even dried my boots in your dryer. They're still warm."

She knelt in front of her nephew to secure the Velcro neck strap and help him with his gloves. She looked over her shoulder at Keeso. "I didn't have the heart to make him wait any longer. He seems to have weathered last night's adventure without a problem—not even a sniffle." Standing, she opened the front door. Levi and Pup didn't waste any time getting outside.

She started to put on her coat, but he laid his hand on her arm and closed the door. "I need to talk to you."

"Can't it wait? I don't want Levi out there alone."

"We'll watch them from the window."

"But—"

"This is important." He pulled her with him to the window where she could watch Levi romp in the snow.

"Frank called a few minutes ago."

She turned to face him. "Frank? Why?"

"The FBI came to the store again this morning. Tom Johnson was there and mentioned seeing you and Levi with me. Frank said the agent acted suspicious."

"How did he get to the store? I thought the roads were closed."

"The plows have been out all night. Frank says they've cleared part of the state highway that runs in front of the store. He didn't know how far they'd made it up the mountain. The snow can drift over the road if the wind's high enough. I doubt it's passable this far up."

"Then he won't be able to make it up here?"

"It's unlikely. The snow is over three feet deep, considerably higher where it's drifted. The pass won't be clear for a day or two.

"He'll come after us as soon as the roads are clear."

"We have time to formulate a plan. Don't worry. I won't let him take you back to a safe house, or anywhere else."

Despite his decision to keep his distance, he put his arm around her. "Em, you're not in this alone. We'll figure something out, I promise. I won't let anything happen to you and Levi."

"I'll call Levi back in." She glanced toward the window, tensed and lunged for the door.

"They're gone!"

# 17

✦

He caught her before she opened it. "Calm down. They haven't had time to go far." He took her coat and helped her slip into it. "We'll follow their tracks." He shrugged into his winter jacket and opened the door.

"I can't see their tracks." Frantic, she glanced across the yard as they stepped down from the porch.

"There they are." He pointed to the Jeep's tire tracks. Small boot prints and the dog's toenail scratches followed the tread marks. "It looks like Pup's leading him toward the mine."

"The mine? He'll get lost in there, or it could cave in." She started to run but slipped on the packed surface and would have gone headfirst into a snowbank if he hadn't caught her in time.

"Slow down." He steadied her. "Levi won't get into trouble. The mine's gated. The boy can't get in."

He pointed to a massive, boulder-like wall of rock. "The mine's on the other side of that outcropping." They circled the perimeter and when she looked up from watching where she stepped, she saw Levi standing inside the gate. The pup was running circles around him.

She said a prayer of thanksgiving. Her nephew was safe—and on the wrong side of a fifteen-foot-high fence with an iron-barred double gate. The fence followed the wide cave entrance and butted up against a sheer rock wall on each side.

She turned a frown on the man walking beside her. "I thought you said he couldn't get inside."

"He shouldn't be inside." They stopped outside the gate. He nodded to a small box on the gatepost. "He can't reach the controls."

They could speculate all day, or she could simply ask him. She opted for the direct method. "Levi, how did you get inside the gate?"

"I'll show you." He turned sideways and pushed between the bars to their side of the gate. He beamed up at them. "See, I can squish through."

Keeso glanced at her and shrugged. "Apparently the engineers who designed the gate didn't take four-year-old escape artists into consideration."

Levi took her hand. "Have you ever seen a big gate like that?"

"No, I've never seen anything like it."

A huge yellow vehicle sat near the wall. The Jeep was parked beside it.

"Uncle Keeso, I found your spaceship."

Keeso knelt in front of the boy and nodded toward the machine next to the Jeep. "That isn't a spaceship, Levi. It's a loader. We use it to haul large chunks of rock.

The boy was shaking his head. "That's not the spaceship. It's around the corner in a really big room. Come on, let's go see it." He was practically dancing in anticipation.

She looked from her nephew back to Keeso. "Do you know what he's talking about?"

Keeso didn't answer but frowned as he moved to the metal lockbox attached to the gate. He removed a key from his pocket, inserted it into the small keyhole, and gave it a twist. The door sprang open revealing a black glass window imprinted with the red outline of a hand. He pressed his palm against the glass.

The gate groaned as it moved. When the opening was wide enough for them to enter, Keeso pushed a button on the side of the box and the gate stopped moving. He led them inside.

Levi grabbed her hand and half dragged her toward the back of the first room. Keeso followed at a more leisurely pace, apparently in no hurry to get to the room Levi was so excited to show her. She glanced over her shoulder at him. His expression gave nothing away and she turned back to watch where she was going.

The mine's second room was huge. The dome-shaped ceiling gleamed as if every inch had been polished to a fine sheen. It was spectacular.

And, smack dab in the middle of the room, was a machine she'd expect to see in a sci-fi movie. The sleek platinum vehicle wasn't like anything she'd ever seen before. It didn't have wheels. But it wasn't a sled—maybe a hovercraft? Granted, she knew very little about mining. But she was pretty sure the elegant piece of equipment had little to do with the operation Keeso claimed to run.

She turned to him, wary now. "Would you like to explain what this is?"

He leaned back against the mine wall and folded his arms across his chest. "Not particularly."

"Do it, anyway."

He shook his head. "Trust me, you really don't want to know."

She tilted her head toward the huge machine. "Try me."

He shrugged. "Okay, I'm an alien."

# 18

✧

"You're an alien."

He nodded.

"From another country?"

"From another world."

"You expect me to believe that?"

"Is it such a difficult concept?"

"You don't look like an alien."

"What are aliens supposed to look like?"

"I don't know. I've never seen one."

He tilted his head and grinned. "You have now."

Emma looked at the ship. "Is this a classified experimental craft? Are you a government agent?" She started backing away, grabbing Levi's hand as she did.

The creaking of the big gate in the outer chamber caught her attention, and she saw the remote in Keeso's hand. Turning, she ran to the mine entrance, practically dragging Levi with her. Keeso followed them into the front room. She swung around to face him, pulling Levi behind her.

"Why did you close the gate?" She could barely get the words past the knot in her throat.

"We need to talk."

"I'll be glad to talk to you once we're on the other side of that gate."

He shook his head. "You're beginning to panic. I can see it in your eyes."

"And you think locking us in here is going to calm me?"

Levi edged to her side and she glanced down. The boy's eyes were wide with confusion. Even Pup was subdued by the tension in the air.

Keeso knelt and motioned the boy to him. "Hey buddy, can you do me a big favor?"

Her grip on Levi's shoulder prevented him from walking toward the man.

"I forgot to give Pup his treats this morning. Do you think you can take him to the house and give them to him?"

Levi glanced at her.

She hesitated, torn between the need to keep him close where she could protect him, or getting him away from whatever was going to happen in the next few minutes. She finally nodded and let go of him. She wanted him far away from whatever Keeso had in mind.

Her nephew turned his attention to the man she no longer trusted. "I don't know where the treats are."

"Look under the kitchen sink. You'll see the box as soon as you open the cabinet door. I don't keep anything else under there. Pup can have two treats." The child started to squeeze through the gate when Keeso called out to him. "And Levi, stay in the house. Your aunt and I will be up in a few minutes."

Emma tried to smile when her nephew looked up at her. "Do as Keeso says. You need to stay inside and warm up. After you've given Pup his treat, wash your hands and you can have a snack too. There's still a granola bar in your backpack."

The boy squirmed between the gate's bars and trudged through the snow toward the house. The pup walked through with no trouble at all and followed close behind.

Both adults watched the pair until they disappeared around the boulder.

Once Levi was out of sight, she turned her attention to her captor. "Please don't hurt Levi. You can do whatever you intend to with me but don't hurt him. He's innocent."

He was on top of her in two strides, grabbing her shoulders and giving her a quick shake.

"Have you lost your mind?" His eyes flashed gold. "Have you forgotten I've been by your side practically since I met you? I intend to protect you, though I should ring that pretty little neck of yours for even thinking I'd hurt that boy." His hands dropped away. He took a deep breath and stepped back.

Some of her panic eased. If he'd wanted to harm them, he could've abandoned them in the snowstorm last night. Instead, he'd gone into the freezing stream to save Levi.

What he'd said made sense. But he'd already lied to her about who and what he was—not that she believed he was an alien. There were far more feasible explanations for the machine in the other room. The change in his eyes gave her pause, though.

"Will you tell me what's going on?"

He shrugged. "What do you think is going on?"

"Obviously, you're not a gold miner."

"That much is true."

"So, who are you really? Even I can tell the vehicle you have hidden back there is high-tech. Are you a scientist?"

"No."

"A technician?"

He shook his head.

"Are you an FBI agent?"

"I am not involved with your government, or any of your world's governments."

He was admitting to being an alien—something she found too incredible to believe. She'd seen most of his body, felt his arousal pressing intimately against her, and tasted his lips. She had no doubt he was human. So, why was he determined to convince her he was from another world?

"Would you like to see the ship?"

"I don't think so. I have a feeling the less I know about that ship, the better off I'll be."

"You're frightened. Why?"

"You're hiding some type of experimental vehicle in a mine that really isn't a mine and you just claimed to be an alien. All sanity aside, if you are an alien, are you going to morph into something unrecognizable?"

He simply tilted his head and raised one eyebrow.

She took a deep breath. "I'm not making sense, am I?"

He smiled. "No, but I'm sure none of this makes sense to you either. Tell me what's worrying you the most."

"How can I trust anything you say?"

"Before you saw the ship, you instinctively knew you could trust me. You trusted me to find Levi, never doubting I would help you. You can still trust me."

He handed her the remote, basically giving her the power to decide whether to leave or stay.

"I'm not trying to make you my prisoner. I only want to talk to you, to make you understand who I am."

He unbuttoned his coat. But when he began unbuttoning his shirt she stepped back, wary.

"Place your hand over my heart." She didn't move. He stepped closer. "You've touched me before. This is no different." He gave her a lopsided grin. "I'm not going to morph into some hideous monster."

That grin tipped the scales in his favor. She suddenly felt foolish, though still a little unsure of who—or what—he was. Tentatively, she lifted her hand and placed her palm on his chest.

"Can you feel my heartbeat?"

She shook her head and looked up at him in question. He placed his hand over hers and moved it to a spot slightly lower and more centered, closer to his diaphragm. The strong, steady beat of his heart met her fingertips and she looked up at him in question.

He lifted her hand to his throat. "Find my pulse."

She touched the spot below his jaw where a normal pulse would be. Nothing. He moved her fingers to a place behind his ear and she immediately felt the strong pulsing of his heart.

"Last night, when you thought I had gone into hypothermia, I was actually in stasis to counteract the hypothermia. My species is blessed with the ability to self-heal under most circumstances."

"You're telling me I didn't have to try to warm you?"

"It was unnecessary, though I appreciated your attempt to keep me alive."

Heat suffused her face. "You're saying I didn't have to get undressed and practically wrap myself around your body? Why didn't you tell me you didn't need my help?"

"I was unconscious, incapable of telling you anything. And what was I supposed to have said? Oh, by the way, I'm an alien. I'll go to sleep for a few hours, and then be perfectly all right."

He was absolutely right, she wouldn't have believed him. She'd have thought he was delusional.

"You know none of this is enough to convince me, don't you?"

"I know." His voice was gentle. "Are you still afraid of me?"

She shook her head, then looked up at him. "Should I be?"

"Never." He cupped her face in his hands. She didn't pull back when he bent his head and touched his lips to hers. The kiss was soft, undemanding—human. He pulled her into his arms and held her close.

"I didn't like it—thinking that you could be afraid of me."

"I couldn't help it. Everything I thought I knew about you was suddenly a lie. I didn't know what to think and then you closed the gate. You shouldn't have closed the gate."

"I couldn't let you take off with Levi in the snow. Closing the gate was the only way to keep you here without traumatizing him."

He stepped back, cleared his throat. "I'm sorry. I shouldn't have kissed you."

His apology irritated her. "And all the other times you've kissed me? Are you sorry about those kisses too?"

"I should be. But no, I'm not." He rebuttoned his shirt and coat. "Kissing you comes as naturally as breathing, though a physical relationship between us is impossible."

"Because you think you're an alien."

"Because I know there's a chance of incompatibility between our species."

She handed him the remote. "Levi's been alone too long. We should go back to the house."

He activated the gate and they stepped outside. The wind had picked up and she pulled the collar of her coat up around her neck as they trudged toward the house.

He held up the remote. "Thank you for trusting me."

"That doesn't mean I believe you're an alien."

"Are you willing to at least keep an open mind?"

"You wouldn't have gotten the remote back if I didn't have an open mind."

"Are you willing to let me help you?"

"Nothing's changed. I still have to leave." She stopped and turned to him. "I promise I won't tell anyone what's in the mine."

He smiled. "Trust works both ways. I know you won't give up my secret." He took her hand as they walked the last couple of hundred feet to the house. He paused at the steps. "Stay with me. I can't keep you safe if you leave. We'll figure something out."

She climbed the stairs ahead of him and turned, bending slightly to answer.

The bullet passed her head and splintered the post beside her. A second later, they heard the crack of a rifle.

# 19

✧

"Get down!" Keeso surged forward, grabbing Emma and shielding her with his body as his momentum carried them to the door. He reached for the knob. Something slammed into her thigh as they fell into the room.

He kicked the door shut, pushed to his feet, and lurched back to slip the deadbolt in place.

Emma rolled in agony, fire scorching her thigh. "My leg…."

"I see it." He sank to his knees, unzipped her coat, and gently pulled it out of the way. His hand settled on her hip as he stared down at her shredded pant leg, blood already seeping into the fabric. "Oh, Em."

She tried to sit up. "Someone shot at us, didn't they?"

"Yes, someone shot at us. Don't move."

"Levi. Where's Levi?" She lunged forward.

He grabbed her shoulders. "Stay put. I'll find him."

Levi was already halfway down the hall. When he saw her on the floor, he began to run.

"Aunty!"

Keeso grabbed him before he reached her, keeping between him and the window. "Whoa, take it easy."

"Did you hurt my aunty?" Levi struggled to get away from him.

"No, son, I didn't hurt her. She's a little banged up, but okay."

Levi scooted closer to her. "I heard that sound again, like when we were home and you made me hide in the closet—only this wasn't loud."

"That's because the sound came from a long way off." Keeso knelt beside him. "No one's close enough to hurt us. I promise."

Levi looked up at the big man, lower lip quivering. "But she already got hurt."

Emma reached for his hand. "It isn't bad, sweetie. Not like before. I'll be fine." She didn't feel fine. Her thigh burned as if a firebrand had been thrust into it.

Keeso patted Levi's shoulder. "Why don't you run into my bedroom and pull the covers down on my bed? She'll be more comfortable there."

Keeso eased her into his arms as Levi ran ahead. Emma wilted against his chest. "You need to get Levi to safety."

"We're all getting out of here, but we need to get you taken care of first. My bedroom is the safest place in the cabin, no outside walls." He carried her through the door.

Levi had dragged the covers to the foot of the bed. When Keeso bent to lay her on top of the sheet, she tightened her arms around his neck.

"Wait. I'll get blood on the mattress."

"I'll buy a new mattress." He placed her in the center of the bed.

"Shouldn't you be watching for the shooter?"

He shook his head. "He isn't close—probably nine-hundred to a thousand yards away. That puts him in the foothills on the other side of a deep gorge. The cliff face on this side is high and nearly vertical. He'll have to backtrack to the highway. The snow has probably drifted across some of the back roads. He'll be lucky to get here before nightfall."

"How do you know he was that far away?"

"The bullets reached us before we heard the shots."

"You're sure?"

"I'm sure. How are you doing?"

"I'm okay."

He glanced down at Levi. "Why don't you sit beside your aunt and hold her hand? She'd like that."

Levi climbed onto the bed and plopped down by her side, his eyes round and full of worry. Pup picked up on her nephew's emotion. He sat at the side of the bed, whining his own concern.

Keeso brushed the hair out of her face. "I need to make sure the doors and windows are locked, then we'll take care of you."

She grabbed his hand. "Be careful."

"I will." He squeezed her hand and walked to the doorway. "Make sure Levi stays with you." The door closed behind him.

He returned a few minutes later carrying her duffel, a quart-sized crock jar, an armload of white linen towels, and a basin for water. "Everything's secure." He set the jar and basin on the nightstand and laid the towels beside her on the bed. "I activated the perimeter beacon. If anything larger than a coyote gets within five hundred feet of the cabin, we'll know about it." He sat down on the bed. "Let's get your coat off." He helped her out of the garment. Once the wrap was gone, they both got a good look at the damage. So did Levi. He whimpered.

Keeso glanced at him. "It's okay buddy. It isn't as bad as it looks. We'll get her fixed up."

She squeezed her nephew's hand. "I'm fine, honey. I promise. Take some deep breaths and you'll feel better." She had to take a couple of deep breaths herself, to ward off the nausea tormenting her stomach.

Levi wedged himself between them and put his small hand on her cheek. She read confusion in his eyes. He was so young—incapable of fully understanding what was going on in his life. Until his parents' killer was found, he wouldn't have a normal childhood—something he could never get back.

She was powerless to help him. But she could take his mind off his worries for a little while. Summoning a wide smile, she patted his hand. "Guess what?"

Levi frowned at her. "What?"

"When I looked in Uncle Keeso's refrigerator, I saw ice cream in the freezer. I'm sure he'll get you a bowl if you ask politely."

"Emma, that can wait. We need to take care of your leg now."

She shook her head. "Levi comes first."

Keeso relented and turned to the boy. "Would you like some ice cream?"

The tension in Levi's small shoulders eased. "What kind of ice cream?"

"Chocolate, my favorite."

"I like chocolate too. Can I have some, please?"

"Sure you can."

"Maybe Uncle Keeso can find your backpack, and you can play a game after you eat." She glanced at the man. "Are you sure it's safe for you to go back out there?"

He nodded and walked toward the door. "The blinds are closed, and the walls are solid, made from pine logs." He smiled at Levi. "Anything else?"

"Can Pup have some ice cream, too?"

Emma shook her head. "Chocolate isn't good for dogs."

"Can he have another treat?"

"I'll find something for him. Stay close to your aunt in case she needs something before I get back. Okay?"

"Okay."

A few minutes later Levi was settled on one of the couch cushions on the floor a short distance from the bed. Her nephew's eyes had widened at the amount of ice cream piled in his bowl. As she'd hoped, the sweet treat and the toys he'd already pulled from his backpack distracted him. He sat with his back to the bed, and headphones over his ears listening to one of his favorite stories. With luck, he wouldn't notice what was going on behind him.

"Now can we take care of you?" He didn't wait for her reply. Instead, he sat on the bed and tried to lift her jeans away from the wound. The material was too tight.

"Take your pants off."

Perhaps shock made her a little giddy, but she found his statement hilarious. It sounded like something out of a seventies B-movie. She giggled. "I can't believe you just said that."

"Said what?"

"Never mind.

"Let's do this before Levi finishes his ice cream and decides to check on us. It'll save a lot of explanation. I'll help you take off your jeans."

"What? No." Apparently her shock had worn off. She couldn't find any humor in his suggestion this time. Despite the compromising position they'd found themselves in this morning, the thought of letting him remove her clothes embarrassed her.

"Forget the modesty, Em. It's wasted on me right now." He slipped his fingers into the top of her jeans, unsnapped them, and tugged the zipper down. She grabbed the elastic waistband of her panties to keep them from following the jeans as he slipped them off her hips. She couldn't prevent the gasp, or the deep breaths she had to take to control the pain when the material slid over the wound.

"Did I hurt you?"

She shook her head. "Only a little."

"I'm sorry. I'll try to be more careful." He unlaced her boots and pulled them off, then slid the ruined jeans down her legs. They followed her boots to the floor. He packed several towels under her hip and thigh to absorb any blood that might drip from the wound.

"You'll need to roll to your side." He helped her turn. When his warm hand slipped between her thighs to lift her leg and place a pillow under her knee, she almost forgot about the pain.

He grabbed the washbasin and headed for the adjoining bathroom, returning a handful of seconds later with the basin and a first-aid kit. He dropped the kit beside her and sat down. The water in the basin was steaming when he squeezed the excess moisture from the washcloth.

"I'll be as gentle as I can, but this is going to hurt a little."

Her entire body tensed the minute he began cleaning the blood away. "The wound isn't dirty, only a few strands of denim from your jeans." She clenched her teeth as he picked out the pieces of material embedded in her raw flesh. Perspiration beaded her forehead, and her leg throbbed by the time he'd finished.

When Keeso lifted the lid off the quart jar, she glanced up at him. "What— What *is* that?"

"An antiseptic and coagulant."

She studied the red powder he was pouring into his hand with a jaundiced eye. "That looks homemade."

"You might call it that. Brace yourself, this is going to—"

"I don't think you should—" Her voice broke when he released the powder into her wound. Air hissed in through her teeth.

"—sting."

*Sting?* The man may as well have poured molten lava on her leg. She jammed her eyes shut and clamped down on her lower lip to keep from crying out.

Keeso draped a clean linen dishtowel across her exposed thigh. He opened a package of gauze pads, and a roll of gauze. "The powder stopped the bleeding."

She didn't doubt it. The stuff had probably cauterized the wound.

"The bullet plowed a groove across your leg, but it isn't too deep." He handed her the roll of gauze. "Hold this for a minute." She complied, and he placed the pad on the wound. Taking the gauze from her, he began winding the strip around her upper thigh.

She tried to relax, but the heat of his touch reminded her of how intimate his ministrations had become. As his hands continued brushing against her inner thigh, she took a deep breath.

"Is it too tight?"

"No, it's fine." Her voice was shaky, but she couldn't help it.

He didn't seem to notice. "Good. Let's make you more comfortable." He moved the first-aid supplies out of the way, removed the pillow supporting her leg, and helped her lean back against the other pillow.

"You have splinters of wood in your hair." He held a sliver up. "The first bullet must have struck the porch post by your head."

She stared at the wood, dumbfounded. How close had she come to dying in that moment? Would it ever end, this constant hiding, constant fear? Would she ever find a haven for Levi and herself, or were they condemned to spending the rest of their lives running, always afraid?

She glanced up at Keeso. "Levi and I need to leave."

"Once it gets dark, we'll get you both out of here, and get you to a medical facility of some kind."

"How? The roads are closed."

"Most of them are. And that's a good thing. The shooter will have to hike back to his vehicle and drive as close as he can. He'll be forced to hike the rest of the way here. It won't be easy and should take him at least a day."

"If he can't get in, how do you plan to get us out?"

"Don't worry about it. I'll make sure we get out."

She couldn't let it go. "We can't take the Jeep." She shook her head. "I suppose you plan to fly out in that—whatever it is?"

He grinned at her.

"You're kidding."

He shook his head.

"That's crazy. I wasn't serious."

"There's nothing crazy about it. The ship is safe and I'm an experienced pilot." Lifting her duffel, he rummaged through the contents.

"What are you doing?"

"Looking for something you can wear."

"There's a long nightgown in there somewhere. It's the only thing I have that won't aggravate the wound."

"Is this it?" He held up her white cotton gown.

"Yes. Thank you." Her hand shook violently as she reached for the garment.

He snatched it away from her. "What's wrong?"

"Nothing. Give me the gown."

"I'll help you with it. You're trembling so hard you'll never get it on. Close your eyes if it bothers you."

"I'd rather you closed yours."

He grinned. "I know."

When he reached for the buttons on her cardigan, she pushed his hands away. "I can do this."

He grasped her hand, turned it up, and kissed her palm. "I'm faster."

She didn't feel up to sparring with him, too tired to even worry about being embarrassed. He'd seen her in her bra and panties before. She wouldn't have to take them off to wear her nightgown.

He was quick, as promised, and had her sweater off in seconds. He'd helped her into her nightgown and was pulling it to her waist when he paused.

"What's this?"

She knew what he was looking at. The top of her panties must've slipped down revealing the puckered scar from her first bullet. It was still an angry pink.

"That's a bullet wound, isn't it?" When she didn't answer, he persisted. "It can't be more than three, maybe four months old."

"Three."

"Frank didn't tell me you'd been shot before."

"Frank doesn't know."

He touched the scar. "How bad was it?"

She rolled her head on the pillow to make sure Levi wasn't listening. His head was bent over something she couldn't see, oblivious to their conversation

Her eyes returned to Keeso. "He left me for dead." She whispered a laugh. "I didn't know I'd been shot—not until someone told me the blood on my clothes was mine." She shrugged. "It could've been worse. The bullet didn't puncture my stomach or damage any major organs. I guess you could say I was lucky."

"Guess? Why guess?"

She saw no reason to keep the truth from him. "I can't have children. He took that away from me. The doctors tried to repair the damage, but it was too extensive." She saw sympathy in his eyes and got angry. "Don't feel sorry for me. Like I said, it could've been worse." She glanced at her nephew. "I might have lost Levi, too."

He nodded, slipped his fingers under the elastic band of her panties and pulled them up above the scar. "I'll take you somewhere safe where he'll never find you again." He adjusted her nightgown, pulled the covers over her, and moved to the door. "I'll be back in a minute."

After he disappeared into the living room, she closed her eyes and tried to calm her racing mind. The pain in her leg made it nearly impossible to focus. The killer had found them again and their rescuer was either an alien—the other world kind—or delusional enough to believe he was. Either way, he was determined to help them. And right now, they needed his help.

He was a complication she couldn't allow. Like a storybook hero, he was big and strong and good-looking—and she wasn't immune to his charm. His cheeky grin did funny things to her stomach. And when he touched her….

"Emma?"

She opened her eyes, surprised to find him standing by the bed. He held up a glass filled with a honey-colored liquid.

"I've been saving this for a special occasion." Putting the glass on the bedside table, he sat down and slipped his arm around her, gently lifting her enough to place an extra pillow behind her shoulders. When she leaned back, he offered her the glass.

She looked at it suspiciously. "What is it?"

"A lightly fermented fruit juice we call *Baquui*. It will give you strength."

"I've never heard of it."

"You wouldn't. The fruit comes from a tree on New Centallus, my recent home world."

She still didn't reach for the glass. He shook his head and sighed, then placed the rim to his own lips and swallowed a mouthful. Tilting his head, he quirked an eyebrow and extended the glass to her once more.

Resigned, she accepted his offering and took a sip. The juice had a slight effervescent tingle and mild flavor that hinted at an unusual mix of melon and citrus. He hovered until she'd swallowed the last drop and took the glass.

"You can rest until we're ready to leave." He gently pulled the extra pillow from behind her head and tucked the covers around her shoulders. "Sleep if you can. I'll watch Levi and get us ready to go."

Closing her eyes, she allowed her exhaustion to take over. She was just dozing off when he brushed her hair away from her face and his lips touched her forehead.

She smiled.

# 20

"Wake up. It's time to go." Keeso's quiet voice gently drew her from the depths of sleep.

She tried to sit up. "Go where?"

"Where you'll be safe. Come on, now. Levi's waiting with the pup in the other room."

Her mind began to clear. "What about the pup?"

"Levi has him on a leash in the living room. They're waiting for us."

"What time is it?"

"Almost seven."

"That late? Why didn't you wake me sooner?"

"There was no reason to disturb you until we were ready." He cocooned her in the quilt and lifted her into his arms.

"The killer could still be waiting for another shot."

"We're going out the back way. If he's still on the hill, he won't be able to see us even with a night scope."

She stiffened in his arms. "Couldn't he or another shooter be somewhere around the cabin?"

"No one's here. Remember the beacon? I'd know if he were close."

He carried her through the mudroom to the back entrance.

"Levi, grab hold of my belt and keep a good grip on Pup's leash. If he takes off on his own, we won't have time to look for him. Ready?"

Levi nodded, and they stepped out of the mudroom into the deepening snow.

Emma leaned closer to Keeso's ear and spoke softly. "Whatever that vehicle in the mine is, I'm not convinced you can drive it, or fly it, or whatever. How do you really plan to get us out of here in this snowstorm?"

"I've never lied to you and I'm not arguing the point when, in a couple of minutes, you'll discover the truth for yourself."

"No sane pilot would take off in this weather." The snow was so heavy, a little wind would create a blizzard. She couldn't even see the gate until Keeso stopped in front of it.

"The remote is in the inside pocket of my coat. Can you reach it?" He loosened his grip enough to allow her to push the blanket aside and reach into his coat. The heat radiating from his body surprised her. No wonder she hadn't felt the chill in the air. The blanket wasn't the only thing keeping her warm.

"Can you find the remote?" Keeso's breath was warm against her ear. She shivered, and not because of the cold.

"Yes, I have it." She pulled the remote from his pocket and placed it in his hand. A second later, the huge gate began to groan open. Levi and the pup had already made it through and were waiting for them inside the second room. The gate reversed course and began to close.

As before, the room seemed brighter than it should have been. The huge vehicle was already open. A wide ramp led from the ground to the interior. Levi ran up the ramp, Pup right behind him. Keeso carried her inside and placed her in one of four seats in the cockpit area. Levi scrambled into the seat directly behind her and Keeso buckled him in. Pup jumped into the seat beside her nephew. He snapped his leash to the seat before leaving the ship.

She heard the Jeep's motor and a minute later, Keeso pulled into the ship. Large crates of varying sizes lined both sides of what appeared to be a cargo hold. He parked the Jeep between them and secured the wheels with some type of metal bar.

He slipped into what she assumed was the pilot's seat. A glass-like panel spread before him with symbols and markings she didn't recognize. His fingers touched several symbols, and the machine came to life. A slight vibration, more like a hum, encompassed the vehicle. The door panel raised like a drawbridge, sealing them inside.

"Tell me this really isn't a spaceship."

"It isn't. It's a *Zaara*-class transport shuttle, designed to carry cargo from an interstellar ship to a planetary surface."

"I thought the shuttle program was over. How experimental is this vehicle? Is it safe?"

"My people have been using shuttles of one type or another for centuries." He glanced at her and smiled. "It's safe, and before you ask, yes, I can pilot it."

She decided to ignore his alien reference. "How are we getting out of here? The passageway's too narrow, and the gate's closed. Come to think of it, how did you get it in here?"

"The same way we're taking it out. We don't need to use the gate." His hands flew across the controls, and suddenly it felt like they had collided with the ceiling, yet they hadn't moved.

"What was that?"

"Snow. I disengaged the barrier."

"Barrier? Wait—what do you mean snow? We're inside a mine."

"Actually, we're not." He nodded toward the front window. Heavy snow swirled around the shuttle. "The barrier protected this ship and anything that was within the holographic field from the elements and intruders."

"A hologram?" She stared out at what appeared to be a snowstorm inside the mine. Heavy snow literally floated from the ceiling.

She looked over her shoulder toward Levi. He didn't seem upset or even surprised, only fascinated. "Honey, what do you see out the window?"

He glanced at her and grinned. "It's snowing in here. Cool."

At least now she could believe her eyes. She turned to Keeso. "I don't understand. I touched that gate out there. It was hard steel and cold, and you were leaning against a solid rock wall inside this room. I'm not at all familiar with them, but aren't holograms illusions?"

"In most cases, yes. But the barrier is solid—and translucent, which necessitated the hologram. We had to hide the ship."

"You're telling me everything out there is an illusion?"

"The gate and the back wall are real, as is the fence running along the perimeter of the barrier."

"If there's a barrier there, how did Levi and the pup get through, or us for that matter?"

"The barrier has a portal as wide as the gate. I use it to truck in supplies for the colony. Normally the portal's closed, but I left it open this morning when I came out to check on the ship. I did take the precaution of closing the gate. I intended to return later and do a systems' check. I didn't anticipate the gate's vulnerability to four-year-olds."

His fingers hovered above the panel, barely grazing the glass. The room evaporated. Only the fence and the loader remained. Keeso nodded toward an opening in the side of the newly configured mountain. "That's the true entrance. We never worked this mine. The gold we used came from New Centallus, my home."

"Barriers, holograms, shuttles with technology beyond Earth's capabilities— I'm having trouble taking it all in." She lifted her shoulders. "I still have difficulty believing you're not human."

"I am human, just not from Earth."

"Uncle Keeso's a spaceman?" There was glee in the little boy's voice. "Are you going to take us up in space?"

Keeso laughed. "For a little while." He turned his attention to her. "I'm taking you somewhere safe."

Her eyes locked with his. "Where?"

He laughed. "Don't worry, it isn't New Centallus, though that's exactly where I'd take you if this shuttle could make the trip. Your pursuer would never find you there."

She might have been tempted if the offer had been more than wishful thinking on his part. "You still haven't told me where we're really going."

"Arizona. The Hopi and the Centallians have been friends for centuries.

There's a state-of-the-art health care facility near First Mesa. We can depend on their aid—and their discretion. The trip doesn't take long."

# 21

Keeso's hands flew over the controls and the shuttle began to hum. Emma grabbed the arms of her chair when the machine lifted away from the ground. Within seconds, they were above the mountains and rising at an alarming rate. One moment heavy snow swirled around them, the next they were above the clouds, a panorama of stars replacing the snow. They climbed higher. The stars waivered, unsettling her stomach, and suddenly focused into brilliant points of light. The ship had passed through the atmosphere.

She'd experienced no pressure from the gravitational force, no discomfort as the ship climbed higher. The Earth seemed to shrink in its wake.

"Wow," Levi cried. "Look at the moon. It's so close I could touch it."

He wasn't exaggerating. The moon seemed to be growing as quickly as the Earth was shrinking. Emma's gaze slid to Keeso and their eyes met. Had he been watching her?

"This is impossible. We don't make anything that can get us to the moon in a matter of seconds."

"We do. Centallians have been creating ships capable of interstellar flight for centuries. A quick trip from Earth to the moon is... how do you say it... a piece of pie?"

"A piece of cake."

"Yes. A piece of cake. I still have trouble with some of your idioms."

He suddenly didn't sound at all like the man she'd come to know. His speech had grown even more formal than the few times she'd noticed the pattern-change before. "You're scaring me." She looked back at Levi, afraid her whispered comment might have frightened him.

Apparently, it hadn't. He was practically drooling on the window in his excitement over their proximity to the moon.

Keeso touched her arm, drawing her eyes back to him. "I did not intend to frighten you. I merely wanted to remove all doubt from your mind. We have become more than simple acquaintances. I care about you and the boy and intend to protect you to the best of my ability. It is only right for you to know exactly who I am and where I come from."

He reached for her hand but didn't grasp it. Instead, he waited for her to meet his gesture. When she cautiously placed her hand in his much larger one, he smiled and closed both hands over hers. "I am simply Keeso, not Keeso Smith. I was born on a now-dead world known to many other worlds as Centallus. My people are struggling to save our species from unknown attackers. Those of us who survived our planet's devastation have established a colony on a young world we call New Centallus. The wooden crates you see behind us are filled with gold from a mine on New Centallus. We use the gold to buy supplies from Earth. The other containers in the shuttle's hold are supplies waiting for our interstellar ship, *Novaria.* It should have arrived months ago. Something has happened, either to the *Novaria* or to my people. Until my people return, if they ever return, I am stranded on your world."

"Uncle Keeso, are we gonna land on the moon?"

He swiveled back to check the control panel before answering him. She guessed he needed a moment after what he'd told her. Finally, he looked over her shoulder at Levi. "Not this time. We need to get your aunt to a doctor."

"Okay." The disappointment in his voice switched to concern when he asked, "Will the doctor make her feel better?"

Emma was quick to reassure him. "Yes, he will. You don't have to worry."

"Will the doctor give you a shot?"

"He might, but that's okay. I'm not afraid of shots."

Her nephew looked impressed and turned to the man in front of him. "Aunty isn't afraid of anything."

Keeso smiled. "I know."

She felt anything but brave—confused, unsure, terrified, even baffled. But brave? If she'd been brave she wouldn't have allowed Keeso to help them.

How often in the last week had she reached out to him? And he'd always been there for her. He was a good man who had allowed her to disrupt his life, even put it in danger.

She couldn't continue to depend on him. He didn't belong on her world. She had no idea if—no, *when*—his people might return. Would he go home to his own world? How soon before she was on her own again?

Keeso focused his attention on the control panel, running his fingers across the glass. The shuttle slowly rotated until they were facing Earth. She'd seen pictures and videos of Earth suspended in space, but the blue planet below them astounded her.

"It's… beautiful."

Apparently satisfied with the readings, he swiveled his chair to face her, temporarily ignoring the panel.

"Yes, it is." His fingers swept across the panel again. The ship changed angle as it moved back toward Earth at a much slower rate of descent.

"It won't take long to get to our destination."

"Do we have to worry about reentering the atmosphere? Is it dangerous?"

He shook his head. "Our shuttles have protective barriers somewhat like the one that protected the mine entrance. We won't feel the heat or any vibration." His hand skimmed over the glass panel again. "We'll descend into the atmosphere and go straight down from there."

She looked over at him. "Won't we be seen?"

"We've probably been seen already, but the barrier I told you about masks our signal and shape. By the time they give up trying to figure out who or what we are, we'll have landed. The area where we'll set down is remote. You'll understand when we drop below the clouds."

It was too dark to see much, but as they flew over the landscape, she had the impression of a great expanse of land, perhaps a desert. The shuttle landed in a shallow, horseshoe canyon.

Keeso released his harness and moved to the door. "We'll take the Jeep from here. You and Levi can stay in the shuttle where it's warm until I get the Jeep ready."

He pressed his palm against a panel on the entry door and the wide ramp lowered, allowing him to drive the vehicle out of the ship. Leaving the motor running, he returned to help Levi and Pup out of their harnesses. After a few minutes, it was Emma's turn. He gently swiveled her chair and disconnected her harness.

"What about our bags and my purse?"

"I stowed them in the Jeep before we left Colorado."

He carried her to the Jeep, securing her seatbelt before returning to the ship. He stepped out of the shuttle a couple of minutes later with two large duffels. Setting them on the ramp, he secured the hatch. Retrieving the bags, he moved down the ramp.

The shuttle suddenly disappeared. Keeso seemed suspended in midair. She wasn't sure what she expected then, but it wasn't his nonchalance as he continued walking until he reached the vehicle.

Stowing the bags in the carrier behind the Jeep's backseat, he grabbed a quilt. He tucked the cover around the boy and double-checked the seat harness before getting behind the wheel.

"So now are you going to tell me you can levitate and make things disappear?"

The grin he flashed her took her breath away. There were times when he could make her forget everything but him.

"Did I impress you?"

She tilted her head and gave him her best impression of a disgruntled look.

His smile broadened. "No?" He laughed. "I initiated a hologram and barrier when I returned to the ship. It activated before I reached the ground."

He turned on the ignition. "The back roads out here can get a little rough, but we'll take it easy. Once we get to the highway, the ride will smooth out and you'll be more comfortable. At that point, it won't be far to the clinic. Let me know if you need to stop for a few minutes."

She glanced around. "Where are we?"

"In Arizona, on the Hopi reservation." He shifted into drive. "I have friends here who will help us."

The rough ride reminded her of the back roads she'd driven during her visits to her grandparents in the Ozarks. Soon, the throbbing in her leg prevented her from thinking about anything but the pain. Keeso took one look at her, pulled the Jeep to the side of the road and shut off the motor.

"Need to rest?"

"I could use a few minutes' break if we can spare the time."

"We can. It shouldn't be more than fifteen or twenty minutes to the medical facility." Reaching into a small cooler tucked between the seats, he retrieved a bottle of water and opened it before passing it to her.

"Thanks." After a few swallows, she glanced into the backseat.

"He's fine." Keeso shifted in his seat to look at her nephew. "He fell asleep about fifteen minutes ago."

She nodded. "He can sleep anywhere if he's tired enough." She took a few more sips, then handed him the bottle. He finished it off and put the empty container in a small trash bag.

"How do you feel?"

"Physically or mentally?"

He smiled. "Both. I realize this isn't easy."

"I've been running scared since the day that monster murdered my family. I close my eyes and see my sister lying in a pool of her own blood. I see the killer's face as he tells me to turn around, so he can shoot me, too. In the middle of the night, I hear Levi calling for his mom and know I can't bring her back to him. I hate feeling helpless." She looked down at her leg. "This wound will heal, but I doubt either of us will ever recover."

Taking her hand, he squeezed it gently. "No one fully recovers from the loss of loved ones. We rage against it, we agonize and grieve. In the end, we accept what we can never change, and rebuild our lives, knowing there will always be regret. We cannot escape the sorrows of our losses, but we eventually begin to live again. It will get better, I promise."

He'd suffered his own losses. The proof was in his voice, in the sorrow she saw in his eyes. She wanted to comfort him but didn't know how.

He reached for the keys, but instead of restarting the Jeep, he leaned forward, resting his arms on top of the steering wheel, and stared out at the dark night. Several minutes passed before he looked at her.

The intensity in his eyes startled her. "What is it?"

He took her hand. "By my honor, I vow to provide for and protect you. I accept Levi as my own issue."

Suddenly wary, she tilted her head. "What was that about?"

"It is the vow a Guardian gives the woman he has chosen for his bond-mate."

"I don't understand...."

"By giving you the words, I am now bound to you by honor. I have joined my life to yours."

She jerked her hand back. "You can't do that. We don't even know each other."

"You know more about me than anyone else on Earth. And I know all I need to know about you." He sighed. "I do not make this vow lightly. I have considered the ramifications. Joining my life to yours is the best way to protect you both."

"It still isn't binding."

"By my own words, you have become mine to keep safe, and Levi as well. My place is now by your side."

"Keeso, you're not listening to me. You can't say you're going to take care of me and consider it a binding commitment."

"It *is* binding—at least for me. And necessary. According to the beliefs and laws of my people, the words I have given you make Levi my son. They are as binding as blood. From this time forward, we *share* the responsibility of his welfare. When he cannot be with you, he will be with me, safe and protected."

"It doesn't work that way here. There are laws that regulate what happens to a child if a parent or guardian dies. If anything happens to me the state will come in and take him."

"Nothing will happen to you! I won't allow it."

"You're not all-powerful, Keeso. Anything could happen to me and the government would take Levi."

His narrowed eyes told her he didn't like what she'd said. "Then what will happen to him?"

"He'll be taken into protective custody and placed with a foster family."

"We can't let them have him."

"If I'm gone, you can't legally keep him with you."

"What must I do to make it legal?"

"I don't know. Denise and John had wills. They each designated me as Levi's legal guardian if anything should happen to them both. Their attorney had me sign an agreement."

"Can you make me his guardian?"

"You're not related to Levi. It would be next to impossible to make it legal."

"The vow I gave you makes him my son."

"On your world that might be true, but this is Earth. Your vow doesn't give you any rights where Levi is concerned."

"What will?"

"It might help if you were married. The court would probably be more open to me assigning a husband and wife guardianship."

"I have a better suggestion. Marry me. That would make me his uncle in truth. No one would question my guardianship of him."

"You're kidding."

He frowned. "I'm deadly serious. We're talking about Levi's welfare."

They were also talking about her future. Marriage vows were as binding for her as his vow was for him. She wasn't willing to go that far—not yet. There had to be more options.

"I'm sorry. I didn't mean to offend you. Your suggestion just... took me by surprise."

"Why should you be surprised? I've already spoken my vow of commitment to you according to my people's laws. Why would I hesitate to extend that commitment to include your world's laws?"

"Keeso, you're also asking *me* to make a lifetime commitment."

"You're unwilling to make such a commitment for Levi's sake?"

"I'm willing to sacrifice anything to keep Levi safe."

He lifted an eyebrow. "And marrying me would be a sacrifice?"

"I didn't mean it that way. I just meant… I… I'm not in any position to make a lifetime commitment to anyone. I feel as if my life has been taken out of my hands. All I can think about is running, keeping Levi safe, and staying one step ahead of the man trying to kill us. I can't pull you into this mess we're in. I can't bear the thought of losing you too. Don't you understand? I don't have the strength to worry about one more person."

She took a deep breath. "This argument is probably futile. The lawyer told me I'd have to petition the court to finalize the guardianship. I didn't get a chance to do it. Obviously, I can't go back. I'm not sure they wouldn't take him away from me. It's why I can't let anyone find us."

He leaned across the console and used one corner of the quilt to wipe the tears from her cheeks. "I know it's hard for you, Em, and I don't want to add to your burden, but you need me. Whether you accept me as your mate or not, I intend to be there for you and Levi. We can speak of the vows later, when your leg is healed, and you've had time to rest and reflect on what I've said." He tucked the blanket around her shoulders.

"For now, I suggest you be admitted to the clinic as my wife, Emma Smith. It isn't a good idea to have your true name on record. And there won't be any question of Levi remaining in my care."

She nodded, suddenly drained of energy.

"Good." He started the Jeep and pulled back onto the road. She shifted to ease the pressure on her wounded leg. Closing her eyes, she willed the constant fear and tumultuous thoughts to the back of her mind. But one question refused to be ignored.

What did you do with a hero who refused to go away?

# 22

✦

The Hopi Healthcare Center lay a few hundred feet off Highway 264. Keeso pulled the Jeep onto a side road, bordered on the right by a fairly new housing development and on the left by the medical facility's large parking area. Turning into the lot, he followed the drive around a walkway and pulled under the sheltering roof of the emergency entrance. A glance through the rearview mirror assured him Levi was still sleeping. Emma's eyes were closed. Was she asleep or unconscious? She hadn't said anything since their talk earlier on the side of the road. He'd surprised her when he gave her the words, and probably frightened her when he suggested an Earth marriage. Her response had stung his ego, but he wasn't giving up. When he'd given her the words, he'd also given her his heart. He walked around the Jeep and opened her door.

She moaned when he lifted her into his arms. "Levi?"

"He's fine. I'll get him in a minute." Drawing her close, he walked through the automatic doors. A nurse and an orderly ran in his direction. The orderly grabbed a wheelchair. "You can put her here."

"I'll take her." He looked around. "Where?"

The nurse shook her head and nodded toward the door to their left. "She'll go into triage first. You're not allowed inside. The waiting room's across the hall. We'll let you know how she is after the doctor sees her."

He didn't like the idea of letting Emma out of his sight, but placed her in the chair, bending down to whisper, "I'll be right in there." He nodded to the door on her right.

"Levi?"

"I can see him from here. Don't worry. I won't let him out of my sight."

The orderly wheeled her through the triage door. When the door closed behind them, the nurse regained his attention. "Can you tell me what's wrong with her?"

"She's been shot. The bullet grazed her leg. It didn't go through."

"When did it happen?" The woman hadn't shown any reaction when he mentioned the bullet.

"A few hours ago." She tensed this time but didn't comment. "Are you related to her?"

"She's my wife. Her name is Emma, Emma Smith."

"We need Mrs. Smith's' medical history." She handed him a clipboard with several forms attached and a pen.

He shook his head. "Emma and I are newlyweds. I'm afraid I can't even tell you her blood type. Is there a reason she can't fill out those forms? Has her condition worsened? She should be able to answer the questions."

"Your wife is as well as can be expected. We've made her as comfortable as we can." She retrieved the clipboard. "We usually get the information from next of kin, but I'll take these back and get the information from her."

She glanced toward the entry doors. "You'll need to move your vehicle. We need the space for ambulances. There's an emergency parking lot to your left as you exit the doors. Stop by the window after you've taken care of it."

She nodded toward a sliding-glass window set in the wall. "I have other forms you'll need to fill out."

Levi roused as soon as the Jeep started. Before Keeso had time to explain, he looked at his aunt's empty seat and started screaming.

"Aunty!" He fought the straps of his seat harness.

"It's all right. She's with the doctor."

"Don't leave her."

He shut the car off and turned in his seat. "We won't leave her." The pup was whimpering and licking Levi's face. He suddenly looked to Keeso and barked.

"Pup's mad at you too." The dog barked again, emphasizing the boy's point. Keeso suddenly felt outnumbered and helpless. How did you reason with a four-year-old and a half-grown hound?

"Levi, listen to me. We're not leaving your aunt. We're only moving the car into a different parking lot, over there by that white truck. Can you see it?"

He glanced in the direction Keeso indicated. "Uh-huh."

"All we have to do is go around the curve and park by the truck. It isn't far. The sooner we get parked, the sooner we can go back inside and wait for your aunt."

"Promise?"

"I promise. Are we good now?" He reached into the console and grabbed the half-sized box of Kleenex he'd stashed there, passing it to the child without mentioning the tears rolling down his cheeks. "Can I pull the Jeep around now?"

Levi dragged a wad of tissues from the box and haphazardly mopped his face and nose. He nodded.

Turning back to the wheel, he restarted the Jeep and drove to the adjoining lot. Levi was intent on keeping the ER doors in sight.

He shut the Jeep down, got out, and opened the back door. "Hey, buddy. Shall we take Pup out for a walk before we go into the doctor's office?" He didn't wait for the boy's agreement, but helped him out, unclipped the dog's harness, and attached the leash. The hound was excited to be out of the Jeep and lunged ahead keeping the leash taut as they moved toward a patch of open ground.

A few minutes later, they were back at the Jeep. Ordering Pup into the vehicle, he told him to stay and handed Levi his backpack.

"Can we bring Pup with us in the doctor's office?"

Keeso shook his head. "He isn't allowed inside, but he'll be comfortable sleeping in the Jeep. We can check on him if you get worried."

He zipped Emma's handbag in the duffel. She'd probably need a change of clothes. Grabbing the quilt Levi had been wrapped in, he locked the Jeep and took Levi's hand, walking him to the ER.

After settling Levi in the waiting room, close to the door where he could see him, Keeso walked to the sliding-glass window to speak to the nurse. She was waiting for him and opened the window as soon as he walked up.

"Do you have your insurance information?"

"I'll pay with cash."

"Mr. Smith, you *do* realize the cost of your wife's medical care will be expensive, correct?"

"I understand. Can you give me a figure?"

"No, sir. Accounting will have to take care of that. You can make arrangements with them in the morning."

She glanced over his shoulder toward the waiting room door. "Your son looks worried."

"If we're finished here, I need to let him know everything is all right."

"Go take care of your boy. We're good here. We'll let you know how your wife is as soon as the doctor examines her." She picked up the clipboard and exited the reception area through a door at the back of the room.

He slipped the money into his wallet and returned to the waiting room. "How's it going, buddy?"

"Can we go see Aunty yet?"

"Probably not for a while. The doctor has to see her first and take care of her leg. Are you hungry? I put some snacks and juice in your backpack." He unzipped one of the compartments. "You've got some games and books in here too. I don't think your aunt would mind if you used your tablet for a while."

He spent the next half-hour entertaining, and being entertained by, Levi. He was in the middle of explaining how Centallian starships got from one planet to another when a law enforcement officer stepped through the doorway.

"Are you the owner of the Jeep in the parking lot?"

# 23

Keeso stood, placing himself between the officer and Levi. "The Jeep belongs to me."

"I'm officer Lenn Chaca. We received a call from this center reporting a possible gunshot wound. Did you bring a woman in who'd been shot?"

"Yes. Can I help you?"

"I'd like to ask you a few questions, sir."

"Let me get my nephew settled and we can go into the hall to talk."

At the officer's nod, Keeso knelt beside Levi. "I'm going into the hall to talk with the officer. You'll be able to see me from here and you can call out anytime you need me. All right?"

"Do I have to be afraid of him?"

"No. He only wants to ask me some questions. You don't have to worry. We'll finish our story when I get back. You can play a game on your tablet until then."

The officer stepped back and inclined his head toward the door, obviously wanting him to step into the hall first. The man's right hand rested on his waist just above the gun at his side. The safety strap was unsnapped.

He preceded Officer Chaca, turning to keep Levi in his line of vision. The boy was still wide-eyed. He gave the child a reassuring smile before turning his attention to the officer.

The man pulled a small notebook and pen from his front pocket. "Can you tell me what happened?"

"Emma and I were standing on my cabin's porch steps when the first shot struck the porch post inches from her head. The second shot grazed her leg before we made it into the house."

"There were two shots?"

Keeso nodded.

"Then it wasn't an accident?"

His eyes locked with the officer's. "No, the man intended to kill her."

"What makes you think that?"

"She saw something she shouldn't have."

"Can you be more specific?"

"Emma will be able to tell you more than I can, but I'm not sure she'll want to."

"And why is that?"

Levi shifted in his seat and he glanced over to make sure the boy was still all right. "Officer, I need to speak with Chairman Mockta. Can you contact him and let him know Keeso Smith is at the clinic, that we have mutual ancestors to speak of? He'll understand what I mean."

The officer raised an eyebrow. "You're acquainted with our chairman?"

"I am. I need to speak with him as soon as possible. It's important."

"I'll see what I can do. Until then, don't leave the center."

"I'm not going anywhere until I speak with the chairman. And I'm not leaving without Emma, so you don't have to worry. I also need to ask you not to make any reports until after you've spoken with the chairman." The officer nodded, and Keeso returned to the waiting room where Levi played.

An hour later, Chairman Mockta entered the waiting room. Levi had fallen asleep on one of the small couches, and the two men moved to the opposite corner of the room to speak with each other in low tones. Keeso quickly explained their situation and need for sanctuary.

"As it has been from the beginning, you will be welcomed as one of us. No Hopi will deny you aid. I will contact the leader of the Tobacco Clan on First Mesa. A house has recently become vacant. It belonged to an elderly woman who outlived her husband and her children. To my knowledge, no woman has petitioned the clan leader for the house. If it is still available, I will request it for you. The house will belong to your wife for as long as you need it."

"You should know that Emma does not yet consider herself my wife. I have given her the words, but she is unsure."

The chairman laughed. "I remember when you first came to visit us with Rhyel, Valdon, and Zitan. Many of our young women would've welcomed the attention of you or your captain. It's difficult to believe you are having a problem convincing her."

"Emma is a stubborn woman, but I am hopeful she will eventually agree."

The chairman left a few minutes later, but the officer returned almost immediately. "Chairman Mockta has asked me to offer you any assistance I can. I have to finish my rounds, but my shift is over at seven." He handed Keeso a card. "I've written my cell number on the back. Call me if there's a problem before I return."

"Thank you. Have you filed a report?"

"The chairman asked me not to. He feels this is an internal matter that should be handled by the Hopi alone. I'm sorry for the misunderstanding earlier. I've accompanied your commander, Rhyel, and several Guardians and Elders to our sacred valley, but I don't remember meeting you."

"I've never been to the sacred valley before."

The officer nodded and sighed. "You should know. I ran your plates earlier."

That was unfortunate. Emma suspected her sister and brother-in-law's killer had ties to law enforcement. If that were true, and he had no reason to believe it wasn't, the killer would soon know where they were. He had to get Emma somewhere safe before her pursuer had a chance to find them.

The mild pain in her left thigh roused Emma from a fitful sleep. Confused, she glanced around. The unfamiliar room was dim, the only light coming through partially closed curtains that covered a standard-sized window.

She had an idea of where she was. Keeso had carried her into the medical facility late last night after a jarring ride through terrain far different from the Colorado countryside.

She remembered a ship capable of taking them hundreds, maybe thousands, of miles in a matter of minutes.

Levi. Where was he? Leaning up on her elbows, she glanced around. Keeso sat dozing in a chair, his head lulled back against the wall. Levi had fallen asleep in the big man's arms.

Resting back against the pillow, she breathed a sigh of relief. Keeso was a mysterious man, yet she trusted him. Instinctively, she knew he would protect Levi with his life. She knew beyond any doubt Keeso would raise her nephew as his own if something happened to her. He'd said as much.

What had he told her last night? That the vow he'd given her had, by his people's beliefs, made Levi his son. She sighed and shifted her gaze to the ceiling. He claimed the words he'd spoken to her were formal and bound him to her for life. He was now her—what had he called it—her bond-mate. She wasn't sure what that meant, but she had the feeling she was stuck with him. And what did that mean? At the very least, he intended to be her bodyguard. And at the most? She suspected that was where her own willingness came into play. She took a deep breath and let it out slowly. It was too much for her muddled mind to consider. She closed her eyes and gave herself up to sleep.

When she opened her eyes again, the doctor was examining her leg. Keeso stood on the opposite side of the bed holding her hand.

"Levi?"

He stepped back so she could see the chair he'd been sitting in earlier. "He's been waiting for you to wake up." She looked across the room at her nephew and smiled. He smiled back but made no effort to come to her. "He's been wary of strangers since we got here." Keeso kept his voice low, hoping Levi wouldn't hear him. "He planted himself in that chair as soon as the doctor entered the room."

She nodded. "It isn't just here, and he isn't wary," she whispered. "He's afraid. I don't know if he'll ever trust a stranger again. I'm not sure he should."

Her attention returned to the doctor and she caught her first glimpse of the damage. Her leg was swollen and bruised, probably from the doctor's prodding—which he was in the process of doing again. A long line of neat tight stitches evidenced the bullet's path. The scar was going to show if she wore shorts. At least no one would be able to attribute it to a bullet wound.

The scar from the first bullet wound told a different story. Fortunately, that one was easy to hide. Only she would know it was there.

She glanced at Keeso, who stared intently at her damaged leg and revised her thinking. He would know. Her cheeks warmed. Everyone here thought they were married. He certainly acted as if he had the right to look at her leg, and she couldn't tell him to stop. Not in front of the doctor.

He replaced the sheet and turned to Keeso. "I assume you're a friend of the Hopi."

"I am. How did you know?"

"The red powder. I've seen it before."

He nodded. "How soon can Emma leave the hospital?"

"I'll sign her release forms and she can be out of here in an hour or so." He patted Emma's shoulder and reached out to shake hands with Keeso. "We'll do a follow-up in a few days."

As soon as the physician left, Levi scrambled out of the chair and ran to her bedside. Keeso lifted him onto the bed. Her nephew hugged her neck and snuggled against her side.

"Did the Doctor make you all better?"

"He did. In a few days, I'll be as good as new." She looked up at Keeso. "Where do we go next?"

"The chairman has arranged for us to stay at First Mesa for as long as we need. My people have ancient ties to the Hopi. They will aid our cause in any way they are able. The leader of the Tobacco Clan has arranged a house for us. According to their customs, the house will belong to you during our stay." He grinned. "Apparently, I will be there at your discretion."

She tilted her head. "And if I decide you can't stay?"

He laughed out right. "Then Pup and I will camp on your doorstep."

"I never said Pup wouldn't be welcome."

His only response was a raised eyebrow.

She glanced around. "I need my purse. My money's in it."

"Your purse is safe in your duffel. Everything you packed is beside the chair."

"The medical bill—"

"Is not your concern."

"Why not?"

"I am now responsible for you. Including your medical expenses."

"That's high-handed and out of the question."

"It's already done."

"Keeso, I'm not taking your charity."

"Does an Earth wife consider what her husband brings to the marriage *charity?*"

"Of course not. But I'm not your wife. You have to stop acting as if we're married. We aren't…." She took a deep breath. "I appreciate everything you've done. But you have to let this go."

"A Guardian does not relinquish his vow. He cannot. Only under the gravest of circumstances will his vow be rescinded by the Elders. Otherwise, once given, the vow becomes a matter of honor. It is the way of my people."

"But your vow doesn't bind me?"

"It binds you only if you are willing to accept my words."

"That's crazy. It's like half a marriage. One partner makes all the sacrifices and the other goes blithely on their way."

"Protecting you is not a sacrifice."

"Please don't think I'm not grateful. I don't know what I'd have done without your help. You saved Levi's life… and mine. The only way I can repay you is to release you from your vow. And I'm doing that now."

He shook his head. "Only death, or an edict from the Centallian Council of Elders, can release me from my vow. Even the Council could not release me were the ceremony completed and the veil rent."

Her eyes widened. "I'm not even going to ask what that means."

He grinned. "We'll have time for explanations later." He took her hand and lifted it to his lips. "For now, you must concentrate on recovering and we must get you out of here. Last night, a Hopi officer ran the Jeep's plates before the chairman could stop him. It may not be a problem, but I'm not willing to chance it. The sooner you're out of this facility and hidden on First Mesa, the better I can protect you. Once you're settled in our new home, I'll return the Jeep to the shuttle."

A nurse walked into the room and came to her bedside. "Sorry to interrupt, but I need to get your vitals."

Emma pushed her sleeve back to let the woman wrap the blood pressure cuff around her arm. "Don't I remember you from last night?"

"Yes. We're shorthanded today, so I'm working a double shift."

Levi's worry-filled eyes caught the nurse's attention. "It's okay sweetheart, I'm not hurting her." She looked over at Keeso. "It's nice to see you're not frowning this morning. These two were so solemn last night I wanted to cry." She smiled. "I could hear the love in his laughter a few minutes ago and I see it in their eyes now. It's in your eyes too. Every family should love each other as much as you do." She typed Emma's vitals into the computer. "Someone will be here in a few minutes to help you get dressed." She turned to Keeso. "The doctor left a couple of prescriptions. I'll have them at the reception window."

Emma leaned against the pillows and closed her eyes. Levi snuggled into her side and hugged her neck. Keeso's hand rested on top of her head in a protective gesture.

Family.

# 24

*New Centallus*

Amber placed eight-month-old Jonathan in his crib, covered him with a light blanket, and turned her attention to her bond-mate. Rhyel stood, half-dressed, at their chamber window watching the lingering stars in the predawn sky over New Centallus.

"Do you miss them?" She joined him and he immediately pulled her into his arms.

"The stars?" He kissed the top of her head. "Most of my adult life was spent among them. Yes. I miss the stars and the *Novaria*. She was my home for many years."

"I'm sorry you lost your ship."

"As am I, *Rishka*. But I will be forever grateful for what we were able to accomplish before her destruction. Our colony can sustain itself. Continuing to augment our supplies from Earth would've made it easier, but that wasn't what I was thinking about."

"You were thinking about Keeso again."

"I don't like leaving a man behind."

"Don't blame yourself for what happened. You were in stasis when the *Novaria* left Earth, and no one knew Celiiel's ship was out there—except Tzorik."

"I don't blame myself, but I am frustrated. There's no way to go back for him."

"From what you've told me, he's capable of surviving back home."

Pulling her closer, he nuzzled her neck. "Do you still consider Earth your home? When I brought you here, you fought so hard to go back."

She tilted her head, giving him better access to her throat, loving the feel of his lips against her skin. "A part of me will always consider Earth home." She turned in his arms and looked up into his beautiful gold-flecked eyes. "Earth is the home of my past and still a part of me. But New Centallus is my home now. I'm happy here."

He lifted her into his arms, carried her to their bed, and fell with her to the mattress, his body covering hers, his arms supporting his weight. "And I, *Rishka*, am also happy you are here."

She gazed into eyes that were full-gold with passion and smiled. Her Guardian could not hide his need for her. She slipped her arms around his neck, her need for him just as great.

A knock sounded at the chamber door. Rhyel touched his forehead to hers and groaned. "Perhaps if we ignore them they'll go away."

"It could be an emergency at the clinic." She pushed against his shoulders to get him to let her up.

His lips touched hers in a quick kiss that conveyed his frustration. "Later."

The knocking began again, louder this time.

"Commander, I'm sorry to disturb you, but Cintar requires your presence in communications. He says it's urgent."

Her mate rolled away from her and off the bed. He sprinted to the door and opened it a crack. "Tell him I will be there momentarily." He closed the door before the Guardian could reply and turned back to the bed.

Jonathan began to fuss, and she got up to quiet him. "What kind of an emergency would they have in communications?"

He lifted his shoulders in a non-answer. "I'll tell you about it at the morning meal." Pulling a tunic over his head, he came around the bed for a brief kiss before leaving the chamber.

✧

Rhyel entered communications a couple of minutes later. Ten pairs of eyes met his. All of the Centallian Elders were there, including Amber's grandfather. Doctor Samuel Donovan, now the unofficial seventh member of the Council of Elders, stood beside Rhyel's father, Zitan. Cintar, Rhyel's second-in-command, hovered in front of the computer with Liiam and Tiinar.

Cintar stepped back and pointed toward the computer. "Readings indicate a ship entering orbit. I checked for anomalies and ghost echoes. It's out there."

"One ship?"

"There's no indication of more than one. If the reading's accurate, it's about half the size of *Novaria.*"

"Have they tried to make contact?"

"I don't believe so, sir, but there's a disturbance in the high-frequency range. It's distorting our reception. We've attempted to communicate—either they can't or won't respond."

Cintar caught His commander's eye. "The Kenchee?"

Rhyel nodded. "I suspect so. The high-frequency distortion fits."

Samuel Donovan glanced from the alarmed Elders to Rhyel. "Who—who are the Kenchee?"

"They are a species called the Kenchee. We share the same general body shape— two arms, two legs and two eyes—but that's the end of the resemblance. They have a flat, almost indiscernible nose, nearly hidden by the long, thick fir that covers their bodies. Their ears set high on their head and are capable of movement, like many of the animals on your planet. We don't know much about their females, but the males fall into two categories, the Senchee-male and the Cho-male. The Senchee are intelligent—they make the decisions. They are cunning, sly, and cannot be trusted. The Cho bear little resemblance to the Senchee. They are taller and burlier, with scruffy fur. Their intelligence is questionable. They appear to fall into the servant-warrior class."

The doctor nodded. "Are they dangerous?"

Rhyel heaved a sigh. "They could be."

He turned to his men. "We've prepared for this, though I would've preferred our discovery happening in the distant future. Our visitors may simply be inquisitive. But we need to be ready for any alternative. Elder Valdon, rouse the fortress. Liiam, monitor communications. Keep us informed of their actions." He turned to his second-in-command. "Cintar, see to arming the Guardians. Half will prepare to defend the fortress and stand ready to meet the Kenchee outside the walls. You will oversee the defense preparations. Assure the women there is no immediate threat. The remainder will go with me."

He turned his attention to Amber's grandfather. "Doctor Donovan, Amber will need you in the clinic, should we be attacked. Tiinar, you are with me." He left the communications room, pausing long enough to stop a passing Guardian.

"Stay with Liiam in communications. Contact me if there are further developments. Liiam will explain."

Amber was halfway down the stairs by the time he'd finished giving the Guardians his orders. Jonathan rested against her shoulder, sound asleep. She looked concerned. He met her at the bottom of the stairs.

"What's wrong?"

"Nothing, I hope. It appears we may have company, but I'm not sure of their intent. They haven't made contact yet and failed to respond to our hails. Take Jonathan to the clinic. Keep him with you. I'll have Cintar send Hiilani to you."

She shook her head. "Her baby's due any time. She shouldn't be working at the clinic."

"Give her something she can handle to keep her busy. Cintar needs to know she's exactly where she should be if her labor begins. I want his full concentration on protecting the fortress."

She nodded. "Can you spare a Guardian for the clinic? I may need someone with a little muscle."

"I'll ask Elder Tzarn to offer his aid. He's strong enough to assist you."

"What will you do?"

"Friend or foe, my men and I will meet them outside the fortress walls. What occurs after that is up to them."

She leaned up and kissed his cheek. "Be careful."

Her admonition had nothing to do with a lack of faith in his abilities. It was her way of telling him she cared. Bending, he touched her lips with his.

"You as well, *Rishka*." He touched his son's head with a gentle hand. "Keep our child safe." He walked away from her, steeling himself for what might come.

Cintar issued the weapons. Each man wore his own personal long-knife and shield, the only concessions to the traditional battle garb of the ancients. The grotesque battle masks and leather armor had been relegated to Centallian ceremonies. The Discourager was now the Centallian's weapon of choice. Whimsically dubbed the Discourager by its inventor, the flexible glove-shaped weapon had a cylindrical barrel mounted over the knuckle area. It attached to the belt at an angle for quick insertion of the hand and easy release from the belt. The weapon fired by aiming the cylinder and flexing a fist. A button on the side of the glove deactivated the safety. Magnetic accelerators fired electrically charged pellets capable of immobilizing or killing the target, depending on the point of impact.

His father, Zitan, came to stand beside him. "I suggest we evacuate the upper floors. If the fortress is attacked, we don't want our women and children trapped in the rooms above."

Rhyel nodded. "Take whatever men you need and see to it now. Women with newborns as well as those in advanced pregnancy should go to the day nursery next to the clinic. The remainder can wait in the Council Chamber. Assure them there is no immediate threat, but make sure they stay out of the Great Hall. If fighting breaks out inside the fortress, it will be there."

Zitan placed his hand on his son's shoulder. "May the Creator of all worlds walk with you this day."

He bowed his respect to his father. "And with you as well." The Elder commandeered four fully-armed Guardians. His instructions were short and the Guardians divided to take the staircases on each side of the hall to the upper level.

"Commander." The Guardian assigned to communications sprinted across the hall toward him. "Commander, Liiam needs you at once." Rhyel raced past the young Guardian and gained the room before the man could catch up.

"Report."

"I'm picking up a shuttle moving toward the surface." He pointed at a blip on the screen.

"Toward the fortress?"

"No, sir." He pointed to the angle of the blip. "If I'm reading this right, their destination point is on the other side of the second mine, near the *Novaria's* debris field."

Rhyel bent closer to the holographic screen. "Is the ship weaponized?"

"It's hard to tell, sir, but I don't think so." His third-in-command was never wrong when it came to interpreting the readings.

Liiam looked up at his commander. "Either they haven't noticed us yet, or they're not interested in us. Why do you think the debris field interests them?"

*The Acqeli.*

A wave of dread almost staggered him. Could he have been wrong? They'd walked every inch of the debris field searching for the black crystal. He had been satisfied the accursed translation stone had disintegrated with most of his ship before reaching the planet's surface.

Even if the crystal had survived, their visitors wouldn't know of its existence. Only the Centallians had known. He left communications to gather his men for the potential confrontation and spotted Siikzo and Sonya. Siikzo held his young son while he and his bond-mate were in deep conversation. The child was agitated, probably by the confusion in the Great Hall. The Guardian patted his son's back and kissed the top of his head before handing him to his mother. The bond-mates shared a kiss. Siikzo placed a gentle hand on her stomach. The couple had wanted a second child right away. Sonya plagued Amber for weeks, to approve their decision to conceive again.

He understood the reasoning. Sonya had lost their first baby to the virus and gone through her second pregnancy believing Siikzo was dead. It had been a dark time for the colony. Siikzo, Kaarz, a Centallian technician, and his own bond-mate, Amber, were thought to have perished in a shuttle accident. Kaarz had died, but Siikzo had succeeded in rescuing Amber. He owed the Guardian a debt of honor he would never be able to repay.

The couple walked to the clinic and Siikzo opened the door for his mate. They shared one more kiss before she carried her child into the clinic and he closed the door behind them.

"Your son is growing."

The Guardian smiled. "At his rate of growth, he will be as big as I am before his brother or sister arrives." He laughed at his own boast. "Sonya tells me I will spoil the boy with my praise."

"Amber is of the same mind. She chides me for my exaggerations of Jonathan's accomplishments to his grandfather and great-grandfather. Her grandfather keeps reminding her it is impossible to spoil a child with love."

Siikzo sobered and fell into step beside his commander. "Do we prepare for battle?"

"We do, but it is my hope our preparations are unnecessary. Perhaps our unexpected visitors will prove friendly."

# 25

✧

*Earth*

The Tobacco Clan leader provided Emma with a home on the Flats below the original First Mesa Village. Though many Hopi preferred the traditional lifestyle, a few of the homes, like the one she'd been given, had electricity, water, and propane. The wood-frame structure was small but efficient, with two bedrooms, a bath, a small kitchen, and living room.

Though she'd offered to share one of the bedrooms with Levi, Keeso had insisted she needed her privacy and opted to sleep on the couch. Levi argued someone needed to sleep with her because she had bad dreams. Keeso promised he would hear her if she needed him.

The couch was large, but Keeso was larger. When she'd checked on Levi the first night, she'd glanced at the couch and seen him lying on his back, his legs dangling over the arm. She'd resisted the urge to tuck the blanket around his feet.

Probably not by coincidence, the home was directly across the road from the officer who'd first spoken with Keeso. According to Hopi custom, their home belonged to Marie, Officer Lenn Chaca's wife. She was a member of the Tobacco Clan. Lenn, born into the Bear Clan, had automatically become a part of the Tobacco Clan when they were married. He would remain a member unless Marie passed before he did.

Their daughter, Sarah, was three months younger than Levi. It hadn't taken long for the two youngsters to become best friends. They played together every day.

Pup was finally growing into his feet. The young dog still resembled a hound, but heavier-chested. He'd appointed himself the children's guardian, planting himself between the children and any passersby. Fortunately, he was watchful without being aggressive.

Emma stood at the window for twenty minutes watching Levi and Sarah play with Pup. She insisted Levi stay close to the house where she could keep an eye on him.

Keeso moved to the window and handed her a cup of hot tea. Over the past few weeks, he'd become more acquainted with her preferences. She had an aversion to his coffee, preferring tea instead—something called Earl Grey. He'd tried a cup and decided he didn't care for her tea any better than she did his coffee.

"Let's go for a walk today. There's a small canyon I'd like to show you. We'll take the new Jeep most of the way, then follow a short trail."

Keeso and Lenn had stowed the original Jeep in the shuttle, away from prying eyes. He'd paid cash for the new one, preventing the possibility of a money trail, and registered it as a Hopi vehicle.

"What about Levi?"

"He can go with us. Lenn and Marie are taking Sarah and invited us to go. The canyon is part of the connection between my people and the Hopi. I want you to see it. We'll take the Jeep and go out early, so we can take our time. I don't want you overtaxing."

"I'm fully recovered. You don't have to baby me."

"Yes, I do. I'll tell Lenn we'll meet them there."

An hour later, Levi came tearing into the house, skidding to a halt in front of her. Keeso followed at a more dignified pace.

"Aunty! Uncle Keeso says I have to ask you. Can I?"

"Slow down, honey. Can you what?"

"Go with Sarah."

She looked at Keeso in question.

"He wants to ride to the canyon with Sarah and her family."

"I'm not sure that's a good idea."

"Please, Aunty."

"Levi, why don't you make sure Pup has water while your aunt decides."

"Okay. I'll be right back." He gave his aunt a pleading look before heading toward the back door.

"I won't undermine your authority with the boy, but I think you should consider letting him ride with the Chacas. He needs some normalcy in his life, a chance to spend the day with Sarah and forget to be afraid."

Tears welled in her eyes. "I know what I'm doing to him. I've dragged him halfway across the country. How many months have we been running? Where do we run to next? I can't give him normal and keep him alive." She turned her back to him, swiping the tears with her fingers.

He came up behind her, put his arms around her waist and pulled her back against his body. When she tried to break his hold, he rested his chin on her shoulder and whispered, "Shhh, Em. Stop blaming yourself. None of this is your fault. You're as much a victim as Levi is. But you do have to loosen the reins a little. He'll be safe with Lenn and Marie. They'll only be a few minutes behind us and there shouldn't be anyone else around for miles." He turned her in his arms and the caring she saw in his gaze brought more tears to her eyes.

She leaned away from him to grab a Kleenex from the box on the stand by the window. "I never used to cry. Now I can't seem to stop. You must think I'm terrible."

He pulled her back into his arms, holding her close against his hard body. "Never think that. You are the strongest woman I have ever known." He pressed his cheek against the top of her head. "Levi couldn't have survived without you."

The back door slammed, and she pulled out of his arms as Levi ran into the living room.

"I gave Pup lots of water. He was thirsty. Can he come with us today?"

Keeso ruffed the boy's hair. "That sounds like a good idea." He glanced at her and tilted his head in question. She knew what he was asking and gave him a quick nod. Turning back to Levi, he smiled. "Do you think there's room in Sarah's dad's car for you and the Pup?"

"I can ride with Sarah?"

"Yes, but you'll need to ask Sarah's dad if it's okay for Pup to go along. Otherwise, he'll have to ride with your aunt and me."

Levi lifted his eyes to her. "Can I go ask him now?"

"Yes, but be careful crossing the road."

"Okay." He started for the door, then turned and ran back to give her a hug. "I love you, Aunty."

The Jeep bounced and bucked over what was more a path than a road. The vehicle hit another pothole and her head would have hit the ceiling if she hadn't been wearing her seatbelt. They drove for a good forty-five minutes, heading for a red-stone mesa that loomed in the distance. Finally, they edged up to the stately rock formation.

Parking the Jeep in the shade of the sheer cliff face, Keeso jumped out and came around to open the door and help her out. She glanced around. The view was beautiful, but not much different from what she'd seen every day for the past few weeks.

"We walk from here. It isn't far." Retrieving a Stetson from the back seat, he plopped it on her head, laughing when the brim of the oversized hat covered her eyes.

"Ready?" They were skirting the Jeep when she saw a small break in the rocks. He adjusted his hat and took her hand to lead her into the shadow-dark fissure.

"Watch your footing."

"Okay." If it hadn't been for the light filtering in from the top of the bluff face, she would've sworn they were walking through a cave.

When she started to look up, he placed his hand on her head. "Not a good idea. Birds tend to nest in the crevices up there. Not many, but enough to warrant caution." He tapped the top of her hat. "Might even be a few bats up there."

"So, the hat's for bat droppings?" She couldn't hide the disgust in her voice.

He laughed. "Yup."

It wasn't until the path curved to the right that she saw light coming from the end of the passageway. The light was so limited, she had trouble judging the height of the distant opening. The exit could've been as low as three or four feet or as high as fifteen or twenty. When they reached the end of the passage, she realized the opening was considerably higher, the gap nearly reaching the top of the cliff face on both sides.

The hemmed-in canyon they entered took her breath away. In stunning contrast to the desert reds and browns she'd grown used to, the hidden valley vibrated with color. A beautiful deep blue pool graced one side of the valley—she guessed a spring or perhaps an artesian well fed it. A trickling stream meandered from the pool around the valley before disappearing underground. Lush, thick-bladed grass surrounded the pool, following the stream's path. Multi-hued blossoms splashed the landscape as if flung from an artist's brush, defying the encroachment of winter.

"Oh Keeso, it's... it's...."

He slipped his arm around her waist and pulled her against his side. "The Hopi consider this valley sacred."

"I can understand why." She looked up at him and smiled. "It feels like we've stepped into another world. Thank you for bringing me here to see this miracle of nature."

"The is only a part of what I wanted you to see." He pointed toward a cluster of boulders on the far side of the valley. "I want you to understand the heritage I share with these people. I have a story to tell you."

He led her through the maze of rivulets until they reached the four tall boulders. Pictographs covered most of the stones. The inscription below the etchings on the largest stone was distinctively different from the drawings.

Keeso knelt and touched the writing with reverence. "This is Centallian—

the language of my people. Five of your centuries ago, three of my people found sanctuary with the Hopi. Riistren, his wife, Wrenn, and his father, Tiines, made their home with these people. They are buried in this valley. Riistren's and Wrenn's children embraced the Hopi culture, and their descendants carry a mix of Hopi and Centallian blood."

"Are you one of the descendants?"

"I bear no Hopi blood, though I would be proud to do so."

They sat for a time in companionable silence until barking and a burst of children's laughter announced the Chacas' arrival. They walked to where Keeso and Emma were.

The children were allowed to run and play for a while. But Lenn had a purpose. His daughter was old enough to learn something about her ancestry. He and Marie thought the best place to begin was the ancient burial place in the hidden valley. In simple words, he explained the story carved in the glyphs, speaking English, so Levi understood the story as well.

Emma enjoyed listening to the Hopi version of the ancient Centallian visit. The officer's rendition was basically the same as Keeso's, but it was fascinating to listen to each man's impression of the event. After his story, the children took off to splash in the stream.

The men sat together on a low boulder and spoke in quiet tones as they watched the children. They shared Centallian blood, a bond neither would ever deny.

Even she felt the family ties. Maybe it was because Marie reminded her of Denise. The young Hopi woman loved to laugh. Her sister had, too.

# 26

✧

*New Centallus*

The Kenchee.

What was that band of marauders doing on New Centallus, far from the central order of planets? Not that they were any more welcome there. It was generally accepted that wherever you found the Kenchee, you'd find trouble. Their prey was always weaker, usually unable to protect themselves. Their world had been banned from the Contingent of Planets centuries ago, due to the inhabitants' marauding tendencies.

Rhyel stepped out of the ground shuttle. Siikzo and Tiinar flanked him as he walked toward the debris field.

The forty or so hulking, fur-covered Cho-males scrambled to assemble behind the five sleek-haired Senchee-males—the alphas. Why were they on New Centallus, digging through *Novaria's* rubble? What were they looking for?

Tiinar moved closer to his commander and spoke softly. "Why are they here?"

Rhyel's voice was equally quiet. "My thoughts exactly." He rested his hand on the hilt of his long-knife. The Guardians immediately fell in behind him. "Contact the fortress. Have Liiam jam any communication between the Kenchee ground forces and the ship. He'll need to use high-range frequencies. Advise Cintar of our visitors' identity and tell him to prepare for a possible invasion. The

Kenchee attack with little provocation or warning, and we don't know how many are still up there." The Guardian nodded and returned to the shuttle.

A subtle movement caught his eye. One of the Cho lumbered forward to speak to the lead Senchee. He fumbled something dark into his leader's hand as he returned to the ranks.

"I am Khad, First Enrow of the stellar ship *Arcave.*" He nodded, his action condescending. "And you are?"

"Commander Rhyel." He offered no other information.

"I am correct, am I not, that you are Centallian?"

Rhyel neither affirmed nor denied his question.

The First Enrow shrugged. "It is believed your species had been wiped out when your world disintegrated. Yet, here you are. Why is that, I wonder?" At Rhyel's continued silence he shook his head. "It's a shame about your world. Did your Elders finally meddle in something they shouldn't have and start a war? Are you in hiding?"

Rhyel's cold stare gave nothing way. "Why are you here?"

He lifted his shoulders. "We were attracted by your debris field."

"You are not the first to find us. There was a firefight."

Khad glanced around. "Your ship?"

"Has the *Arcave* in its sights." Rhyel told the lie with enough confidence to make the Kenchee uncomfortable. The Cho shuffled from one foot to another. A Senchee-male lifted a small object to his lips and muttered something. A moment later, he called out to Khad in the Kenchee language. What he had to say didn't make the leader happy.

Rhyel's translator allowed him to understand everything the Kenchee had said. Liiam had succeeded in blocking their communication system.

"You need not fear our aggression," Khad was quick to assure. "We were only mildly curious. If you will allow us to board our ship, we will leave without further delay."

"After you return what you have taken."

"You must know there's nothing of value in the debris field."

"Valuable or not, I want what the Cho gave you. Now."

"Calm yourself, Commander. I will be happy to relinquish the worthless souvenir." He reached into the packet at his side and jerked out a hand-sized silver, cylindrical object.

Rhyel grabbed his own weapon and was dropping to the ground when Siikzo leapt in front of him. The Senchee must have fired his weapon. Siikzo flinched and lurched back, screaming. In milliseconds, his body expanded to three times its normal size then instantaneously imploded. A dry, pebbly residue covered the ground where he'd stood.

*No, not Siikzo!*

"Take cover!" He fired at the Kenchee and rolled behind a nearby boulder. A second Guardian suffered Siikzo's fate.

"Gravitational wands. Get behind something big." His shout galvanized the stunned men, and they dove for cover. Tiinar hovered just inside the shuttle door. Rhyel waived him farther back. "Warn Cintar." The Guardian headed for the cockpit but returned in a matter of seconds.

"The com's down. Whatever Liiam did to jam their communications took care of ours, too. Ground-to-ground is out as well. You'll have to shout your orders. I've activated the blast shields, but I can see the Kenchee on the vid-screens."

Rhyel leaned his back against the boulder and glanced around. Only a handful of his men were in sight. Hopefully the rest of his Guardians were within shouting distance.

"Target the Senchee-males. They have the wands." He moved to the other end of the rock that protected him. Another boulder rested beside his, with a three-foot gap separating the two. Weapon in hand, he leaped across the gap, firing as many times as he could in the general direction of the Kenchee. Two high-pitched, pain-filled snarls pierced the air at the same moment a small tree behind him expanded and imploded. He wondered if the wounded were Senchee or Cho. Whichever, they were no longer in the battle. Their own weapons, like the gravitational wand, were silent. The battle was surreal, the only sound the cries of the wounded and dying.

"Good shooting, Commander." Tiinar stood inside the doorway again.

"Two Senchee are on the ground. I can't tell if they're alive or dead. I don't much care." He disappeared into the cockpit for a second or two then returned to the entry. "Don't move, Rhyel. Khad is using the Cho as shields. His wand is aimed at that gap. He's waiting for you to appear again."

"I am indeed, Commander," Khad purred. "Would you care to wager which of us is faster? I will admit your stakes are a little higher than mine. You risk your life whereas I… lose a Cho."

He glanced at the ship. Tiinar was out of sight. When he returned to the entry, he looked stunned. "Khad used his wand on the wounded Senchee."

Rhyel was outraged. "How can you kill your own men?"

"Don't condemn me, Commander. They expect no less. Any Kenchee, Senchee or Cho, who cannot defeat the opponent who wounded him deserves death. There is no honor in losing."

"To my knowledge, the Kenchee have no honor. I doubt you understand the meaning of the word."

Tiinar came into sight again. "Several of the Cho are down, Commander. When one goes down, another moves in front of his leader. They have no sense of self-preservation."

Rhyel nodded. "And the Senchee-males no honor. What about our men? Have we taken more casualties?"

"I'm not sure. With the blast shields down, I'm only picking up a few of our men."

"Why don't you try talking to our friends, Tiinar? You have a *flair* for diplomacy. All you need to do is *flash* a smile, and they'll be your friends."

The Guardian tilted his head and shrugged his shoulders, obviously trying to figure out his meaning. Rhyel pointed a finger skyward. After a minute, Tiinar smiled, nodded, and returned to the cockpit.

Weapon ready, he waited for the low boom of the signal flare launcher. The flare shot high and exploded. The sky lit red and Rhyel jumped out from behind the boulder, firing twice. Both Senchee dropped to the ground screaming.

"Guardians, now!"

His men swarmed the battleground.

Yowling with rage, the Cho attacked, their sharp, club-like weapons swinging. His Guardians opted for their long-knives and shields.

Rhyel sprinted from behind the boulder to where the Senchee lay and confiscated their wands. He pocketed one and tossed the other three to Tiinar. "Don't let them near the shuttle. I need to secure their ship before someone decides to go for help."

The intense hand-to-hand combat between the Guardians and the Cho allowed him to skirt the battlefield unchallenged. His hand gloved in the Discourager, he used the cover of trees and brush as he approached the Kenchee ship.

The hatch was open, the ramp extended, but no one, Senchee or Cho, lurked at the entrance. He circled the craft, avoiding the cockpit windows, and hunched at the opening. No sound emanated from the interior. Staying low, he ascended the ramp on silent feet, alert to the slightest hint of activity. Still nothing. Pressing his back to the side of the doorway, he pivoted and lunged through the hatch, arm extended, ready to fire.

The craft was empty. The troop carrier had four seats in the cockpit area, and a long, stout bench on each side of the craft. There was no place for an attacker to hide.

Why they'd left the ship unprotected was beyond his comprehension.

By the time he'd secured the vessel, the distant battle sounds had stopped. Bodies littered the area, most of them Cho. None of the Kenchee were standing. He walked toward the battleground, taking in the scene. His Guardians were milling around, some checking the Kenchee, others helping their Centallian brothers.

Tiinar had left the shuttle and was kneeling beside one of the Guardians. He stood as Rhyel approached.

"Report?"

"We've lost four Guardians, Siikzo and Sandriis were killed by the Kenchee wand, Jaadel and Kaaden in hand-to-hand combat."

Rhyel tamped down his anger and sorrow. He had a world to defend. "How many wounded?"

"Nine severely. They're in stasis. Another seven with minor wounds. It could have been worse."

"The Cho?"

"All dead."

"All?"

"Every member of the landing party. I don't know why. Some of their wounds were superficial, and yet they died."

"It probably has something to do with Kenchee honor. Apparently, the Cho are expendable. How they accomplished their own deaths is unimportant. Our main concern is getting our wounded Guardians to the fortress."

For a long moment, he stared at the pebbled remains of his two friends. Tiinar had posted a Guardian to protect each site.

"Place Siikzo's and Sandriis's remains in containers. Mark each for identification and entrust them to the Elders. See that Jaadel and Kaaden are properly covered before they are returned to the fortress. No one is to know who we've lost until their bond-mates are informed in private. Shuttle our wounded to the fortress. The Guardians capable of fighting will remain with me. Have Cintar divide his men. Half will return here to join our forces."

He lifted the gravitational wand from his belt. "Hopefully, the remaining Kenchee will come to check on their shipmates." He aimed the wand at a Cho corpse and fired. As if it had been given life, the Cho body raised from the ground, expanded to a macabre caricature of itself, and imploded. Pebbled dust fell to the ground. He aimed the wand at a second body and fired. He knelt beside Khad and took the pouch the Senchee had used to contain his find. He stepped back and fired the wand twice more.

"I'm concerned about the number of Kenchee still aboard their ship. If this was a small landing party, we could be facing hundreds more. If we are fortunate, they will assume the residue belongs to our men and assume the landing party has moved on to the fortress. It should give us the advantage of surprise. Remove anything Kenchee from the battlefield. Scatter a few of our swords and shields near the piles of residue. The wands don't affect metal."

Liiam continued to jam their frequencies. After several hours with no communication, two Senchee-males and no more than twenty Cho landed the second ship next to the first. Evidence of the wands' use, scattered across the surface of the ground, gave them confidence, and they walked into the Centallian trap.

Rhyel took out the Senchee-males using the gravitational weapons. Guardians rushed forward, expecting another furious battle. But before they could reach their adversaries, the Cho began dropping to the ground, dying within seconds. He handed the wand to Tiinar, who had returned to fight alongside him.

"Get rid of them."

# 27

✧

Amber removed her latex gloves and glanced over at Hiilani. Cintar's mate was pressing her hands against her lower back.

"Are you in pain?"

"No. But my back is tired."

"We're finished here. Why don't you go find a bed in the other room and lie down for a while? We'll let you know if you're needed."

The nurse nodded. "Tell Cintar where I am and that I'm fine. The closer my time gets, the more he hovers. It's sweet, but sometimes he drives me crazy."

Sonya set the used instruments in the clinic sink to be washed and put in the sterilizer. "Siikzo behaved in much the same way when we found out I carried our son. I believe it was because we had lost our first child. Cintar is probably having the same misgivings. He remembers when you and Keeso lost your baby." She patted her slightly rounded midsection. "I can only hope my Guardian is calmer with this child."

Hiilani laughed. "I don't see that happening. Admit it, Sonya. You wouldn't have him any other way." She opened the door and abruptly stepped back to allow Rhyel, Zitan, and Valdon to enter.

Amber looked up at her mate, but the smile died on her lips. "Rheyl? What's wrong?"

"We need to speak with Sonya." She nodded and started to brush past him, but he caught her hand. "Stay."

Sonya took one look at the men's grim faces and started shaking her head. "No. Not again." She stumbled back.

Valdon reached out to steady her. "I'm so very sorry, child." Zitan pulled out a desk chair and the chief Elder eased her into it.

Amber pulled away from her bond-mate and grabbed a blanket from one of the clinic beds. She draped it around her friend's shoulders.

Hiilani brought her a glass of *Baquui*. "Drink this."

Sonya pushed the glass away and looked up at Rhyel, her eyes brimming with tears. "How?"

He knelt beside her chair and took her hands in his. "The Kenchee are, for the most part, a renegade species. Why they're in this quadrant, I have no idea. But they were close enough to New Centallus to find something of interest among the *Novaria*'s debris and brought a shuttle down to investigate."

He took a deep breath and slowly released it. "The Kenchee are marauders who prey on the weak. They are without honor. Their leader, Khad, had a concealed gravitational weapon, a weapon banned by the Contingent of Planets.

"Khad was aiming the weapon at me when Siikzo jumped between us, taking the shot. It will comfort you to know his death was instantaneous. Siikzo died a hero. He saved my life."

"I want to see him."

Rhyel shook his head. "It's best if you do not. Siikzo would want you to remember him with your heart." He took the glass of *Baquui* from Hiilani and placed it in Sonya's hand. "Drink this for your baby's sake and let Amber go with you to your room. You should rest."

Hiilani shook her head. "I'll go with her. Amber needs to stay at the clinic." When Sonya finished the *Baquui*, the nurse helped her to her feet. Amber walked with them to the door. Hiilani paused and looked back at Rhyel. "Did we lose anyone else?"

"Jaadel, Sandriis, and Kaaden were also lost. Kroyda and Tiinar are with Sandriis's mate, Rija. Jaadel and Kaaden were unbonded."

The nurse nodded and opened the door. Amber walked through with the two women, intending to make sure they made it up the stairs, but Valdon moved forward to take Sonya's arm and lead her across the hall, Cintar aiding Hiilani.

A double row of Guardians formed a wide line leading from the clinic, up the steps to the door of the room Sonya and Siikzo had shared with their son. Every man stood with arms crossed in front of their chests and heads bowed, honoring the bond-mate of a fallen brother. Amber swallowed back the tears as Sonya straightened and held her head high—her way of acknowledging their action and honoring the man she loved.

Amber returned to the clinic and closed the door. Rhyel was only a few feet away. They were the only two in the room. Zitan must have left through the infirmary door. Rhyel pulled her into his arms. She grabbed the front of his shirt in both fists and buried her face in his neck. "It isn't fair. They were so happy. She lost him once and went through her son's birth believing he was dead. She's pregnant again, and this time she's truly lost him. He won't show up unexpectedly, to make everything right. I don't know how she'll get through this."

He rested his cheek on the top of her head and rubbed her back. "Sonya is a strong woman and she has the love and support of the colony. We can't take away her grief. I'm not sure she'd want us to. She owes that to Siikzo. It's a manifestation of her love for him. But we can help her, and we will. She won't face the future alone, and neither will Rija. Both are valued members of our colony and will continue to be so."

"I know." She turned and reached for a tissue from the box on her desk to wipe the tears from her eyes. "I can't believe Siikzo's gone. He'd become such a good friend, it's hard to remember I once considered him an enemy. I would've died if he hadn't risked his life to get me out of the shuttle."

"He gave his life to save mine today. Future story-keepers will remember his name and keep his deeds alive in the hearts of all Centallians."

She leaned back and looked up into his eyes. "Please tell me he didn't suffer."

"He was gone in a matter of seconds."

"Good. Sonya will be relieved to hear it happened so quickly."

Glancing around the clinic, he raised an eyebrow. "You have no patients?"

"You know the number of wounded better than I do. I assume the more severely wounded are in their own chambers and have placed themselves in healing stasis. I saw a few cuts and abrasions. Some of your men let me apply a little antiseptic and most of them requested the red powder."

Rhyel smiled. "And did you use the red powder?"

"Of course. It has proven to be beneficial. I'm not adverse to using what works, even if it is unconventional." She patted his chest. "I think I need to sit down."

With no warning, he lifted her into his arms and carried her to the nearest chair, but instead of sitting her in the chair, he took the seat and settled her on his lap. She leaned into him. He rested his cheek on top of her head and seemed content to simply hold her.

After a moment, she whispered, "Why am I on your lap?"

He kissed her brow. "Because I want to hold you in my arms. I need to be close to you."

She understood the feeling. She knew he'd come close to death probably more times than he was willing to admit to her. Siikzo's death made her realize how temporary life could be, and how fleeting a lifetime together truly was. She wrapped her arms around his waist and held him with all her strength. She never wanted to let him go. Several minutes passed before she took a cleansing breath.

"Are you sure there's no one left on the ship?"

"I'm sure."

"How can you know?"

"It was the way the Cho behaved. When the first group came down, the Cho continued to fight, even after their Senchee leaders fell. When the second force landed on New Centallus, we quickly killed the Senchee-males. As soon as they were dispatched, the Cho dropped their weapons and collapsed to the ground, dead. The only explanation for their behavior was that there were no longer any Senchee-males to follow. That meant there were no leaders left on the ship, and I doubt they would leave any Cho on board without the presence of a Senchee."

"What will you do now?"

"Liiam will continue to monitor the ship and watch for any additional Kenchee stellar ships, while our technicians study the transport shuttle we've captured in hopes of unlocking their technology. Once we know how their shuttle functions, we'll fly it to the orbiting vessel and learn everything we can about it. Hopefully, its interstellar capabilities are similar to what we were familiar with aboard the *Novaria.*"

"And then?"

"We return to Earth and find Keeso."

Tiny hand-cut stones marked the final resting places of twenty-eight stillborn babies and one bride who had died in childbirth—and now four new graves had been added. The small burial site had far too many graves for such a short existence.

The struggling colony could ill afford the loss of even one member. Less than a hundred Centallians had survived the mass annihilation of their species.

The colonists gathered along the rim of the bluff overlooking the emerald Centallian Sea for the joint memorial service. They had each partaken of the cup of sorrow and sprinkled the sands of time into the wind. Bouquets and wreaths woven from the abundant exotic flowers growing near the fortress were tossed into the frothing waters below. Many Centallian brides wept quietly, and the two widows were surrounded and supported by love.

Hiilani leaned against her bond-mate as the solemn group returned to the fortress. She made him stop twice so she could catch her breath. When she stopped a third time, Amber came up beside them.

"Is there a problem I should know about?"

The nurse shook her head. "I'm okay."

Cintar looked over at Amber. "Is she....?" He didn't wait for an answer but swooped his bond-mate into his arms and began striding toward the fortress.

She couldn't help but be reminded of a time, not so very long ago, when he'd done the same for her. Amber scurried after them.

The nurse's labor pains had begun earlier that day, but she hadn't wanted to disturb the ceremonies. She'd started hard labor during the ceremony, but the contractions were far enough apart for Amber to predict the baby wouldn't make an appearance for a few hours.

Sonya came into the clinic a few minutes after they'd arrived. She'd taken her son to the nursery where Amber's baby and several other infants were being cared for. She insisted on helping Amber with the delivery. The three women were close friends, and Sonya had become an expert midwife. Amber didn't argue. She had a feeling Sonya needed to keep busy. Sometimes doing normal things was a way to cope with sorrow.

Cintar wanted to hover. Hiilani wanted him to leave her alone and let her do her job. In the end, they compromised. She did the hard work, and he let her squeeze the feeling out of his hands. Half an hour later, their child was born—a perfect little girl with her mother's dark hair and eyes. One more precious life and the promise of a new world.

# 28

*Earth*

Emma screamed and fought the arms that pressed her into the mattress. She couldn't let him get to Levi.

"Stop fighting me." Her attacker caught both of her hands and held them tight. She screamed again.

His hand covered her mouth. "It's me, Em. Sweetheart, listen, it's Keeso." She stilled. After a moment, his hand left her mouth and began stroking her cheek. "You're safe. I've got you."

His familiar voice penetrated the haze of fear. "Keeso?" Her voice shook so hard she could barely get his name out. Reality slowly returned with a relief so great she shuddered. "Keeso...." She whispered his name like a prayer, throwing her arms around his neck, holding him as if her life depended on their connection.

"I'm here, baby. I'm here." His voice trembled, as if he'd been frightened too. He lifted her and slipped into bed, drawing her so close his heart seemed to pound in her chest. She didn't pull away, needing the bond while she struggled to free herself from the terror of the dream.

"I'm okay." She couldn't control the tremor in her voice.

"You don't sound okay." He eased her back against the pillow and gazed down at her, his eyes full of concern. "Levi wasn't exaggerating the severity of your nightmares. No wonder he didn't want you sleeping alone. You must scare him to death."

"The dreams don't occur that often." A tear escaped and she swiped it away. "But you're right, they do scare Levi. I hate putting him through that, but I can't control them." She started to get up. "I need to check on him."

His hand on her arm stayed her. "I'll go." He slipped out of bed and drew the covers up over her shoulders. "I'll be right back."

"Okay." She pulled the blankets higher, suddenly chilled without his body heat. "If he's awake, bring him in here. He can sleep with me." He nodded and headed for Levi's room.

Moments later, he was back. "Levi's fine. The pup's snoring so loud I doubt he can hear anything else."

"Good. Thank you. What are you doing?" He'd pulled the covers back and climbed in beside her.

"Getting in bed."

She leaned away when he reached for her. "I'm okay now. You don't have to worry about me."

"You shouldn't be alone tonight, or any other night as far as I'm concerned. Besides, your bed's more comfortable than the couch."

"I don't think it's a good idea—"

His kiss, over before she had time to gather her thoughts, stopped her protest. "You are safer in this bed with me than you will ever be in this bed alone." He settled himself in, stacking his hands behind his head.

"Do you remember your dreams?"

"I don't think I'll ever forget them. They're always about Levi. He's in trouble and I can't find him. I'm searching a dark maze—sometimes it's rooms in a big house with endless hallways. I know someone's in the dark, watching me. I can feel him and then I see the man standing over Denise with a gun aimed at Levi. He looks at me, smiles, and tells me he's a good shot just before he fires."

Turning, he faced her and raised her chin, forcing her to look into his eyes.

"No wonder you wake up screaming." He brushed a strand of hair out of her eyes. "Are you still frightened?" When she shook her head, he smiled. "That's good. Try to go back to sleep."

"I'm not sure I can."

"Close your eyes and try. Remember, I'll always be here to protect you and Levi. I won't break my vow to you." He eased her against his shoulder. "I'll know if the dream comes again and wake you before it gets bad."

"How will you know?"

"As long as you're in my arms, I'll know." He snuggled her against his warm body.

His heat was seductive. Her body relaxed and she yawned. "This probably isn't a—"

He gave her a quick hug to stop her protest. "Pretend we're a complacent old married couple who want nothing more than a good night's sleep."

A minute passed. Then another. "I can't...."

"Can't what?"

"Imagine we'll ever be complacent."

His lips tickled her ear. "Neither can I."

"Why did you do it?"

"Do what?"

"I was wondering why you would commit yourself to me knowing I would probably never make the same commitment. You could have protected me without the vow. You're sleeping on the couch—at least you were. I would have let you sleep there without any promises."

"You were running scared. You needed to understand I was serious about keeping you safe. The commitment was my way of reassuring you."

"As far as you're concerned, you've made a lifetime commitment. You don't even know me that well. Someday you'll want a normal life and family. You'll want children, and I can't give them to you. You deserve better."

"I want no more than to remain by your side and watch Levi grow into a good man."

"You say that now, but you might fall in love someday and regret your vow to me." The thought of Keeso with another woman bothered her more than she wanted to admit.

He kissed the top of her head. "Let me tell you a story. When my people established our mine in Connor, I was put in charge of the operation. I met a young woman, Hiilani, a nurse from the clinic in Connor. We became friends, and eventually I asked her to be my bond-mate. She agreed to let me say the words. She was the first Centallian bride. Almost immediately, we discovered she carried my child. Another Guardian, Miilar, took my place at the mine and I traveled from New Centallus to Earth on a regular basis to handle the business. Everyone believed Miilar and I were business partners.

"I spent most of my time on New Centallus, since Hiilani oversaw the new clinic. Our ship, the *Novaria,* made weekly trips between New Centallus and Earth. Each trip home brought new brides. The colony was growing fast."

He rolled to his back, pulling her against his chest. When he finally spoke, his gruff voice was no more than a whisper. "Hiilani collapsed one afternoon. A few hours later, she lost our son. The baby was severely deformed, would never have lived. We were devastated. The entire colony was. Our technicians ran tests and genetics scans. Incompatibility markers were identified through blood-screening. Though most Centallians and humans are compatible, we were not. We couldn't stay together.

"Fortunately, we had never taken time to finalize our vows. She had agreed, and I had given her the words, but the final act, the rending of the veil, was never completed."

"What's the veil?"

"A thin, translucent cloth placed between the couple at the beginning of the ceremony. After the Guardian has given his bride the words, he uses a long-knife to slice the material from top to bottom. It is symbolic of their unification and final. Once the veil is rent, nothing and no one can dissolve their bond, not even the couple themselves. There is no divorce in Centallian society.

"Hiilani and I couldn't stay together. Conceiving another child was unthinkable. In the end, there was only one possible outcome. The Elders allowed our bond to be dissolved. Leaving Hiilani was the hardest thing I've ever done, but time heals. And though she will always be a part of me, we have both moved beyond the pain. Rhyel's second-in-command, Cintar, asked for my approval of his intention to take Hiilani as his bond-mate. I gave my approval and my blessing with no regret. Eventually, I would've chosen a compatible bride to become my bond-mate. But the *Novaria* may never return. I have no way of knowing if it ever will. Without the genetic test devised by our technicians, I didn't dare find a bond-mate on Earth.

"And then I met you." He pulled her closer. "And you told me you couldn't have children—that the doctors were certain you could never conceive. It was probably selfish of me, but I saw it as an opportunity for both of us. You would have someone who cared about what happened to you and Levi, and I wouldn't have to spend the rest of my life alone."

He placed his cheek against the top of her head. "I was drawn to you from the moment we met. But as the days and weeks passed, and I got to know you, my feelings ran deeper. I love you, Em. You mean more to me than any woman I have ever met, even Hiilani. My love comes not from loneliness, or a sense of responsibility, but from the depths of my being. You have become my sustenance, the air I breathe, the center of my lifeforce. You are *Aamyia*, my one true love."

# 29

✧

Emma sat alone at the kitchen table, nursing a cup of chamomile tea and enjoying the quiet. Keeso had gone across the street to visit with Lenn. Levi, who never passed up an opportunity to play with Sarah, had gone with him. Even the pup had abandoned her. It was blissful.

She hadn't really been abandoned. Keeso had invited her to join them, but she opted for some badly needed alone time.

Keeso's revelations last night had left her confused and uneasy. He'd had an Earth-born wife—a bond-mate he'd loved and lost due to their genetic incompatibility. They'd lost a child. She'd ached for him and for Hiilani, too.

Now, he was stranded on her world, cut off from the few remaining members of his species. He'd lost so much, and yet had committed his life to her and to Levi—before she told him she couldn't have children—before he knew he had anything to gain. His apologetic admission, that he'd found hope in the revelation, had opened her own eyes.

She'd be a hypocrite if she didn't admit his confession had removed one of her reasons for denying his claim. Her inability to give him children no longer mattered. She would, in fact, be giving him a child to raise as his own—Levi.

There was still the danger. Her main reason for denying his claim was still out there, still searching for her and Levi. She'd thought of running again, disappearing, leaving him. She ached at the thought.

But she sensed her efforts would be futile. Somehow, he'd know where she'd gone. He would find her. There was an inexplicable sense of awareness between them. They shared a connection. Her parents had experienced such a connection. After thirty years and two daughters, they read each other's emotions like a book. But she and Keeso hadn't been married thirty years, hadn't shared children. Would never share a child.

The sound of the front door slamming pulled her away from her thoughts. Levi raced into the kitchen. She smiled. He never walked anywhere.

"Aunty. Guess where we're going!"

She looked up at Keeso as he walked into the room. "Where?"

"We're going to the Grand... the Grand...."

"Canyon," Keeso finished for him.

"Yeah, the Grand Canyon. We're going with Sarah."

Alarm bells went off in her head. The Grand Canyon was huge, with thousands of visitors every day. How could she keep Levi safe in a place like that?

Keeso must've seen the fear in her eyes. He sat in the chair beside hers while Levi crawled into her lap.

"Lenn and Marie want to take Sarah to the Grand Canyon. The Hopi have a deep connection with the Canyon. Their ancestors originated there. Sarah's too young to go into the canyon but Lenn wants her to see it, despite the commercialism. They've invited us to go along."

"It can't be safe. What if—"

He reached over to tuck a stray wisp of hair behind her ear. "If it upsets you, we don't have to go."

Her nephew grabbed her hand. "No, Aunty please."

Keeso lifted her nephew off her lap and stood him on the floor. "Why don't you go give Pup some fresh water and give your aunt time to think about it?"

Levi tilted his head up at the big man. "You're always telling me to give Pup water when you don't want me to hear what you and aunty talk about." But he obeyed, calling the dog to his side as he stepped out the back door.

"That boy is getting wise to me."

She laughed. "You're probably going to have to use the direct method from now on. Simply tell him we need to talk and he needs to give us some privacy."

"That works?"

"Usually, I think." She shrugged. "I honestly don't know. I'm new at this, too." She got up to refresh her tea. "Coffee?"

He shook his head. "I'm good. Let's figure this out before he gets back. I won't push you to go if you don't want to."

"Don't you think it's dangerous?"

When she sat back down, he took her hand, his thumb caressing her wrist. "Because of the killer or because of the canyon?"

"The killer. He could be anywhere."

"Em, the chances of him being at the Grand Canyon are astronomical. You know that."

"He could be watching for us—hanging around the hospital, or any number of places."

"We don't know he's followed us this far. Lenn ran the Jeep's plates, but nothing ever came of it. No law enforcement office, state or federal, has made contact. My Jeep's out of sight—has been since we arrived. The new one can't be traced to us. It's a different style and color and registered to the Hopi. No one's looking for it."

"Do you think it's safe for us to leave the protection of the reservation?"

He shook his head. "I can't promise you it's safe even on the reservation. There are too many variables. But we can't protect Levi at the cost of his childhood. No one can predict the next moment, but I can promise to keep Levi as safe as possible regardless of where we are."

They both heard the backdoor slam. He gave her hand another squeeze. "The choice is yours. I'll stand by your decision."

Lenn had arranged the use of a minivan for the day-long trip. The two families piled into the vehicle at dawn. Even Pup went along, since dogs were allowed at the Canyon if they were leashed.

Once they were on state Highway 264 headed west toward Second Mesa, Emma began to relax. The likelihood of anyone looking for her and Levi in a group of people was low. She sighed. Prey animals instinctively congregate en masse. Fish schooled and birds flocked to confuse predators. Apparently, humans were no different—there was a certain safety in numbers.

The minivan had three rows of seats. Sarah and Levi sat together in the second row in booster seats that allowed them a clear view of the surrounding countryside. In his own harness, Pup was already snoozing in a corner beside them. Emma and Keeso climbed into the back seat.

As they passed the Hopi Healthcare Center, she tensed and studied the distant parking lot. Keeso put his arm around her in a half-hug. His hand kneaded the tense muscles of her neck and shoulders, letting her know he was there, would always be there.

The two-plus-hour drive from First Mesa to the Grand Canyon fascinated her. The flat desert expanse between First Mesa and Second Mesa gave way to a steep, cliff-side drive. To their left, sheer, ledges towered high above the road. To the right, a deep canyon plunged straight down, ending hundreds of feet below in a rubble of ancient rockfall, some boulders two and three times larger than houses.

She held her breath as their vehicle followed the winding highway to Second Mesa's summit, praying the short metal barrier lining the road's edge was strong enough to prevent a plummet into the abyss. The children loved it, each straining to see as far over the embankment as their harnesses allowed.

It wasn't until Keeso gently squeezed her shoulder that she realized she had a death grip on his thigh. Letting go of him wasn't easy, not when she'd rather be safe in his arms.

The breathtaking views from atop the Second and Third Mesas gave way to a long expanse known as Desert View Drive. Though not as spectacular, there was a quiet beauty in the vast, simple landscape.

They stopped for a late breakfast at Tuba City, parking their car in front of the small restaurant. The interior was neat and the food delicious. The three waitresses on duty busied themselves with restocking condiments and refilling sugar shakers at each table but took enough time to visit for a few minutes. Tammy, the waitress who took their orders, had a special rapport with the kids. She seemed as excited as they were about their trip to the Grand Canyon. Rena talked about her own grandchildren, her love for them obvious. Shelley spotted Pup in the driver's seat of the car and laughed. A couple of minutes later she returned from the kitchen with a doggie bag of meat scraps for our "chauffeur."

It had been a pleasant break, but they were soon following highway 160 to junction 89, turning south toward Cameron and the Highway 64 turnoff to Grand Canyon Village. As they approached Cameron, Lenn pointed to a line of rock formations that continued into the horizon.

"We're on the northwest edge of the Painted Desert."

Apparently, Arizona had badlands too. The knobby outcroppings clustered together, some resembling huge Easter eggs striped in hues of red, tan, orange, brown, and green. The formations huddled close enough to seem impenetrable. The colorful striations continued in volcano-like cones, mesas, and buttes.

At Cameron, they turned west on Highway 64 and began the climb toward the Grand Canyon. Lenn explained the air was thinner since the Grand Canyon Village sat at an altitude of over eight thousand feet. They might find themselves a little breathless at times.

Their first glimpse of the Canyon came when Lenn pulled into a parking area near an overlook beside the highway. Emma grabbed Levi's hand the minute they stepped out of the car. Marie had Sarah's hand as well. The few bucket-sized rocks placed along the canyon rim couldn't have deterred a box turtle and wasn't at all comforting.

When Keeso lifted Levi to his shoulders, she was finally able to quit worrying and take her first good look at the Grand Canyon. Magnificent was the single word that came to mind. From their position, the canyon lay slightly below them, offering a spectacular view that continued for miles. Striated canyon walls, some thousands of feet high, followed meandering valley paths cut through the stone by ancient rivers. Below, a silver thread of water snaked its way between the monoliths. The immensity of the canyon struck her when she realized she was looking at the raging Colorado River.

Another car pulled in, breaking her concentration, and she watched an older couple walk to where artisans sat at tables positioned a few feet from the canyon's edge. The vendors presented a startling image with the Grand Canyon as their backdrop. Lenn explained the Navajo often displayed handcrafted jewelry at this location.

Keeso slipped an arm around her shoulder. "Let's see what's there." They headed toward the booths while Lenn and Marie continued to take in the canyon view with Sarah.

A man who looked to be in his mid-fifties stood and smiled as they approached his table. His dark, sun-toughened skin bespoke a lifetime of exposure to the harsh southwestern elements. Smiling, the vendor spread his arms wide, indicating the table in front of him. "Feel free to get a closer look."

She glanced at the table with its variety of jewelry, polished stones, and agate slices—turquoise, rose quartz, jade, and rocks she couldn't identify. Her eyes were drawn to a piece of Tigers-eye, in the shape of a humpbacked man playing a flute. It was attached to a delicate silver neck chain. She'd seen the image several times since coming to the Southwest.

The Navajo vendor, apparently a shrewd salesman, recognized her interest and picked up the necklace, handing it to her.

"You like *Kokopelli?*" He grinned and edged a pair of matching earrings in her direction.

"*Kokopelli?*"

"The flute player. *Kokopelli* has been a part of our culture since the time of the Anasazi. The Navajo, Hopi, and most Pueblo tribes call him the trickster, but welcome him. He brings good luck to our people."

"This is lovely." She started to replace the necklace, but Keeso's hand on her wrist stopped her.

"How much?"

"Keeso you don't have to—"

"Thirty dollars," the vendor interrupted, lifting the box containing the earrings. "With the necklace, these would only cost fifteen dollars."

"We'll take them." Keeso jostled Levi on his shoulder while he reached for his wallet. Her nephew giggled. "What about you, buddy? See anything you like?"

Levi leaned so far over to look at the contents of the table, Keeso was forced to grab his arm to keep him from tumbling to the ground.

"Those." He pointed toward the tray of polished agates. "The blue ones."

He'd chosen two halves of an agate slice, the whole close to the circumference of the rim of a teacup. Like the rings of a tree, the agate's lacey pattern alternated between ice blue and crystal white. At the center, a wide layer of blue bordered a white crystal-encrusted hollow. Eye-screws had been inset at the top of each half-piece to accommodate a neck chain.

"Your son has a good eye for nature's beauty. You can have the two for fifteen dollars." At Keeso's nod, he wrapped the stones in newspaper and placed them in a Ziploc bag. He added two neck chains, to the bag before handing it to Levi.

She noticed Keeso didn't correct the man's assumption that Levi was his son. But then, she reminded herself, the big man already considered her nephew his son.

Keeso handed her the box containing the earrings but insisted on fastening the necklace around her throat. When he finished, the Navajo man raised his arm, the side of his hand pointed toward them as if in blessing.

"May *Kokopelli* give you your heart's desire."

*Their heart's desire.* If the man had, indeed, given them a blessing, Kokopelli was in for a long, complicated time of it.

# 30

✧

Keeso watered Pup and took him for a walk while everyone else settled into the car. On their way again, Levi removed the wrapped packets from the bag. Emma felt a surge of pride when he handed one of his treasures to Sarah, mumbling, "This one's yours." After unwrapping the slivers of shiny, polished stone, the youngsters spent the next twenty minutes comparing the two halves. They handed them over long enough for Emma to attach the chains and suggest they wear the agates around their necks to keep from losing them.

At the park entrance, Keeso paid for the passes. She'd worried about the possibility of being asked for identification at the gate, but Lenn's information was all the Ranger requested.

A few minutes later, they pulled into their first stop—the Desert View Watchtower. Lenn explained the architect, Mary Coulter, had hired Hopi men to help build the tower in the 1930's. "She designed it to look ancient—handpicking many of the stones." He opened the heavy wooden door and they entered a large circular room.

"This depicts a Hopi kiva. Most kivas are round, with a fire pit in the center. But you don't enter a kiva through a door. Kivas are built below ground, with rock walls to support a rough wood-beamed roof." He nodded toward a handmade ladder beside the fire pit. "Anyone coming in or going out of a *kiva* uses a ladder lowered through the smoke-hole."

Lenn led them toward one of the large picture windows set along the perimeter of the room. "Were this a true kiva, there would be no windows. But the view of the canyon reminds the Hopi of our unique connection with this place."

They moved to a set of stairs that angled from the kiva room to the watchtower's first level. The walls of this room, as well as the two above, were covered with southwestern tribe pictographs. According to Lenn, most of the renditions were painted in the 1930's by renowned Hopi artist Fred Kabotie.

The late October day was on the chilly side, and Emma was glad they'd included heavier jackets when they'd packed for the trip. The pup's excited bark greeted them when they returned to the parking lot. Keeso took him for a quick run before they headed on to Grand Canyon Village.

It was close to noon by the time they reached their destination, but the kids were too excited to even think about eating. Parking was at a premium, and they decided everyone would wait at the visitor center near the Hopi house while Lenn found a place to park. He had pulled up to the curb when Marie spotted a car backing out of a prime parking spot. Lenn took full advantage and pulled in as soon as it was vacated.

Emma's first view of the canyon took her breath away, and for a moment, she was suspended in time, lost in the beauty of an eternal landscape.

Lifting Levi into his arms, Keeso pointed to a large bird in the distance, surfing the wind currents with a dancer's grace. "Can you see the condor? Sarah's dad said we might see one." He turned to her. "Lenn mentioned their numbers had declined over the years. It had become a concern, but recently the number of mating pairs have increased, giving them hope for the bird's full recovery."

They spent most of the day following the canyon's Rim Trail and exploring the various shops and museums. Keeso and Lenn took turns waiting outside with Pup while the ladies admired the beautiful paintings, woven baskets, and pottery.

In the Hopi House—a Mary Coulter representation of a traditional Hopi home—Lenn described the legend of the dreamcatcher and its ability to keep nightmares away. Emma had given Levi spending money, and he insisted on buying her a dreamcatcher "to stop her nightmares."

He'd also pulled her aside to ask if he had enough money to purchase a beautifully crafted, suede sheath to hold the Hopi knife Lenn had given uncle Keeso. Long strips of braided leather secured the narrow pouch to the thigh or calf. Though simple in design, his intended gift cost considerably more than she'd given him, but she nodded when he held the money out for her to count. Considering the amount of money Keeso had spent on them without accepting repayment, she felt no qualms about standing behind Levi and holding up the additional bills needed as he stood on tiptoe to shove his money toward the clerk. Transaction completed, and treasures in hand, he practically dragged her through the exit to where Keeso sat on the wide rock wall overlooking the canyon.

"Uncle Keeso, look what I got you." She gasped when Levi threw himself into Keeso's arms, momentarily envisioning the two of them going over the side. It was a reflex reaction. It would take more than a four-year-old to push this big man off balance.

Levi shoved the bag into Keeso's free hand. "Open it."

Keeso glanced her way, his head tilted in question. She merely shrugged. Opening the bag, he withdrew the handstitched sheath.

"Do you like it?" Levi was practically dancing with excitement. "I picked it out all by myself."

After examining the workmanship, he held the child's gift up. "How did you know this was exactly what I needed?"

The boy beamed and scrunched his shoulders. "I jus knowed."

Keeso stood and handed Pup's leash to her. "Shall we try it out?" At Levi's nod, he shook the laces out and tied them around his jean-clad thigh, securing the knife holder to his right leg.

He tilted his head toward Levi. "How's it look?"

"Good."

Her mouth nearly dropped open when he reached into his boot and withdrew the Hopi knife, placing it in the suede sheath. "You keep the knife on you?"

"It won't be of much use if it stays in a dresser drawer. Don't worry, I'm not a stranger to knives. On Centallus, we were trained in the use of a long-knife as soon as we were strong enough to hold one." He hoisted Levi onto his shoulder, and they joined Lenn, Marie, and Sarah at a raised stage-like square to watch Navajo dancers perform the graceful Eagle and intricate hoop dances.

The youngsters were winding down. After eating sandwiches from a deli-style shop, they didn't argue when Lenn suggested they rest at the car for a while. He let down the van's rear seat and spread out a thick quilt. The kids scrambled in through the back door, Pup climbing in and wriggling between them. Within minutes, all three were sound asleep. Marie covered them with another quilt.

Keeso put his arm around Emma's shoulders. "How are you holding up?"

His hand moved to the back of her neck, gently kneading the tense muscles. She laughed. "I don't mind telling you a nap sounds good right now."

He glanced into the back seat and raised an eyebrow. "Doesn't look like much room back there."

She smiled. "Resting back against the seat and closing my eyes will suffice."

"I think we can do better than that." He glanced across the top of the car at Lenn and Marie. "If you two want some time to yourselves, we'll stay with the kids. I'll call your cell when Sarah wakes up."

Lenn grinned, slipped his arm around his wife, and nodded. "We won't be far away."

Keeso opened the door and moved the booster seats out of the way so Emma could slide in. He followed her in and quietly closed the door to keep from disturbing the kids. Leaning her head against the seat, she closed her eyes and heaved a sigh. A moment later his low chuckle drew her attention.

She opened one eye. "What?"

"You sound as if you need a nap more than they do." Pulling her into his arms he settled her against his chest. "Better?"

Though she probably should've protested, she snuggled closer. The steady beat of his heart calmed the thrum of anxiety she'd experienced all day, as if she walked a thin line between safety and danger.

She was beginning to relax when the sudden acceleration of his heartbeat and subtle tensing of his body warned her something wasn't right. She stiffened and tried to straighten up.

His arms tightened, and he pressed his lips close to her ear. "What's wrong?"

It was then she noticed her hand rested high on his upper leg—too high. She jerked it away, realizing she was the cause of his reaction.

He still wouldn't let her pull back. "You were frightened. Why?"

What was she supposed to say? *I thought you were reacting to a threat and instead it was my hand where it shouldn't have been.*

"I wasn't frightened, not really."

"Your entire body went rigid."

*So did yours.*

"Honestly, I'm not frightened, just on edge. I'm uncomfortable in a crowd. I find myself constantly watching for middle-aged, slightly balding men."

He laughed.

"Keeso, it isn't funny."

He did stop laughing, but he couldn't hide his smile. "It is a little. Probably half the men in the park are middle-aged and slightly balding."

She sighed. "I know. I probably stared at every one of them too, some to the point of being rude. A couple of them even flirted with me. One was with his wife and kids." She couldn't keep the disgust out of her voice.

"So, you've spent the day looking for the killer."

She nearly cringed at the sympathy in his voice. "It wasn't that bad. Levi's having fun. He and Sarah have been wide-eyed since we arrived. I've enjoyed the museums and shops, and I'd have to be dead not to be inspired by the canyon."

"But?"

"A couple of times, I thought I'd seen him. I'm sure it was the same man both times, but he was too far away. I know I sound obsessive, but the way he moved...."

He drew her closer. She was practically on his lap now. "You're not being obsessive. After everything you've been through, your family's murder, being shot—twice." He brushed the hair away from her face and touched his lips to her brow. "You wouldn't be normal if you didn't experience fear. But you need to remember there's no way he'd know you and Levi are here. No one followed the van. I was aware of every vehicle on the road. None of them stayed with us for long."

She leaned up and kissed his cheek. "Thank you for taking care of us."

He bent his head, his lips touching hers in a kiss that was all too brief. "It's my job. Remember?" He lifted her onto his lap, spreading his denim jacket over her legs.

"Close your eyes and rest while you can." He nodded toward the back of the car. "Those two will be ready to head out as soon as they wake up."

She nodded. For now, the tension was gone. He'd keep her safe while she slept, keep them all safe. He was a good man—this person who called another world his home. She yawned. His arms tightened in a brief hug, and she smiled against his chest. He'd be an easy man to love.

Childish giggles woke her. She opened her eyes and blinked at the three faces smiling down—make that four. The dog seemed to be grinning too.

"Aunty, we're gonna go do more stuff as soon as Sarah's mama and daddy get here." Levi giggled again. "You fell asleep on Uncle Keeso's lap."

She wasn't exactly on his lap, but almost. She moved out of his arms and sat up. "Did I sleep long?"

"Nearly an hour. Feel better?"

"I think so." She finger-combed her hair and gave him a hesitant glance. "Did I snore?"

He laughed out right. "Yes, the entire time—provided you call the cute little snuffling noises you always make in your sleep snoring."

"There's mama." Sarah waved furiously.

Keeso stretched and retrieved his jacket from the floorboard. "I called them a few minutes ago. Ready to continue this adventure, or do you want to head home? I'm sure Lenn and Marie would understand."

"No, Aunty please. We want to stay and see the sunset."

Levi's plea and Sarah's round, expressive eyes were her undoing. She gave them a bright smile. "We'll stay. I don't want to miss the sunset either."

They spent the next hour and a half following the Rim Trail, eating ice cream, and generally enjoying the view. They were returning from Bright Angel Lodge when Levi stopped abruptly and pointed in the direction of El Tovar Lodge's well-manicured back lawn.

"Deer! Can we go see them?"

She glanced in the direction he indicated and saw three animals nibbling grass. "I don't think those are deer, honey."

"They're not." Lenn knelt in front of the two children. "They're elk, and we don't want to get too close. See the big one with the antlers?" Both kids nodded. "Well, he's a bull and it's his job to protect the cows. If you get too close he might try to chase you away and you could be hurt." He glanced at Emma. "A large bull can weigh up to twelve hundred pounds."

She was sure her eyes had grown as round as the children's.

Pup viewed the small group of animals with curiosity but didn't attempt to investigate. He was a smart dog, and Keeso had trained him well. Still, he was young, and she was glad Keeso had a firm grip on the leash. She could only imagine the chaos one dog and three elk might instigate.

Earlier in the day, Keeso had arranged to house Pup in the on-site kennel while they took a shuttle to Hermit's Point, then backtracked to Hopi Point to watch the sunset. The kennel usually closed at five o'clock, but he'd arranged to pick Pup up after sunset. The kennel was less than a mile from El Tovar Lodge and Keeso decided to walk the pup rather than take the van and lose their parking space. He'd meet them at the Lodge and they'd eat before boarding the shuttle to Hermit's Point.

Pup whined and balked when he realized most of his people were staying behind. A word from Keeso started his tail wagging again and he followed his master as they took the stairs leading down to the train station—a shortcut to the kennel.

Marie left with Sarah to find a public restroom while she, Lenn, and Levi waited in front of the Lodge. The rocking chairs on El Tovar's sprawling stone-pillared front porch were occupied. The porch was crowded, and they decided to wait on the less congested sidewalk.

A tour bus pulled into the circle drive behind a car parked in front of the porch steps. As soon as the bus doors opened, the driver stepped down and opened the luggage compartment. Passengers scurried behind him, some moving to where the luggage was being lined up on the sidewalk, others heading directly to the Lodge.

Lenn took her elbow, moving them away from the bus and closer to the front steps.

"Another elk!" Levi pulled his hand free and ran toward the edge of the circle drive.

"Levi, wait!" She lunged after him, colliding with a large man lugging an oversized suitcase. She may as well have hit a brick wall. His own momentum sent her careening off the sidewalk into a line of bushes. Lenn tried to break her fall and ended up on the ground beside her.

"Lady, I'm sorry." The man with the suitcase was climbing over the hedge to get to her.

Lenn rolled to his feet and helped her up. "Are you okay?"

"I think so." She glanced around. "Where's Levi?" Bystanders crowded in on her, blocking her view. She pushed past the man who still held his suitcase, Lenn right behind her.

"Levi!" She thrashed through the gawkers, trying to locate him.

He wasn't on the sidewalk.

Running into the street, she barely noticed the squeal of brakes and the curse of an irate driver. The elk was still there, placidly munching the little bit of grass across from the Lodge.

But Levi wasn't in sight.

She lurched from one direction to another. He couldn't go far. How long had it been? Two minutes... three? Not enough time for him to disappear. He had to be close.

"*Leeeviii!*" She waited for his answer, for the sound of his feet running to her.

All she heard were the frantic hoofbeats of the startled elk.

She sank to her knees. He was gone.

"Please God, no."

# 31

✧

Emma blinked away the tears blurring her vision and focused on Lenn. He was running toward her, his phone against his ear. Behind him, the crowd watched. A few people held their cell phones high, recording the excitement. She turned away.

Lenn knelt beside her. "Are you okay?"

She clawed at his arm. "I can't find him." Her voice shook so hard she had trouble getting the words out. "You have to help me find him."

"I will. Let's get you out of the street." He put his arm around her waist.

"Get Keeso." She walked on wobbly legs, leaning on Lenn for support, as they moved closer to the crowd. Bending her head, she used her hair to bar their invasion of her privacy. "Keeso will find Levi. He has to."

"I've already called him. He'll be here in a few minutes. He isn't too far away." A park ranger pushed through the crowd, took one look at Emma and turned to order the crowd aside. Lenn guided her to the foot of the stairs leading to El Tovar Hotel's porch.

She climbed halfway up then shook her head and sagged to the step.

The ranger pulled her two-way radio from the holder at her waist and spoke into it, pausing to listen to the static response. She moved closer. "I'm Ranger Elaine Juarez. The Emergency Medical Services team is on their way."

Marie and Sarah were suddenly beside her. Her friend took her hand and brushed the hair back from her face. "Your cheek is swollen. What—"

"Where's Levi?" Sarah whispered the question, but both women heard her. Marie shook her head and swung back to Emma, her eyes questioning.

"He isn't here."

Ranger Juarez bent closer. "What happened?"

"We have a missing child situation—a four-year-old boy." Lenn's voice took on a professional, no-nonsense tone. Though he had no jurisdiction in the park, he pulled his wallet from his pocket and flipped it open to reveal his identification and badge.

The ranger nodded. "Can you give me his description?"

Lenn complied, giving a brief but concise description of Levi's height and weight. "Dark brown hair, blue eyes."

Keeso's arrival interrupted them. Ordering Pup to sit, he dropped down beside Emma.

She threw her arms around his waist. "Levi's gone. Vanished. I was right. The man I saw... It was him, wasn't it? He has Levi."

"Shh, *Aamyia*. Don't jump to conclusions and don't panic. The Ranger can tell you this isn't anything new. Kids get lost at the Grand Canyon all the time." He kissed the top of her head and pulled her closer. "We'll find him, I promise."

"Please tell me you've never broken a promise."

"I've kept every promise I've ever made. I'll keep this one too."

The two-man EMS team arrived, interrupting them. Marie and Sarah moved a few steps higher to give them space.

One medic snapped on sterile gloves. "I'm Rob. Can you tell me your name?" He reached for her wrist and looked at his watch.

She drew her arm back. "We don't have time for this. My nephew is missing. We have to find him."

Keeso's arm tightened around her. "Let them check you out. I want to know you're okay. Someone else will do the searching. They're probably already looking for him."

"He's right, ma'am. Search and rescue's setting up a perimeter right now. The rangers at the gates have been notified. They'll keep in touch with us. In the meantime, let's see how you're doing."

She took a deep breath and nodded. "Please hurry."

"I will. Like I said, I'm Rob and this good looking fellow behind me is Anders." He carefully lifted her chin to examine her cheek. "How did this happen?"

"I collided with someone and fell. Please, we don't have time for this."

"It won't take much longer." He retrieved a pen light from his med kit and flicked it in front of her eyes. "Pupils are reacting normally." His partner scribbled something in a small black book. This time when he reached for her wrist, she didn't protest. "Heart rate ninety-four." He patted her hand. "I know you're upset but you need to take some deep, calming breaths. You won't do that little boy any good if you collapse on us." He cleaned her face and applied antiseptic to the abrasion.

The ranger touched Lenn's arm. "The boy's name is Levi?"

Lenn nodded. "Yes."

"What was he wearing?"

"Jeans and a bright yellow hoodie. He should be easy to spot."

Emma shook her head. "No, no. He took the hoodie off. He's wearing a tan jacket now."

Keeso suddenly pulled his hand free of her grasp, bringing her fingers to his lips.

"I'll be right back." Grabbing the dog's leash, he moved to the sidewalk, pausing long enough to say a few words to Lenn. His friend fished the van keys out of his pocket and handed them over. Keeso and Pup took off toward the parking area. He probably intended to put Pup in the car to keep him away from the excitement.

A couple of additional rangers showed up to help disperse the crowd. Rob and Anders were packing up to go. "Take it easy for a while." Rob took her arm to help her stand. "Let's see if we can't get you into one of those rockers on the porch." He led her up the steps to the porch where several roughhewn, wicker rocking chairs provided respite for weary visitors. When they reached the top, a boy, not much older than Levi, jumped up from the nearest one and gave her a shy smile.

She returned his smile. "Thank you."

Rob knelt in front of her and patted her hand again. "We'll be close by if you need us. We'll also check your nephew once he's found."

Nodding, she smiled at him too. "Thank you for your help."

He shook his head and stood. "It's what we do. Try not to worry. Our search and rescue teams are the best in the country." He left her then, sprinting down the steps to meet Anders.

Marie and Sarah had followed her to the porch. An older man, sitting in the rocker next to hers, stood and offered Marie his chair before walking into the hotel. Sarah, eyes glistening with unshed tears, climbed into her mother's lap and pressed her face against her chest. Marie patted and rocked the child, but neither woman could offer her words of comfort.

Lenn finished his conversation with the ranger and shook the woman's hand before climbing the steps of the hotel. The crowd on the porch had thinned out and there were several available chairs, but Lenn shook his head when Marie suggested he sit down.

Squatting in front of Emma, he told her everything he'd learned thus far. "Search and rescue is setting up grids across the area and has started searching. Volunteers are walking the Rim Trail and rangers have alerted the businesses and lodges. The ranger told me the Grand Canyon has a fleet of drones used during search and rescue. They're generally used in the Canyon, along trails and in places it's difficult to get to by foot. They're not as effective in wooded areas, but they'll probably be brought out if we can't find Levi soon."

"There's Keeso." Emma jumped to her feet and started down the steps, with Lenn right behind her. Keeso still had Pup with him and she was confused until she saw the yellow hoodie in his hand.

Fresh hope sent adrenaline pumping through her system. She was breathless with anticipation by the time they met at the foot of the stairs. "He can find him, can't he? He's done it before."

Keeso pulled her into his arms and kissed the top of her head. "There's a chance, but you need to remember he's young and untrained. He'll have to find Levi's scent out of thousands of others. He might not be able to."

"I know, but he's Levi's best friend and right now, he's our best chance of finding him."

Lenn had followed Emma down. "I agree. I'm going with you and I think we should let Ranger Juarez know what we're doing." At Keeso's nod, Lenn sprinted toward the ranger he'd spoken with earlier. After a few words he returned. "She agrees it's worth a shot and she's coming with us. She can call for assistance if we need it."

The ranger joined them a moment later. "Are we ready?"

At his nod, the group moved to where Emma had last seen Levi. Keeso bent and held the hoodie out for Pup to sniff. The young dog plunged his face into the garment, snuffling and whining in sudden excitement. He lifted his head and looked around as if he expected to see Levi. His whining grew louder, sharper, when he couldn't see the boy. He stuck his nose against the garment again.

Keeso stood. "Where's Levi? Find him. Find Levi."

Levi's name seemed to galvanize the animal. He lifted his head in the air and sounded a yodel-like bay that reminded her of a beagle. His nose touched the ground and he ping-ponged from one direction to another, running in circles before he stopped and suddenly flattened his nose against the sidewalk. Letting go a bugle of what could only be interpreted as triumph, he followed the scent into the road and stopped. Whimpering, the dog ping-ponged again, his nose in the air, then back to the ground.

Apparently, he'd lost the scent. She ran to the curb and watched the dog's obvious frustration. Fear numbed her mind. Had someone grabbed Levi and forced him into a car before taking off with him?

Pup's bark wrenched her from the debilitating thought. He'd left the street. Nose to the ground, the dog headed for the stairs, pulling at his leash, practically dragging Keeso in his wake.

She turned to follow. Lenn took her arm as they headed back up the hotel steps. At the door, Pup bayed and scratched at the door.

Keeso paused, giving them a chance to catch up. When his gaze landed on her, he frowned. "Are you all right?"

"I'm fine. Open the door, let's go."

Nodding, he pushed the door wide. Pup rushed into the building, his excited bark echoing in the large foyer. On he went, sniffing the wide runner leading to the reception desk in the next room.

A tall, balding clerk hurried around the desk toward them, stopping directly in front of Keeso. "I'm sorry. You can't bring that dog in here."

Ranger Juarez stepped forward. "It's okay, we're looking for a missing child."

The man relaxed a little. "We've been informed. Our staff has searched the entire lodge. We called his name but there was no answer. He isn't here."

"The dog seems to think different." From the set of his jaw, Keeso had no intention of letting the man stop them.

The ranger appeared torn. They needed her cooperation. Emma laid a hand on the ranger's arm. "Ms. Juarez, something traumatic happened a few months ago, causing Levi to be terrified of strangers. He'll hide if he believes someone is after him. He won't answer anyone but me or Keeso. The dog believes he's here. Right now, it's our only lead and we're taking it." She looked the clerk directly in the eye. "Please get out of our way."

The clerk glanced at the ranger before stepping aside.

Keeso held the hoodie out and let the pup sniff it again. The dog took off in a frenzied search for the scent. He bugled once more at the red-carpeted staircase, forging ahead and racing up the stairs two at a time as if the scent were more apparent.

But on the mezzanine level, he came to an abrupt halt. At the landing there were three options—turn right and follow a long hall with doors on each side, take the stairs in front of them to the next floor, or go into the mezzanine lounge with its octagonal banister protecting those who wanted to view the room below. Across the mezzanine, another hall led to more guestrooms. Nose practically buried in the carpet, Pup circled the landing twice, bayed his excitement, and lunged up the stairs.

Twenty minutes later, she was beginning to doubt Pup's ability to find Levi.

They'd followed the dog from one hall to another, upstairs and down. The halls seemed to blend together.

The longer they searched, the less confidence she had in their ability to find him. Where was he? Who was he with? Was he alone and frightened? How long before someone decided to give up?

The ranger was in constant contact with search and rescue. The sun would be setting soon. Would they keep looking once it was dark, or was the terrain treacherous enough to halt the search until morning?

Excited barking pulled her out of her reverie. Pup was scratching at a door. Keeso pulled him back and handed the leash to Lenn. Taking Emma's hand, he gave it a squeeze before trying the knob. It wasn't locked.

She held her breath as he opened the door wide and ran his hand along the wall to find the light switch. The room brightened to reveal a large linen closet—but no Levi.

Pup whined and tugged at his leash, wanting in the small room. He obviously believed Levi was in there.

"Levi?" Her voice shook. He didn't answer.

Maybe he couldn't.

"Levi, it's Aunt Emma. Answer me, honey."

"Aunty?"

"Levi!" Her heart slammed against her ribs with her sudden rush of joy. She'd found him. He was alive. She pushed a linen cart out of her way. Keeso shoved it into the hall. "Baby, where are you?"

A small foot appeared from under a tall shelf in the corner, then another as Levi wriggled out of his hiding place. Her legs refused to support her and she sank to the floor. Scrambling to his feet, Levi threw himself into her arms. She pulled him close, never wanting to let him go again. "Dear God, thank you."

"Don't cry, Aunty." She hadn't known she was and reached up to touch her cheek, brushing at the unchecked tears.

Keeso dropped to the floor behind her. Wrapping them both in his arms, he took a long shuddering breath and pressed his cheek to the top of Emma's head. Pup pulled free of Lenn's loosened grasp, skittered into the closet, and plopped down beside them, giving her arm a quick swipe of his tongue before resting his head in Levi's lap.

Cocooned in Keeso's embrace, holding her nephew close, she rested her hand on Pup's neck.

They were all safe.

But for how long?

# 32

Keeso carried Levi to El Tovar's mezzanine lounge where they were to meet the EMS team. Emma walked beside them holding her nephew's hand. She was amazed by Keeso's sense of direction. He'd known exactly where they were and how to get back to the unique circular room. Lenn had gone on ahead to find Marie and let her know Levi was safe.

Rob and Anders were waiting when they descended the stairs into the room. Levi buried his head in Keeso's neck, unwilling to acknowledge the strangers, but Rob's calm, friendly voice, and a bribe—a Grand Canyon Fire Department's EMS patch—won him over. After thanking the fireman, Levi held his prize out for her inspection. The blue and gold emblem depicted a canyon scene. Lenn had arrived with Marie and Sarah. Anders knelt in front of Sarah, offering her a patch as well.

While Anders finished checking out Levi, Rob moved to Emma's side. "How are you holding up?" He touched her wrist with his fingers and glanced at his watch. After making a notation in his notebook, he checked the bump on her head. "Your heart rate's still a little rapid, but considering everything you've been through, that's expected."

He nodded toward Levi. Her nephew still clutched the patch, but his arms were around Keeso's neck, holding tight. "That boy looks like he's had more than enough adventure. I suggest you pack it in for the day. I imagine you're ready, too." He stood, slipping the notebook into one of the many zippered pockets of his jacket. "Looks like you're good to go."

Keeso reached out and shook his hand, then shook Anders'. "Thank you for everything you've done."

Anders looked uncomfortable with the attention. "It's our job." He gave Pup a pat. "From what I've heard, this fellow deserves the thanks and an extra treat."

The firemen took their leave. Lenn spent a few minutes speaking with Ranger Juarez before the group left El Tovar and headed for the car. By unspoken agreement, sunset at Hopi Point would be postponed to another time.

Levi and Sarah had been strapped into their booster seats. All she wanted to do was hold her nephew close, but common sense overrode the natural inclination. He was safer belted in, but her own restraints didn't keep her from leaning close and holding his hand. She never wanted to let him go.

He was unusually quiet on the trip home, but then so was Sarah. Did his silence indicate his need for answers to questions he couldn't voice?

She patted his hand. "Are you okay?"

He looked away. "I guess so." He wasn't at all convincing.

"Tell me what's wrong."

He glanced toward her but didn't make eye contact. "Nothing."

She slipped her hand under his chin and gently brought his face up until their eyes met. "You can talk to me about what's bothering you. I won't get mad or upset." He was silent for so long she didn't think he was going to answer.

"Why did you leave me?"

Her heart nearly broke at the anguish in his voice. "I didn't leave you, baby."

"Yes, you did. I wanted to look at the elk, but you didn't come with me. When I turned around, I saw you go into the big building, so I ran after you. I hollered at you, but you wouldn't stop. I runned after you but you went up the steps and I didn't see you anymore. I couldn't find you."

"Sweetie, that wasn't me. I never went into the building. I was still outside. You couldn't see me because of all the people."

"But you had on your special bright hoodie." She'd purchased the iridescent, lime-green jacket to ensure Levi would be able to spot her if they were temporarily separated in a crowd. Ironically, that had been the cause of the problem.

"You need to understand something. I will *never* leave you alone. *Never.*"

He looked up at her, his eyes full of hope. "Promise?"

"Yes, I promise. If I have to go anywhere without you, I'll tell you, and Keeso will stay with you until I get back." She glanced toward Keeso, knowing he was listening. His nod was all the assurance she needed.

Levi pulled her attention back to him. "Like he took care of me when you were hurt and in the hospital? Uncle Keeso and Pup stayed with me the whole time."

"Yes, exactly like that time. Does it make you feel better?"

His face brightened. "Yes."

"From now on you need to remember what we've talked about before, how if you get lost, you'll stay right where you are until I find you."

"Yeah, but I wasn't lost. You were."

Sometimes it was impossible to reason with a four-year-old. Hopefully, he'd gotten the message she was trying to convey.

Levi seemed to be fine, but she couldn't get past the terror she'd felt when she'd lost sight of him. A debilitating fear buzzed through her body like a low electric charge. She drew a sudden, shuddering breath. Keeso glanced over his shoulder, his eyes full of concern. She gave him a weak smile and turned her attention toward the window.

They stopped at Tuba City for sandwiches and ate in the car. Levi's adventure didn't affect his appetite. He ate his sandwich and half of hers. She wrapped the other half and put it back in the bag.

Keeso noticed. "You're not hungry?"

"Not right now. I'll save it for later." He looked like he wanted to argue but didn't say a word.

By the time they reached home, both children were asleep. Lenn pulled into his drive and shut off the engine. Keeso lifted Levi, who snuggled against his shoulder without waking. She grabbed Pup's leash and Keeso put his arm around her shoulder. Together, they walked across the road to the house she considered home. She unlocked the door and turned on the light as they entered.

He paused before walking down the hall. "You look exhausted. I can get him settled in. Why don't you get ready for bed?"

She didn't argue. Her body protested every move she made and the headache she'd held at bay all evening could no longer be ignored. Hopefully, a couple of Tylenol and a hot shower would help. Grabbing the sweats she'd taken to wearing since Keeso insisted on sleeping in her bed, she made her way down the hall toward the bathroom.

Pausing at Levi's door, she watched Keeso tuck her nephew in. Levi never woke, even when Pup jumped on the foot of the bed and belly-walked to his side. Their four-footed hero stuck his muzzle under his best friend's arm, closed his eyes, and sighed. Obviously, all was right with his world. She took a deep breath and continued down the hall. If only that were true.

Emma's sigh caught Keeso's attention, but she'd moved away from the door by the time he'd looked her way. He flipped Levi's nightlight on, shut off the lamp, then walked to the door. The hall was empty. She must've gone into the bathroom. He closed Levi's door and headed toward their bedroom but pulled up short. He couldn't get her sigh out of his head. There was a hopelessness to it that tore at his heart. Retracing his steps, he stopped at the bathroom door. The barrier didn't mute her sobs, but it did prevent him from consoling the woman he vowed to protect, the woman he loved. He raised his hand to knock but paused when the shower came on. His hand dropped to his side and he headed back to the bedroom. Hopefully, the hot water would sooth the agonies of the day. There would be time after her shower to comfort her.

Lying on his side of the bed, his hands stacked behind his head, he stared into the darkness. He'd been blessed to love two amazing women from this planet—both had demonstrated courage far beyond the average woman, on any planet. Hiilani, his first love, had experienced the devastating loss of their child, but she hadn't let it destroy her. Instead, she made her home with his people on a world as alien to her as Earth was to him. He'd loved her, but he'd been able to let her go.

Then there was Emma. He'd sensed an immediate connection with her, something unexpected. Something strong enough to draw him back to Frank's store with any implausible excuse he could find. He smiled in the dark. Frank hadn't been deceived and became an eager conspirator in getting them together.

She'd felt a connection too, he was positive of it. But as courageous as she'd proven to be, she feared dragging someone else into her nightmare. He'd taken that decision out of her hands by committing himself without requiring a like commitment from her. He'd remain by her side, and Levi's as well. There was nowhere else he wanted to be.

When he remembered how close she'd come to dying on his mountaintop, the bullet inches from her head, he shuddered. Terror, like none he'd ever experienced, overshadowed his thoughts—terror and anger. He would've cheerfully put an end to the killer's existence. He still might. Bullets can travel in both directions.

What he wanted to do was get Emma and Levi off-planet, take them to New Centallus where they wouldn't have to be afraid of every shadow.

But that was unlikely. He would probably never know what happened to his people. Was he the last living Centallian? There was a chance at least a few other Centallians had been off-planet when their world was destroyed. He prayed it was so—he didn't want to think his species would cease to exist at his passing.

He glanced at the clock on the nightstand. Twenty minutes had passed since he'd climbed into bed—enough time for her to shower and dress. Slipping out of bed, he walked barefoot to the bathroom and listened at the door. The shower was still running. It didn't make sense. The water heater wasn't big enough to keep the water hot this long.

"Emma?" He knocked. No answer. He knocked again, louder.

"Emma, answer me." She should have heard him, even with the shower on. He tried the door. It wasn't locked. "I'm coming in."

Emma was huddled on the shower floor.

*"Aamyia!"* Grabbing a body towel from the shelf, he opened the shower door, and reached in to turn off the water. The spray, cold as winter rain, pelted his arm and shoulder before he shut it down.

Emma sat in a tight, shivering ball, arms around her legs, head resting on her knees. He knelt beside her, unmindful of the chilled water soaking into the legs of his sweatpants and covered her with the towel. She refused to look at him.

*"Aamyia,* open your eyes. Are you hurt?" When she didn't answer, he nudged her shoulder.

"I—I'm fine… I need to be alone." Her shivers and chattering teeth made the words difficult to understand, but he got the message. Well, she didn't look fine and he wasn't about to leave her alone.

"Come on, Em, let's get you out of here." Securing the oversized towel around her body, he lifted her into his arms and backed out of the shower. Grabbing another towel from the shelf, he carried her down the hall to the bedroom.

Not bothering with the light, he sat her on the ladder-backed chair just inside the room. Draping the dry towel over his shoulder, he knelt in front of her to dry the excess water from her hair.

He tugged on the wet towel she wore. "Let's get rid of this."

"Don't." She clutched the sodden terrycloth to her shaking body.

*"Aamyia,* it's soaked. It'll only make you colder. You have to take it off."

She shook her head. "Don't call me that. I'm not your one true love and I don't have anything on underneath."

How she could remember the meaning of his endearment, and forget he'd been the one to cover her nakedness, was beyond him. "Forget the modesty, Em. We need to get you dry and warm. You don't want to get sick. Levi needs you, especially now." He pulled her to her feet. "Let go of the towel. I'll look away and we'll wrap this one around you." To his surprise, she cooperated, and he secured the dry towel around her body. He carried her to the bed and briskly dried her hair.

Still shivering, she leaned into his side. The fresh towel wasn't damp enough to worry about. He pulled the covers back on the bed and settled her in, pulling them back under her chin.

"I'm going to check on Levi. I'll be back in a minute." She didn't respond.

He sprinted down the hall to Levi's room. Pup looked up, thumped his tail once and went back to sleep. Levi never moved.

Emma, on the other hand, was still shivering. Peeling the water-soaked sweatpants off his legs, he slipped into bed, turned her to face him and pulled her against his warm body. She didn't resist. Her head lay against his chest, his cheek resting on top of her head. His hand circled her back in a slow, comforting motion. Neither spoke for a long time.

She finally relaxed against him. He brushed the hair away from her face and touched his lips to her brow. "Better?"

Suddenly, she pulled her arms free of the towel and wrapped them around his neck. "Say the words."

"What?"

"I nearly lost Levi today. I can't do this alone. I need you to say the words." She leaned up and kissed him—her lips softening, beckoning. He didn't deny her. His mouth slanted across hers, his tongue seeking entrance. She moaned and opened for him. She tasted like ambrosia.

He wanted more.

She pulled her lips away. "Make love to me. Say the words."

He stilled.

Grabbing his hair, she tried to force his lips back to hers. "Please."

The desperation in her voice sobered him and he grasped her hands, pulling them in front of him. "Em. I've already given you the words."

"Then—"

"No, don't say anything else. Just listen. Long before I gave you the words, I committed my life to your protection. And Levi's. I will never leave you to face your enemy alone. You don't have to accept my words or my body to hold me to that promise."

She stiffened and tried to push away from him. He wouldn't let her. "Don't take offense. I'm not accusing you of anything. And I'm not rejecting you. You are *Aamyia*. I will always want you. But when we come together, I want it to be for the right reasons." He leaned above her and waited until she met his gaze.

"When you give me permission to say the words again, I don't want it to be because you're afraid."

He lay back against his pillow. "I'm a patient man, Em. Ask me to say the words when you know I am your one true love."

He drew her against his chest, cocooning her in his heat. "For tonight, let me hold you. Together we'll keep the nightmares at bay."

# 33

✧

"Good morning."

Keeso walked through the front door and hung his Stetson on the Elkhorn hat rack on the wall beside the door. Levi had found the old, bleached-white antler not long after they'd moved to the reservation when he and Keeso had gone to check on the shuttle. The two had spent an entire afternoon polishing and mounting it on a foot-long board they'd scrounged up from somewhere and painted. Levi beamed with pride every time he passed the door. His ballcap held a place of honor in the center.

Emma tightened the belt on her robe as she walked out of the bedroom. "Good morning." Avoiding eye contact, she glanced down the hall toward her nephew's room. "Where's Levi?"

"He's at Lenn and Marie's house, playing with Sarah. Lenn doesn't go to work until one today." Walking to the propane range, he lit a fire under the coffee pot and adjusted the flame to low. "Don't worry about Levi. The kids won't be going outside. It's cold and the wind's high, so there's lots of dust in the air. Lenn promised to keep a close eye on them."

She pushed the hair away from her face but didn't look at him. "I didn't mean to sleep so long. Did Levi have his breakfast?"

"He had cereal and juice."

"What time is it?"

"A little past nine-thirty. After yesterday, I'd hoped you'd sleep later." He moved to stand in front of her. "Emma, look at me." When she refused to meet his eyes, he gently lifted her chin with his hand. "What's the matter?"

"Nothing." She brushed his hand away and backed up. "Nothing. I need to get dressed."

Returning to the bedroom, she pulled underwear from the top drawer of her dresser and grabbed jeans and a blue pullover sweater from the closet. She felt his eyes on her back. Sure enough, when she turned around, he was standing in the doorway watching her, his arms crossed and eyes full of concern. He stepped back to keep her from running over him as she headed to the bathroom.

She spent an inordinate amount of time getting ready for the day. Not that she was concerned about her appearance. The man in the other room waiting for her to come out of hiding was responsible for her behavior.

How could she face him after last night? She'd practically begged him to make love to her. And he'd refused. She wasn't sure how she felt about that.

Shaking her head, she pulled on the sweater and straightened her shoulders. Of course, she was glad he'd refused. They didn't need to complicate an already tenuous situation.

But had he really refused, or put off the inevitable? Since they'd left Colorado, he'd made no secret of his feelings for her.

And his kisses… what was she going to do about the way they made her feel? She may have initiated the first kiss, but he'd quickly taken over and demonstrated the difference between the few mundane kisses she'd shared with other men and the toe-curling passion she shared with him. The hot taste of him was still in her memory—would probably haunt her forever.

Her emotions were in such constant turmoil it was difficult to separate one feeling from another. She cared about him. How could she not? He'd appointed himself their own personal guardian. Wasn't that what he'd called Centallian warriors—Guardians?

He was that. He'd saved them from their stalker—whisking them out of Colorado, carrying them to Arizona, hiding them in a Hopi village. It was the stuff of heroic stories. A smile touched her lips. Science fiction stories if you considered his mode of transportation.

Did her feelings for him stem from gratitude alone? Her physical attraction to him disproved that. She liked him as a person, too. Stepping into her jeans, she fastened them. He was brave, smart, sometimes funny, and always loyal to those he cared about. And he was gentle.

Levi, Sarah, and Pup trusted him. As a teacher, she'd spent an inordinate amount of time with children. The old adage was true. You can't fool children or animals. It was as if they could see through to a person's soul. His must be something special.

She trusted him as well. If she hadn't, he wouldn't be sleeping in her bed every night, regardless of her nightmares. Their intimate proximity made her aware of him, not only as her protector, but as a man. He had made it plain he wanted to be more than her protector. He wanted to be her mate. Sometimes she wondered what it would be like to feel his hard body pressed to hers in passion, fully aware of what they were doing.

"Emma, please tell me you're not in the shower again." His unexpected voice took ten years off her life. A glance in the mirror revealed bright red cheeks and she had to remind herself he couldn't hear her thoughts, though sometimes he seemed capable of it.

"Emma?"

"I'm all right. Just trying to do something with my hair." She turned on the hairdryer and reached for a washcloth, holding it under the cold water before pressing it to her face. Turning the hairdryer off, she ran the brush through her hair and took a deep breath before stepping into her shoes and opening the door.

The hall was empty. She peeked around the doorway and saw him sitting at the kitchen table, a cup of coffee in his hand.

He burst into laughter. "It's safe to come out, Em. I'm not planning an attack."

She snorted. It was the least ladylike sound she could think of. Had she honestly listed his sense of humor as an attribute?

"I plugged in your hot pot a few minutes ago. The water should be ready for your tea."

"Thank you." She still hadn't looked at him, but fortunately he'd given her an excuse not to. She fished a package of Earl Grey out of the box and tore open the foil pouch. He'd placed her favorite cup and saucer on the counter beside the pot. Resting the teabag in the bottom of the cup, she poured near-boiling water over the bag. While the tea steeped, she retrieved a carton of milk from the refrigerator. When the tea was strong enough, she disposed of the bag and drizzled milk into the cup until the color suited her. She carried the cup to the window and looked out at the wind-whipped morning.

"We live in the same house, *Aamyia*. You can't avoid me forever."

She sighed, carried her cup to the table and sat down. "I'm not trying to avoid you. Not really. After last night...."

"Nothing happened last night."

"No, but it could have. I was willing." She studied the tea swirling in her cup, still unable to focus on him.

"You were distraught and needed comforting. Things got a little carried away, that's all."

"I would have let you make love to me."

"That remains to be seen. I have a feeling you would have come to your senses before that happened."

She finally looked up at him. "Thank you for... not taking advantage of the situation."

He frowned. "Do you think I would have?"

She knew she'd inadvertently insulted him. "No, of course not, but I'm still grateful you stopped me before I lost complete control."

She pushed away from the table and carried her still full cup to the sink, dumped the contents and rinsed it. Setting the cup in the draining rack, she turned and leaned back against the sink as she dried her hands on the dish towel.

"I know you want me to commit to this relationship." She laughed, but there was no humor in it. "I don't even know if you can call what we have a relationship. It makes me uncomfortable to be so dependent on you."

He moved to her side, leaned against the counter, and folded his arms across his chest. "Not so long ago, I was completely dependent on you for survival."

She glanced up at him. "When?"

"The night of the blizzard. I could've died of hypothermia, but you took care of me."

"But I didn't do anything. You'd gone into healing stasis."

"That's probably true, but I could have been in hypothermia and in trouble. You were there for me, compromising your modesty, sharing your heat. It was such an unselfish act."

He turned her to face him, both hands on her shoulders. "Do you understand what I'm trying to say?" He didn't give her enough time to answer. "Everyone born on this planet depends on someone at one time or another, and not just as babies or children. And not only on this planet. Every species my people and I have contacted has its own form of interdependency."

"How many other inhabited planets are out there?"

"Lots. Don't change the subject. I'm trying to make a point." He slipped an arm around her waist and walked her to the couch. "Sit down." She didn't argue and when they were both seated, he continued. "You're going to have to depend on people. You need to stop letting it bother you. Especially when it's me you're depending on."

He angled forward and cupped her face in his warm palm. "You need to understand something else. Last night, when you asked me to make you mine, I didn't reject you." His lips touched hers, warm and whisper soft. "I only want you to be sure. Once you've accepted my words, our bond will never be broken. I intend to rend the veil, sealing my commitment to you." His lips covered hers again, and he pulled her against him, deepening the kiss. His teeth gently tugged at her lower lip, encouraging her to open for him. She did, and his tongue swept in to let her taste him. She moaned, her arms circling his neck to draw him closer.

He raised his head, ending the kiss, and took a couple of shuddering breaths. "I think we'd better stop."

She leaned back against the couch and realized she was breathing hard, too. She nodded, unable to speak quite yet.

He brushed the hair back from her face and placed a chaste kiss on her brow. "Don't take too long to realize you love me." He unfolded himself from the couch, grabbed his Stetson, and left the house.

# 34

✧

*Don't take too long....*

Emma adjusted her pillow and leaned back against the headboard. How long did it take to know you loved someone? Years? Months? She'd never really thought about it, had never been interested enough in the men she'd known to commit to the relationship—physically or emotionally.

It was different with Keeso. From the beginning, she'd felt this curious connection to the man, an immediate attraction she'd never experienced before. An attraction she knew beyond a doubt he shared.

Every time he walked into a room, she'd experience palpitations usually associated with a high school crush. After months of close association, his unexpected appearance still sent adrenaline shooting through her system. It didn't make any sense.

They'd been sleeping in the same bed—at least until he challenged her to come to terms with her feelings about him. That night, he'd taken his pillow and an extra blanket to the couch. He hadn't explained why. It hadn't been necessary. The kiss they'd shared on the very couch he presently slept on was explanation enough.

He wanted her.

She wanted him, too.

Or maybe she only missed his solid presence beside her when she slept. She felt safe with him next to her. She hadn't slept well the past few nights.

Sleep was just as elusive, maybe more so, this evening.

Leaning forward, she rested her arms on her upraised knees. Did she love him? She seemed to have all the symptoms—including a strong physical attraction. She wasn't dead, after all, and that alien-turned-cowboy possessed all the attributes she'd ever fantasized in a husband.

But it wasn't just physical. She liked him, for his gentle response to Levi and Sarah, for his respect for the Hopi people and their traditions, for his loyalty to those he considered friends… his loyalty to her. He was steadfast—the man had promised to stand beside her to his dying day.

So, did she want to spend the rest of her life with him? She sighed and rested her head against her arms. Maybe the real question was, could she imagine spending it with anyone else?

"Aunty!" Levi's terrified scream wrenched her from her thoughts. She rolled out of bed and headed for the door.

Keeso was already halfway down the hall. "Stay there," he shouted back at her.

She didn't slow down. By the time she reached the bedroom, he had Levi in his arms, holding him close, muttering soothing words as the child sobbed against the crook of his neck. Pup circled their legs, whining and jumping up to sniff her nephew.

She reached out. "Let me have him." Levi threw himself into her arms, staggering her. Keeso braced his arm against her back to steady her.

"I thought I told you to stay in the hall," he growled. "There might've been trouble—"

"Levi needed me."

"The man was chasing me." Levi rambled bits and pieces of what had to be a half-remembered nightmare. "He was gonna hurt me."

She hugged him closer, her heart aching at the fear in his voice. "It was only a dream sweetie. Only a dream."

Keeso held them both close, one arm around her shoulders the other gently rubbing Levi's back. "We're here now, buddy. Nothing can hurt you."

Levi leaned back, gazed up into her eyes, and put his small hands on her cheeks. "I don't wanna go to sleep again. He might come back."

Her arms tightened around him in a fierce hug. "It was just a dream, remember? He won't come back, honey."

"Will you sleep with me tonight?"

"Of course I will." She moved toward his bed.

His arms tightened around her neck. "Can Uncle Keeso sleep with us too?"

She wasn't sure what to tell him. Keeso had been clear. He was uncomfortable sleeping with her. He had decided against doing so until she committed to a permanent relationship.

"Sure, I can, buddy. Let's go sleep in the big bed." He simply shrugged at her sharp look and steered them down the hall toward the master bedroom.

A few minutes later, Levi was tucked into the center of the queen-sized bed with her and Keeso on either side, the pup curled up at Levi's feet.

Levi finally calmed down and closed his eyes. After a few minutes, she thought he'd fallen asleep.

"Sarah wanted to know why I have an aunty and uncle instead of a mommy and daddy. She says mommies and daddies and little kids are forever families. Is she right?" Emma wasn't sure where the question came from or where it was leading.

Levi didn't give her a chance to answer. He leaned closer. "Mommy and daddy and me... we were a forever family, right?"

Brushing his hair back, she leaned down and kissed the top of his head. "Yes, sweetheart. You were a forever family."

His sigh bordered on a renewed sob. "Forever isn't a very long time, is it?"

"Oh, honey." She blinked back tears and pulled him into her arms, holding him close, praying for the right words to comfort him. How did you explain forever was never forever to a four-year-old? At least not in this lifetime. Keeso's arms came around them both, cradling them, offering silent comfort and support.

"You still are a forever family, baby. Your mommy and daddy will always be with you." She put her hand on his chest. "They're right here in your heart. All you need to do is remember the happy times."

"What if I don't remember?"

"I won't let you forget, honey. I'll tell you stories, and we'll look at the pictures in my wallet."

He wriggled out of her arms and gazed up at Keeso for long minutes before returning his attention to her. "Joey says when you get 'dopted you get a new mommy and daddy."

The sudden change in topic caught her off guard. "What made you think about being adopted? Who's Joey?"

"He's my friend back home in daycare. He got 'dopted 'cuz his mommy and daddy got in an accident. He says when your mommy and daddy go away, you have to get a new mommy and daddy." He was quiet for a moment or two, then looked up at her. "I don't want a new mommy and daddy. I want my real mommy and daddy back."

"I know you do, sweetie." She brushed the hair back from his face. "I want them back too, but they can't be with us like that anymore."

He looked up at her, his eyes shimmering with fresh tears. "Do I have to get a new mommy and daddy?"

He was breaking her heart. How long had he worried about forever families and being adopted? He'd never mentioned his friend Joey before tonight.

She hugged him closer. "No, sweetie, you have me to take care of you."

"And Uncle Keeso, too? Are we a forever family?"

His question jarred her. Were they? In this moment, with her snuggling Levi close and Keeso's arms keeping them safe and protected, it felt like a family—had for a while. She caught Keeso's intense gaze. It was past time for her decision.

"Yes. Uncle Keeso and I are your forever family. You don't need another mommy and daddy."

"Good." He snuggled against her side and pulled Keeso's arm closer before closing his eyes. A few minutes later, his deep, even breathing told them he was sound asleep.

When she glanced at Keeso again, the intensity in his gold-flecked eyes told her what he was about to do. "Don't say the words yet."

His eyes narrowed. "You didn't mean what you told the boy?"

"Don't misunderstand. I meant what I said, about our being a family. I've given you permission to say the words, but not tonight. I want a wedding, in a church, with Levi participating so he will never doubt we are a family."

"You keep mentioning Levi, but you haven't said anything about us. Don't misunderstand me. Levi is important, but you will be my bond-mate. By allowing me to say the words and rend the veil—which I intend to do—you bind yourself to me forever. You can't make this commitment out of a sense of duty to Levi."

"I know what I'm doing, and it isn't because of duty or gratitude—though I am grateful for everything you've done for us. You make me feel cherished and safe. You make me laugh and hold me when I cry. You've become my best friend. You're not perfect, but I have a feeling you're as close as I'm ever going to get."

"I'm not perfect, huh?" There was laughter in his voice.

"No one's perfect, Keeso. Get over it."

He did laugh then. "There's a small church nearby. I'm sure Lenn can make the arrangements for us and see to any necessary paperwork. With your agreement, I would like to incorporate a few Centallian traditions."

She smiled. "I'd like that."

"I'll speak to Lenn in the morning. It shouldn't take long to make the arrangements. A few days perhaps."

She nodded. "Good. For Levi's peace of mind, we should be married as soon as possible."

Gently pulling his arm free of Levi's grasp, he leaned over and cupped her chin in his hand. "For mine as well." Leaning down, he touched his lips to hers.

"Aunty?"

Like opposite poles on a magnet, the two sprang apart. Keeso took a deep breath before settling back against his pillow. She did the same. Levi was mumbling in his sleep, blissfully unaware. She shook her head and giggled, suddenly feeling like a teenager caught necking in the backseat of a Chevy.

Keeso reached for the lamp on his side of the bed and the room darkened. His drawn-out sigh was full of frustration.

"A few more days."

# 35

✧

How did you plan a wedding in a few days? Emma had asked Keeso that very question. He'd smiled, told her not to panic, and promised to take care of all the arrangements.

She wasn't comforted.

Marie's promise was far more reassuring. She told Emma she'd keep an eye on what the men were planning and offer a suggestion here and there. "We also need to consider what you're going to wear."

That brought her up short. She hadn't even thought about a dress. Didn't even own one. When you bought clothes on the run, you didn't think about nice dresses. Marie must have read the renewed panic in her expression.

"Don't worry. We have time. Lenn and Keeso are planning a trip out to the shuttle and they're taking Levi with them. Keeso mentioned needing something for the ceremony. He also told Lenn he needed to go to town. They'll probably be gone all afternoon. That'll give us a chance to go into Winslow and find something for you to wear."

"I don't know. It might not be safe."

"We can make it safe. I'll invite my sister and her children to go with us. No one would think to look for you in a group of women, especially if you're carrying a toddler around."

She nodded. "Okay, but we need to get back before the men do. I don't want Levi to worry."

"I'd be more concerned about Keeso if I were you. He won't be happy if you're not here when he gets back."

"You could be right. I'll meet you at the car in ten minutes."

She should've known they wouldn't make it back in time. Shopping for something as important as the gown to get married in took time. She lost track of the number of stores they'd gone to and the number of dresses she'd tried on. She'd finally chosen a floor-length basic satin sheath of pearlescent ivory. The delicate material hugged every curve of her body.

Fortunately for their time crunch, the bridal shop carried matching shoes in a variety of sizes. The gown was carefully boxed with tissue paper to prevent wrinkling and they were soon on their way back to the reservation.

Keeso was standing in the doorway of their home when they pulled into Marie's drive. He didn't look happy. They carried her things into Marie's house before she crossed the road to face him. One look at the scowl on his face and she felt like a kid coming home after curfew.

She wasn't about to let him get away with that. "Have you been back long?"

"Long enough to be worried about you."

"I left you a note."

"I read it."

Enough with being civil. "Don't growl at me. I'm not your wife yet, and even if I were, I wouldn't stand for your attitude. I won't be told what I can and can't do. This isn't the dark ages. You'll be my husband, not my keeper. It can't—it won't—be any other way."

He grabbed her shoulders and pulled her up against his body. His voice was deceptively quiet, but his eyes were full gold. "There's a monster out there determined to kill you. I'm just as determined to keep you alive. Get used to this attitude. It isn't going to change until he's dead." He kissed her. It wasn't gentle, but filled with passion, possession, and frustration. Pulling away, he turned and walked into the house, leaving her to lean against the doorframe wondering what had just happened.

Emma's wedding day dawned cold, with snowflakes drifting to the ground. But, by early afternoon, the clouds dispersed and the sun eased the morning's chill. The ceremony was to be held at four o'clock. She would dress at Marie's and ride to the church with her. Keeso and Levi would prepare at home and drive to the church with Lenn. Marie had sent Levi a beaded sash and moccasins to wear with the white pants and shirt Emma had purchased.

She still didn't know what Keeso intended to wear. He'd brought a large ornately carved wooden chest back from the shuttle. The dark burgundy grain had been buffed to a high gloss. She assumed his traditional bonding clothes were inside. She couldn't imagine what else it held but Keeso's muscles had bulged with the weight of the chest when he carried it from the living room into the bedroom.

Lenn knocked on the door and announced that Marie had decreed it was time for her to get ready for the wedding. She laughed and opened the door wide for him to enter. Planting a kiss on top of Levi's head, she left the men to their own preparations.

Levi watched in fascination as Keeso pulled each item from the chest and laid it on the bed. He encouraged the boy he already considered his son to touch and examine each piece as he put them on.

"I am a Centallian. We are peacemakers. Do you know what a peacemaker is?" Wide-eyed, Levi shook his head. "We try to teach people how to get along with each other. But, a long, long time ago, when my world was very young, Centallians were not peaceful. They were warriors. And their disagreements were settled in battle. Centallians had to be prepared to defend themselves, even during celebrations and ceremonies. Do you understand what I'm telling you?"

Levi looked up from the helmet he'd been examining and nodded. "They got in fights all the time."

Keeso smiled. "That's right, buddy, but after a while my people discovered it was better to talk than to fight. Today, Centallians are not warriors. We are Guardians—protectors of the weak."

"Like you protect me and aunty."

"Yes, like I protect you and your aunt." He accepted the helmet from Levi and turned to Lenn. "Is it time?"

Lenn looked at his watch. "We have about ten minutes to get to the church. Marie and Emma have already left."

Keeso knelt in front of Levi and removed the wrapping from a box he'd been saving for last. The child's eyes rounded as the small lacquered chest, covered with precious stones, was revealed.

"Do you remember what we talked about yesterday, how you will carry a box to the front of the church and hand it to me when it's time?" Levi nodded. "This is the box you will carry. On Centallus, my closest relative, the person I trust the most, would be given the honor of carrying this for me. According to the laws of my people, you are my son, my closest relative. Will you carry it for me?" Levi nodded solemnly and accepted the tiny cask, holding it close to his body in a protective gesture as they walked out the door.

# 36

✧

Emma waited for Keeso at the altar—according to Centallian tradition, he would come to her. That and the rending of the veil was all she knew regarding a Centallian bonding. The minister was aware of the additions to the usual marriage ceremony, though he had not been told of their alien origin.

This stage-like upper level only had room for a small choir box, the pulpit, and two chairs. The pulpit, as well as the altar table, had been moved back. The minister stood at the edge of the foot-high banister spanning the raised area. She stood at floor level, in front of the minister.

Marie and Sarah sat in the front pew, with Pup resting at Sarah's feet. Levi had insisted Pup was part of the family, and therefore, should be at the ceremony. Neither she nor Keeso had argued the point.

Footsteps in the vestibule caught her attention. The small group attending the wedding turned to face the inner doors. She transferred the bouquet Marie had surprised her with from one hand to the other, suddenly nervous.

Two blanket-draped Hopi drummers stepped into the sanctuary. Each man moved to opposite sides of the door, placed a reed mat on the floor and sat down. Pulling the small drums onto their crossed legs, they began a steady, triple-beat cadence, one beat, then two, one beat, then two—the rhythm of the human heart.

Lenn and James, the tobacco clan leader, stepped into the room and walked side by side down the center aisle, in tempo with the drumbeat. Lenn's outstretched hands held a folded, translucent wisp of cloth.

Levi came next. His loose, white pants and tunic were belted at the waist with the beaded blue and gold sash. He held a small, deep-blue lacquered box encrusted with what she was certain were semi-precious jewels and diamonds. He was so intent on his part of the ceremony he didn't acknowledge her until he'd reached the front of the church. Then he looked up and grinned before turning around to face the entry doors.

She followed his gaze and stopped breathing.

Keeso. Like she'd never seen him before.

He paused briefly in the open doorway. A warrior dressed for battle, his thigh-length tunic reminded her of a garment a Roman soldier would have worn. Steel arm and shin guards protected his forearms and legs, a breastplate emblazoned with a grotesque beast-like image, covered his chest. The same image decorated the shield strapped to his left arm. He carried a helmet-mask in the crook of his right arm, its image as unique as the Hopi glyphs. A long, curved knife hung from a braided belt at his waist. His boots, though not moccasins, were some type of soft leather.

He walked toward her, broad-shouldered, with thick-muscled arms and thighs—a man aware of his ability to protect himself and those who depended on his strength.

He was magnificent… and frightening.

Until he stepped in front of her. She looked into dark eyes filled with love and satisfaction.

Her Keeso.

No more room for doubt—she belonged to him.

Lenn and the clan leader spread the translucent cloth between them. Levi took his place beside Keeso, still holding the lacquered box. The minister stepped forward to begin the ceremony with a prayer and a few brief words on the sanctity and responsibility of marriage. He explained the bride and groom's desire to speak their own vows. He turned to her, giving her the opportunity to speak first.

Everything she had prepared to say disappeared from her mind. Panicked, she looked toward Keeso, his features only slightly distorted through the gauzy film of material between them. As he had so many times in the past, he seemed to know exactly what she was feeling. His smiled his encouragement. Suddenly, everything was as it should be. She took a deep breath and in a strong voice, gave him her vows.

"From the moment we met, my life changed for the better. You gave me a reason to laugh, to hope. A reason to dare to believe in a future for Levi and me. You have become our champion—my champion—my *Aamyia*. I love you. Give me the words."

The minister turned toward Keeso.

"Sweet Emma. From the moment you fell into my arms, we've shared a connection, an immediate bond few ever achieve. You complete me. I vow to love and respect you, to stand by your side, to share the responsibilities of our bonding." He placed his hand on Levi's head, a possessive gesture no one could mistake. "I vow to acknowledge, protect, and provide for any child of this bonding. As long as my body draws breath, I am bound by honor to these promises."

The minister cleared his throat. "Emma and Keeso have spoken their vows before God and these witnesses. By the power vested in me, by God and the state of Arizona, I pronounce you husband and wife."

Taking a step back, Keeso drew his sword, and raised it above the gossamer veil. The narrow diamond-hard blade glided downward through the fabric as if it were made of mist. The severed cloth drifted to the floor.

Handing the knife and his helmet-mask to Lenn, he took Emma into his arms. "This is forever," he whispered just before his lips touched hers, sealing his final vow. He pulled away, took her arm and turned to Levi.

Her nephew lifted the ornate box in her direction. She bent to accept the gift and Levi placed a wet kiss on her cheek. "Uncle Keeso said I should give you this. It's from both of us."

"Thank you, sweetheart." She straightened and looked at Keeso.

"Every Guardian gives his new bond-mate the gift of life, a small seed symbolic of his promise to give her children. There is a seed inside as tradition requires, but there is another symbolic gift inside as well." He raised the latch and opened the lid. Beside the seed, a silver necklace—three hearts entwined—rested on deep-blue velvet.

He lifted the piece from the box and leaned forward to clasp the chain around her neck, centering the cascading hearts at her throat. "As the seed would have been symbolic of the family I would have given you, this necklace is symbolic of the family we have become." He lifted Levi into his arms and turned with her to face those assembled in the sanctuary.

The minister's voice rang clear in the silence. "May I present to you Keeso, Emma, and Levi Smith. A forever family."

# 37

Marie and Lenn prepared a celebration dinner and insisted Levi and Pup spend the night with them. Their intention, of course, was to give the newlyweds privacy. Levi hesitated, but Sarah soon convinced him a sleepover was fun.

Marie helped Emma change out of her wedding dress while Keeso changed out of his armor at home. A considerable amount of time had passed before he returned with Pup at his side. She wondered if there was some type of ritual connected with removing and repacking a Guardian's wardrobe.

After dinner, the children left the table to play with Pup in Sarah's room. Keeso stood. "It's getting late. We should go." He offered Lenn his hand. "Thank you for making this happen so fast."

Lenn shook his head. "It was no problem. The blood of your people's ancients runs through my veins. I am honored to call you brother."

"And I as well."

Marie came around the table and hugged Emma. "I'm so happy for you and Keeso."

"Aunty, don't go." Levi threw his arms around her legs.

She knelt eye-level with him. "It's getting late, sweetheart."

"Maybe I should go home, too."

"You can, if that's what you want, but I thought you and Sarah were going to have a sleepover."

He nodded. "We were, but I don't want you to be alone."

"I won't be alone, sweetheart. Keeso will be with me."

Keeso lifted Levi into his arms. "I'll take good care of your aunt. I promise."

Levi grabbed Keeso's neck for a hug. He leaned over to reach for her as well, hugging them both before squirming to get down. "Bye." He ran into Sarah's room.

She laughed. "I think we've been dismissed."

"You could be right." He slipped his arm around her shoulder. "Let's go before he changes his mind."

Keeso caught Emma off guard when he swooped her into his arms as soon as he'd opened their door.

Laughing, she wrapped her arms around his neck. "What are you doing?"

He grinned. "I believe I'm supposed to carry you over the threshold." He walked inside with her, kicking the door shut, but instead of putting her down, he continued through the hall, standing her on her feet at the entrance to the bathroom. "When I came home to change earlier, I left a gift for you in here." He cupped her face in his hands and gave her a lingering kiss. "I'll be waiting in our bedroom." Turning, he walked down the hall.

A white gift box lay on the counter. She lifted the lid to find an eggshell-white silk nightgown, as translucent as the veil that had separated them earlier. Since she had a nice, never-worn nightgown in her dresser, she hadn't given much thought to what she'd wear tonight.

Apparently, he had.

She showered, dried her hair and brushed her teeth before slipping into the gown. One glance in the mirror and she swallowed hard. The revealing material clung to every curve of her body.

She was dressed for seduction—Keeso's.

Reaching for the necklace he'd given her at their wedding, she paused. The three hearts beautifully represented family. But tonight wasn't about family, it was about her new relationship with Keeso. She reached instead for the necklace he'd bought for her on the road to the Grand Canyon. It had been his first personal gift. The satin-like sheen of the tiger-eye figure complemented her gown.

*Kokopelli.*

The little humpbacked flute player was a symbol of fertility and abundant harvest. Fertility. She was barren, and Keeso dare not father a half terran baby. Still, she wondered what a child of their making would be like. Shaking her head, she opened the bathroom door, ready to face her future.

The bedroom door was closed. She knocked, waited a few seconds, then walked inside and stopped short. The bed had been moved against the wall on the far side of the room. In its place lay a large, oval, silver-gray, fur rug. Candles circled its perimeter, giving the darkened room an otherworldly feel.

Keeso stepped into the sphere of light, and her breath caught in her throat. The braided leather band holding his breechcloth in place rode low on his hips, his nearly nude body glistening bronzed-copper in the flickering candlelight. His dark, unbound hair touched his powerful shoulders, and again she was reminded of the Native American she'd once taken him for.

He was perfect—glorious—and daunting.

She took a deep breath. Then another. Why hadn't she realized how big he was? Huge was a better word. He could easily....

"Emma?"

She jumped. "What?"

"Be calm, *Aamyia*. I won't bite." He tilted his head and smiled. "Unless you want me to."

Suddenly he was her Keeso again.

She laughed, relieved. "That line's as old as I am."

His smile widened. "It worked though, did it not? You're laughing instead of thinking about running." He moved closer, extending his hand palm up.

"Come to me."

Gathering her gown and her courage close, she stepped past the candles, took his hand, and followed him to the center of the rug.

"You're trembling." He opened his arms and she stepped into his warm embrace, the heat from his powerful body easing her shivers.

He nudged her chin up. "Better?"

"Yes."

"Were you really afraid of me?" His voice echoed the concern in his gold-flecked eyes.

"Not afraid, overwhelmed. I've never seen you like this, so... untamed."

"Untamed, huh?" He grinned and traced her collarbone with a finger. "Afraid I'm going to pounce?"

"That isn't funny."

"Yes, it is."

She stiffened at the humor still lacing his voice and struggled to pull out of his arms. "You're making fun of me."

He wouldn't let go. One hand pressed her head against his chest. "Not making fun of, *Aamyia*, having fun with. There's a difference."

"Not much of one from my stand point."

"That's because you're too nervous to find the humor in your reactions."

She pulled her head free of his grasp and looked into his eyes. "I told you I'm not afraid of you."

"True, but you are uneasy tonight. Do you deny it?"

"I'll admit I'm edgy." She took a deep breath and expelled it slowly. "Giving someone else control over my body is a little unnerving."

His fingers glided through her hair to brush it away from her face and his lips touched hers in a chaste kiss. "What makes you think I intend to be in control?"

"You're the one with the experience."

"Love is not about control, Em. It's about sharing, about giving." His arms dropped to his sides. "You set the pace and I will follow your lead." He took a step back. "Do what you will, *Aamyia*."

She gazed at him—took in his wide, muscular shoulders and arms, his massive chest and heavy-muscled thighs. He was such a beautiful man and not just physically. He had a beautiful spirit as well. He was strong, gentle, compassionate, and steadfast. And he was hers.

"May I touch you?"

"We're bond-mates, Em. My body belongs to you." He bent closer, his breath warming her ear. "As your body belongs to me."

His words shivered over her, his invitation impossible to resist. She centered her hands on his chest, gliding them slightly lower until she felt his heartbeat, strong beneath her touch—if not quite steady. The crisp sprinkling of hair teased her fingertips as she skimmed upward, grazing his shoulders, tracing the muscles of his biceps and forearms.

She inched around him, her fingers trailing a path to his wide, strong back. His gaze followed her, his head tilting to look over his shoulder.

She used both hands to braille the steel-like muscles encased in feverish skin, and breathed in his scent—exotic... male... Keeso. Pressing her face to the center of his back, she flicked the tip of her tongue against his skin, tasting him, and grinned as goosebumps rose on his shoulders. She slipped both arms around his waist, holding him close as she pressed her face against his back, loving the feel of him. Her fingers moved restlessly against the skin of his lower stomach as she rained quick kisses down his spine to the braided band holding his breechcloth in place.

He groaned, a shudder coursing his body. She smiled before moving to stand before him once more. Leaning up on tiptoe, she kissed his lips, moving lower to plant butterfly kisses on his chest, and lower still to his hard, flat stomach. Her fingertips delved inside the band draped low on his hips.

He grabbed her wrist, roughly pulling her up against his chest, trapping her hands between their bodies. She gazed up into the scorching heat of his full-gold eyes.

"It's my turn to touch."

He buried his face in the hair at her neck and inhaled. "Your scent heats my blood. Since the night we met, *Aamyia,* you've invaded my dreams and haunted my fantasies. I've craved your hands on my body, your lips...." He splayed his fingers through her hair to cup her head with both hands. His gaze swept her face, centering upon her lips. "You are lovely beyond imagining. Exquisite, truly."

Nervous, she licked her lips.

Air hissed through his teeth, and he groaned. His mouth covered hers, his tongue following the path hers had taken, tracing her lower lip before seeking entrance.

She moaned and wrapped her arms around his neck, tangling her fingers in his hair, to pull him closer, deepening the kiss until they were both breathless.

His mouth found her ear, his tongue tracing the delicate shell. His harsh breathing fanned her hair and throat as his lips forged a path to the ultrasensitive spot where her neck and shoulder joined. He nipped her. She gasped and straightened, but he didn't allow her to pull away from him. His mouth covered the abused area, his tongue sweeping over the sensitized skin. It was her turn to feel goosebumps. His teeth found the thin strap of her gown, and he tugged it past her shoulder. His fingers hooked the other strap, easing it down as well.

The gown hung on the thrust of her breasts. He paused and gazed into her eyes. She had time to deny him, knew a shake of her head would be enough. She didn't move. With a quick nod, he bent his head to place a kiss in the hollow between her breasts. Sinking to his knees, he tugged the gown to her waist.

She held her breath.

Another tug and the diaphanous garment floated to the rug. She tried to cover the ugly scars marring her body.

Shaking his head, he lifted her hand to his lips, kissing her palm before pressing his face against the puckered flesh.

"You're beautiful, Em. You have no reason to be ashamed of these scars. They're evidence of your strength."

His hands glided down the back of her thighs to her knees and pulled them to either side of his waist. She fell forward, grasping his shoulders as he rolled her onto the rug, his lower body resting between her thighs.

"*Aamyia.*" His mouth found hers, his tongue tracing the soft inner recesses, sinking in to taste her, retreating and sinking in again.

Heat coiled low in her belly, expanding until every sensitive part of her body felt the fire.

She moaned at his erotic play, squirming beneath him until he snuggled his arousal where she needed it most.

Surging against him, she tried to get closer, frustrated by the cloth separating them. Pushing up against him, she reached for the tie securing his breechcloth, desperately needing to touch him.

He must have guessed her intention. His hand covered hers, and she glanced up into his intense gold eyes. He shook his head. "You may look, *Aamyia*, but you cannot touch—not this time. Your innocent hands have already strained my control." Releasing her, he slipped his hand between them to free the lacings. She didn't stop him.

When the breechcloth fell away, she wished she had. Heaven help her, he was bigger than life—certainly bigger than normal, or was that normal where he came from?

"We can't possibly… You're too… We won't.…"

His fingers touched her lips. "Don't panic, *Aamyia*. We'll make sure you're ready for me." His words might have been comforting if she hadn't been so aware of his arousal pressing against her belly.

"Keeso I don't think—"

"Shh, we'll go slow. We have all night to discover each other." He nibbled her lips, licking and teasing them. "Open for me. Give me your tongue." His hand caressed her cheek, her neck, then he slanted his mouth over hers, sucking her tongue into his mouth, letting her taste him. Her body tingled in response to the slow rhythm of his tongue stroking hers. She moaned.

"You taste good." He licked a path to her throat. His hand palmed one breast, his thumb skimming the taut peak. He brought his face closer, his lips no more than an inch away. His tongue flicked out—a bolt of lightning striking her straining nipple. She cried out, arching into his waiting mouth. He suckled, then moved to give the other orb equal measure.

Leaning up, he brushed back her hair and nuzzled her neck. His lips touched her ear and he whispered words she couldn't understand yet knew were passionate promises of what he meant to do. His warm body surrounded her. She shivered in anticipation.

Keeso slipped his hand into the curls at the junction of her soft thighs, his fingers sinking into her liquid heat. Emma whimpered and bucked against his erotic touch.

"Patience *Aamyia*. I've only just begun touching you." He eased his fingers out, then slowly pushed into her again—and again and again. His mouth covered hers in a tongue-thrusting kiss. His hand pulled away from her moist heat to caress the soft skin of her hip, snuggling her more intimately beneath him and gently pressed into her.

She was hot, wet, tight—ready for him. He pushed deeper, gaining only an inch or so. Gritting his teeth, he buried his face in her hair.

She was exquisite.

"Keeso?"

"It's okay, Em. It doesn't hurt, does it? Please tell me I'm not hurting you."

"No." She didn't sound sure and shifted, inadvertently drawing a little more of him into her. She whimpered.

He groaned and grabbed her hips to hold them still. "Give it time, sweetheart. I promise it will feel as good to you as it does to me." He pulled out until only the tip of his arousal remained inside her. His hands glided up her body to cup both breasts, his thumbs teasing her nipples into hard buds. His lips found a peak, his tongue circling it before he sucked it into his hot mouth. She moaned and slashed her fingers through his hair, grasping the thick strands to pull him closer. Her response and her sweet, beckoning body drove him over the edge. He surged deep.

She cried out, stiffened and push against him. He knew why, had felt the membrane tear. He hadn't been gentle and was now buried full hilt in her tight, hot sheath, his pelvis flush against hers.

"You're a virgin."

Not anymore.

Emma closed her eyes against Keeso's astonished expression and pushed against his chest. He wouldn't budge. His arousal, hot and hard, throbbed deep inside her and she tried to ignore the pain that came with each swell of his manhood.

"I thought because of your bullet wound… the damage it caused…." He brushed the wetness from her cheeks. "I should have been more careful. I'm sorry I hurt you, Em."

"I'm all right."

He shook his head. "No, you're not. We can stop." He was already pulling out of her.

"No! *No!*" She threw her arms around his neck and raised her hips, preventing his retreat, embedding him deeper. She gasped when their bodies slammed together.

He pressed his pelvis against hers, preventing her from moving again.

"Stay still, Em. I don't want to hurt you any more than I already have."

She tangled her fingers in his hair. "I don't think I can. You make me want to move."

It was all the encouragement he needed. His mouth covered hers, his tongue sinking in to tease and taste her. Bracing his arms, he eased out and entered her again in one long excruciatingly slow thrust. Grabbing his shoulders, she rolled her hips forward to meet his, encouraging him to pick up the pace. Passion smoldered in his golden eyes as he gave in to her desire, thrusting faster, deeper. His voice rasped against her ear, sexy, throaty, exciting. His touch, his taste, his exotic male scent drugged her. A delicious warmth coiled in her belly, expanding until the exquisite pressure nearly drove her mad.

"Keeso!" Shattering pleasure pulsed through her body. She sobbed his name again and threw her arms around his neck.

"I've got you, *Aamyia*. I'll keep you safe."

Her climax triggered his own and he buried himself deep, the pulsing release of his seed joining her own sweet throbbing.

He rested his face against her neck, his body sated, his breathing still harsh. Her breathing was as out-of-control as his. He was arrogantly pleased by that realization.

He rolled to her side, pulling her into his arms. She gazed up at him, her eyes misty, her lips swollen from his kisses. She was the most beautiful woman he'd ever known.

He kissed her, gently now. "I'm sorry I hurt you." He didn't hide the regret in his voice.

She smiled up at him. "I don't remember."

He raised an eyebrow. "Why do I find that difficult to believe?"

"Really. The pain got caught up in what you were making me feel. I can't explain it. It was as if we were one person. Inseparable."

"I felt the connection too, *Aamyia.*" He got to his feet. "I'll be right back." He left the bedroom and spent a few minutes in the bathroom. Retrieving a basin from under the sink, he filled it with warm water and dropped in a washcloth. He stopped in the kitchen long enough to grab the bottle of *Baquui* and a glass. In the bedroom, he set the basin on the floor beside the rug before filling the glass and offering it to her.

Sitting up, she took the glass. "I recognize this. What did you call it?"

"*Baquui.* I have a few bottles stored on the shuttle." He sat down beside her. "Drink it all. It should help alleviate some of the discomfort I've caused."

"It wasn't that bad. Honest." She emptied the glass and handed it to him.

"The *Baquui* will still help." He set the glass aside and pulled her into his arms. His kiss was gentle, as he laid her back against the soft rug. Reaching into the basin, he picked up the cloth, squeezed out the excess water and sponged the perspiration from her body.

She grabbed his hand when he reached the junction of her legs. "What are you doing?"

"Taking care of you, *Aamyia*. Let me do this."

Her hand fell away. He dipped the washcloth into the basin once more.

*He'd never shot a dog. He liked dogs, always had. Pulling the silencer out of his pocket, he attached it to the barrel of his gun. Dogs were honest, up front. They didn't pretend to be something they weren't, like most humans.*

*The mutt was friendly most of the time. But he was watchful when the boy was with him, always standing between the kid and people he wasn't sure of.*

*The dog would raise a fuss when he came after the boy. He couldn't have that. Few people would miss a stray and that was probably what this one was.*

*The boy would miss him. But not for long. He wouldn't be worrying about anything after tonight, and neither would the kid's aunt. He should have put another bullet in her when he had the chance. Now she wasn't an easy hit, not with that big cowboy looking out for her. He'd put a bullet in him too if he got a chance.*

*The dog was still gnawing on that meaty bone he'd used to lure him into the shed, his tail whipping the dirt floor fast enough to raise dust. He released the safety and aimed the gun. The pup wouldn't know what hit him. Here one minute, gone the next. That's the way he did his marks. He was a good shot.*

# 38

✦

The pounding threatened to break the door down. Keeso jumped from the bed, grabbed his pants, and headed into the living room.

He looked over his shoulder at Emma. "Stay here."

She was already on her feet, wrapping the sheet around her body. She ignored his order and followed him out. He'd managed to get his pants on and zipped before reaching for the knob.

"Keeso, wake up. Open the door."

Lenn.

She grabbed Keeso's arm for support. "Levi."

Keeso swung the door wide. Lenn leaned against the doorframe, half bent, gasping for air, his unbuttoned shirt hanging off one shoulder.

"Levi's gone."

Her knees buckled.

Keeso grabbed her waist, pulling her into his side. "How?" He stepped back to let Lenn into the house and headed for their bedroom.

Lenn followed. "I don't know. Pup's gone, too—didn't come back after I let him out. I figured he came here."

"He didn't." Keeso pulled a shirt from the closet and slipped it on, not bothering to button it while he searched for his boots. "Is Sarah all right? Does she know where he went?"

"Whatever happened, she slept through it." He cleared his throat. "This was on Levi's pillow." He held out a sheet of paper.

Keeso practically ripped it from his hand. Emma leaned closer as he studied what appeared to be a crude map with a message scrawled below. Keeso read it out loud. "Emma Kent, if you want your nephew to live, come get him—alone."

Relief and terror vied for control. Levi was alive, but with the killer. "I'll go change."

Keeso caught her arm. "Don't even think about going out there with us. It's too dangerous."

"The note said—"

"I'm not letting you anywhere near that—"

"We're talking about Levi's safety. The note says I'm supposed to go and I'm going. If you don't take me with you, I'll find a way to go alone." She left the bedroom for the bathroom before he could argue. She'd left her clothes and shoes there last night.

When she returned to the living room, the two men were leaning over the table studying the paper. Lenn traced one of the lines on the map with his finger. "I recognize the area. It skirts the upper level of Second Mesa, below the village of Mishongnovi." He pointed to another line veering away from the heavier one. "If this is where I think it is, that side road edges the Mesa. The cliffs drop straight down in several places along there. It's treacherous in the dark."

"Can we look at the map on the way? We need to leave now." She picked up her jacket and a throw from the couch. "Levi will be cold."

Keeso nodded. "We'll take the Jeep."

Lenn handed Keeso the paper. "I'll get a few things out of my truck and let Marie know we're leaving. I won't be long." He opened the door and took off running.

Grabbing his jacket, Keeso stuffed the paper in his pocket and bent to strap on the knife holder Levi had given him.

"Maybe you should take the knife you used at our ceremony."

He shook his head as he slipped the knife Lenn had given him into the sheath. "It's too big. I can't keep it out of sight. The Hopi blade will be enough." He took her arm and pulled her around to face him. "Em, there's no reason for you to go along. I don't need to worry about both you and Levi."

"You don't have to worry about me. Just save Levi."

"He wants to kill you, too. That's why he's insisting you go out there. You know that."

She pulled out of his grasp and hurried out the door. That was when she heard it.

Keeso caught up with her. "Emma—"

"Listen. Can you hear that?

"Hear what?"

"There's a dog whining."

He paused for a moment, then nodded. "I hear it." Turning in the direction of the sound, he cupped his lips and shouted, "Pup!"

Frenzied barking and scratching answered his call.

"It's him. Get his leash." He disappeared in the dark.

She retrieved the leash and ran toward the Jeep when she saw Lenn crossing the road.

"Where's Keeso?"

"Going after Pup. We heard him barking. Maybe Levi's with him."

Keeso appeared, hanging onto Pup's collar. The dog tried to pull ahead, dancing on his hind legs. Levi wasn't with them. Fighting back tears, she bent and snapped the leash onto Pup's collar.

"Let's go." Keeso fished the keys out of his pocket and tossed them to Lenn. "You drive."

They reached Highway 264 and headed west. It wasn't long before Lenn made a fishtail right onto a secondary blacktop.

Emma panicked. "This is the wrong turn. We haven't gone far enough."

Lenn never took his eyes off the dark road. "Apparently Levi's kidnapper doesn't know the area—probably got his directions off a tourist map. This leads to Mishongnovi, but it's closer. We'll save a few miles going this way." He glanced over at Keeso. "Do we have a plan?"

"He's got to know Emma won't be alone, but he might not expect two of us. If I can get around behind him, I might be able taken him by surprise. It depends on where he's taken Levi."

"Sounds reasonable, but I should be the one to circle around. I know the area, you don't."

Keeso shook his head. "That won't work. You've got the gun. You need to stay close to Emma."

"I can give you the gun."

"I've never shot a gun in my life. Never even held one."

"All right. I'll stay with Emma. Open the bag at your feet. I brought along something that might help."

Keeso lifted the bag to his lap and unzipped it. "What am I looking for?"

"Night goggles. A friend of mine gave me a pair a few months ago. Said it would give me an added advantage when I'm after poachers at night. It's amazing what you can see."

When they reached the village of Mishongnovi, everything was quiet, the houses dark. The Jeep was still climbing as they passed through. She couldn't see more than a few feet beyond the car lights, but her mind conjured images of steep cliffs above them and heart-stopping drop-offs across the Highway. Outside the village, a low rock barrier lined the opposite side of the road, following the curve that angled right. The wall ended just before she saw the side road.

Lenn turned and slowed to a crawl. "He'll be somewhere along here. The question is where. It's secluded—only a few houses and they're spread out. It's open though. He won't be able to ambush us." He glanced at Keeso. "It will be harder for you to get around him."

"We'll figure it out." He released his seatbelt, leaned back, and reached up to snap the plastic cover off the dome light.

She leaned out of the way. "What are you doing?"

"Making sure he won't see me getting out of the car." He dropped the small bulbs in her hand. "Put these in the glove box." He removed two more bulbs from the front and handed them to her. "That should take care of it."

A minute later, they spotted headlights in the distance. The vehicle sat in the middle of the road, its bright lights preventing them from seeing anything else. She couldn't seem to catch her breath. Levi was out there somewhere with the man who'd murdered his mother and father. Keeso reached back and grasped her hand. "Stay in the car. Lenn can let him know you're here. You don't have to make yourself a target."

She didn't argue, but she didn't make any promises. Instead, she squeezed his hand. "Be careful. He won't hesitate to kill you."

"I'll be careful. We'll get Levi back. Lenn, keep the Jeep's headlights on bright. He won't be able to see you any better than you can him."

Keeso slipped the goggles over his eyes, adjusted the head strap, and glanced outside the car. The green cast distracted him momentarily, but he was soon amazed at his ability to identify the surrounding area. When he glanced at the other car, a green explosion of light jarred him back against the headrest. He closed his eyes. They burned as if he'd stared into the sun. He ripped the goggles off and wiped his face with his sleeve.

"Sorry, I should've warned you about that." Lenn hadn't stopped the car. "Are you gonna to be able to do this? We don't have much time. He'll see the door open if we get much closer."

Keeso replaced the goggles. "I know. My vision's beginning to clear." He opened the door and stepped out on the running board. Moving back, he quietly closed his door. Grasping the rear door handle in one hand for balance, he stepped off the running board and took a couple of steps before turning it loose to run alongside.

Boulders dotted the side of the road, some the size of buses. He stayed close to the Jeep, using the glare of its lights for cover. Lenn drove five, maybe eight miles an hour. He was dropping behind. A string of good-sized boulders lay ahead. He veered away from the Jeep and sprinted in their direction. Jogging from one boulder to the next, he drew closer to the parked car. The goggles had stopped him from tripping over box-sized rocks or sideswiping clustered boulders, but the glare from the headlights finally forced him to toss them aside. If he couldn't find them later, he'd buy Lenn a new pair.

The Jeep's brake lights came on and a moment later, the motor shut off and a door slammed. Lenn stepped in front of the vehicle's lights, making himself a target. Twenty, maybe twenty-five feet separated the two cars, with the sedan edging what was probably a sheer drop-off. From this distance the car looked empty. Hoping Lenn's appearance was enough of a diversion, he jogged to the last boulder in line. From his new position, he could tell the sedan was empty, but a shadowy figure hunched on the other side of the vehicle just outside of the light's beam.

Bending low, he inched toward the sedan, praying he'd get close enough to stop whatever happened next.

"I told the woman to come alone." A medium-sized, balding man stepped into the light. Levi dangled limp in his left arm. He held him like a shield against his body. His right hand held a gun to the boy's head.

Lenn shook his head. "You didn't really believe I'd let her meet you alone, did you?"

"I didn't believe she was stupid enough to defy me. Not with the boy's life at stake. And he is alive. He's sleeping. Did you know you can still buy ether? Not for medical use, of course. But it's around. First things first." He waved his gun toward Lenn. "I'd be more comfortable if you dropped that gun on the ground. And don't try to be a hero. If you got off a lucky shot and hit me without hitting the boy, we'd both go over the cliff." He laughed, the mirthless sound sending chills down Keeso's body. "I'm bettin' you grew up around here, probably know this country by heart. How far down is it, do you think—fifty, a hundred feet to the bottom? Now get rid of the gun before I decide I can drop the kid over the edge and blow your head off before you get your gun out of its holster."

Lenn raised his right hand and slowly reached across his body with his left hand to lift the gun from its holster, dropping it on the ground at his feet.

"That's good. Now I want the woman where I can see her."

Keeso tensed. *Don't do it, Em. Stay in the car.*

A door slammed. Emma appeared in the glare of the headlights, moving to stand beside Lenn.

Keeso's heart slammed against his ribs. Intentional or not, she'd made herself an easy target, giving the killer exactly what he wanted.

Pup was beside Emma, lunging at the leash she held, barking and snarling, intent on getting to Levi—and the killer.

"I see you found the dog. He's a good one. Thought I might go back and get him when this is over." He heaved an exaggerated sigh. "Keeping him is impossible now that he's seen me with the boy. Look at him. That mutt would tear me apart if I gave him the chance. I suppose he'll have to go too."

"Please don't hurt Levi. He's just a baby."

"You're not stupid, lady. You had to know it was gonna end this way. You should've been dead months ago—the kid, too. For a while I thought the fire took care of you both. But you were identified at the bank. Have to admit, you did a good job of staying ahead of me. If it hadn't been for that cowboy, I'd have finished you in Colorado. Where is he, by the way?"

"I don't know who you're talking about."

"We both know that's a lie." He shrugged. "No matter. With you and the boy in my sights, he can't do a thing. I'd still like to know how he got you to Arizona in the middle of the Hopi reservation. They've treated you like a long-lost relative, haven't they? Closed ranks around you. If it hadn't been for that little incident at the Grand Canyon, I'd still be looking for you. It's amazing how much information you can get from the media these days. There must've been a dozen or more pictures of you and the cop on Facebook alone. It didn't take me long to find out who he was or where you were." He heaved an exaggerated sigh. "And here we are, out in the middle of nowhere. I think we'll take care of the dog first." The barrel of the gun lowered toward the dog, then suddenly raised to Emma. "Or not."

"No!" Keeso was on his feet and running, knowing he couldn't make it in time.

"Emma, get down!"

The gun discharged. Lenn jumped in front of her and they both crumpled to the ground.

Keeso went after the killer. Pup got there first, knocking the man off balance. He tossed Levi toward the cliff and grabbed the dog's throat.

Levi rolled twice before going over the edge. Keeso lunged and slid on his belly, grabbing his son's shirt as he went over, praying the material would hold.

Pup yelped and was suddenly quiet. Keeso couldn't spare the dog a glance as he struggled to get a better hold on Levi and pull him to safety.

"I wondered where you were hiding."

Keeso tensed and slowly rolled onto his back, Levi dangling by an arm, and stared into the barrel of the man's revolver.

"This is convenient. One bullet, two bodies."

Keeso yanked Levi up behind his back, shielding him with his body and stared into the dead eyes of a monster.

"Still playing the hero? The boy's still getting a bullet, you know. Right after you get yours."

The gun cracked.

Keeso flinched.

The killer's eyes never changed—not even when blood trickled down between them from the bullet hole dead-center in his forehead. The man's arm fell to his side and he toppled over the edge of the embankment. The sickening sound of his flesh striking rock echoed up a few seconds later.

Pulling Levi into his arms, he checked for a heartbeat. It was thready, but there. He glanced toward the Jeep. Emma sat on her knees beside Lenn—his gun in both hands, her arms stretched straight out, still aimed at a man who was no longer there.

# 39

✧

Keeso struggled to his feet, clutching Levi to his chest. "Em? It's okay. He's gone. You can put the gun down." Emma didn't move. "*Aamyia.* Levi's alive, but he needs you."

She took a deep breath and set the gun on the ground. "Levi?"

"He's still asleep." Keeso moved to her side and settled Levi into her arms. He knelt beside Lenn who was only now regaining consciousness. The wound in his shoulder didn't look as serious as the gash on his head. He must've slammed into the car when he jumped in front of Emma.

Leaving his friend for a moment, he ran to the back of the Jeep to grab a blanket and the first-aid kit. When he returned, Lenn was trying to sit up. Slipping an arm under his shoulders, Keeso supported him as he leaned against the Jeep's wheel, tucking the blanket behind him and around his shoulders.

Lenn pulled his wounded arm against his chest and sighed. "Where is he?"

Keeso had unbuttoned his friend's shirt and splashed disinfectant into the bullet hole. He reached for several thick gauze pads to pack against the wound. "The killer?" Tearing strips of tape from a spool, he secured the packing. "He's dead. Went over the edge."

Lenn grunted his satisfaction. "Levi?"

Keeso nodded toward Emma. "He's safe." Dousing a cotton ball with disinfectant, he cleaned the gash on Lenn's head. The wound wasn't as bad as he'd first thought. There was a good-sized knot, but the cut wasn't deep. The bleeding had already stopped.

"Where's my revolver?"

Keeso reached over and picked up the gun, handing it to his friend.

Lenn took it with his left hand, paused for a second, and lifted it close to his nose. "It's been fired. Who...?"

"Emma." He lowered his voice. "Clean shot to the head. I'll tell you about it later."

Lenn's eyes rounded. He nodded and flipped on the gun's safety before shoving it toward Keeso. "Wipe her prints off. Make sure you get them all. Wipe yours too." He leaned against the tire to watch him use a corner of the blanket to buff the metal before using the material to hand it back.

"Someone's coming." Keeso stood and watched two sets of headlights moving toward them.

"Probably someone from the village." Lenn slipped the gun into its holster. "They must have heard the shots. Let me do the talking."

"Good idea." Keeso moved to Emma's side, bending to help her to her feet. "Let's get you and Levi into the Jeep." The less contact they had with anyone right now, the better.

Emma leaned into his side as they walked to the Jeep. "What about Pup?"

He'd forgotten about the dog. "I'll find him soon as I get you into the Jeep."

He'd just gotten them settled into the back of the Jeep when several car doors slammed behind him. He moved to stand beside Lenn.

Four men with rifles aimed at the ground approached cautiously.

Lenn recognized one of them. "Thomas, my friend, have you come to check out the noise?"

The man gave Keeso a wary glance before hunkering down in front of Lenn. "You get yourself shot up?" He pulled Lenn's shirt back to check the wound, and eyed Keeso. "You do this?"

"The bandage? Yes. The bullet? No."

His attention returned to Lenn. "You know who shot you?" The other three moved in closer and squatted beside Thomas.

"Not really. You don't have to worry about him, though. He's at the bottom of the ravine."

The men grunted their satisfaction.

Keeso touched Lenn's good shoulder. "I need to find Pup."

Lenn nodded and waved him on. "Go. We'll make sure Emma and Levi stay safe."

"Thanks." He sprinted to the killer's car, praying the dog was still there. He was. Pup lay on the opposite side of the sedan. He growled, but a word from Keeso immediately set his tail thumping. He raised his head and whined as he tried to sit up.

"Easy boy." Dropping to his knees, he ran his hands over the dog's body, not sure of what had happened to him. He'd been too busy keeping Levi from falling over the cliff to pay attention to the dog's struggles with the killer. He touched the dog's head and Pup yelped. "Sorry, fella. Let's see what's wrong." He found a knot as big as the one on Lenn's head over Pup's left ear. "Got you with something big, didn't he?" Using as much care as possible, he lifted the dog into his arms and carried him back to the Jeep.

"How bad is he?" Lenn's voice seemed weaker.

"Better than you, I think. As far as I can tell, he was only hit in the head. How are you feeling?"

"I've been worse."

"Yeah? Well, we should probably let a doctor decide that. As soon as I get Pup in the Jeep, we'll get you to the healthcare center." One of the Hopi men opened the back door for him, and he gently eased the dog onto the seat next to Emma and Levi. "Don't touch his head. There's a good-sized bump on it." Before he got the door shut, Pup had crawled forward to rest his head against the boy.

Lenn was standing, supported by Thomas. "Take your family home, Keeso. Thomas will make sure I get to the health center. I'll probably end up in Phoenix before morning. They don't do bullets at the center."

"You're sure?"

"Take your wife home, brother. This is a Hopi matter."

Keeso understood. Lenn intended to protect them. Their presence at the hospital would complicate the situation—someone was bound to remember Emma's visit and the fact that she too had been admitted with a bullet wound. Their caution might still be a wasted effort. If Levi didn't show signs of recovering from the anesthesia soon, he wouldn't hesitate to bring his son to the center.

One of the men pulled the sedan to a wider area of the road and parked it on the side. While Thomas settled Lenn into his truck, Keeso helped Emma get Levi into his booster seat. The boy moaned and muttered something under his breath. It was a good sign.

Emma buckled herself into the seat next to Levi. Pup, unable to reach Levi, put his head in her lap. She stroked the dog's soft coat, careful not to touch his head.

Keeso turned the Jeep around and followed the three vehicles back to the main highway. The car and one of the trucks turned off the main road at the village. Keeso continued to follow Thomas's truck until he reached Highway 264. When Thomas turned right toward the medical center, Keeso swung the Jeep to the left, heading home. Emma closed her eyes in prayerful gratitude. So many things could've gone wrong out there tonight. Every one of them had barely escaped death.... All but one.

"I killed a man." Her throat had tightened. The words barely escaped her lips.

Keeso heard anyway. "You killed a monster."

"I took a life that wasn't mine to take. He'd be alive now if—"

"Levi and I would be dead if you hadn't pulled that trigger. You traded one life for two—a psychopathic killer for your bond-mate and our son. He would've killed you as well and made sure Lenn was dead. You stopped him, Em. Don't you dare feel bad about it."

They pulled into the drive and he shut off the motor. "Who taught you to shoot like that?"

"No one. I've never shot a gun before. I hate them."

"I was looking into the barrel of his revolver. His finger was on the trigger when you fired that gun. Some people would call it a lucky shot. I prefer to believe a higher power guided your hand—and the path of the bullet. Think about that whenever you doubt what you did was right."

She didn't move until he'd come around the car and opened her door. Leaning in, he released the catch on her seatbelt. When she still didn't move, he brushed the hair out of her eyes. "Are you okay? Can you make it into the house?"

"Yes."

"Good." He kissed the top of her head before handing her the key. "Go open up. I'll bring Levi and come back for Pup.

"Marie needs to know what happened."

"Her car isn't there. Lenn probably called her." He lifted Levi out of the Jeep. Pup managed to follow him. After relieving himself, the dog followed Keeso on wobbly legs.

She ran ahead to Levi's room and turned down the covers. Keeso slipped the boy into bed and drew the blanket to his chin. Pup, still wobbly, couldn't make it onto the bed. Keeso gave him a hand and the dog snuggled against the boy's side. Levi pulled an arm out from under the blanket and wrapped it around Pup's neck. She breathed a relieved sigh. It was another good sign.

Levi would be all right.

Keeso slipped an arm around her shoulders. "Let's get you back to bed."

"I don't think I can leave him right now. He almost died."

"But he didn't and the man's dead, Em. He can't hurt Levi anymore." He hugged her closer. "Pup may be groggy, but he's not going to let anyone near that boy tonight. Neither will I." He walked her to the door, flipped the light switch, and the room darkened, with only the nightlight for illumination.

He paused at the entry to their bedroom. "If it'll make you feel better, I'll check outside, then double-check the doors and windows." She nodded. He touched the sleeve of her blouse. "You have blood on your clothes."

"It's Lenn's."

"I know. I can't get the image out of my mind. When you both went down, and I saw a flash of blood, I didn't know which of you had been shot. I couldn't stop him. I couldn't get to him in time."

She threw her arms around his waist, hugging him. His arms went around her, drawing her against his body. They held each other for long moments before she realized he was trembling. "Keeso, you can't second-guess yourself. You saved Levi. You were exactly where you were supposed to be. Let this go. For my sake."

He cupped her face in both hands and tilted her head up for his kiss. "I don't ever want to come that close to losing you again, *Aamyia*." His lips slanted across hers before he pulled away. "Go have a shower, Em. I'll check around the house and be back in a few minutes."

She didn't bother turning on the bedroom lights, just grabbed a nightgown and headed down the hall to the bathroom. A quick shower later, she slipped on her gown and dried her hair. Leaving the bathroom, she looked in on Levi. She doubted he had moved since they'd tucked him in bed. Pup didn't rouse when she ran her palm along his neck, but his tail wagged.

Keeso wasn't in their room. When she couldn't find him in the house, she began to worry. It didn't take this long to check the yard.

She'd reached for the switch on the bedside lamp when something moved on the back porch outside her window. Clutching her gown at her neck, she leaned on the sill and nudged the curtain open.

Keeso.

He was all right. The tension drained from her body so quickly her knees nearly buckled. She opened the curtains to see him better. He should have noticed her, but he didn't. Leaning against the porch rail, he stared at the endless expanse of stars. The sky was so big and wide, the full moon couldn't wash out their brilliance.

He shifted, and his face caught the moon's glow. Stark. Vulnerable. The anguish she read in his features tore at her heart. Had nearly losing her and Levi tonight heightened the pain of not knowing what had happened to his people? Any doubt she might have harbored about his origins died in that moment. The emotion overwhelmed her. Vision blurred, she reached up to wipe the tears away. The action finally caught his attention and they were suddenly eye to eye.

He turned and moved out of her sight, and the back door opened and closed. She pivoted to face the bedroom door and waited. He took his time coming to her. Ten… fifteen minutes passed. Still, she waited.

And then he was there, stepping into their room. He paused when he saw her. He'd expected her to be in bed, hopefully asleep. She read it in his expression.

The need to go to him was powerful, but she stayed in place. He was unapproachable, a man apart from this planet and the people who inhabited it—but not alien. Her eyes, and her body's reaction to him, attested to that.

Even now, the attraction was strong. He'd showered while she'd waited. His damp hair was tied at the nape of his neck. Loose pajama bottoms replaced the breechcloth he'd worn a few hours ago, but the muscles of his bare chest and arms reminded her of his raw strength.

But he was still Keeso, the man who had vowed to keep them safe, this man who longed to go home. A sob caught in her throat. She needed to go to him, to comfort him.

And still, she couldn't move. It was as if he had erected a barrier between them and only he could lift it. The need to go to him, to somehow make things right, surged through her like electricity, humming in her mind and in her blood. She couldn't stand still, nearly danced with the need to run to him, to hold him, to heal the void in his heart.

"Emma." He opened his arms, and suddenly the barriers were gone. Crying out, she threw herself into his arms, the need to touch him overwhelming.

He buried his face in her hair and whispered words she didn't understand. He found her lips. She opened her mouth and his tongue swept in to taste her.

Groaning, he lifted her into his arms and carried her to their bed, climbing in without turning her loose, pulling the covers over them both. She was surrounded by his body, cocooned in his embrace.

He nibbled her ear, sucking the lobe into his mouth. His teeth grazed her neck, his tongue teasing the sensitive place between her neck and shoulder. She moaned and slashed her fingers through his hair as his mouth moved to the pulse point at her throat. He found the buttons on her gown, loosened them, and slipped his hand inside to cup her breast, his thumb brushing the taut nipple. He pushed the fabric aside and his lips closed over the tender flesh. She cried out and pulled his head closer. His hot mouth sent scorching sensations to her core.

He tore his mouth free and rolled between her thighs. She gasped. Her nightgown had worked its way above her hips and his pajama bottoms were open. His hard manhood throbbed against her. His lips claimed hers in a long, drugging kiss that left her wanting more.

He dragged his lips away, threw the cover back and pulled her nightgown over her head. She reciprocated, sliding his pajama bottoms over his hips, caressing him as he kicked the offending garment away. His mouth found hers again, his tongue dueling with hers, his hot body settling on top of her. He urged her legs farther apart, caressing her thighs as he lifted her hips to push his thick arousal into her.

She tried to ignore the discomfort as he slowly embedded himself. It had only been a few hours since she'd given him her virginity. She was bound to be sore. But she'd wanted this—no, she needed this, needed him.

His mouth glided from her lips to her ear. "I was going to wait before we did this again, give you time to heal. Am I hurting you?" He started to pull out.

She raised her hips, keeping him deep inside her. "Don't leave me. I need you right where you are."

He growled, capturing her lips for a tongue thrusting kiss and sank deeper into her liquid heat. She was so tight, so perfect for him. She thrust her hips up, rocking against his pelvis, taking every inch of him in. Shuddering, he grabbed her hips to still them and fought for control.

Tearing her lips free, she threw her arms around his neck and panted against his ear. "I can feel you swelling inside me. I want to move."

"*Aamyia*, if we continue this conversation, or you grind against me one more time, we'll be finished before I can bring you to pleasure." He withdrew until only the tip of his arousal remained, and ever so slowly pushed deep into her once more. She moaned and trembled beneath him. He withdrew again and again, burying himself in her exquisite depths, increasing the mating rhythm.

Her body stiffened, tightening around him. She tore her lips from his and gasped. "Keeso."

He growled her name and thrust twice more before giving himself up to the glory of his own orgasm.

They held each other, hearts pounding, bodies trembling, their breathing harsh. He rolled to her side, pulling her against him. She sighed and rested her hand in the center of his chest—over his heart.

He placed his hand on top of hers. "I love you. You know that, don't you?"

She nodded against his chest. "I know. I love you too. I hadn't realized how much until I thought that monster was going to kill you."

His arms tightened around her. "Don't think about it. Not now."

She didn't say any more. He thought she'd fallen asleep and was about to doze off when she broke the silence. "Out there tonight, when you were standing on the porch, you were thinking about your home, your real family, weren't you?"

"My home, yes. But you and Levi are my family. I was thinking of the circumstances that brought me to this planet." He brushed the hair out of her eyes and touched his lips to her forehead. "That brought me to you."

"I felt your anguish, as if what had happened to you had happened to me. I wanted to comfort you."

He rose up on an elbow. Moonlight slanted into the room through the parted drapes, catching his solemn expression. "We share a connection, *Aamyia*. I believe we were destined to be together. You will always be in my heart, in my soul." He tangled his fingers in her hair and pulled her head up for a gentle kiss.

"It's hot in here and we're both covered with perspiration." He rolled out of bed, giving her an uninhibited view of his magnificent body as he reached across the nightstand to open the window.

"What, no basin of water for a sponge bath?"

He laughed at her teasing and swooped down to catch her up in his arms. "I'm in the mood for a shower."

# 40

✧

Emma held stone still, willing the queasiness away before she got out of bed. So far, she'd been able to control the nausea she'd experienced every morning for the past few days. The nausea, sore breasts, and exhaustion were all symptoms her sister had experienced when she carried Levi. If she didn't know better....

Impossible. The doctors had been emphatic. There would be no children in her future—at least no biological children. Levi was as close as she was going to get biologically.

Besides, the symptoms were way too soon. Not even a full two weeks had passed since her wedding night. According to her menstrual cycle, she would've been fertile only a day after the wedding. She would've had to conceive the first night they'd made love. Not that there wasn't ample opportunity for conception. Her lusty Centallian was most attentive.

Her last period had been two weeks before the wedding, and she was never late.

She'd bought a pregnancy test yesterday when she'd shopped for groceries. According to the instructions, it was too early to get a positive, even if she were pregnant. But Denise had tested at the onset of her first symptoms and gotten a positive. She'd test now to ease her mind and test again later if—no when—she got a negative, just to be sure.

She tried to climb out of bed, but Keeso's arm tightened possessively around her waist. Patting his hand, she whispered, "I'll be back in a minute." He mumbled something and let her go. A few seconds later, his breathing was deep and even again.

She returned from the bathroom, slipped back into bed, and stared up at the ceiling.

Positive. It didn't make sense.

Keeso reached over, pulling her against him and nuzzling her neck. "Something wrong?"

What was she supposed to tell him?

He leaned up on an elbow and kissed her. "You know you can talk to me if you have a problem."

"I know. I promise I won't keep anything important from you." She put on a smile. "Pup's up. I let him out on my way back from the bathroom. And if Pup's up, Levi won't be far behind. Breakfast?"

"I'd rather spend a little more time in this bed with my beautiful bond-mate. If we're quick enough—"

"Aunty. I can't find Pup."

Keeso sighed and swung his feet over the edge of the bed. "So much for what I'd rather do." He pulled her over for a quick kiss and brushed the hair out of her eyes. "You look tired. Go back to sleep. I'll make Levi's breakfast this morning."

She didn't argue. A little more sleep might alleviate the nausea and ease her exhaustion.

Voices woke her. How long had she been asleep? Climbing out of bed, she put on her robe and moved to the door, opening it a crack. Keeso and Lenn sat at the dining room table drinking coffee. Slipping into denim jeans and a long-sleeved flannel shirt, she sat on the side of the bed to put on her socks and shoes. She was fastening the last button on her blouse when she walked into the front room.

Both men stood. Lenn still wore the sling that protected his wounded arm. Marie insisted he wear it until his doctor's appointment at the end of the week.

Keeso pulled her into his arms for a hug. "You didn't sleep long. Can I get you some breakfast?"

"I think I'll wait for lunch, but a cup of mint tea sounds good. Where's Levi?"

"He and Sarah are in his room playing cowboys and Hopi."

She tilted her head and raised an eyebrow. "You're kidding."

Keeso grinned. "Nope. I think Pup's the cowboy."

A glance at the kids on her way to the bathroom confirmed Keeso's account. The two were sitting in the middle of the floor. Sarah concentrated on weaving reed strips while Levi squinted through a hole in a bead he attempted to thread. Pup lay on Levi's bed, his head on his paws, sound asleep, with Levi's Stetson tilted precariously on top of his head.

Her husband had a cup of hot mint tea waiting for her when she returned to the table. He stood at the stove, hot pad in hand reaching for the coffee pot. "Lenn came by to tell us about the investigation."

She sat at the table and waited for Keeso to fill their cups with coffee. Lenn seemed to appreciate the unique blend of coffee grounds and egg. He always accepted a cup and she'd never once seen him grimace after swallowing a mouthful, so he wasn't just being polite. She admired the man's fortitude. "How are you feeling?"

"The arm's a little stiff, but the doctor says it's healing well. I could do without the therapy, though."

"I never had the chance to thank you. You saved my life and nearly got yourself killed doing it. You saved all of our lives that night."

He shrugged and winced. "Keeso and I share ancestors. We are brothers and you are my brother's wife. We Hopi protect our own."

"You were telling Keeso about the investigation?"

"You didn't miss much. When I got out of recovery after the surgery, my boss and the tribal chairman were waiting in my room. I told them about Levi's kidnapping and the note demanding you go to the killer. I told them everything except who fired my gun. No one else needs to know it wasn't me.

It took two days to find the killer and take him out of the ravine. And another day before they found the gun. His wallet was still in his pocket. He was FBI."

She took a sip of tea and set the cup back in the saucer. "That doesn't surprise me. When the safehouse was compromised, I knew someone connected with the case had to be responsible."

"By the time we identified him, the feds had listed him as missing. As soon as the department filed our report, they contacted us. They knew he was in Arizona and they knew he was looking for you and Levi. He hadn't mentioned where in Arizona he was, or that he had seen the photos of us posted in the media. The gun he used that night was a small caliber pistol, probably a twenty-two—not an FBI-issued weapon. We'll have to wait for ballistics results, but I'm guessing he used the same gun to kill your sister and brother-in-law. The same one he used on you."

Keeso reached over and took her hand, squeezing it before turning his attention to Lenn. "Has the FBI asked about Emma?"

"I don't know. I've been on medical leave and haven't been at the office much. I do know they've sent a couple of agents to take over the investigation. This may be Hopi land but a federal agent's dead. It's gonna look suspicious if we don't cooperate."

He ran his fingers through his hair. "Look, as far as the Hopi are concerned, he tried to murder one—no, two—of our own on Hopi land. If I hadn't gotten shot, we could've made this go away. But a bullet wound gets reported and my department's playing damage control. Hopefully, what an FBI agent was doing on Second Mesa, and why he'd shoot a Hopi police officer with a non-issue weapon, will remain a mystery. But I don't think they're going to let it rest, and there are too many ties to you waiting to be discovered."

Fear closed her throat and she had to swallow twice before she could speak. "What ties?"

Lenn leaned back in his chair. "The FBI's good at putting things together. It's what they do best. They know Billingsley—that was the killer's name—was looking for you. I don't know how he managed to get assigned to your case, but he did. They have his handgun and the bullet that came out of my shoulder. I'm sure they have a file on your sister and her husband with the bullets that killed them, and one on your shooting as well. It won't take much to tie the crimes to that weapon. There's always the chance he got rid of each gun after he used it, but I don't think so. He was arrogant and probably believed he wouldn't be connected to the murders. And he was determined to see that the only witnesses to the original crime were dead, too. Unfortunately, his cell phone was still on the body when we brought it up. He'd downloaded several pictures of us from the Grand Canyon. That's how he found you. Once the feds get a look at his phone, they'll discover them. They'll want to talk to you."

Keeso scooted closer and put his arm around her shoulders. "Don't panic, *Aamyia*. You haven't done anything wrong."

"He's right, Emma. You're not in trouble and now that Billingsley is gone, you're probably no longer in danger. The most they can do is put you in protective custody until everything is cleared up."

"That's not gonna happen." Keeso's arm tightened around her. "Billingsley wasn't the only one involved."

"But Billingsley was the only one she and Levi could identify."

"I still don't trust them."

Lenn shrugged "They might only want to make sure Billingsley didn't get to them before he died."

"Whatever the reason, my bond-mate and son are not going with them."

Lenn nodded. "My people and I will do everything in our power to protect you and your family." He drew a deep, agitated breath and stood. "We may be anticipating something that will never happen." He looked down at her, his eyes sympathetic. "I admire your strength, my friend. But I see the strain is taking its toll. Hopefully this will be over soon and you, Keeso, and Levi can begin new lives."

Keeso stood and offered him his hand. "Thank you for everything. Please extend my thanks to the chairman."

Lenn paused for a long moment, eyes locked with Keeso. Nodding once, he turned and left the house.

She stood and set the teacup in the sink before turning to face her husband. "Why did that feel like goodbye?"

He moved to where she stood, pulling her into his arms. "Perhaps because that is what it was. The Hopi have given us as much protection as they can. It's time to leave."

# 41

"Leave? Now?"

He gave her a quick kiss. "Don't panic. We have time to get ready. We won't leave until it gets dark."

"That's only a few hours. We have to pack our clothes and food—what about Levi and Sarah? And I haven't had time to tell you about—"

"Take a deep breath, *Aamyia.*" He walked her to the couch and sat down, pulling her into his lap. "Stop worrying. Levi and Sarah are fine where they are. Let them play. They're going to miss each other after we leave. Only pack the necessities. Lenn will see that what's left is distributed to those who need it." He pulled her against his chest and kissed her forehead. "Now, what haven't you told me?"

She looked into his eyes. "I think I'm pregnant."

'What!" He stood so fast he nearly dumped her onto the floor. Only his quick reflexes kept her from falling. "Tell me I didn't hear you right. You can't be pregnant. The doctors—"

"I know what the doctors said. I didn't believe it, either, but I tested this morning. It came up positive."

"I don't care what came up, Em. You *can't* be pregnant." The horror of what he and Hiilani had suffered—the loss of their terribly deformed child, the near loss of Hiilani—flashed through his mind. "We should never have taken the chance. The risk was too great. If we're genetically incompatible…."

She took his face in both hands. "We have better than a fifty-fifty chance of being compatible. We have to cling to that hope."

He hugged her against him. "I can't stand the thought of you suffering through what Hiilani did." Lifting her into his arms, he headed for the bedroom.

"What are you doing?"

"You need to be in bed."

"Why? I'm pregnant, not sick. And I may not be pregnant. Tests can be wrong." He eased her onto the mattress and began unlacing her shoes. "Keeso, stop that." She jerked her foot away. "It's your turn not to panic. I'm fine." She started to leave the bed, but he pressed his hand against her shoulder, keeping her in place.

"Let me up."

He shook his head. "There's more than our incompatibility to consider. Do you know if you can carry a baby to term? Did the doctors say anything about the internal damage the bullet caused?"

"The doctors repaired the damage to my womb, but never speculated on my ability to carry a child to term. They were convinced I couldn't conceive." She placed her hand on his. "You need to be reasonable. Even if I did suffer damage, the baby won't be big enough to cause any problems for three, maybe four months."

"With an ordinary child from two Earth parents, that might be true. But our baby is half Centallian, and as improbable as it seems, our child's development will be controlled by its Centallian genes. A Centallian baby is fully developed in five Earth months. You'll have to reevaluate your timeframe." He bent, touching his lips to hers, then left the room and closed the door behind him.

She'd looked stunned. He understood the feeling.

✦

Emma was having trouble processing what he'd just told her. Five months?

That would explain the early symptoms. But shouldn't the mother's body dictate the gestation period of her baby? She hadn't thought much about it—actually, hadn't thought about it at all. She slipped her legs over the side of the bed and bent to retie her shoelace. She might have to reconsider when she had to start taking precautions, but her pregnancy—if it was real—shouldn't be in danger yet.

She pulled her duffel bag off the top shelf of the closet and set it on the bed. Staring at it, she suddenly felt overwhelmed. How many times would she be forced to stuff this piece of luggage with clothes, take Levi and run? Now, thanks to her, Keeso was forced to run, too. He didn't deserve another complication in his life, not after all he'd been through.

Emptying her underwear drawer into the duffel, she ran to the closet and slid the hangers across the rod. She grabbed two short-sleeved blouses, one long-sleeved, and a sweater, folded them, and slipped them into the duffel. A pair of jeans and two pair of slacks followed. She managed to squeeze in two nightgowns—one warm cotton, and the other Keeso's favorite.

Spotting the chest where Keeso kept his armor, she grabbed an arm-load of his clothes and placed them inside. As a last thought, she grabbed the garment bag holding her wedding dress and lay it on top. She needed a few personal items from the bathroom and she'd be ready to pack Levi's things.

Keeso looked up from the cooler he was loading and frowned when she came out of the bedroom with the duffel. "You're supposed to be resting."

"I promise I'll rest later. I packed some of your things in the chest. It's ready to go to the Jeep."

"What do you have left to finish?"

"Not much. I need a few things from the bathroom and to get Levi ready."

"That's all?"

"That's all."

He gave her a quick nod and closed the lid on the cooler. "I'll get the chest."

After stuffing the items from the bathroom into the duffel, she set it beside the cooler on the couch and went to Levi's room where he and Sarah were still playing. She dreaded telling him they had to move again. Grabbing his backpack from the closet, she began packing his clothes. But when she put his favorite toys in, his eyes rounded with worry.

Sinking onto his bed, she patted the place beside her. "Come sit by me for a minute." He took his time. He obviously knew what she was about to tell him and didn't want to hear it.

"Honey, I'm sorry, but we have to leave."

"Is the bad man coming back?"

"Oh, no. No." She pulled him onto her lap and hugged him close. "He can't ever come back, I promise you. But it's time for us to leave our Hopi friends and go on another adventure."

"Will Keeso and Pup go, too?"

"Of course they will. You, Keeso, Pup, and I are a family now. Remember?"

"Can Sarah come with us?"

"No. Sarah needs to stay with her mommy and daddy. They would be very sad if she went away."

"I don't want to leave."

"I don't want to leave, either, but sometimes we have to do things we don't want to do." She stood and finished filling Levi's backpack.

"Do you have the necklace Keeso bought you?"

Levi nodded and fished inside his shirt, pulling the agate out for her to see. "Me and Sarah always wear our necklaces 'cuz they match." Sarah pulled her own necklace from beneath her blouse to show her. The two children held their half-agates together, making a whole. It was something else they'd have to remember each other by.

On a sudden thought, she pulled her cell out of her pocket. "Why don't you and Sarah stand by Pup and I'll take your picture?" She took several, thinking to have prints made. She'd mail Marie a set when she got them copied.

Keeso walked in from outside as she re-entered the living room with Levi's backpack. "Everything's in the Jeep."

She sank to the couch with a tired sigh. "I told Levi. He's not happy about the move. He and Sarah have grown close. It's going to be tough on him to leave his best friend."

"I know. I wish we didn't have to leave, but I can't let the FBI find us."

"Why are we waiting until tonight to leave?"

He sat down beside her and pulled her into his arms. "You were beginning to panic. I thought you'd be calmer if you weren't rushed. We can leave whenever you're ready, but I would prefer you rest first."

She was in the mood to cooperate. "A nap right now sounds wonderful."

"Good. I'm glad you're being reasonable." He stood and pulled her to her feet. "I'll make sure you're not disturbed."

"You're not always going to get your way."

He laughed and put his arm around her. "Sure I am. You love me, remember?"

"I know exactly what—"

The front door flew open, bouncing against the wall. Marie hadn't bothered to knock. "Keeso, they're almost here. Lenn says you need to leave now."

# 42

✧

Emma couldn't move. Keeso gave her a gentle shake. "Grab the backpack and get in the Jeep. I'll get Levi."

Marie leaned against the doorframe, breathing hard. "Where's Sarah?"

Keeso glanced over his shoulder as he headed down the hall. "Sarah's with Levi in the bedroom. I'll bring her."

Snatching Levi's backpack, Emma headed for the door, stopping to give Marie a hug. "Thank you for everything. You've become a dear friend and I'll never forget you."

Marie tightened the hug. "We are like sisters. My heart goes with you." She pushed her toward the doorway. "Now hurry."

Keeso carried both children into the living room. He handed Sarah to Marie and put his arm around Emma. "Tell Lenn thank you."

Marie nodded. "He's going to try to delay them to give you more time."

They raced to the Jeep with Pup keeping pace. Levi had a death grip on Keeso's neck, but one hand waved toward the house. At the Jeep, Emma looked toward the house. Sarah was leaning her head against Marie's neck, waving back. Both children were frightened and forlorn. She blinked away tears as she tossed Levi's pack and her duffel onto the rear floorboard. They were leaving good friends behind. She thought of Frank and Molly, the way they'd taken Levi and her in, and helped them escape. How many future good Samaritans would they have to depend on? How often would they be forced to hide like common criminals?

Where would they go—another state, maybe another country? Keeso's shuttle could take them anywhere they needed to go.

But what if she were pregnant? Running would be close to impossible.

"Em." Keeso's voice pulled her away from her dour thoughts. "*Aamyia*, it's going to be okay." He snapped Levi's seatbelt in place, and Pup nudged past her to jump into the seat beside the boy.

"Get in the car." He slammed Levi's door and opened his. She climbed in and reached for the seatbelt. Keeso pulled the Jeep out of the drive and gunned the motor. There was only time for one last wave.

He glanced over at her. "We'll be on a good road for a couple of miles, then it's pickup and bike trails. But we'll have the advantage out there. I know the area, they don't. Once we leave the main road, they'll be forced to slow down to avoid hitting the large rocks and losing control on uneven ground. I won't be able to drive as fast, but we can still outrun them."

He glanced at his rearview mirror. "Anyone behind us yet?"

She twisted around to look through the back window. "No, but a dark sedan just turned onto the road leading to the house. I don't recognize the car."

"It's probably the agents. Hopefully Marie or Lenn can delay them. We'll pick up speed when we clear the village."

Once they'd passed the last house, the road angled to the right and straightened. Keeso floored the accelerator, slowing only when the Jeep fishtailed on loose gravel.

"Are they following us?"

She glanced behind them. "There's something back there, but it's too far away. I can't tell if it's the same car, but it's moving fast enough to catch up with us."

"It's them." He increased their speed.

Her heartbeat increased as well. She'd heard somewhere that Jeeps were notorious for rolling over, something about being top-heavy. She glanced back to double-check Levi's seatbelt, then looked over at her husband. He didn't show any signs of stress. She took comfort in his calm attitude. If anyone could get them through this, he could.

She looked at her side mirror and caught her breath. "Keeso, they're getting closer. I'm pretty sure it's the sedan."

"Brace yourself, we're going off-road." He slowed the Jeep and pulled to the opposite side before leaving the road entirely. The vehicle bounced high a couple of times before settling into the bumpy terrain. It felt like they were driving over an old-fashioned washboard.

Keeso picked up speed and Emma's heart slammed into her throat. She thought they'd already been going too fast. Late afternoon sunlight slanted across the vast flatland, causing scrub brush and rocks to cast confusing shadows. "Are we going the right way? I don't see anything that looks like a path."

"It's there." He swerved to miss something she couldn't see. "Don't worry. Are they still behind us?"

It took her a second to find them. "They've left the road too, but farther back. They must've turned off the road when we did. I think they're angling across to cut us off. I don't think they've slowed down. They're gaining on us."

"I thought the FBI hired intelligent people. Keep an eye on them."

The sedan bounced high and came down hard but didn't slow. At that rate of speed, they'd be on top of them in a couple of minutes. The car bounced again. She was pretty sure it wasn't built for off-roading. With any luck, maybe they'd break an axle or something and be forced to give up the chase.

She glanced at Levi. His eyes had rounded with worry. "It's okay, honey. They're not trying to hurt us. They just want us to stop, but we don't want to."

She checked the sedan. "Oh no!"

He didn't take his eyes off the road. "What's wrong?"

"I'm not sure. They must have hit something. The car is on its side."

He kept driving.

"Keeso!"

"I'm not stopping until I get you to the shuttle. When you're safe, I'll go back and check."

"Keeso, stop the Jeep. No one's chasing us." She touched his arm. "We can't leave them. We don't know how badly they're hurt. Someone could bleed to death before you got back."

Keeso balanced the need to protect his family against his honor-bound duty to make sure his pursuers were not dying. Expelling an exaggerated sigh for Emma's benefit, he slowed the Jeep. She was right. He shifted gears and made a U-turn.

The sedan was on its side, but barely. Its side had come to rest on a low outcropping that had, fortunately, prevented it from rolling and probably saved their pursuers' lives.

"Stay in the Jeep." He opened his door and stepped out. As soon as he slammed the door, someone inside the car shouted for help. Going around to the back of the car, he leaned against the trunk and levered himself onto the outcropping. The vehicle rocked precariously.

"What's happening?" The voice inside the car was more than a little tense.

Keeso followed the outcropping to the front of the car and squatted down, peering through the windshield. Two men stared up at him, squinting against the sun at his back.

"Nothing's happening at the moment. Are either of you hurt?"

The driver nodded toward the man in the passenger's seat. "Ward might have broken his shoulder. He took the brunt of the impact when we went over."

"You?"

"My head bounced off the door frame. I'll probably have a headache for a couple of days, but I don't think it's serious."

"Are you both buckled in?"

"Yes. Why?"

"We need to get the car upright."

"How?"

He didn't bother explaining, but walked to the center of the car, grabbed the front and back door frames and lifted. Easing off, he allowed the car to roll back, then lifted again. On the third lift, he bent his back into the effort and the car teetered off the outcropping. All four tires hit the ground, causing the vehicle to rock like a spring horse on a playground. From the condition of the crooked wheel on the passenger's side, it wasn't going anywhere.

"How did you do that? It wasn't human."

"Never said I was human." He jumped down from the outcropping, walked to the driver's side, and looked through the open window. "Anyone bleeding?"

The driver glanced at his partner who shook his head. "No."

"You have a cell phone?"

"It's in my pocket. Why?"

"You'll need it to call for help." The agent unsnapped his seatbelt and started to get out of the car. "I'd stay in there if I were you. The lump on your head looks serious."

"I'm fine." The agent climbed out of the car and grabbed the door for support.

Keeso shook his head. "Figures."

"What's that supposed to mean?"

"It means you don't have the brains you were born with. You'd have to be stupid to tear out across this terrain in that vehicle."

"You didn't seem to have a problem with it."

"I was in a Jeep and I knew where I was going." He turned his back on the man and walked away.

"Where are you going?"

He kept walking. "Where I was headed before you turned your car over."

"I can't let you do that."

Keeso stopped. The hair on the back of his neck raised. He slowly turned.

The agent leaned against his open car door, his arms braced against the top, a revolver in his hand. The second agent had scooted across the seat and struggled to stand behind his partner. He cradled his injured arm with his left hand. Keeso figured they shared the same IQ.

"You're not taking the woman and boy anywhere."

"The woman is my bond-mate and Levi is my son. Where I go, they go."

"What's a bond-mate?"

"His wife." Emma stepped around Keeso. "I'm his wife."

He shoved her behind him. "I told you to stay in the Jeep."

"I'm not very good at taking orders."

"I've noticed."

"Miss Kent, why don't you and your nephew come over here by me? All I want to do is make sure you and the boy are safe."

"It's Mrs. Smith—Mrs. Keeso Smith, and believe me, I'm perfectly safe with my husband."

Multiple motors drew their attention. Five, maybe six vehicles—most of them pickups—had pulled off the road in the distance, heading cross-country in their direction.

"Aunty!" Levi threw himself at Emma's legs. She staggered, then swung him into her arms.

"Sweetie, you were supposed to stay in the Jeep."

Keeso shot her a look. "Just like his aunt."

She shrugged. "Pup wanted out, so I came with him."

Snarling at the agents, Pup scrambled around Keeso, positioning himself in front of his family. Hackles raised, his low, menacing growl warned them away. Keeso grabbed his collar.

The vehicles pulled up and stopped. Men scrambled out of truck beds, and car interiors. At least forty Hopi formed a circle around them—a human barrier against the man with the gun.

Lenn placed himself directly in front of Keeso. "It is good to see you are not harmed, brother."

"I'm most pleased to see you, as well." Pup was still growling and pulling at his collar.

"He seems to have taken a dislike to our friend over there."

Keeso shrugged. "I believe he has an aversion to men with guns."

"Understandable. I'm plagued by that attitude myself." Lenn turned and took a couple of steps toward the agent who stiffened and took aim.

"I'm a Hopi police officer. I'm reaching for my identification." Hampered by the sling on his right arm, he retrieved his wallet with his left hand and flipped it open to reveal his badge and identification. "In case you have forgotten, you are on Hopi land and have no jurisdiction here. Put away your weapon."

The agent complied, slipping the gun into the holster at his side. "Your chairman promised us full cooperation in this case."

"I don't remember him agreeing to holding a gun on one of us. Are you arresting these people?"

"We just want to take Miss Kent and her nephew into protective custody."

"Protection from who?"

The agent nodded toward Keeso. "Right now, from him."

"Has Mrs. Smith asked for protection from her husband?"

"Do you have proof they're married? He might be coercing her into saying they're married."

"I was at their wedding. Is that proof enough for you?"

Neither agent answered. They weren't even looking at Lenn. Mouths agape, both men stared past him. Lenn pivoted, releasing the safety on his handgun to face whatever danger the agents had seen.

Keeso felt the familiar tingle of static electricity and a sudden surge of relief and joy. A blue-tinged silver haze enfolded the immediate area and a formidable half-circle of Centallian Guardians materialized behind the Hopi.

He doubted Lenn's people, though aware of the Centallian's existence, had ever witnessed an actual bio-transfer. Some of the men tensed, tightfisted, while others placed their hands on or near the knives on their belts. None of them took their eyes off the two agents.

Pup lost his courage and tried to crawl behind Keeso. He let go of the dog's collar and gave him a pat. "It's okay, fella. They're friends."

Emma moved closer.

One of the men turned. Keeso smiled and bowed his respect to his commander. "Rhyel, I thought never to see you again."

Rhyel grasped his shoulders and pulled him into what the locals called a bear hug. "There was that possibility, my friend." He stepped back and glanced toward the two agents and the line of Hopi. "Is this your idea of keeping a low profile?"

"The situation became complicated in your absence."

"Obviously. I assume our Hopi friends are protecting you and...." He nodded toward Emma and Levi.

Keeso pulled her into his arms. "Emma, my bond-mate, and Levi, my son."

Rhyel bowed his respect. "I am honored."

Levi decided to be shy and buried his face in his aunt's neck.

She smiled. "I'm happy to meet you."

Nodding, he returned his attention to Keeso. "Is there business that needs completing before we depart?"

"That will be up to our Hopi brothers."

Lenn left the agents and stepped through the Hopi circle, his men closing ranks as he joined the Centallians and Emma. His mind eased, knowing Emma and Levi would never have to run again. They would be safe with Keeso's people.

He turned to Rhyel, bowing his respect in the Centallian manner of greeting. "I am pleased you have returned to us."

"And I am grateful for the aid your people have given our Guardian and his mate."

"Keeso is my brother. His family became ours to protect."

"Do you need further assistance?"

Lenn grinned. "These men do not belong on Hopi land. They will be taken before the chairman and he will decide what must be done."

Rhyel nodded and bowed his own respect. "Then we will leave you to your duty. If all goes well, we will meet again soon."

Keeso gave Lenn a final nod. Emma leaned over and kissed Lenn's cheek. There were tears in her eyes when she stepped back. "Thank you."

He flushed and reached out to pat Levi's back. "I will tell Sarah you have gone to live among the stars. She will understand."

He stepped away from the group.

Rhyel glanced toward the back of the Jeep and spotted the chest. "I assume you'll want your armor." He looked down at Pup who now sat beside Keeso, tail thumping. "Does he stay or go?"

"He goes." Keeso reached down and patted the dog's head. "He's part of the family." He opened the Jeep's back door and leaned in. When he straightened, he held Levi's backpack and Emma's duffel, setting both on top of the chest.

He put his arm around her. "Ready to go?"

Emma suddenly looked wary and tightened her hold on Levi. "Wait a minute. Go where?"

The silver-blue haze enfolded the Centallians and Keeso's family, then dissipated. They were gone.

Less than a minute later, Keeso reappeared. He opened the Jeep's front passenger door and retrieved a leather handbag. "She wanted her purse." Grinning at Lenn, he touched the small box on his belt and vanished.

Lenn spared a moment, wondering if he would ever see his Centallian brothers again. He knew that regardless of your planet of origin, life was uncertain.

His attention returned to the men still standing in the doorway of their vehicle, disbelief etched on their faces.

"I'll drive you to the health center. You can arrange to have your car towed from there."

"What just happened?" The agent's voice was unsteady.

Lenn shrugged. "That is entirely up to you to decide."

The younger man leaned toward his partner. "What do we put in our report?"

"Exactly what happened. They simply disappeared off the face of the Earth."

# 43

✧

All she'd said was, "I forgot my purse." Emma hadn't asked anyone to go after it, didn't even know why she'd mentioned it. The commander had smiled, removed this belt-thing from around his waist, and handed it to Keeso—who'd snapped it on, pushed a button, and disappeared.

What was she supposed to do now?

Levi hugged her neck and Pup plastered himself against her legs. They needed comforting. She needed comforting too and her husband wasn't here to give it. Did he really just go after her purse?

The static tingling she'd experienced when her husband vanished in the blue fog returned. A second later, Keeso appeared in front of her, holding out the purse. She took it, feeling a little disoriented, probably from the haze that hadn't completely dissipated. She swayed. Keeso grabbed Levi and slipped an arm around her.

"I need to sit down." There wasn't a chair in the huge room, but he led her to one of the chair-sized boxes lining the walls. It wasn't the softest of seats, but she gratefully sank onto it.

Setting Levi on the box too, he knelt in front of her. "Is it the baby?"

"Baby?" Rhyel had followed them and was within earshot. "There's a baby?"

The curt question and a hard stare were directed at Keeso.

She answered. "It's too soon to tell."

Rhyel still didn't look at her. His gaze was fixed on Keeso. "Have you…?"

Her husband's quick nod forestalled him.

The commander's dark eyes finally locked with hers. "There's a baby."

She violently shook her head and her stomach rebelled. "I think I'm going to be sick." They all took a step back. Even the dog moved. Rhyel had the presence of mind to grab a small container and stick it under her nose. He gave Keeso a scathing glance.

The nausea abated. She took a couple of deep breaths and handed the container back to the commander. "You don't understand. I can't get pregnant— it's physically impossible. The doctors were adamant."

Levi jumped down from the crate and threw his arms around Pup. She lowered her voice so only the men could hear her. "My symptoms are probably psychosomatic. They didn't start until after Levi was kidnapped and I killed the FBI agent."

"You did what?" Rhyel didn't bother to lower his voice. Pup growled. Levi raised his head, his eyes growing wider.

Keeso placed a hand on his friend's shoulder. "I'll explain everything later."

He glanced around the unfamiliar cargo deck. His eyes met and held Rhyel's. "I'm guessing we both have a lot to explain."

The commander nodded and turned his attention to Emma. "If you're feeling better, we can take the lift to the upper deck where our crew quarters are located."

"Crew quarters?" She grabbed Keeso's hand. "This isn't a shuttle?" She took in the large storage facility and shook her head. "Of course, it isn't." Her frantic gaze returned to him. "Are we on the *Novaria?*" She let go of him, snatched Levi into her arms and stood. "Keeso, why does your friend think we need quarters?"

He took Levi from her trembling arms and pulled her close. Her entire body was shaking. "Don't panic, Em. It can't be good for our baby. You're right, this isn't a shuttle. It isn't the *Novaria,* either. Her cargo bay is double the size of this one. But it is a Steller ship capable of traveling between solar systems." When she started to open her mouth, he shook his head. "Don't let that upset you. We're not going anywhere until you and I talk and agree on a plan of action. Until then, you and Levi will need a place to rest. Okay?"

"Okay."

On the next level, they turned left when the lift door opened. The corridor was much smaller than the *Novaria*'s, the walls dark, polished metal instead of the light bio-luminescent green he was used to. There were no intersecting passages—only one long hall with doors on each side and a door facing them at the end of the passage.

Rhyel led them toward that door. "We lost the *Novaria* in a stellar battle over New Centallus. It happened shortly after we returned from our last trip to Earth.

Keeso shook his head. "If you lost the *Novaria,* how did you manage to take the enemy ship?"

"Both ships were lost during the battle. We were as stranded on New Centallus as you were on Earth."

"And this ship?"

"Became a prize in a very costly battle."

Rhyel stopped walking and, resting his hands on his hips, stared down at the metal grates that composed the hall floor. "Close to three months ago, Kenchee mercenaries found our planet. We discovered them searching through the *Novaria*'s debris field. They'd found the *Acqeli.* We'd sifted through that field multiple times without locating the artifact and assumed it had been incinerated in the planet's atmosphere. We demanded its return. They chose to fight. Four good men died recovering the Crystal—Jaadel, Sandriis, Kaaden, and Siikzo."

"Siikzo?"

"He became a good friend. He died saving my life. The Senchee or alpha-males were killed. Without their leaders, the Cho-males ended their own lives before we could stop them. Their perverted sense of honor didn't allow them to live in defeat."

Rhyel resumed walking. "It took time to learn their ship's functions—we still don't know everything the vessel is capable of, but, fortunately, the technology is similar to ours."

"The *Requiem* is less than half the size of the *Novaria,* but it suits our purpose for the moment."

*"Requiem?"* Keeso tilted his head in question.

Rhyel lifted his shoulders. "The name seemed appropriate."

A double door automatically slid open to reveal a large octangular room with three doors on either side.

"The corridor we just passed through contained Cho crew quarters."

He gestured to the doors around the perimeter of the room. "The doors in this room lead to larger, more elaborate quarters. We believe they belonged to the Senchee-males since it was unlikely their mercenary ships carried VIPs. While our technicians became acquainted with the ship's inner workings, the living quarters were thoroughly cleaned and disinfected. We added a purification system to the water supply, refurbished the bathroom facilities to meet our needs, and raided the fortress supply rooms for Guardian-sized beds and furnishings."

He nodded toward the double door in front of them. "The bridge is through there. We're standing in the Commons area, where the men can relax when they're not on duty. There's a kitchen of sorts directly across from us. One of our Guardians is a decent cook. It's a far cry from the convenience and comfort of the *Novaria,* but we're grateful to have the ship."

He turned toward the closest door to the bridge. "These are your quarters. If you'll place your hand on the panel, I'll activate the recognition code." Keeso pressed his hand on the glass rectangle beside the door and Rhyel punched a few buttons.

The commander glanced at Emma. "Your turn."

She hesitated only a moment before touching her palm to the cool glass. Rhyel entered the code. After entering one more code, he smiled. "Try it."

The minute her hand touched the glass again, the door panel slid open, allowing them to walk into the room.

Rhyel remained in the Commons. He glanced at Keeso. "I'll be on the bridge. When you're finished, find me." He stepped back and the panel closed.

Keeso stood Levi on the floor. The boy and dog began a tentative exploration, Pup sniffing every corner of the odd-shaped room.

He took her hand. "You look overwhelmed."

"I feel overwhelmed. Keeso, what are we doing here? We were supposed to take the shuttle somewhere safe."

He led her to the bed, pulling her down to sit with him on the edge and gently squeezed her hand. "Take a deep, calming breath." When she did, he smiled. "Better?"

She nodded. "Are you going to answer my question?"

"You are here because it is the safest place we can be. But you don't have to stay here if you don't want to. Originally, the choices of where to go were limited. We could find a secluded place to live in your country until we were forced to hide again. Or, we could buy new identities and live somewhere outside of the country. It would be a difficult adjustment, yet it's less likely the authorities could find us. But now we have a third choice. We can return with Rhyel to New Centallus."

"Leave Earth?"

"Yes. And I can't pretend it isn't my first choice. But this is your decision. Whatever you decide, we'll be together. I won't leave you alone."

"What about your friends? You've only just found them."

"We won't lose contact."

He brought her hand to his lips. "We will have a problem, though, if you carry my baby. And for that reason, I want to offer you a compromise. Rhyel's bond-mate, Amber, is a physician. She is highly qualified in both trauma and obstetrics. She is the only physician I know of who can handle potential complications arising from an interspecies birth. Come to New Centallus with me. Allow Amber to examine you, and if you do carry my child, stay on New Centallus. Let her care for you until the baby arrives. If you want to go home when the baby is strong enough to travel, that's what we'll do."

Levi tugged on her sleeve. "Aunty, I have to go to the bathroom."

"Okay, honey. We'll—" She realized she had just no idea of where the facilities were.

Keeso glanced around the room. Obviously, he didn't know, either. Walking to the only door other than the entryway, he opened it and turned back with a smile. "Here you go, buddy. Just like at home."

Her nephew ran to the door and peeked in before going inside. He giggled when Pup tried to squeeze into the small enclosure with him. Keeso grabbed the dog's collar and backed him out before closing the door. A couple of minutes later, Levi returned to the larger room.

"Did you wash your hands?" The boy made a U-turn at his aunt's reminder and went back into the bathroom. A few seconds later, he ran back to his aunt and held up his hands. "See? They're all clean. I even dried them."

Just barely, but at least they weren't dripping wet. She smiled her approval.

He smiled back. "I'm hungry."

Keeso put his hand on the boy's shoulder. "Why don't we go to the kitchen and see what we can find? We'll get something for Pup, too." He glanced at her. "Join us?"

She shook her head. "I don't think my stomach could abide food right now."

He frowned. "You're still not feeling well?"

"I'm not feeling bad, really. Don't worry about me."

"Maybe you should rest for a while?"

The bed took up a good percentage of the room. "It's a big bed isn't it?"

"Guardians are big men."

Remembering the line of large men suddenly materializing in front of her, she smiled. "I noticed."

Keeso returned her smile. "It's the only bed in the room. Take advantage of the space while you can. It'll be crowded later. While you're resting, think about what I've said." He started for the door with Levi and Pup.

"Keeso."

He turned.

"I don't have to think about it. You're right. If there is a baby, I need to be close to someone who knows what they're doing. We'll go to your home for now and decide on our future later." She glanced down at Pup and grinned. "We'll have to stop somewhere for a supply of dog food."

He smiled and nodded. "I'll tell the commander."

Emma walked to the bed and sat down, slipping off her shoes. She was leaving Earth. Did New Centallus have flowers? Did the air smell as fresh and clean as Colorado on a brisk morning? Were there sunsets?

What if there was a baby.... She wrapped her arms around her flat midsection. She put her feet up and rested back against a very Earth-like pillow. There was a good chance she and Keeso were compatible and their baby—if there was a baby—would be healthy. She needed to concentrate on that. At least no one could find them on New Centallus. Levi would be safe. Rolling to her side, she drew a deep, cleansing breath and allowed herself to sleep.

She didn't know how long she'd been sleeping when Keeso nudged her awake. Levi was snuggled against her side and Pup had sprawled across the foot of the bed.

*"Aamyia,* wake up."

"What? Is something wrong?"

"Everything's fine. We're ready to leave orbit. I thought you'd like to see Earth one more time before we go. It may be a while before we return."

She nodded. He helped her out of bed and walked with her to the convex wall. When he pressed his hand to a small panel she hadn't noticed before, a window-sized portion of the wall slid into a well-hidden notch. They seemed to be standing among stars so bright they took her breath away. She didn't see Earth at first, but the stars began to move, or the ship did. Then there it was— the big, beautiful blue world she called home. Everything she'd ever known, everything she'd experienced in her life, had happened there. People she loved and might never see again— Lenn, Marie, little Sarah, Frank, and Molly were there, probably sleeping right now.

Her vision blurred. Keeso brushed a tear from her cheek before pulling her into his arms. She nestled her head under his chin and watched her world slowly disappear as the ship turned to leave orbit.

His arms tightened around her in a fierce, comforting hug. He was her world now. He, Levi, and even Pup. As long as they were together she would be home.

# 44

✧

"It's too early to be absolutely certain, but there's every indication you're pregnant." Rhyel's bond-mate, Amber, had boarded the *Requiem* as soon as the ship established orbit around New Centallus. Her priority had been blood samples, both Emma's and Keeso's. Those had been sent to the lab on the planet. Then she'd shooed Keeso and Levi out of the room so she could examine their colony's newest Centallian bride.

"The doctors were adamant. The damage the bullet caused was too extensive. I can't get pregnant. It's impossible."

"I'd have to look at your files to verify their findings, but doctors are known to be wrong on occasion." She smiled. "I've been wrong a couple of times myself, especially where the big guys are concerned."

"Big guys?"

"The Guardians. I'm still trying to figure out what makes them tick." She was suddenly all business again. "In your case, we'll take our cue from an old saying and err on the side of caution." She opened her bag and extracted a filled and capped hypodermic needle. "One of the first things you'll notice about New Centallus is the lack of mammals. We thought it had something to do with the planet's young age. Unfortunately, the colonists discovered a virus, one capable of infecting a mammalian fetus regardless of the species. More than twenty brides miscarried before the cause was discovered. The Elders declared a moratorium on physical relations between the Guardians and their bond-mates until a cure could be found."

"Who are the Elders?"

"They govern New Centallus. You'll meet them when you reach the colony."

Emma nodded toward the hypo. "What's that?"

"We eventually discovered a vaccine for the virus. If I'm right about you being pregnant, this will protect the baby. If I'm wrong, no harm done." Amber uncapped the needle and motioned for her to push up her sleeve. A moment later, the doctor stretched a Band-Aid over her forearm where the needle had entered.

She glanced down and laughed. "Yellow ducklings? Really?"

"You should see the look on the big guys' faces when I slap one of those on a bulging muscle. Hiilani accuses me of ordering what she calls the 'cutesy' bandages on purpose. She thinks I'm attempting to control egos as big as the men themselves, but she's wrong. These good men lost everything when their world disintegrated—parents, mates, children, their home, and their heritage. The loss is with them every moment of every day. Establishing this colony and striving to save their species has given them a sense of purpose. Their Earth brides have also blessed their lives with love and with children. Upon occasion, my little ducks bless their lives with laughter—never in front of me, mind you, but sometimes I hear chuckles and good-natured ribbing on the other side of the clinic door."

Emma grinned. "It sounds like life is finally smoothing out for the Centallians. I'm glad."

"It isn't always smooth. Some of the bondings have been a little rocky, but the couples knew they had to find a middle ground. There is no divorce or annulment on New Centallus—with one exception." Amber hesitated.

Emma didn't. "Keeso and Hiilani."

"He told you."

"Yes."

"Even though he gave her the words, the final act of the bonding ceremony, rending the veil, had never been performed. That single action binds the couple for life."

"You're trying to tell me we could dissolve our marriage."

"Yes. If your blood tests prove incompatibility and if you can become pregnant, it's an option you might want to consider."

She pushed the hair back from her face and looked up at Amber. "Keeso and I were married in a small church on the Hopi reservation a few weeks ago. It was a traditional ceremony with a couple of Centallian exceptions. He stood before me as a warrior, dressed in armor, carrying a sword and shield. After he gave me the words, he used his longknife to slice through the gossamer veil stretched between us. He made certain that we could never be separated."

"Did you understand that the commitment was for life, that there was no going back?"

"I knew. He made sure I understood. The vows I spoke were as binding for me as rending the veil was for Keeso. I love him."

Amber stood and picked up her bag. "For the time being, we won't worry over problems that may not exist. We'll tackle each obstacle as it comes."

Emma recognized the shuttle the second she entered the docking bay. Apparently, the Centallians had made sure to retrieve the small ship from the Hopi reservation.

For some reason, the familiarity of the vehicle gave her a sense of well-being. Right now, anything familiar was a comfort.

Amber had transported to the surface, and hopefully, would have the blood test results by the time they reached the fortress.

*Fortress.*

It sounded imposing, like the ancient ramparts in England and Scotland.

Keeso elected to fly the shuttle himself. As they had the night they'd fled Colorado, Levi and Pup took up the back two seats, with her riding shotgun, as her husband was fond of saying—probably a carryover from the time he'd spent in the West.

The flight was short, but long enough for her to notice the subtle differences between New Centallus and Earth. The sky was blue but with turquoise tints, their ocean an emerald green.

The shuttle landed alongside three other shuttles of varying sizes. A ground transport waited to take them to the fortress. The pilot, Tiinar, grabbed Keeso in a man-hug that would have broken the bones of a normal man—or at least normal by Earth standards.

Keeso pulled her to his side. "Tiinar, meet my bond-mate Emma. Em, Tiinar is Rhyel's chief navigator and a close friend." He swung her nephew into his arms. "And this is Levi, my son."

Tiinar bowed his respect, then gave Levi his full attention. "I am pleased to make your acquaintance, young Guardian." He glanced at Pup, who watched him with cautious eyes. "And who is this?"

Levi squirmed to get down and immediately threw his arms around the dog. "This is Pup." Suddenly shy, Levi buried his face in the fur on the dog's neck.

Tiinar smiled at his friend. "You're blessed with a fine family. They will be a welcome addition to our colony."

As they transferred from the shuttle to the transport, she noticed the fortress in the distance and nudged Keeso as they climbed into the transport. "Why is your landing area so far from the fortress?"

He settled in beside her. "It's a safety concern. The shuttle's Initial Sequence Fuel, or ISF, is volatile. You don't have to be concerned. The possibility of an explosion is negligible, but we prefer to be cautious."

"What about this vehicle?"

"The ground transport is only powered by solar cells."

"That's good."

Her eyes were drawn to the distant mountains to her right and the vast rows of green vegetation running from the base of the mountains to within a few feet of their vehicle as they skimmed past.

"You're farming." It stood to reason. Centallus must've been like Earth to some degree. Keeso's people couldn't have survived on Earth or been biologically compatible with her species if it were otherwise. With so much in common between her people and Keeso's, it wasn't surprising both would plant and harvest.

Two women and four men, all of them older, stood in front of the huge fortress entry doors. Keeso nodded in their direction. "The Elders have come to welcome you." He stepped out of the transport as soon as it stopped and helped her down, then lifted Levi into his arms. Pup scrambled out and took his place beside them, nudging Keeso's hand. He gave the dog a comforting pat.

Keeso bowed his respect to the group. A man stepped forward to grasp his arm in greeting. He looked older than the others—deeper lines etched his face, his back a bit more bowed. But his clear eyes were bright with intelligence and laugh lines etched the corners of his eyes. His solemn demeanor made her wonder how long it had been since he'd truly laughed.

"We had feared never to see you again, Keeso. Welcome home."

"I had feared the same. It is good to be home." He placed an arm around her shoulder. "This is Emma, my bond-mate." He gave her an encouraging smile and she bowed her head to the Elder. "Aadrok is our Seer. You might call him our priest."

The holy man took her hand. "Welcome to New Centallus." He turned his attention to Levi. "And who is this young Guardian?"

Keeso answered for her. "This is the child of Emma's late sister. When I gave Emma the words, he became my son."

The priest nodded and glanced at Pup. "What manner of beast is this?"

Keeso laughed. "Pup is a canine, more commonly called a dog."

"Sentient?"

"It depends on who you ask. Some consider them dumb animals, others believe they can reason. I personally believe they are amazing animals. This one is a member of our family."

Aadrok nodded. "Then he will be welcomed as such." His attention returned to Emma. "My fellow councilmembers are anxious to meet you." Gently grasping Emma's arm, he led her to where the others waited. Keeso followed, Levi holding tight to his neck.

The priest stopped beside the two women in the group and bowed his respect to the taller of the two. "Kroyda is our Storykeeper. She is gifted with perfect memory and has been taxed with committing Centallian history and legends to our fortress database. She is also adding the history of each of our brides to the records."

Kroyda embraced her, then leaned back. "Welcome, Emma. I look forward to learning about your history and that of your nephew."

Aadrok bowed to the woman next to Kroyda. "Zsaor is gifted with a talent for linguistics. She interprets each new language we encounter and aids the technicians with the translations." Zsaor was as petite as Kroyda was tall, but her hug was just as fierce. She glanced at Keeso and smiled. Levi, still hugging his neck, grinned at Kroyda and Zsaor. The lady's smiles indicated they were suitably charmed.

Aadrok guided her to the three men who stood together. "Emma, this is Valdon our chief Elder, Zitan, our administrator, and Tzarn, the youngest member of our council." Each Elder bowed in turn. Zitan seemed vaguely familiar, though she knew she'd never met him.

Keeso joined them, exchanged greetings with the three men, then put his arm around her. "Are you ready to see your new home?"

She took a deep breath and nodded. "Yes. I'm ashamed to admit I'm exhausted. I don't suppose they have chamomile tea here?"

He laughed and gave her a squeeze. "There are close to a hundred women inside the fortress, all from Earth. What do you think?"

Leaning into him, she sighed. "I'm too tired to think."

"Come on then."

Tiinar and Tzarn sprinted ahead, prepared to push open the huge entry doors. Aadrok motioned Keeso and his family ahead. The Elders followed.

Her husband's arm slid to her waist and he bent close. "We'll find a quiet corner and get you settled."

A quiet corner sounded wonderful.

There was no quiet corner. Keeso gently urged Emma into bedlam— though babble might have been the better description. The residents of that ill-fated biblical town couldn't have been any more confused than she was at the moment. Everyone was laughing and shouting in what seemed like a hundred different languages. Pup added his voice to the cacophony and Levi covered both ears with his hands. Keeso thrust Levi into her arms and knelt to calm the dog.

When he straightened, the crowd closed in. Men were pounding Keeso's back, apparently welcoming him home. She wasn't sure. She couldn't understand a word they said. She couldn't even understand Keeso. Several women approached her, all of them smiling, none of them making any sense as they patted her arm and cooed at Levi.

She couldn't get enough air and took a deep breath. It didn't help. She inhaled so forcefully it hurt her lungs and throat, then inhaled again. The more air she took in, the more her body craved. She knew what was happening and glanced around for a paper bag, anything she could use. Then it struck her. She was looking for a paper bag on an alien planet because she was hyperventilating and because she couldn't understand a word anybody was saying—not even Keeso.

She started laughing and gasping. Flecks of black swirled across her vision in a dizzying display. Keeso swung around and looked at her. The world got darker.

"Keeso, catch Levi."

# 45

✦

He caught them both.

Kroyda took Levi. "Let's get her to the clinic."

Keeso nodded and lifted Emma into his arms, cradling her against his racing heart. He followed the Elder as she made her way through the now silent crowd. Amber opened the clinic door. He hadn't realized she was in the hall.

The doctor reached for her lab coat, slipped it on, and pulled a stethoscope out of the pocket. "Put her on the exam table."

"What's wrong with her?"

"Don't panic, Keeso. I'm sure Emma's only fainted." She wrapped a blood pressure cuff around his bond-mate's arm. "You do know this is another indication of pregnancy?"

He took his son from Kroyda, nodding his appreciation for her help. She smiled, patted Levi, and quietly left the room.

Turning to the exam table, he brushed the hair away from Emma's face. "She looks so pale. Are you sure she's all right? If there is a baby…."

Amber met his gaze directly. "If there is a baby, we'll deal with whatever situation arises. Right now, she's fine. Her blood pressure is normal, and I expect her to wake up at any moment."

"Aunty?" The boy's voice was full of tears.

"It's okay, buddy. Did you hear the doctor say she'll be okay?" Keeso swung Levi onto the exam table. "Why don't you sit here beside her? She'll be glad to know you're close."

He looked over the boy's head at the doctor. "The compatibility tests?"

"Haven't been completed. I'll let you know the minute we have the results."

"Levi!" Two sets of hands kept Emma from pushing up off the table.

"Calm yourself, *Aamyia*. He's fine. He's sitting right here."

She relaxed back with a sigh. Levi threw himself against her chest, grabbing her neck with both arms. She held him close, returning the hug. She glanced from Keeso to Amber. "Did he fall?"

"No." The doctor's voice was soothing. "Keeso kept you both from hitting the floor." She stepped back and slipped her stethoscope into her pocket. "Guardians are blessed with quick reflexes."

"Let me sit up."

"Are you dizzy or disoriented?" She shook her head and Amber smiled. "I'm sure you'll be more comfortable in the chair." She indicated an overstuffed chair situated halfway between the exam table and the large desk.

Keeso peeled Levi away from her neck, lowering him to the floor. "Why don't you stand with Pup and I'll bring your aunt over to you." Pup had already staked out a place beside the chair. He was out of the way and still where he could keep an eye on his family.

Levi ran to where the dog waited. Keeso lifted her into his arms.

"It's ten feet away, Keeso. I'm capable of walking that distance."

He nodded dutifully and carried her to the chair, anyway, gently depositing her in the soft cushions.

Amber chuckled and shook her head. "Guardians."

Rhyel walked into the room to his wife. After planting a quick kiss on top of her head, he pulled her into his side. "What were you saying about Guardians?"

"Only that you are stubborn and arrogant in your belief that you know what is best for your bond-mate."

"True. Those are two of my many traits you find appealing."

Amber didn't try to hide her exasperation. "Like I said, arrogant."

The commander glanced at Emma. "When I returned from the *Requiem* a few minutes ago, I was told you are unwell. I'm relieved to see you aren't as ill as I feared. What happened?"

She'd like to know the answer as well. "I'm not sure. I think I might've been hallucinating. People were shouting and laughing, babies cried. Everyone was talking at once, but I didn't understand a word they were saying, not even Keeso."

Amber touched the small gold square embedded in her ear. "You weren't hallucinating. You don't have a translator yet. We'll make sure you get one by the end of the day."

"But I understood everyone before I entered the fortress."

"They were speaking English for your benefit. When you walked through the doors without the translator, it must've been chaotic."

Keeso sat on the edge of the chair and took her hand, bringing it to his lips. "I should've anticipated the problem. I'm sorry, *Aamyia.*"

"It wasn't your fault. I don't understand why I reacted the way I did. I knew I was hyperventilating, but I couldn't focus enough to control it."

"You were having a panic attack."

Emma slashed her fingers through her hair, pushing it out of her face. "I've never had one before."

Patting her bond-mate's chest, Amber left his side and pulled a desk chair close to Emma. "From what you've told me about your experiences over the past few weeks, I'd say this one was way overdue. The human psyche can be fragile at times."

"Is that why I fainted?"

"Perhaps, but there is also the possibility you're carrying Keeso's child. Fainting is not unheard of during pregnancy."

Levi crawled into Emma's lap and she hugged him close before returning her attention to the doctor. "Do you have the test results yet?"

"Genetic scans take a little time, but it won't be long before we know if you and Keeso are genetically compatible. The lab is only a few doors down." Amber glanced over at Keeso. "Fortunately, we relocated it from the *Novaria* to the fortress before Rhyel's ship was destroyed.

A brisk knock sounded at the door. An older gentleman stepped into the clinic. He clasped Rhyel's shoulder in greeting as he walked toward Amber. Bending, he gave her a quick peck on the cheek before nodding to Emma. His eyes were immediately drawn to Levi. "And who do we have here?"

Amber stood and took his hand. "Grandpa, this is Keeso, Emma, and her nephew, Levi. Emma and Levi are the newest members of our colony." She glanced up at the older man, her eyes filled with love and respect. "This is my grandfather, Doctor Samuel Donovan."

Keeso extended his hand. "I'm honored to meet you, sir."

The Doctor chuckled. "I haven't enjoyed a good handshake in some time. You must be the young man who runs the mine on Earth."

"Ran the mine. The responsibility will now fall to another. My place is here on Centallus, with my bond-mate and son."

Pup chose that moment to stick his head above the side of the chair. The doctor's eyes widened before a smile broke out on his face. "Where on Earth did you find him? It is a him, isn't it?"

"Yes, sir, it is, and he found me."

"What's his name?"

"I called him Pup at first. I assumed he belonged to someone around the area, and by the time I realized he was a stray, it was all he'd answer to."

"Pup, huh?" The dog must have decided the doctor's response was an invitation. He trotted over and sat down in front of the man. Doctor Donovan squatted down and scratched Pup's ears. "I'd say he's mostly hound with maybe a little German Shepherd."

"You're right about the hound. He has a good nose."

The clinic door opened and the doctor stood. A lovely dark-haired, dark-eyed woman hurried into the room.

The entire room fell silent with expectation. Keeso kissed the top of

Emma's head and squeezed her shoulder before moving to stand in front of the woman.

"Hiilani."

The name was a bare whisper, but Emma heard the deep affection in her husband's voice. Levi squirmed in her arms and she realized she was crushing him against her chest. Easing her hold, she murmured an apology.

"Keeso!" The young woman's face brightened. Even from the distance between them, Emma saw tears in her eyes when she leaned up to kiss his cheek. "I was afraid we'd never see you again. Cintar assured me you would be all right, but I worried anyway."

Keeso gave her a hug, then held her at arms-length. "Are you well?"

"Very well, and happy."

"Cintar spoke with me on his last trip to Earth. Did he mention our conversation to you?"

"Yes, just before he asked to give me the words. He told me you wished us happiness. We're bond-mates now, and have a daughter, Kalani."

"I'm happy for you." He took her hand and led her to the chair. "Hiilani, this is Emma, my bond-mate, and her nephew, Levi, who is now my son."

Hiilani took Emma's hands in hers. "I'm glad he found you. Keeso deserves a full and happy life. I hope you know how fortunate you are."

The door opened before Emma could respond. If she'd harbored any misgivings about the young woman's feelings for Keeso, they ended when Hiilani set eyes on the man filling the doorway. The obvious love of her life held a sleeping baby in one arm and a sealed envelope in the opposite hand. He gave the baby to his bond-mate and handed the envelope to Amber.

"I met Malur at the door. He said you were anxious to receive this."

Keeso reached for Emma's hand as Amber opened the envelope and read the report.

She looked up, smiling. "Your scans are compatible."

Keeso laughed and knelt, taking Emma's face in both hands, kissing her despite their audience.

"Wait a minute." Hiilani frowned and handed the baby back to Cintar.

"Emma, you're pregnant?" She didn't wait for an answer but swung around to give Keeso a fulminating glare. "How could you touch her without making sure you were genetically compatible?"

Emma took umbrage. "Don't yell at Keeso. We're not even sure I'm pregnant."

The nurse turned puzzled eyes on Amber. "What does she mean she's not sure? He's Centallian. Of course, she's pregnant."

"This isn't Keeso's fault."

That brought Hiilani up short. "The baby isn't his?"

"Yes, it is—I mean no." She stood and sat Levi in the vacated chair. "I'm trying to tell you there is no baby. I can't have children. It's physically impossible."

"Then why is Keeso so relieved about the scans?"

"Because I've had symptoms, the same kind my sister had when she was pregnant with Levi. At first, I thought it might be possible, but the more I thought about what the doctor told me, the less sure I became."

Hiilani shook her head. "What makes it impossible?"

"I was shot." Only Amber and Keeso knew the story. The gasps and horrified looks she received weren't unexpected, but still made her uncomfortable. "He used a small handgun—at close range. The doctors said a larger caliber bullet would have killed me. They also told me the damage the bullet caused to my reproductive organs was massive. I can't have children."

Keeso put his hands around her shoulder, pulling her against him. "I should've taken precautions, regardless of what the doctors said."

Amber folded her arms across her chest and leaned against the desk. "Fortunately, genetic incompatibility is no longer a worry. Her pregnancy test results should arrive in a few minutes. If Emma is pregnant, we still have a problem, one we need to address sooner rather than later."

# 46

✦

Emma was still amazed at how easy it had been for the Centallians to obtain her medical files, but she was grateful they had.

After looking at the x-rays and going over the records, Amber had agreed with her doctors. It was impossible for her to be pregnant. Yet, a little over four months after arriving on New Centallus, here she was, as big as a house and waddling like a duck.

Both Amber and her grandfather worried about her ability to carry a child to full term. When Doctor Donovan suggested she stay off her feet as much as possible, Keeso insisted she stay in bed—in the clinic. The doctors explained her need for exercise, but in moderation.

Everyone in the colony knew her complicated condition and held their breath whenever she descended either of the two curved staircases leading to the second level and the living quarters. Someone always happened to be going down or coming up the stairs at the same time she was. Occasionally a Guardian would make a U-turn on the staircase to walk with her. Honest to a fault, they never fabricated an excuse for their sudden change in direction. She had noticed Guardians doing the same for any expectant mother. It was sweet, really, the way the men behaved—even though they were constantly underfoot.

She eased into one of several comfortable rocking chairs in the Great Hall. Her back hurt—had been bothering her all day—though most of the time the ache wasn't much more than an irritation.

She glanced around. The size of the room amazed her. If you removed the multiple trestle tables and benches, the Guardians could have played a game of football between the fireplace at the end of the room and the great doors—well, maybe basketball.

The last meal of the day had been served, the tables cleaned. Keeso had taken Levi and Pup outside to play with the new kite Keeso had made for his son's fifth birthday.

Sonya entered the Great Hall holding her son's hand as he toddled beside her and cradling her infant daughter in the crook of her other arm. She sank into the next chair with a weary sigh and looked at her. "How are you feeling today?"

It was a question Emma heard a lot. "Like I just ate a horse. You?"

"Like I was just kicked by one." She inclined her head toward little Kiial, who was trying to climb on one of the benches. "He hasn't slowed down since he took his first step." She nodded toward the cooing baby. "And she never sleeps."

Excluding Levi, Sonya had both the oldest and youngest child on New Centallus.

One of the large entry doors opened. Keeso held it, allowing Levi and Pup into the room. Spotting her, the boy and dog ran full throttle in her direction, Levi grabbing the chair to stop himself, the pup skittering past, doing a full turnabout as he attempted to gain his footing. He trotted back and plopped down at her feet. Kiial immediately stumbled toward the large canine. Pup was content to let the toddler crawl all over him. Levi dropped down beside them, laughing when the smaller child rolled over Pup's back and tumbled to the floor. Eventually the difference in the children's ages wouldn't mean much. They'd probably be fast friends in a year or two.

The permanence of the thought wasn't lost on her. She felt at home on New Centallus. No longer fearing discovery, she knew a peace and contentment she'd given up hope of ever having again. And she'd found a future purpose— teaching the children how to read and write.

BOUND BY EARTH 295

Since the mining operation and their supply contracts were in the United States, the Elders had decided the children should learn to read and write English as well as Centalese. She and Kroyda would be responsible for seeing that the children were fluent in both languages.

Keeso joined them a moment later and bent to place a quick kiss on her lips. "Ready to go upstairs?"

She glanced at Levi. He was having difficulty keeping his eyes open. "More than ready, I think." She tried to angle herself out of the chair and finally looked to Keeso for help. He smiled, kissed her again, and took her hand. He would've carried her up the stairs if given the chance. She'd disabused him of that idea early on. Instead, he lifted Levi to his shoulder and put an arm around her. Emma turned to Sonya. "If you need some help getting the children to your chamber, Keeso can return."

Sonya grabbed her son when Pup stood. "Thank you, but it isn't necessary. Tzarn has promised to help get them settled. He insists Kiial is old enough to hear stories of his father's heroism. Have a restful night."

The climb up the curving stairway seemed to take longer each evening. Obviously, the men who designed the fortress hadn't taken pregnant ladies into consideration. If they had, family living quarters would have been situated on the ground floor.

Emma clasped Keeso's arm for support and looked up. "Have you noticed how much time Tzarn spends with Sonya?"

Her husband shrugged. "He stands in for Siikzo."

"I know, but he spends a lot of extra time visiting with Sonya."

He stopped suddenly and Pup ran into the back of his legs. "Are you suggesting he's interested in Sonya?"

"It isn't unreasonable. As Siikzo's stand-in, they're thrown together a lot. It's only natural they'd become close."

"Tzarn is an Elder. They decided from the beginning not to seek mates."

"Yes, but he's young, and he isn't the only Elder interested in someone. Amber's grandfather appears to be courting."

"Doctor Donovan is not an official Elder."

"He may not be, but Zsaor is."

She laughed at his stunned expression. "I'm not making this up. Watch them at breakfast tomorrow. You'll see."

Keeso opened the door to their chamber and stepped aside, allowing her to enter first. "Lie down for a few minutes and get your feet up. I'll get Levi ready for bed."

She didn't argue. That routine had pretty much become the norm. Keeso saw to teeth brushing, baths, and pajamas while she rested. When he was ready, Levi climbed up on the bed beside her for a story while Keeso showered. As usual, her nephew fell asleep before she'd finished the book. While Keeso settled his son into the alcove bedroom adjoining theirs, she waddled to the bathroom for her shower.

Keeso was in bed when she emerged from the bathroom. When she reached the bed, he lifted the sheet, inviting her in beside him. Settling her into his arms, he bent and touched her lips with his in a long, satisfying kiss.

"You look tired tonight, Em."

"It's a common occurrence with pregnant women. My back hurts tonight though, which, I understand, is also common at this stage."

"Have you mentioned the pain to Amber?"

"No, but I promise I will in the morning. Did you have any trouble getting Levi down?"

"He woke up long enough to ask for his necklace. It was on the nightstand."

She started to get out of bed. "He shouldn't have anything around his neck while he's sleeping."

Keeso tightened his hold. "I didn't let him put it on. He fell asleep hugging it."

"He misses Sarah."

"I know."

"Were we wrong to let them get so close?"

"I don't think so. By the time we ended up at the Hopi village, he'd experienced more trauma than any adult should bear. Pup helped take his mind off the fear, but I think Sarah taught him how to be a little boy again. Love, even innocent love shared by children, is a powerful healer."

He leaned up on an elbow and pressed his lips to her brow. "Your love saved me from despair." Pulling the covers aside, he slid her nightgown above her waist and cradled her swollen belly, planting butterfly kisses where his child nestled. "You gave me hope for the future." The baby chose that moment to kick and she giggled at Keeso's startled expression.

"Does that hurt you, *Aamyia?*" He sounded appalled by the prospect.

She laughed. "It's uncomfortable occasionally, especially if I'm trying to sleep, but it doesn't hurt. Every hard kick tells me our baby is strong and healthy."

He tugged her gown back in place and stretched out beside her, his hand resting possessively over their baby. She ran her fingers through his hair when he bent to kiss her again.

"Keeso, I've been thinking…."

"That cannot be a good thing, *Aamyia.*" He nuzzled her neck. Goosebumps cascaded from her head to her feet. "It usually means you have decided on a task I must accomplish."

Secretly smiling at the laughter in his voice, she snuggled against him. "I'm serious. I have something to tell you."

"You're not having twins, are you?"

She did laugh then. "No. No twins. When we first came aboard Rhyel's ship, you told me the decision of where we would spend our lives was mine. The thought of leaving my world and traveling to yours nearly overwhelmed me. But I've found peace here and friends. It's a simple life, but that appeals to me. No more looking over my shoulder. No more staring at faces in crowds. Levi and I are safe. We belong here with you."

"You're sure, *Aamyia?* You won't have regrets?"

"No regrets as long as we're together." She groaned and rolled to her side pressing her face against Keeso's chest.

"Em, what's wrong?"

"It's my lower back. The pain is getting stronger. It's almost constant now. I think something's wrong."

He scrambled out of the bed and reached for her. "I'll carry you down to the clinic."

She felt a ping and suddenly her gown was soaked. The pain intensified, and this time she felt the tightening in her womb.

A contraction.

The truth would've knocked her down if she hadn't been in bed already. She was in labor, probably had been all day. She should've told Amber about the back pain as soon as it started this morning.

Another intense pain gripped her, and less than a minute later, another.

"It's the baby. I'm having the baby now."

"Now?" He lunged for the door. "I'll go for help."

"Keeso, you're naked. Put on your pants. And don't leave me. I feel the urge to push."

"But you need help." He was hopping around on one leg trying to shove the other into his pants.

"Go out to the rail. There must be someone in the Hall below. Send them for help."

He was still fastening his pants when he opened the door, crossed to the railing, and shouted orders to someone below.

She was panting by the time he rushed back to the bed. "Wash your hands," she gasped between puffs of air. "And bring all the clean towels we have."

The urge to bear down was intense. She panted so hard her face tingled. "Keeso, hurry!"

He skidded out of the bathroom, his arms full of towels and linens. He dropped them on the bed. "I brought you a fresh nightgown."

She almost laughed—almost. "No time." She grabbed her knees and leaned forward to bear down, emitting a loud, unladylike grunt.

Amber opened the door in time to see Keeso catch his daughter.

He didn't know what to do with her. The tiny beet-red infant splotched with white goo was furious. She'd been screaming, her little lips trembling, since she'd slipped into his hands.

He looked to Emma for help. His bond-mate rested back against the pillows still panting, her hair damp and stringy. Tears rolled down her cheeks, but she smiled. "What do I do now, Em?"

Her smile broadened. "Give her to me." As soon as he laid his daughter on Emma's chest, she stopped wailing. He grabbed a towel and covered her.

Only then did he notice Amber and Hiilani. He found the nearest chair and sank into it, more than happy to let the women take care of what needed to be done.

Doctor Donovan entered the room and checked the baby to make sure she was okay. While Amber finished with Emma, and Hiilani bathed the baby, he moved to where Keeso sat.

"You could use a little cleaning up yourself." Then he got a better look at him and laughed. "You might want to fix your pants, too. They're inside out."

Once mother and baby were more comfortable, Amber decided to let Emma rest before moving her and the baby to the clinic where they could be monitored.

Emma had experienced back labor, a common condition usually brought on when the baby's head pressed against the mother's tailbone. The damage Emma had sustained from the bullet wound and subsequent surgery had probably caused her difficulty. During back labor, the intense pain often masked contractions. A few women suffered mild pain between contractions and a few inexperienced mothers failed to realize they were in labor until it was almost too late.

Levi had miraculously slept through the ordeal and through the night. He stood beside Keeso's chair, staring at his new sister.

He folded the blanket away from the baby's face, giving Levi a better view. "What do you think of your new sister?"

"She's little."

"She'll get bigger."

"What's her name?"

"She doesn't have one yet."

His son glanced up. "How come? Everybody has a name, even Pup." The dog sat up in response, his ears perking forward when the baby emitted a squeaky gurgle. Keeso held his daughter closer, letting Pup sniff the blanket. Apparently satisfied with the introduction, he nudged Levi's hand for a pat.

"She doesn't have a name because she's brand new. We haven't given her a name yet."

"We should probably do that now, don't you think?" Emma pushed herself up on the pillows and reached out.

Keeso placed the baby in Emma's arms and brushed the hair out of her face before kissing her. She was so beautiful. "Did we wake you?"

"I was only dozing." She glanced at Levi. "What do you think of the baby?" They'd prepared him for the coming birth—as much as a five-year-old could be prepared.

"She gots wrinkles, like Elder Aadrok."

Emma laughed. "Don't worry. She'll smooth out. What should we name her?"

His face scrunched as he thought for a moment. "How 'bout Sarah?"

"Sarah's a fine name, but I was thinking, if Keeso agrees, we could call her Denise."

"That's Mommy's name."

"Yes, it is. And I think she would be very happy if we name the baby after her. What do you think?" He didn't say anything but nodded as he leaned over the baby to kiss Emma's cheek.

"Will the baby call you Mommy?"

"Maybe, when she's old enough, but she might call me Mama."

"Do you think Mommy will care if I called you Mama too, so the baby knows what to call you?"

Tears made her eyes glisten. "I'm sure she would be very happy if you called me Mama. I would, too."

"Uncle Keeso tells everyone I'm his son. Can I call him Papa? Sometimes Sarah calls her daddy Papa."

Keeso lifted the boy into his arms. "I'd like that."

The uncertainty in his son's eyes cleared and the boy wiggled to get down. "I'm hungry. Can I go downstairs and get something to eat?"

"Why don't we find Sonya and Kiial? You can have breakfast with them while your mama and I get a little more rest."

Emma shook her head. "I don't think—"

"He'll be fine without us for a while. No one's going to let anything happen to him." He took Levi's hand. "I'll be right back."

Emma leaned her head back on the pillows and took a deep breath. Had it only been a year since her life had changed so dramatically? So much heartbreak, and fear—not just for her but for Levi as well. She missed Denise and John, missed watching them play and laugh with their son. If only she could somehow turn back time and stop them from being killed....

Would she and Keeso have found each other? She was enough of a romantic to believe so. She couldn't imagine not spending the rest of her life with her tall alien-cowboy.

The door opened a few minutes later and quietly closed. Keeso walked to the side of the bed, took off his boots, and climbed in, cradling her and the baby in his arms.

"Levi's with Sonya and Tzarn. They insisted on watching him until the noon meal. Sonya also told me I looked terrible. She instructed me to go back to my chamber and take a nap with my mate and daughter." He shrugged. "I was in the mood to obey." He nuzzled her neck. "How do you feel?"

"Exhausted, but happy. She's beautiful, isn't she?"

He touched the baby's head. "She looks like her mother. She cannot help but be beautiful."

"She has your dark hair and eyes."

"She still looks like you." He snuggled them both a little closer. "Are you happy here, *Aamyia*, or do you miss your home?"

"I do miss Earth, but I love New Centallus."

"But are you happy?"

She leaned up, and touched her lips to his, pouring all the love in her heart into the kiss. When she drew back, their eyes met, his still full of questions.

"It doesn't matter where we go, Keeso. If we walk the path together, I'll be happy."

# EPILOGUE

Earth's sun had descended into late afternoon by the time Rhyel gained the approval of the Hopi leaders and traveled with Lenn to the valley of the ancients. After paying their respects to the Centallians buried in the valley five centuries ago, they searched for the fissure hidden in the cliff face by huge chunks of rockfall. Sidestepping through the crack in the wall, they came to a cave-room no wider than the span of his arms and twice that length.

Loosening the drawstrings on the pouch in his hand, he extracted the black crystal for Lenn's perusal. "The *Acqeli* is no longer safe with us. New Centallus has been compromised. The Elders believe it fitting for the crystal to abide with our ancients."

He returned the *Acqeli* to the pouch, drew the strings tight, and handed the bag to Lenn. "For your protection and that of the *Acqeli,* we will not visit your people again. To do so might draw unwanted attention to your tribe. Thank you, my brother, for your help."

Lenn nodded, accepting the pouch and placed it against the far wall of the tiny cave.

"We will protect your secret with as much care as we do our heritage." He looked up at the light pouring through an opening in the rock more than a hundred feet above them. "Only the eye of heaven will see its hiding place."

Rose Sartin was born in Illinois, raised in Iowa, and has spent most of her life in the Missouri Ozarks. She and her late husband, Gary, raised two daughters, Melissa and Angela, and a son, Eric, while building businesses as beekeepers, leathercrafters, and managers/tour guides in a show cave. Ms. Sartin is also proficient with the mountain dulcimer, performing in radio, television, and documentaries. Today she lives in their family home on an Ozark ridgetop that overlooks the Mark Twain National Forest. She is currently finishing the third novel in her Centallian Guardians trilogy. Her life is filled with family and friends, music, good books, and plotting adventures for characters who show up on her mind's doorstep.

www.ingramcontent.com/pod-product-compliance
Lightning Source LLC
Chambersburg PA
CBHW031551240626
47153CB00002B/464